HARPERALLEY IS AN IMPRINT OF HARPERCOLLINS PUBLISHERS.

FGTEEV PRESENTS: INTO THE GAME! COPYRIGHT © 2020 BY LAFFTER INC. ALL RIGHTS RESERVED. PRINTED IN THE UNITED STATES OF AMERICA. NO PART OF THIS BOOK MAY BE USED OR REPRODUCED IN ANY MANNER WHATSOEVER WITHOUT WRITTEN PERMISSION EXCEPT IN THE CASE OF BRIEF QUOTATIONS EMBODIED IN CRITICAL ARTICLES AND REVIEWS. FOR INFORMATION ADDRESS HARPERCOLLINS CHILDREN'S BOOKS, A DIVISION OF HARPERCOLLINS PUBLISHERS, 195 BROADWAY, NEW YORK, NY 10007. WWW.HARPERALLEY.COM

LIBRARY OF CONGRESS CONTROL NUMBER: 2019947145
ISBN 978-0-06-293368-3

TYPOGRAPHY BY ERICA DE CHAVEZ   22 23 24 25 26 LSB 12 11 10 9 8   ❖ FIRST PAPERBACK EDITION, 2021

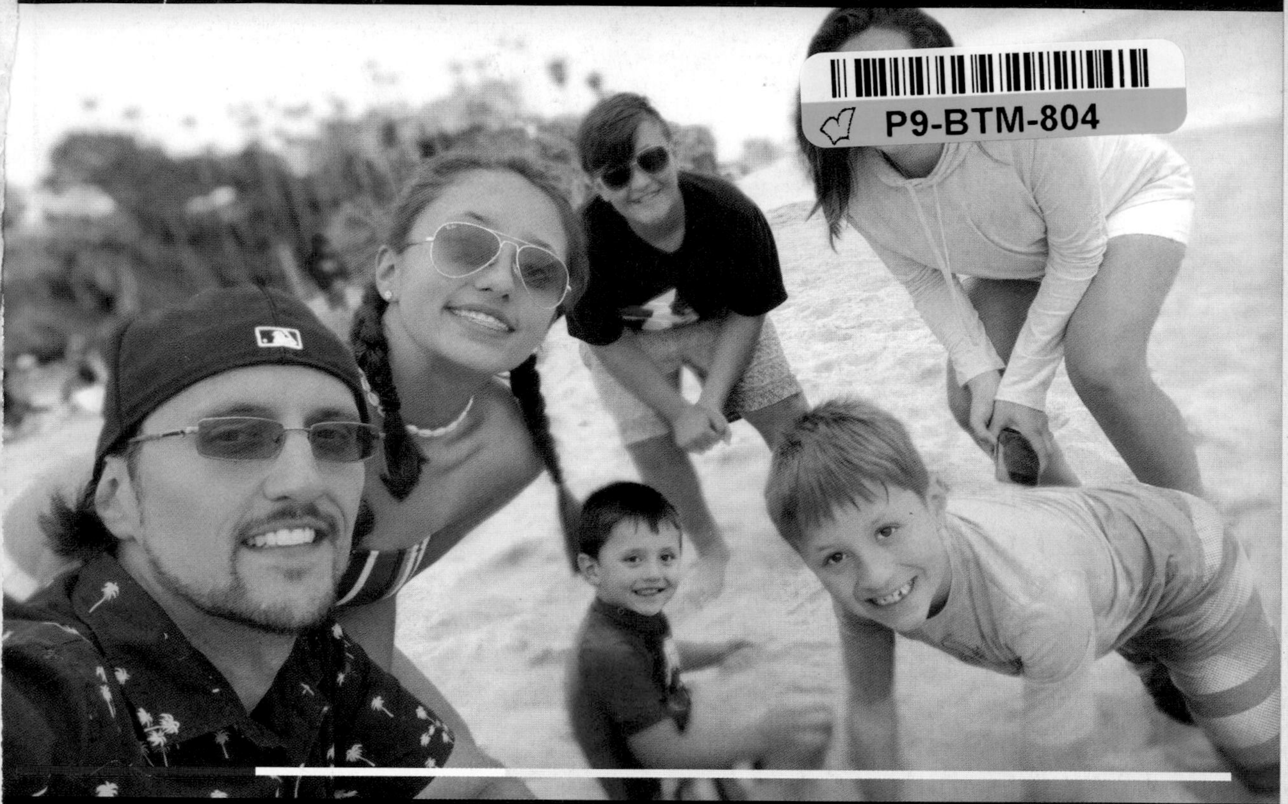

▶ ▶| 3:45 / 13:05

FGTeeV FAMILY BIOGRAPHY

3,601,748 VIEWS 5.6K 41 SHARE ADD •••

FGTeeV 4 DAYS AGO

Duddy, Moomy, Lexi, Mike, Chase, and Shawn are the stars of FGTeeV, one of the most popular family gaming YouTube channels in the world, with more than 12 million subscribers and more than 12 billion views. This family of six loves gaming, traveling, and spontaneous dance parties. To learn more, visit them on YouTube @FGTeeV.

4,120 COMMENTS

YOU Add a comment...

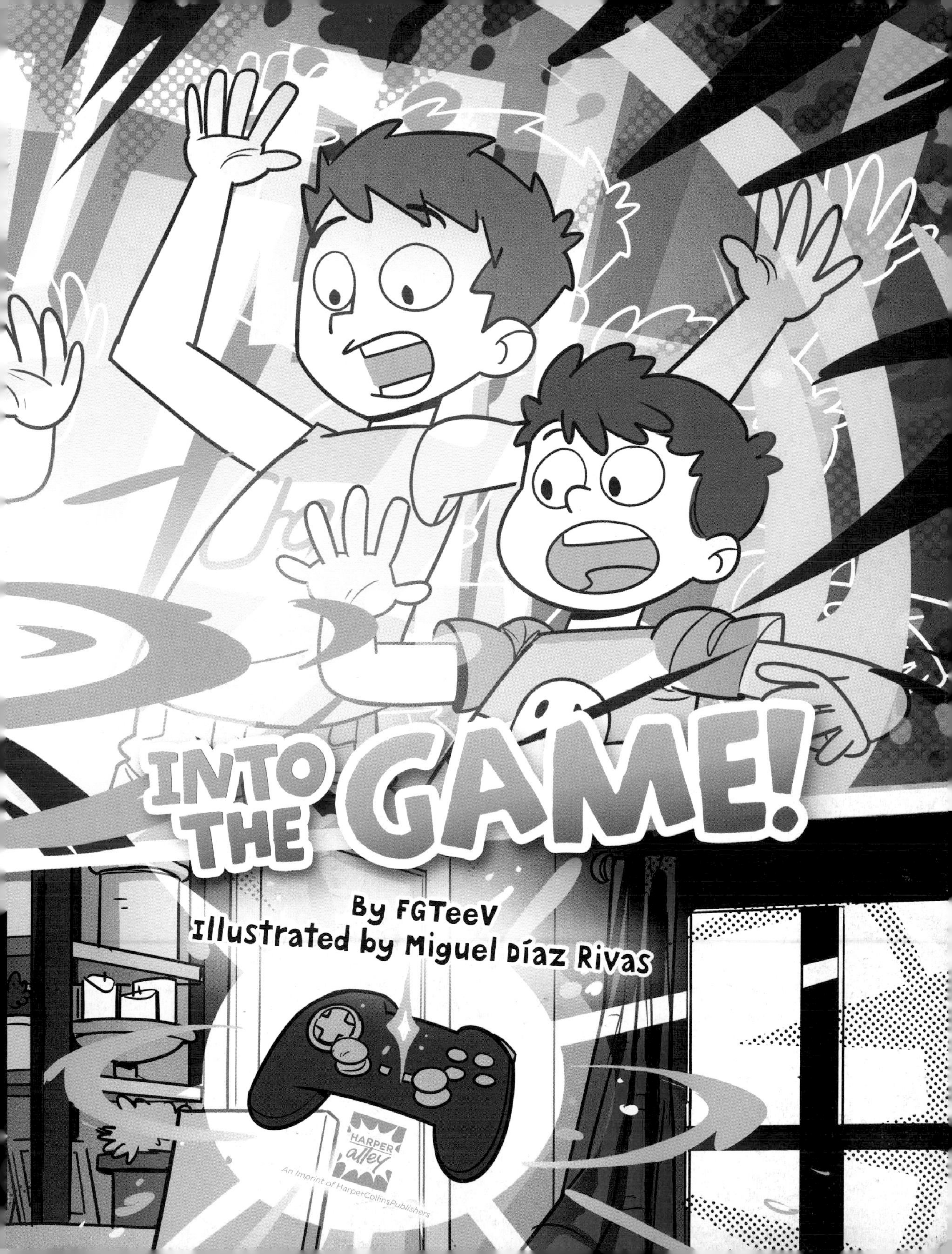
INTO THE GAME!
By FGTeeV
Illustrated by Miguel Díaz Rivas
HARPER alley
An Imprint of HarperCollinsPublishers

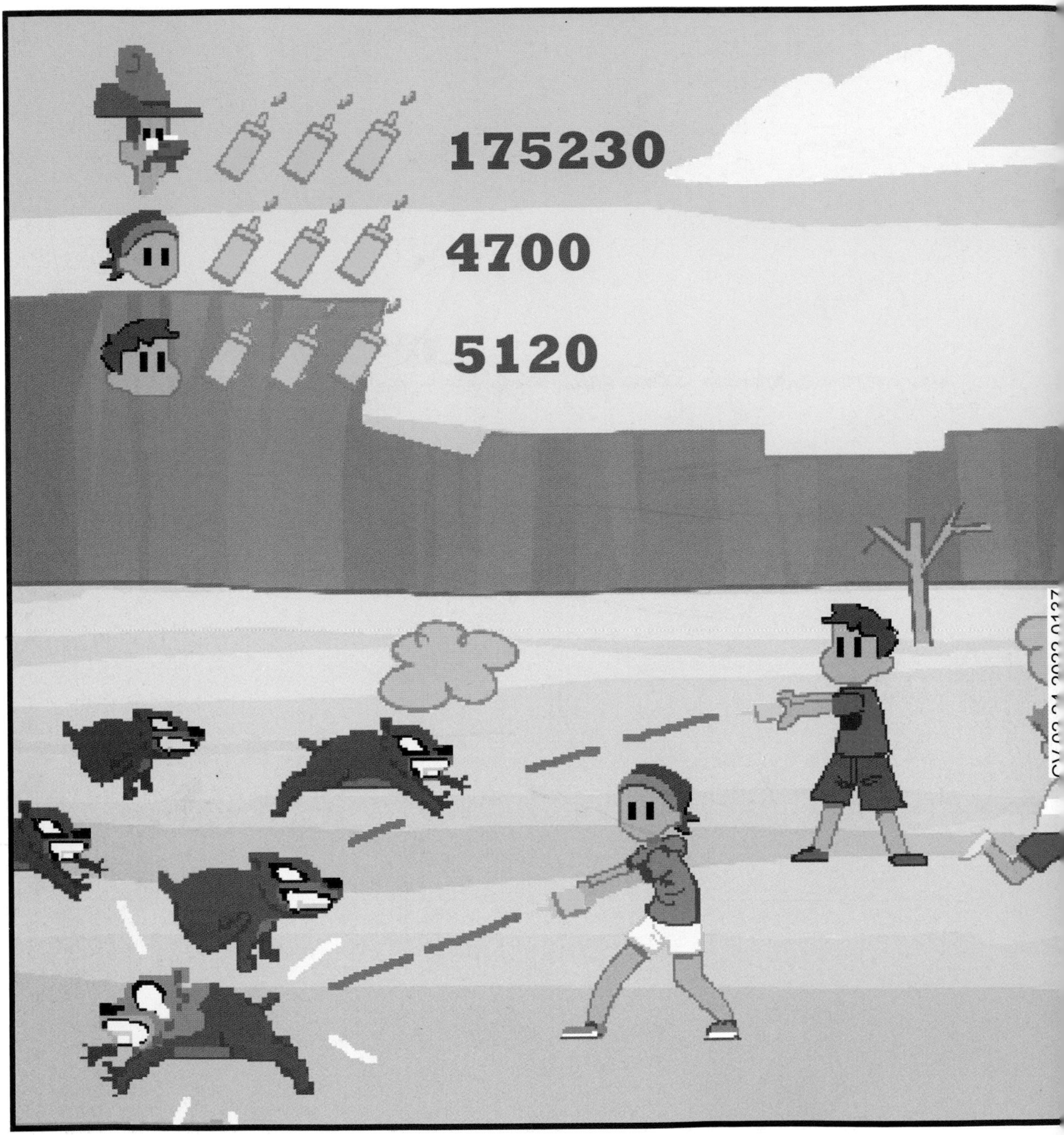
175230
4700
5120

WOW! FGTeeVERS, look how far we've come. We have a book! We are so grateful for all of you who have supported us over the years to bring us to this moment, where you can now enjoy over 100 pages of FGTeeV Action-Packed Fun! We love to entertain and are constantly thinking of new ways to do so. When we found out about the opportunity to create a book for our fans, we jumped

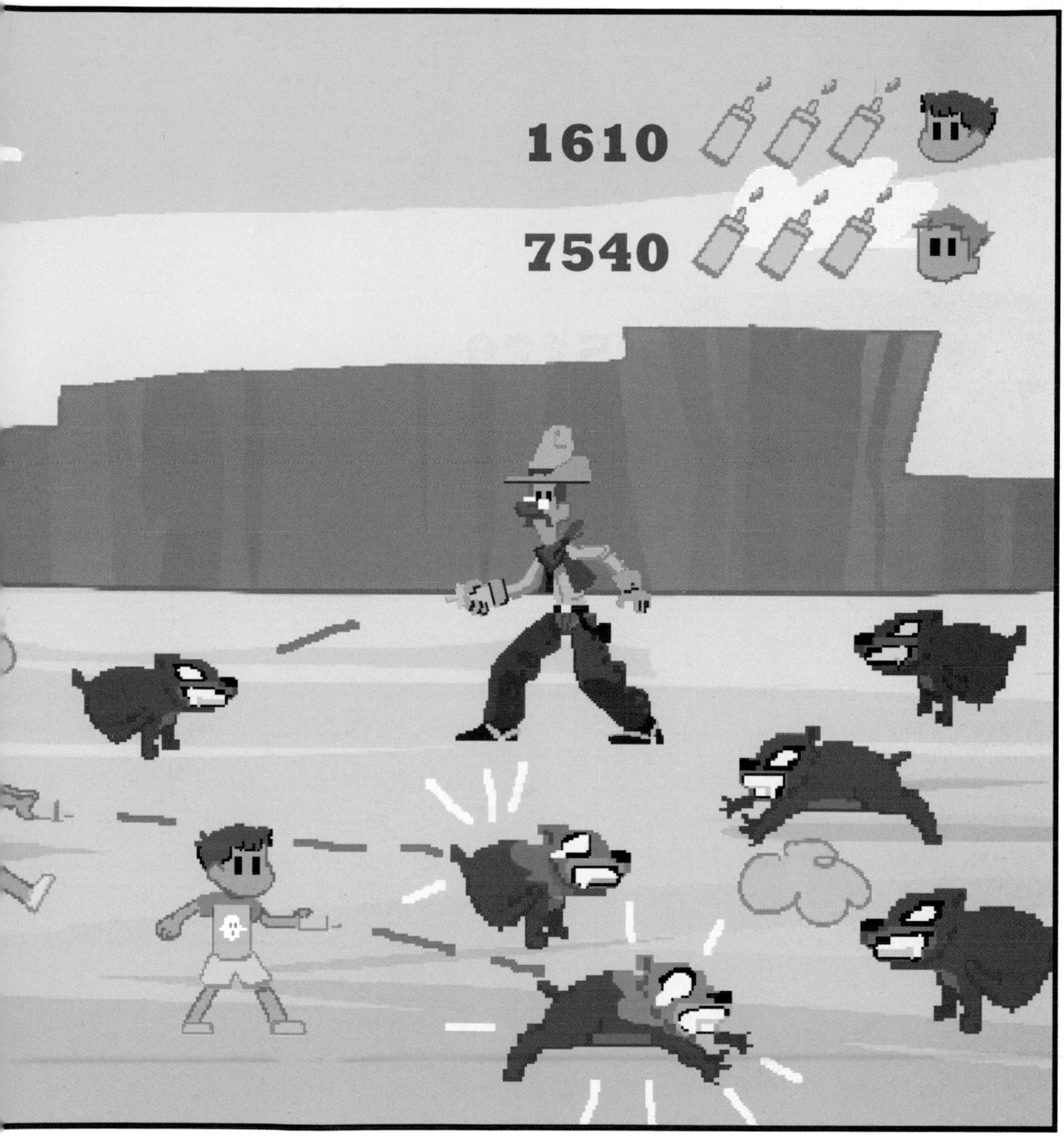
1610
7540

for joy. We hope you all love this book as much as we do! Follow your dreams. Do what you love. Don't let anyone hold you back! You're a superstar! Enjoy the book.

Love, FGTeeV Fam!

P.S. . . . Remember when we said we jumped for joy? Well, we're still in the air and landing now—quick, catch us. . . . **BOOM!**

CHARACTERS

DUDDY/ DUDSTER

The fun-loving dad is always optimistic and wants to turn every bad situation into a funkadelic dance party! But has he met his match in My Boring Pet Fish?

MOOMY

Moomy keeps the fun train from going off the rails, but she's also sweet, as you can see by her chocolate-chip freckle!

LEXI/LEXO

The boss of the children; the master strategist who takes control with the confidence of her gaming know-how.

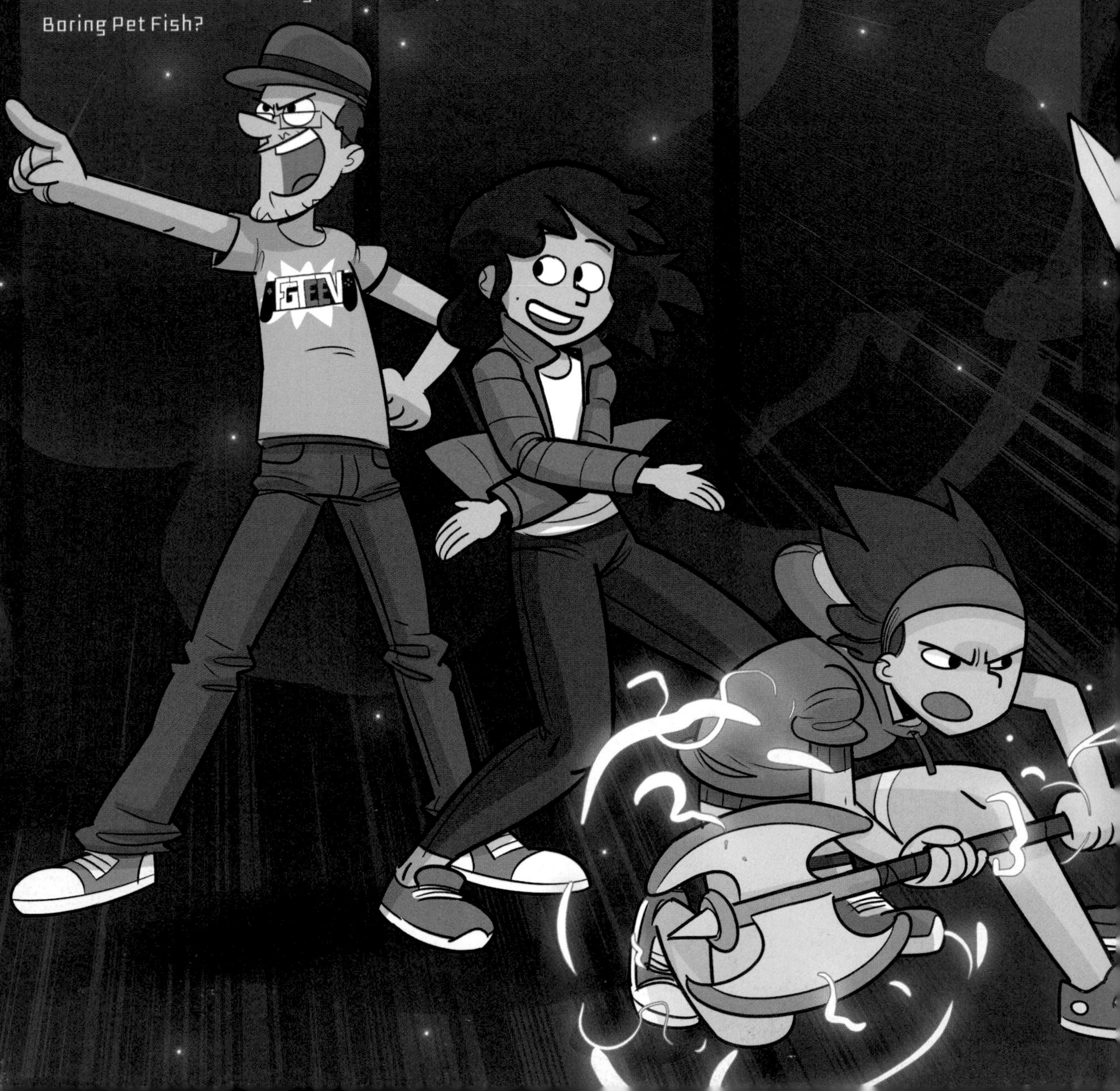

MIKE/ MICKSTER

The second-in-command. Mike respects Lexi's rules . . . but that doesn't mean he always follows them.

CHASE/ DRIZZY

He's the fearless sharp-shooter of the family—even when he's wielding a bottle of relish.

SHAWN/GHOST PUNCHER

Shawn is curious about everything, which sure keeps the family on its toes! He also thinks everything, no matter how dire, is hilarious!

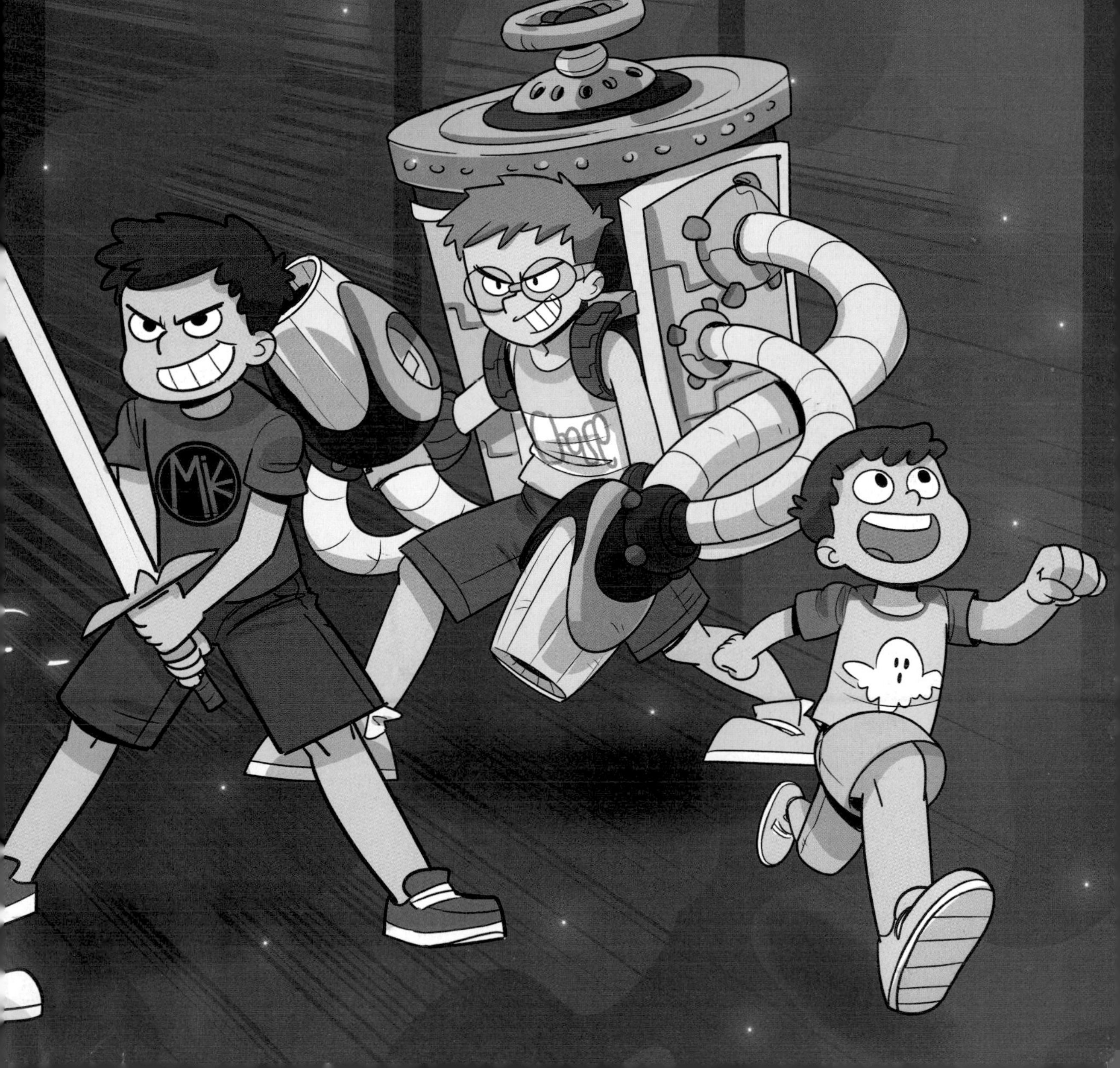

CHARACTERS

FRANKLIN GARFUNKEL TeeV

The prairie man who helps the kids find their inner relish cowboy.

BIG BABY

A big old baby who dirties an unhealthy number of diapers.

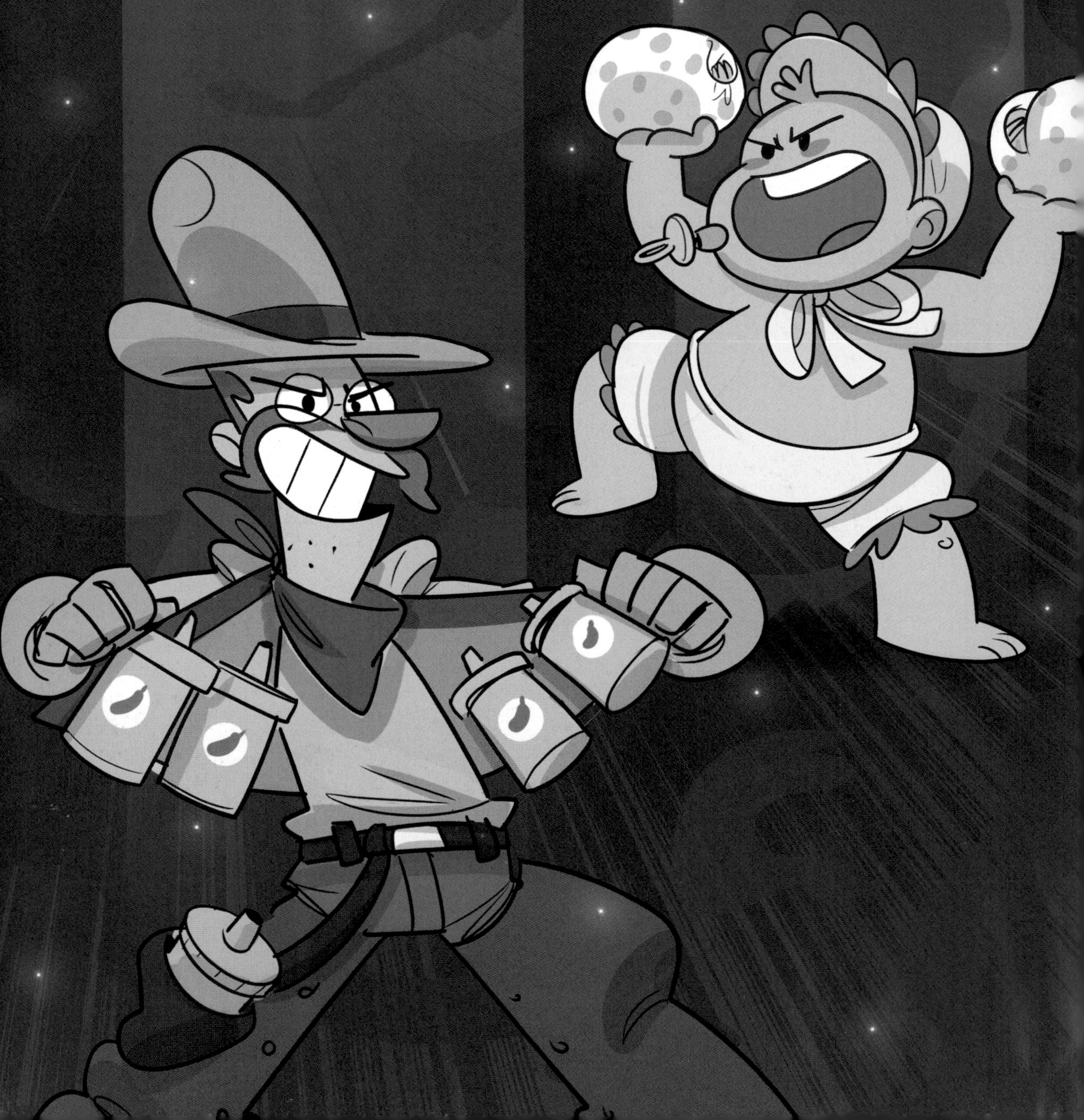

GAMER BRAT

He's always up for a game—any game, any time. But cover your ears if he loses!

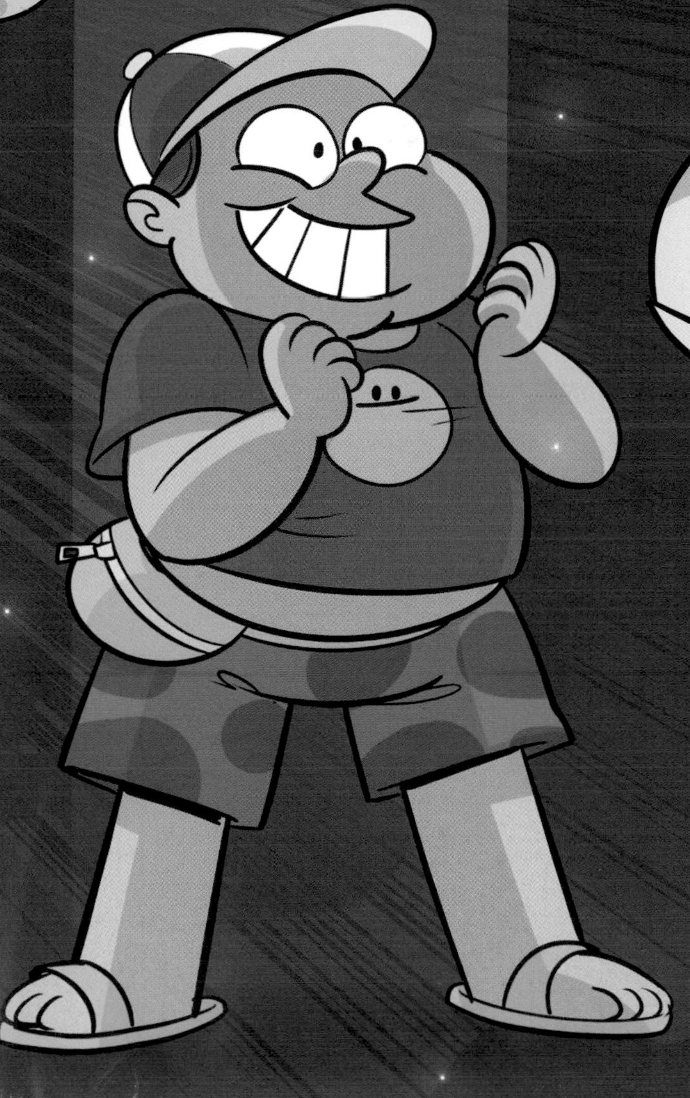

MY BORING PET FISH

. . .

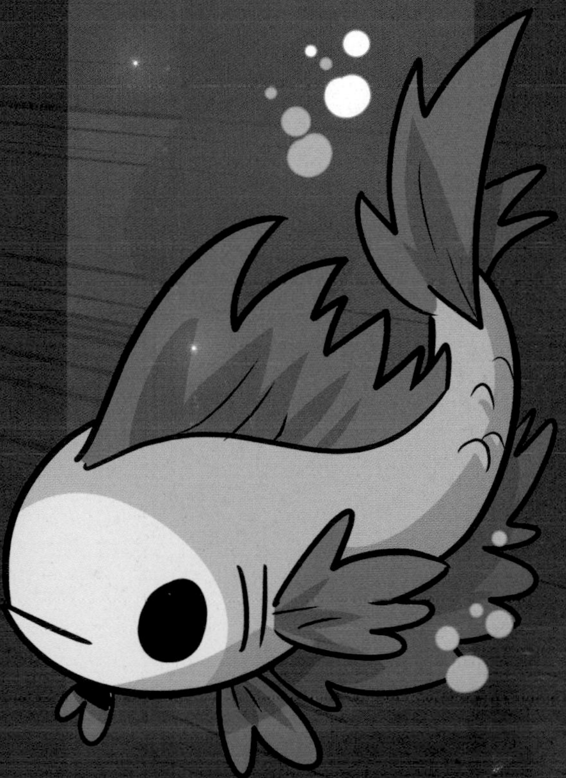

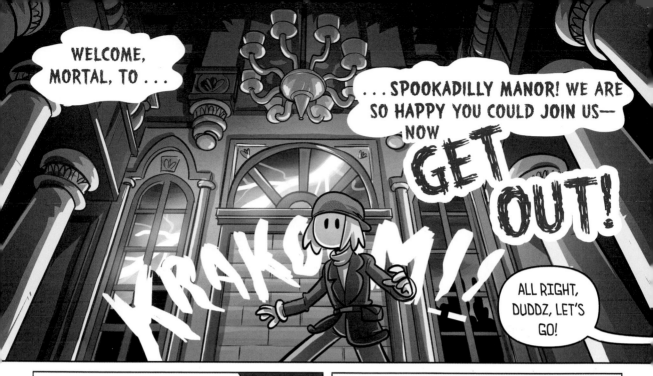

WELCOME, MORTAL, TO...

...SPOOKADILLY MANOR! WE ARE SO HAPPY YOU COULD JOIN US— NOW **GET OUT!**

KRAKOOM!!

ALL RIGHT, DUDDZ, LET'S GO!

YO, LEXI, LISTEN UP—NO ONE'S **EVER** BEATEN THIS GAME BEFORE, OKAY?

WE'RE GONNA NEED A **PLAN**.

THE FRONT DOOR— *POOF!*—JUST DISAPPEARED.

THE OBJECT OF THE GAME IS TO FIND ANOTHER WAY OUT OF THIS FREAKY HAUNTED HOUSE. IF IT GETS TOO SCARY FOR YOU, I'LL TAKE OVER, ALL RIGHT?

WHATEVER! GOT IT! GO!

WAIT UP!

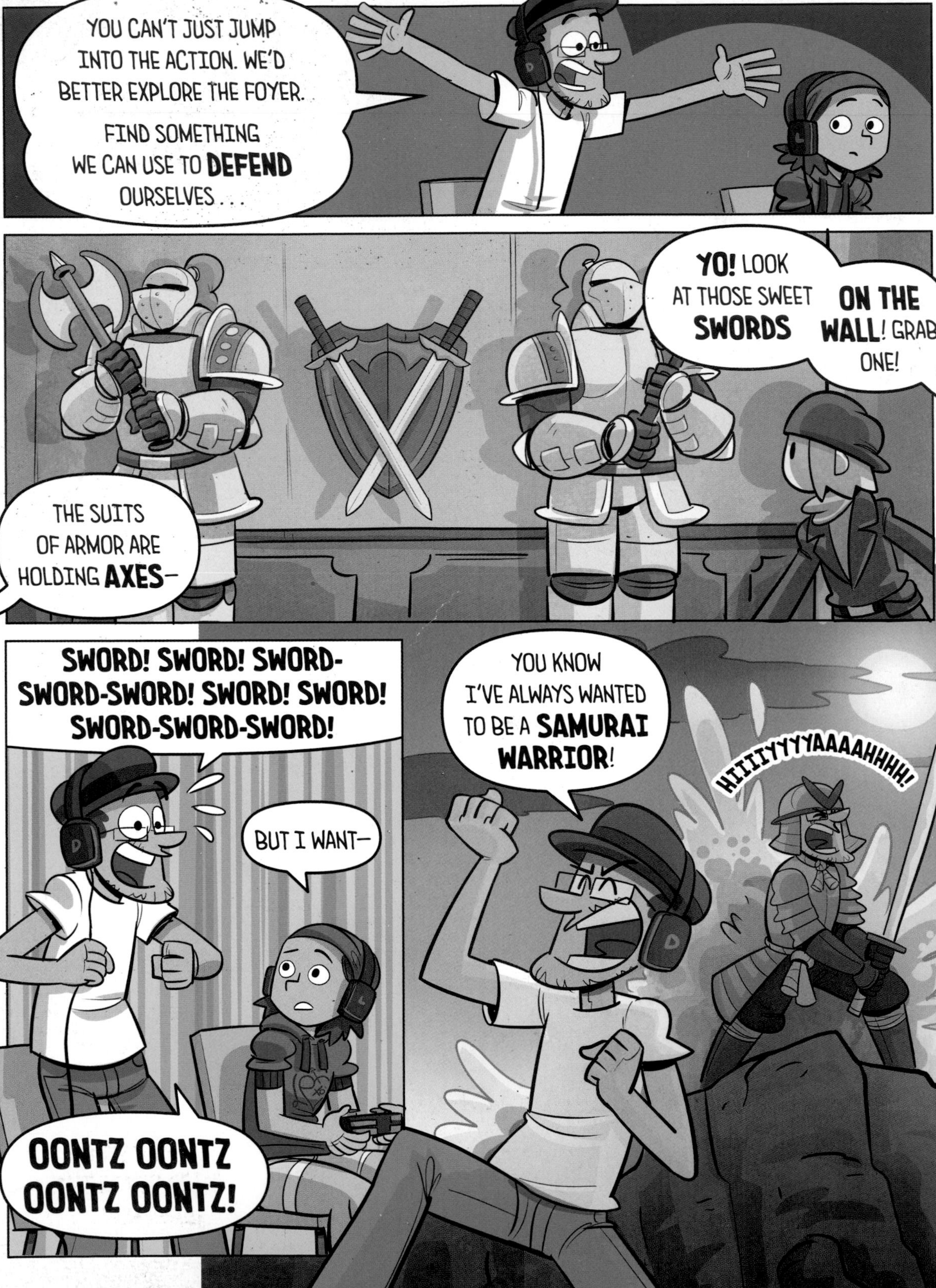
YOU CAN'T JUST JUMP INTO THE ACTION. WE'D BETTER EXPLORE THE FOYER.
FIND SOMETHING WE CAN USE TO **DEFEND** OURSELVES . . .
YO! LOOK AT THOSE SWEET **SWORDS** **ON THE WALL**! GRAB ONE!
THE SUITS OF ARMOR ARE HOLDING **AXES**—
SWORD! SWORD! SWORD-SWORD-SWORD! SWORD! SWORD! SWORD-SWORD-SWORD!
BUT I WANT—
OONTZ OONTZ OONTZ OONTZ OONTZ!
YOU KNOW I'VE ALWAYS WANTED TO BE A **SAMURAI WARRIOR**!
HIIIIYYYYAAAAHHHH!

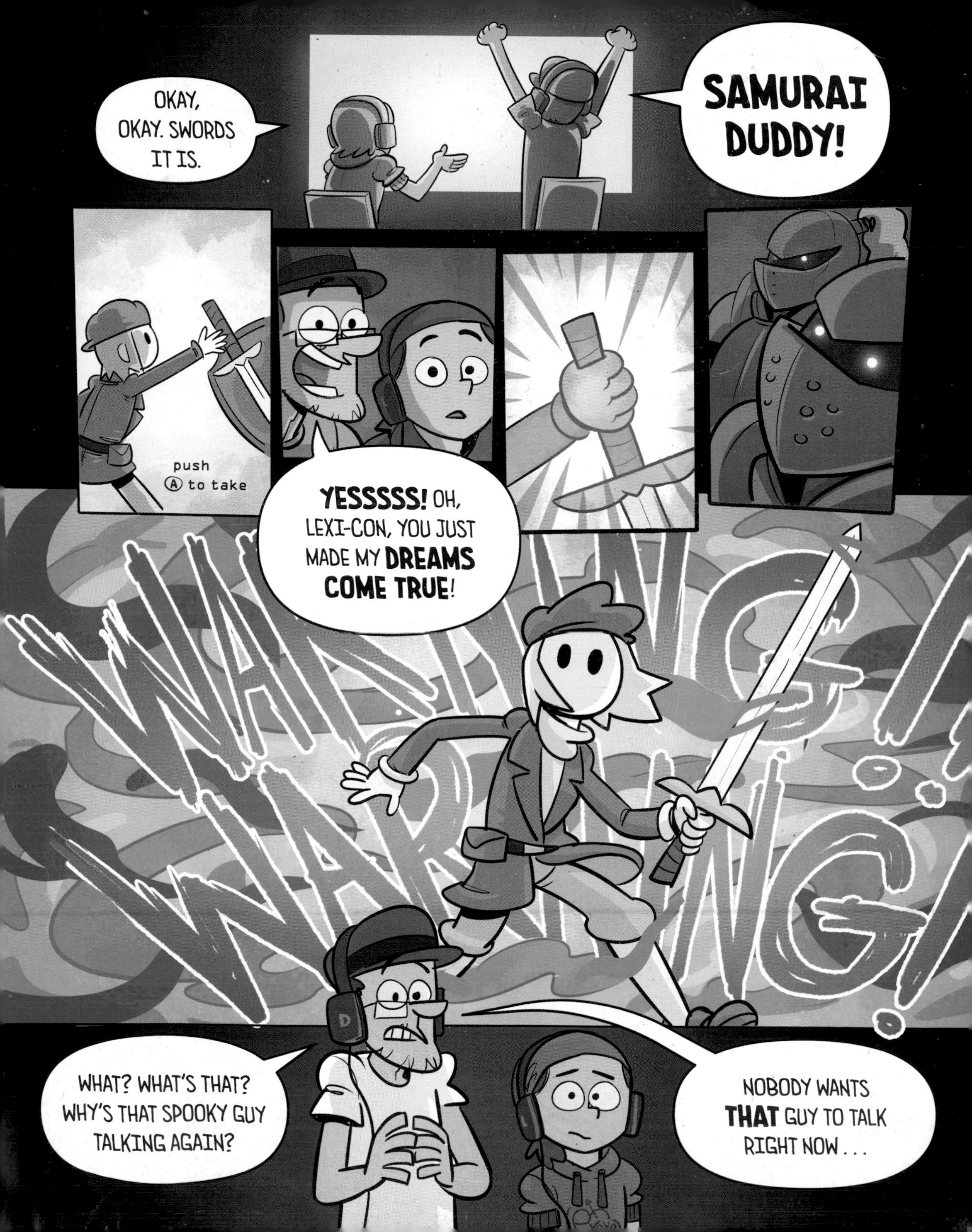

OKAY, OKAY. SWORDS IT IS.
SAMURAI DUDDY!
push
Ⓐ to take
YESSSSS! OH, LEXI-CON, YOU JUST MADE MY DREAMS COME TRUE!
WARNING! WARNING!
WHAT? WHAT'S THAT? WHY'S THAT SPOOKY GUY TALKING AGAIN?
NOBODY WANTS THAT GUY TO TALK RIGHT NOW . . .

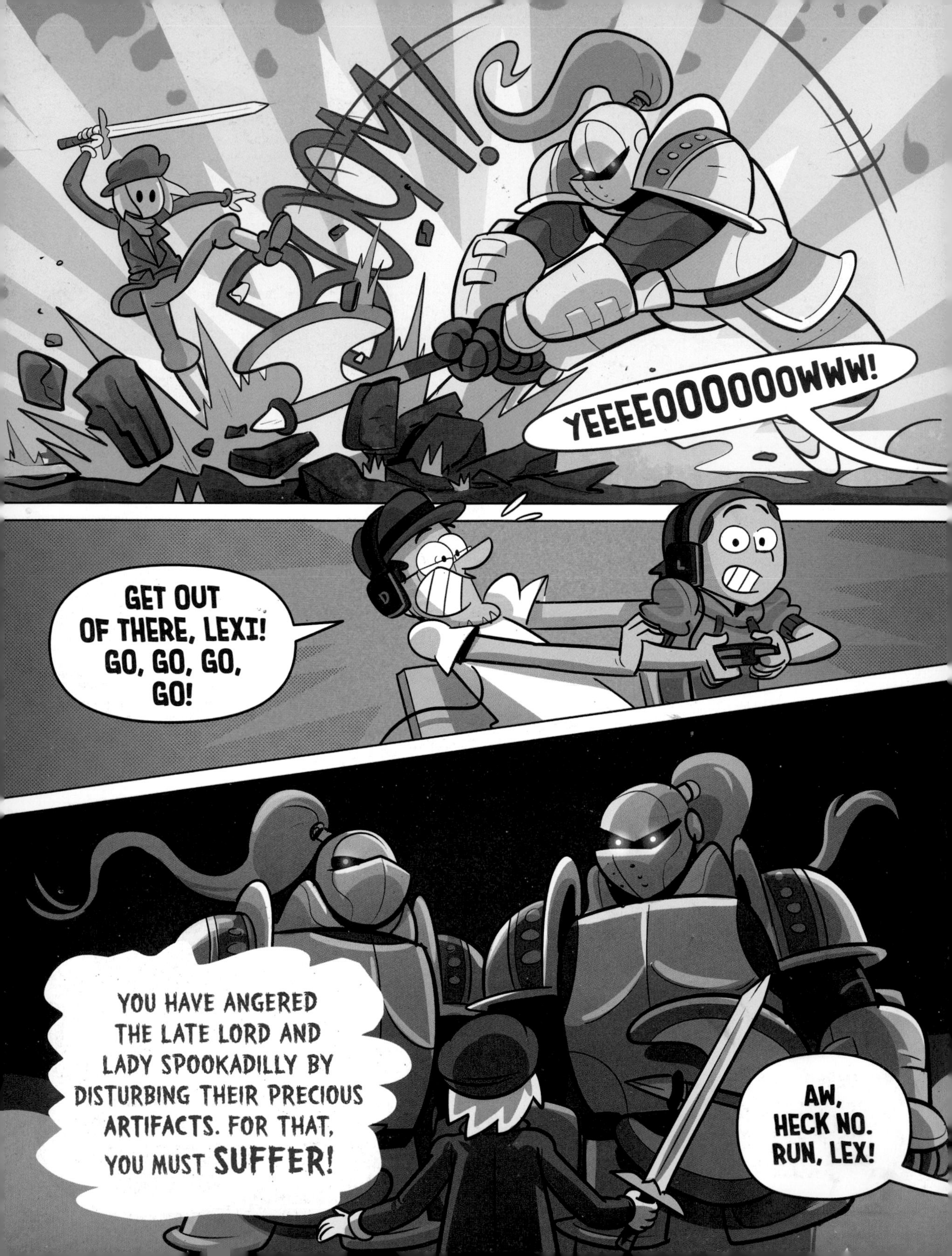
BOOM!
YEEEEOOOOOOWWW!
GET OUT OF THERE, LEXI! GO, GO, GO, GO!
YOU HAVE ANGERED THE LATE LORD AND LADY SPOOKADILLY BY DISTURBING THEIR PRECIOUS ARTIFACTS. FOR THAT, YOU MUST SUFFER!
AW, HECK NO. RUN, LEX!

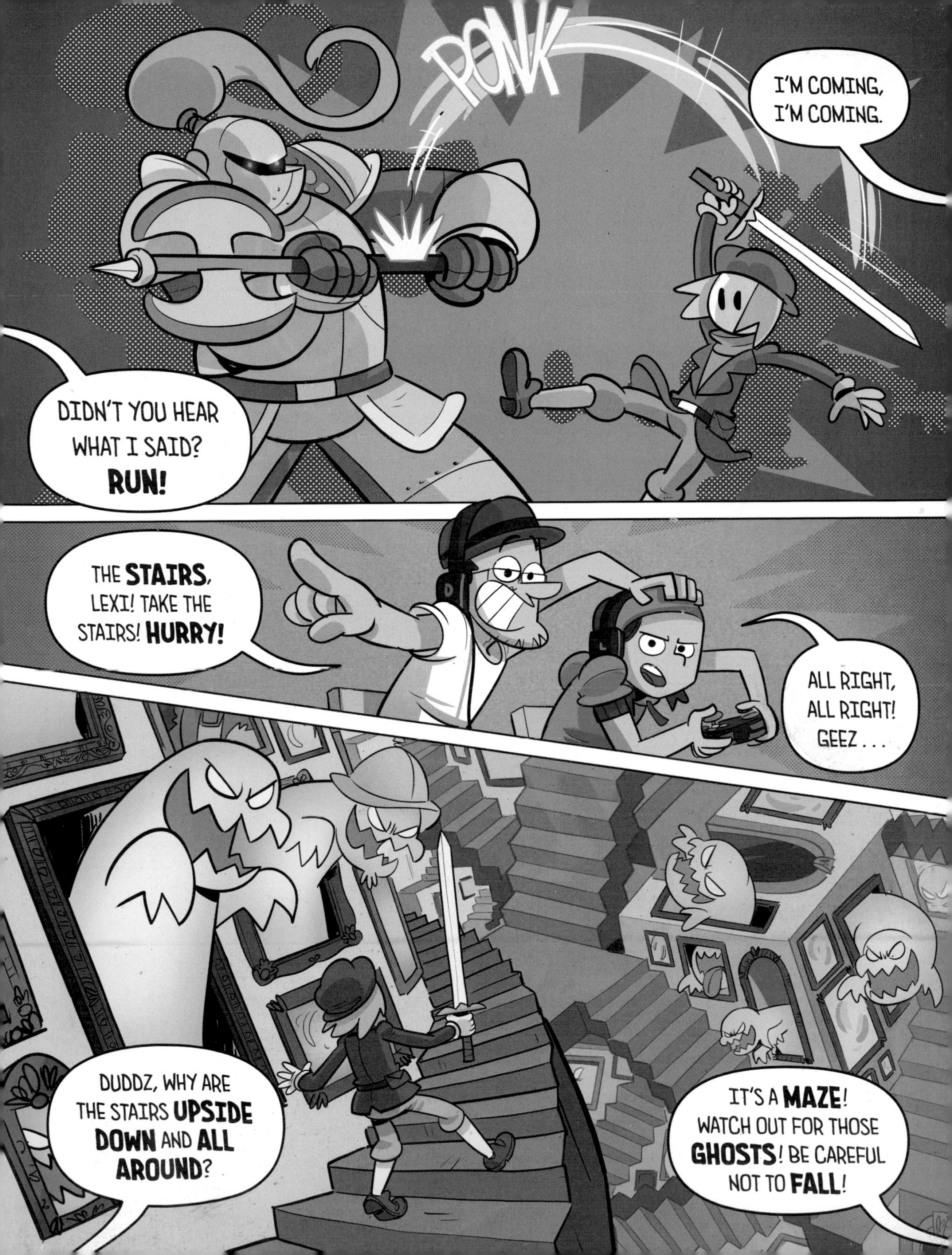
PONK
I'M COMING, I'M COMING.
DIDN'T YOU HEAR WHAT I SAID? **RUN!**
THE **STAIRS**, LEXI! TAKE THE STAIRS! **HURRY!**
ALL RIGHT, ALL RIGHT! GEEZ . . .
DUDDZ, WHY ARE THE STAIRS **UPSIDE DOWN** AND **ALL AROUND**?
IT'S A **MAZE**! WATCH OUT FOR THOSE **GHOSTS**! BE CAREFUL NOT TO **FALL**!

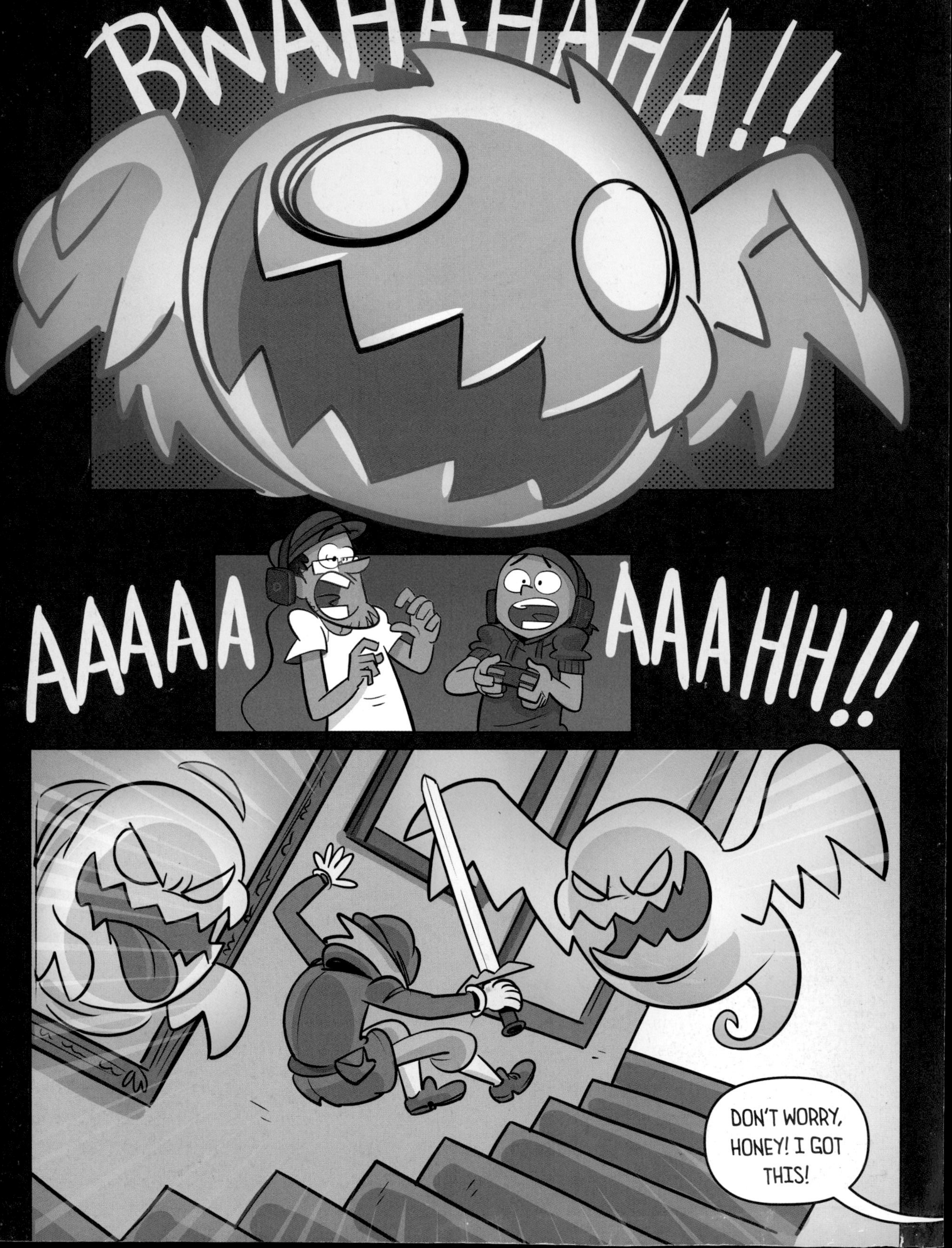
BWAHAHAHAHA!!
AAAAA
AAAHH!!
DON'T WORRY, HONEY! I GOT THIS!

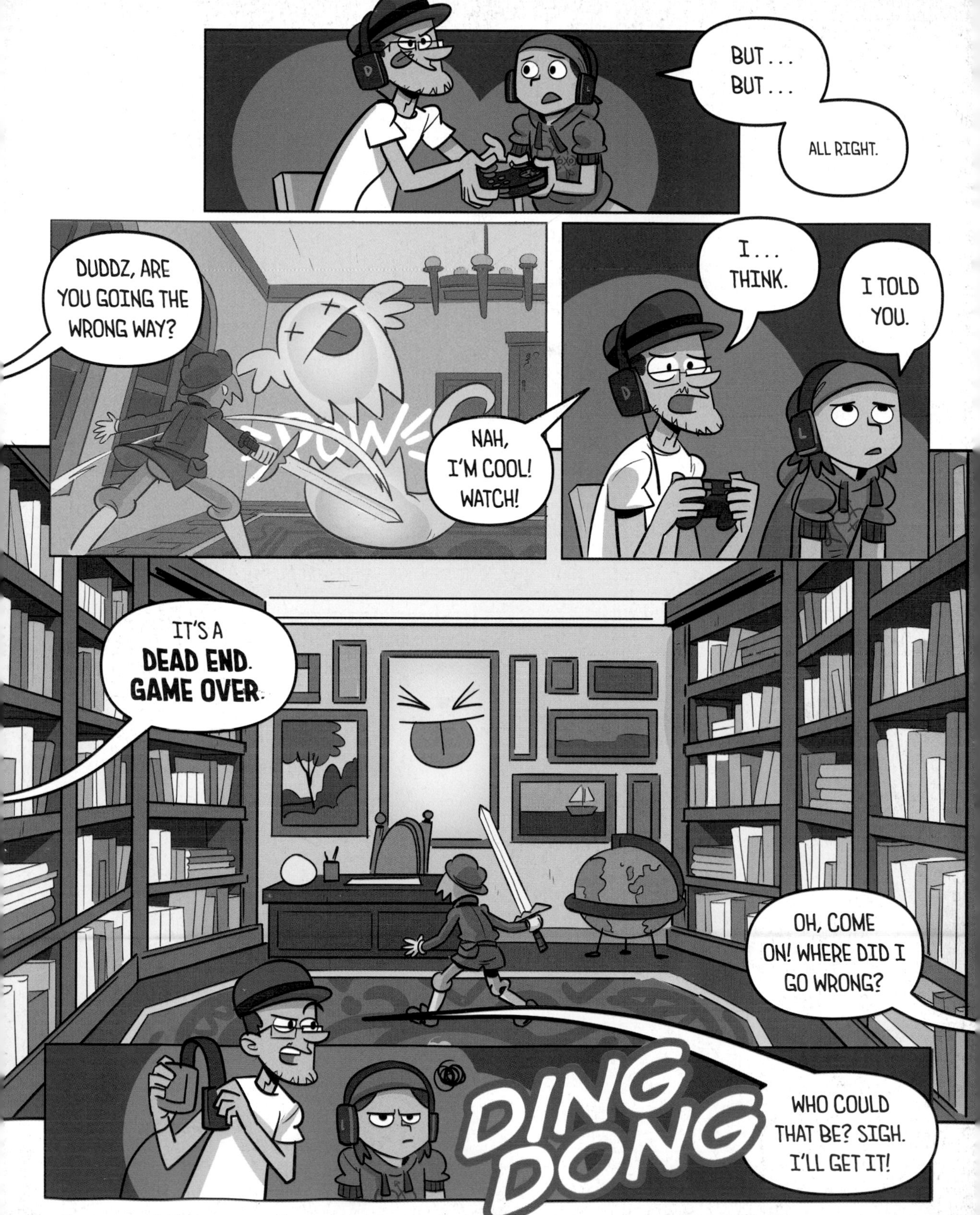
BUT . . .
BUT . . .
ALL RIGHT.
DUDDZ, ARE YOU GOING THE WRONG WAY?
POW
NAH, I'M COOL! WATCH!
I . . . THINK.
I TOLD YOU.
IT'S A **DEAD END. GAME OVER.**
OH, COME ON! WHERE DID I GO WRONG?
DING DONG
WHO COULD THAT BE? SIGH. I'LL GET IT!

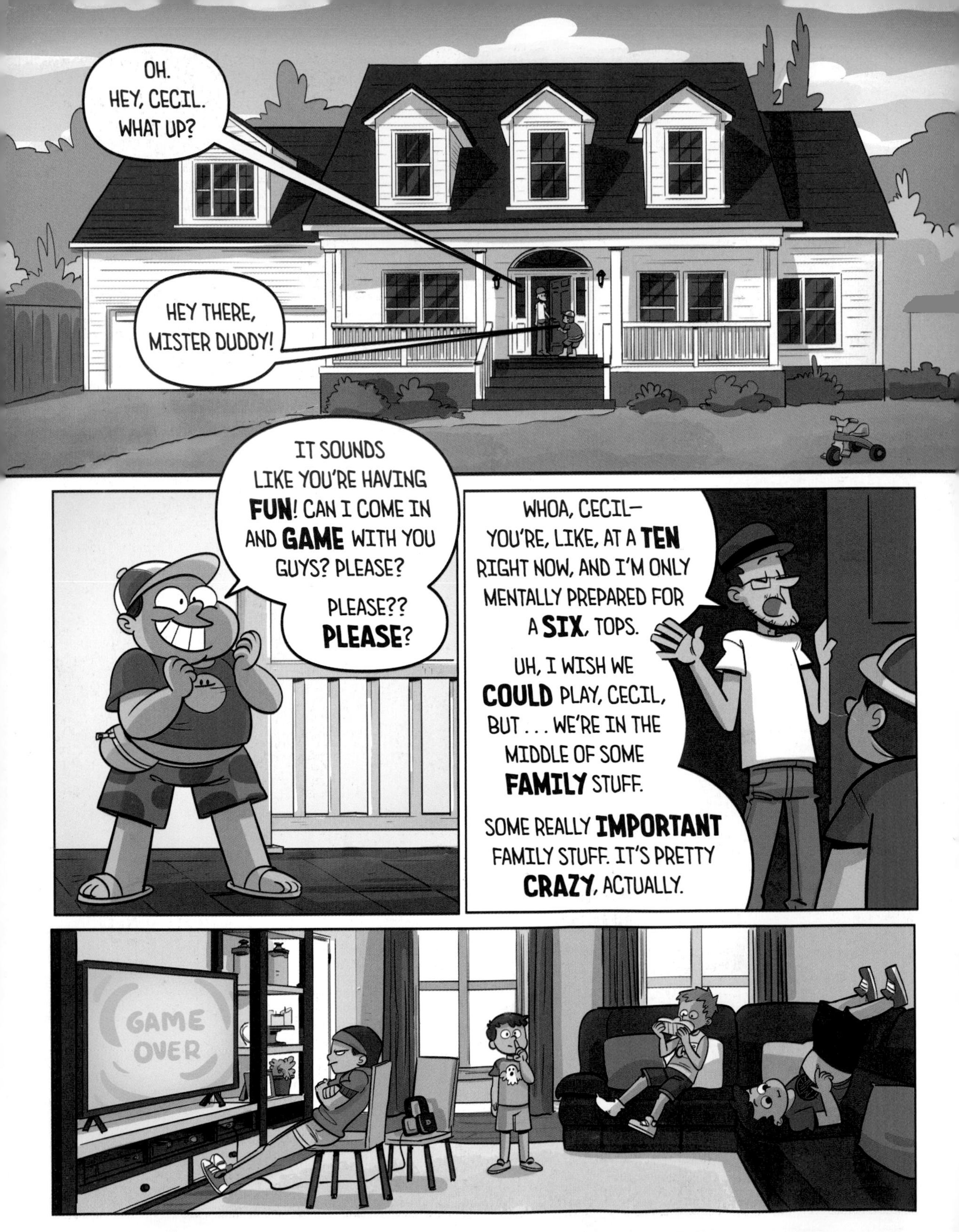

OH. HEY, CECIL. WHAT UP?
HEY THERE, MISTER DUDDY!
IT SOUNDS LIKE YOU'RE HAVING FUN! CAN I COME IN AND GAME WITH YOU GUYS? PLEASE?
PLEASE?? PLEASE?
WHOA, CECIL— YOU'RE, LIKE, AT A TEN RIGHT NOW, AND I'M ONLY MENTALLY PREPARED FOR A SIX, TOPS.
UH, I WISH WE COULD PLAY, CECIL, BUT . . . WE'RE IN THE MIDDLE OF SOME FAMILY STUFF.
SOME REALLY IMPORTANT FAMILY STUFF. IT'S PRETTY CRAZY, ACTUALLY.
GAME OVER

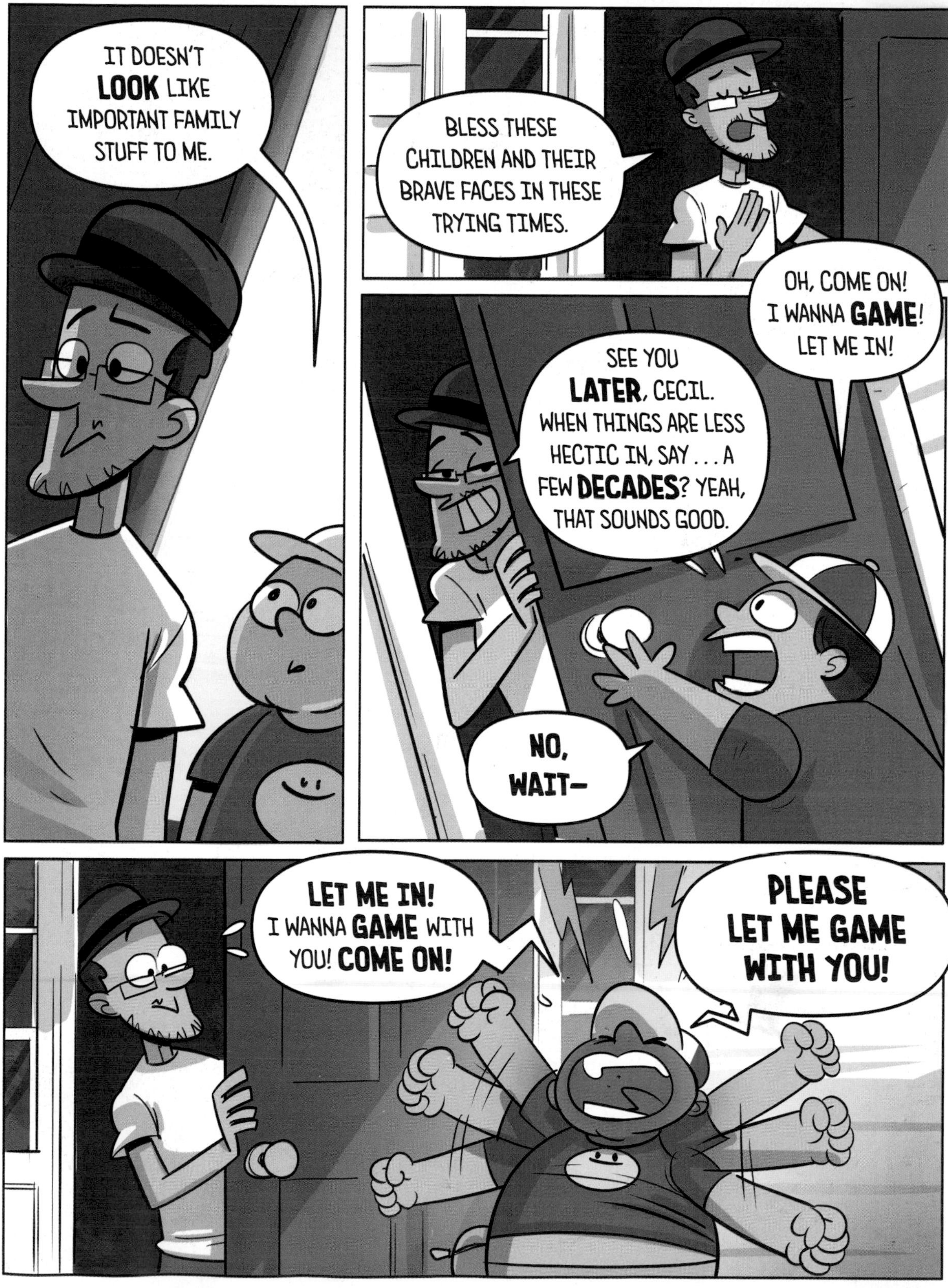
IT DOESN'T LOOK LIKE IMPORTANT FAMILY STUFF TO ME.
BLESS THESE CHILDREN AND THEIR BRAVE FACES IN THESE TRYING TIMES.
OH, COME ON! I WANNA GAME! LET ME IN!
SEE YOU LATER, CECIL. WHEN THINGS ARE LESS HECTIC IN, SAY . . . A FEW DECADES? YEAH, THAT SOUNDS GOOD.
NO, WAIT—
LET ME IN! I WANNA GAME WITH YOU! COME ON!
PLEASE LET ME GAME WITH YOU!

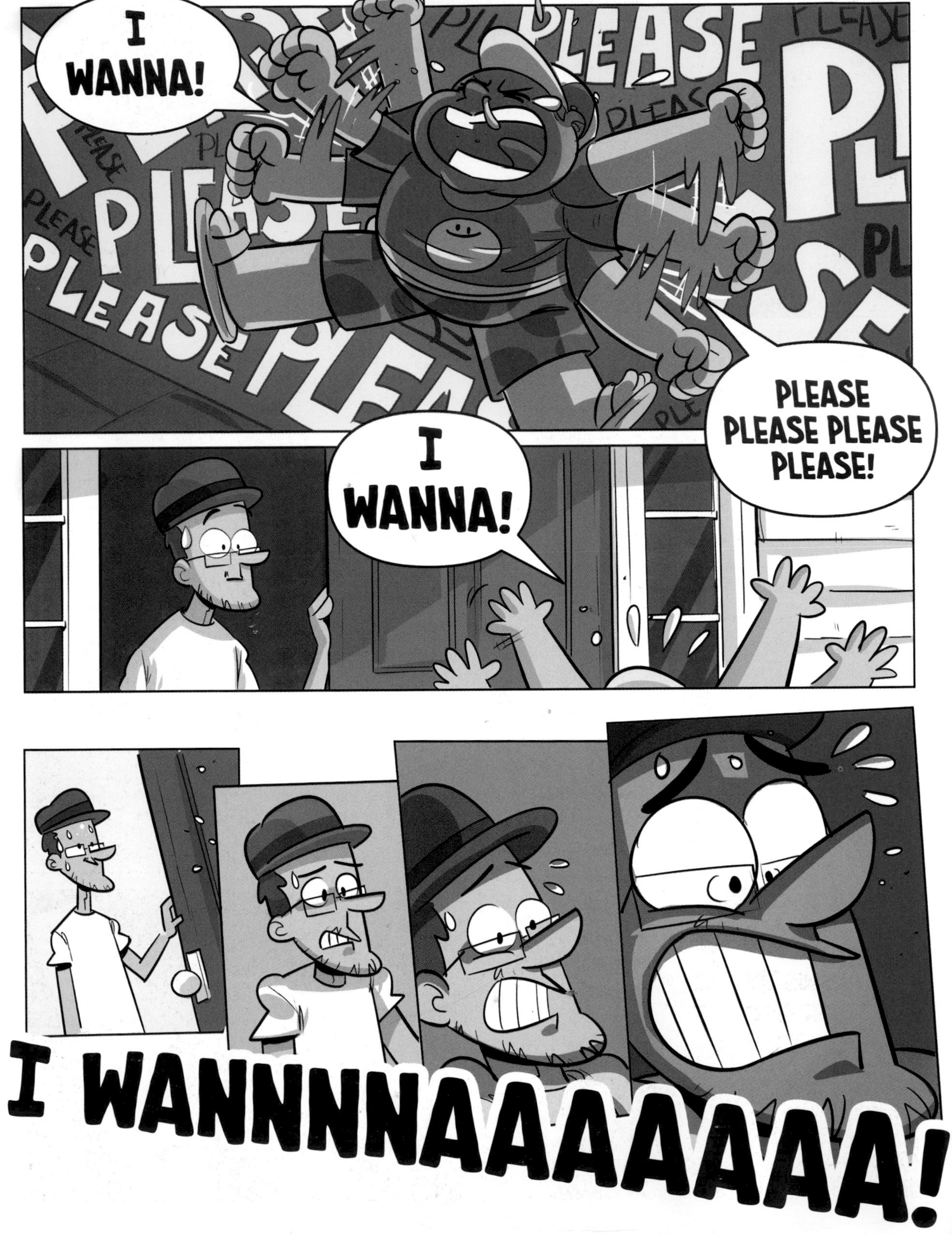
I WANNA!
PLEASE PLEASE PLEASE PLEASE PLEASE PLEASE PLEASE PLEASE PLEASE PLEASE PLEASE PLEASE
PLEASE PLEASE PLEASE PLEASE PLEASE!
I WANNA!
I WANNNNAAAAAAAA!

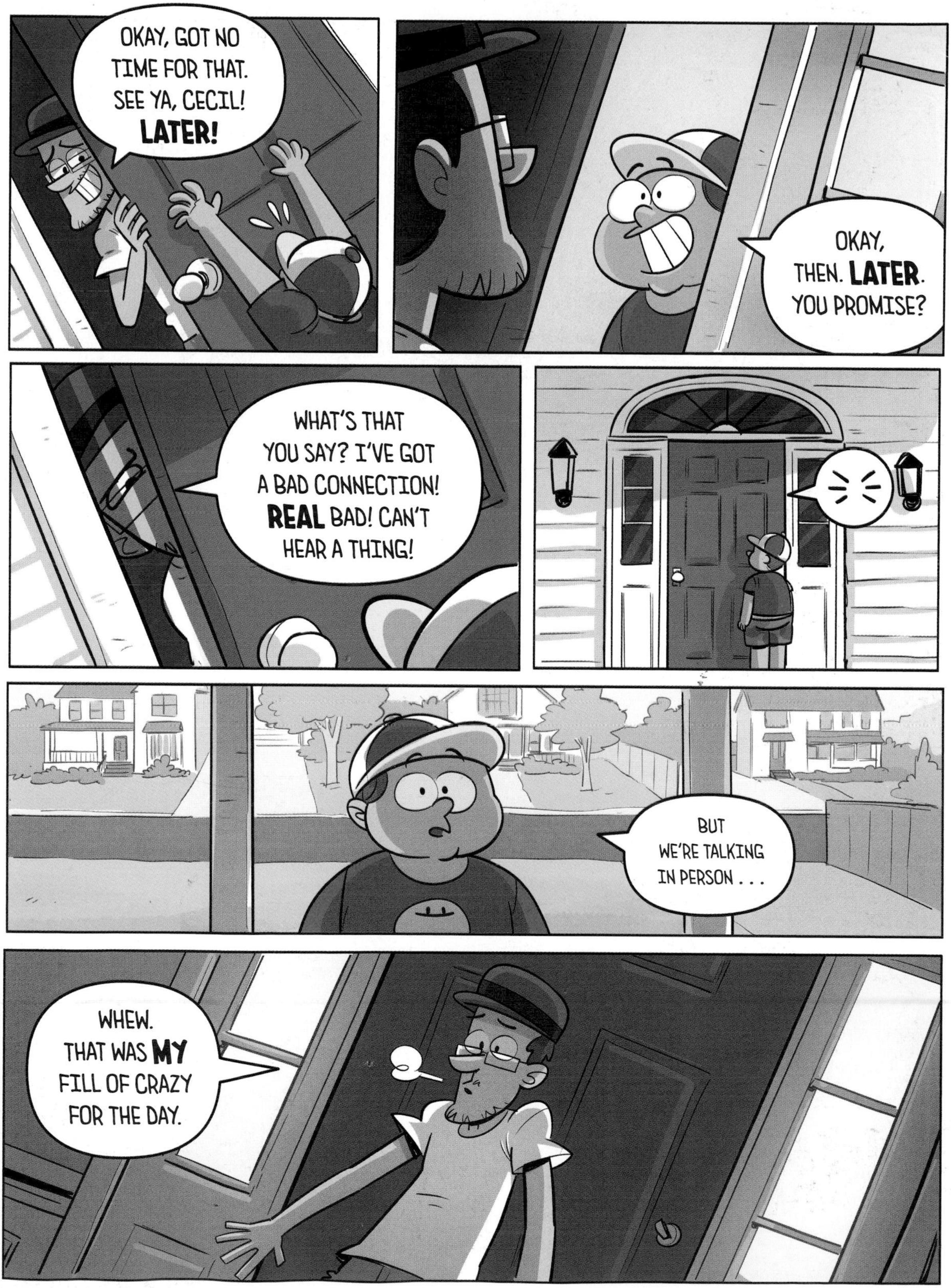
OKAY, GOT NO TIME FOR THAT. SEE YA, CECIL! **LATER!**
OKAY, THEN. **LATER**. YOU PROMISE?
WHAT'S THAT YOU SAY? I'VE GOT A BAD CONNECTION! **REAL** BAD! CAN'T HEAR A THING!
BUT WE'RE TALKING IN PERSON . . .
WHEW. THAT WAS **MY** FILL OF CRAZY FOR THE DAY.

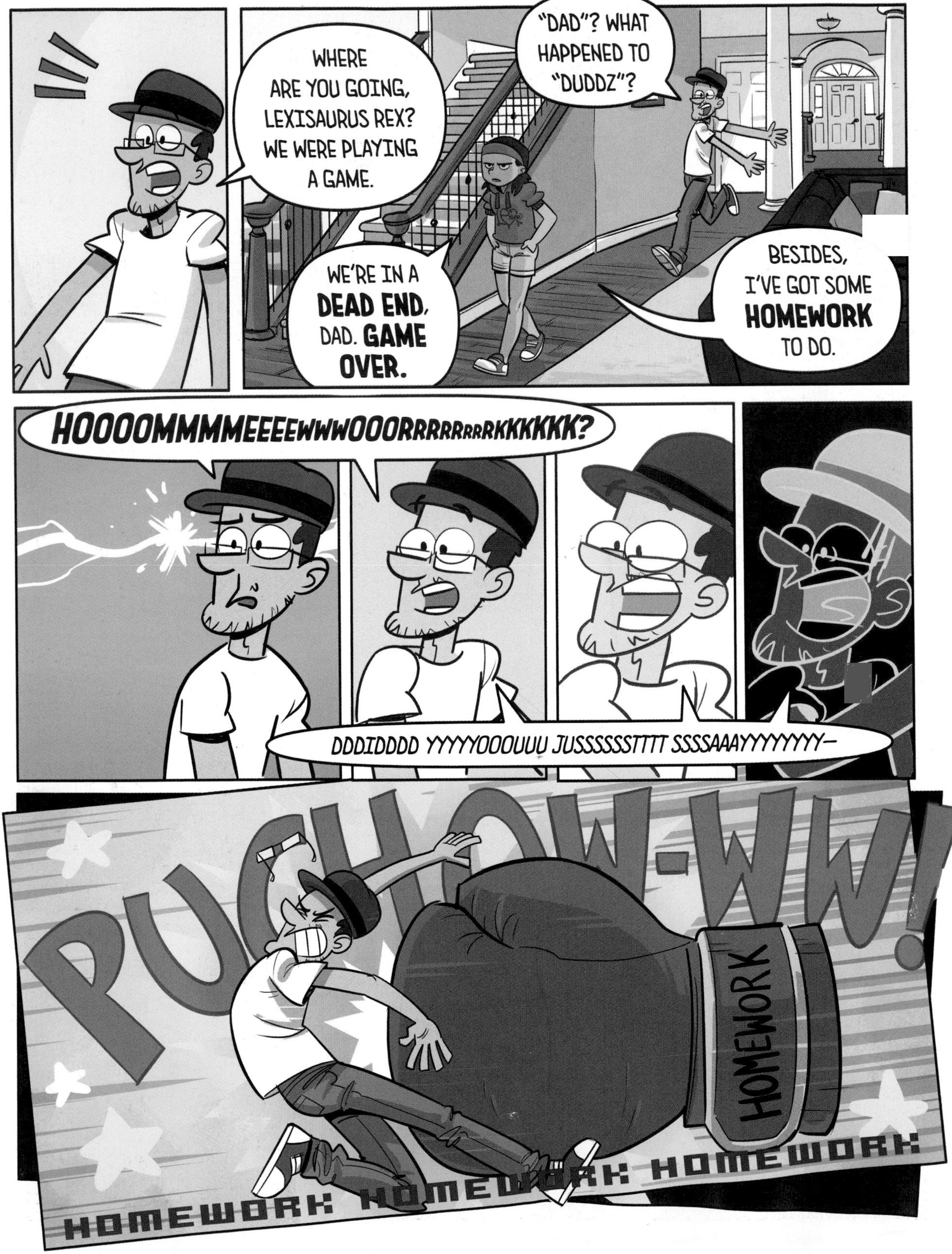
WHERE ARE YOU GOING, LEXISAURUS REX? WE WERE PLAYING A GAME.
WE'RE IN A **DEAD END,** DAD. **GAME OVER.**
"DAD"? WHAT HAPPENED TO "DUDDZ"?
BESIDES, I'VE GOT SOME **HOMEWORK** TO DO.
HOOOOMMMMEEEEWWWOOORRRRRRRKKKKK?
DDDIDDDD YYYYYOOOUUU JUSSSSSSTTTT SSSSAAAYYYYYYYY—
PUCHOW-WW!
HOMEWORK
HOMEWORK HOMEWORK HOMEWORK

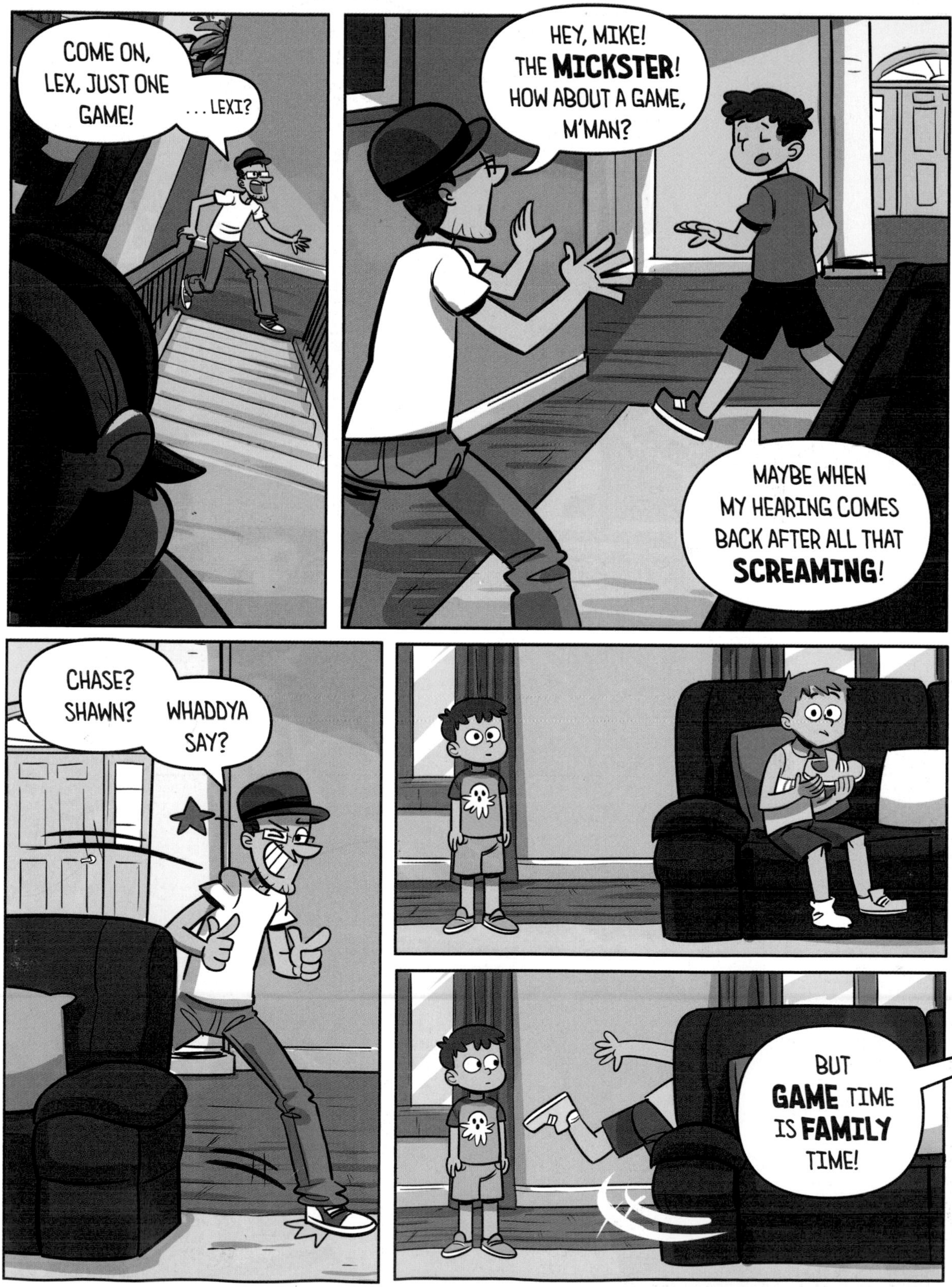
COME ON, LEX, JUST ONE GAME!
. . . LEXI?
HEY, MIKE! THE **MICKSTER**! HOW ABOUT A GAME, M'MAN?
MAYBE WHEN MY HEARING COMES BACK AFTER ALL THAT **SCREAMING**!
CHASE? SHAWN?
WHADDYA SAY?
BUT **GAME** TIME IS **FAMILY** TIME!

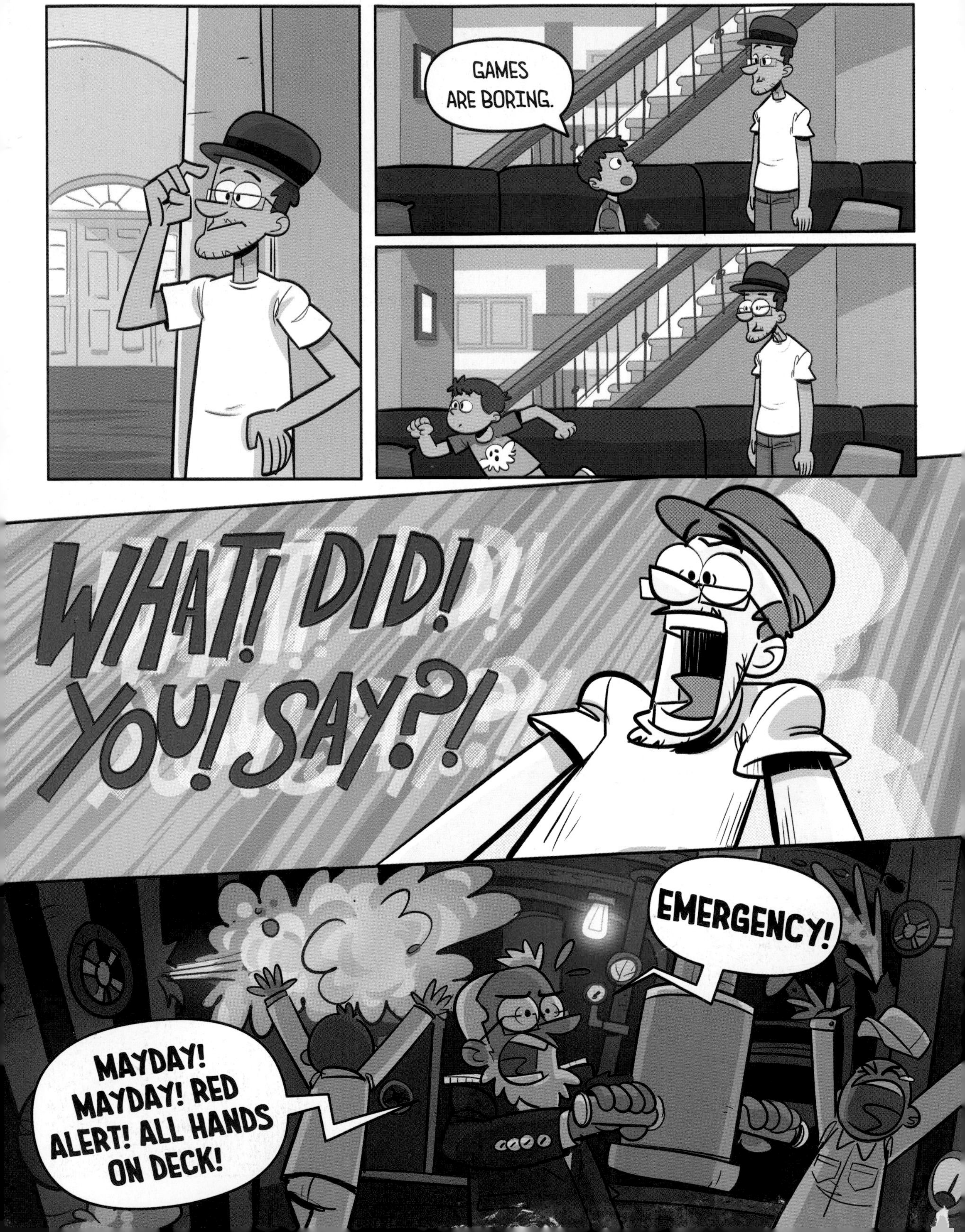
GAMES ARE BORING.
WHAT! DID! YOU! SAY?!
EMERGENCY!
MAYDAY! MAYDAY! RED ALERT! ALL HANDS ON DECK!

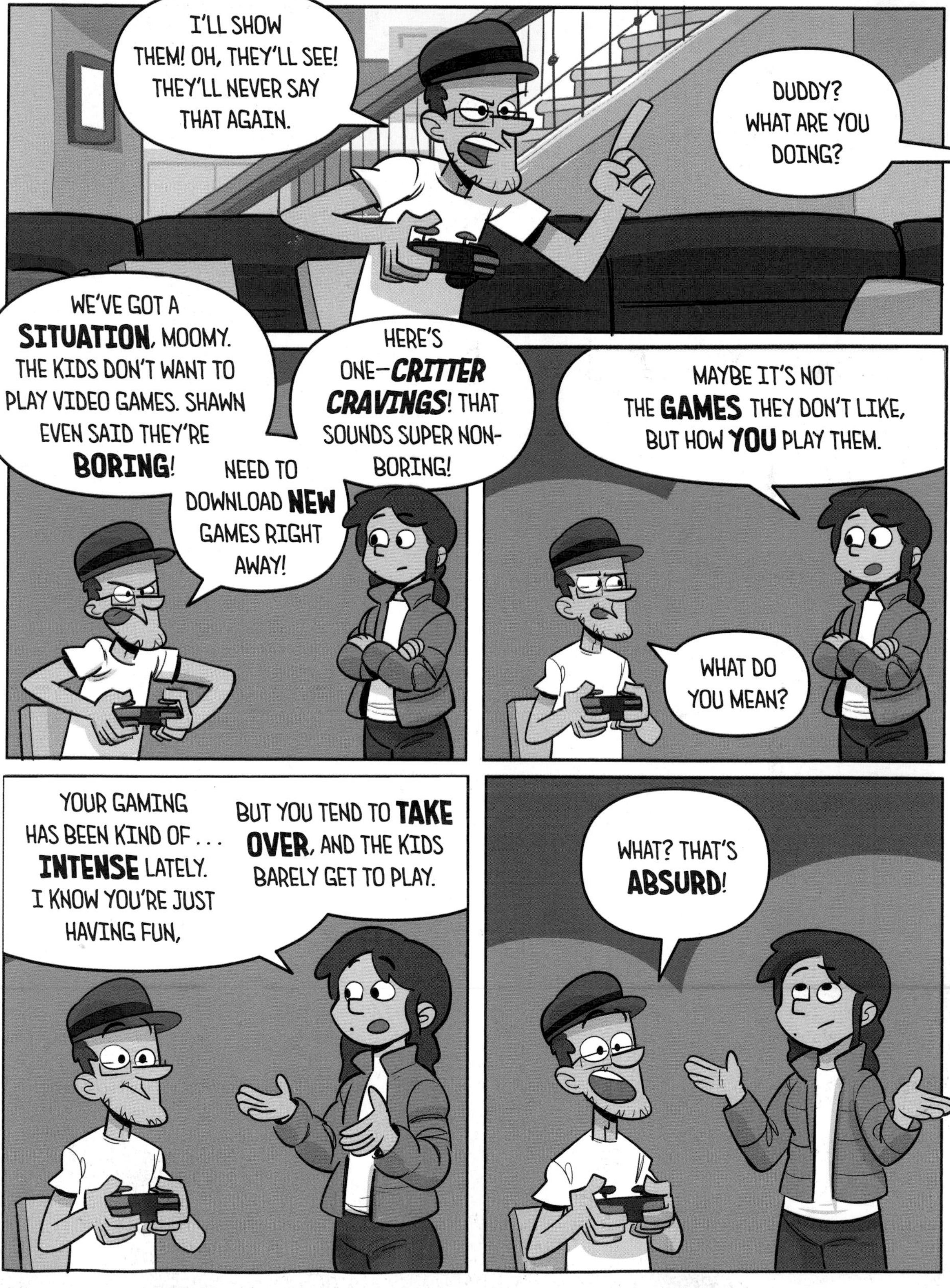

I'LL SHOW THEM! OH, THEY'LL SEE! THEY'LL NEVER SAY THAT AGAIN.
DUDDY? WHAT ARE YOU DOING?
WE'VE GOT A SITUATION, MOOMY. THE KIDS DON'T WANT TO PLAY VIDEO GAMES. SHAWN EVEN SAID THEY'RE BORING!
NEED TO DOWNLOAD NEW GAMES RIGHT AWAY!
HERE'S ONE—CRITTER CRAVINGS! THAT SOUNDS SUPER NON-BORING!
MAYBE IT'S NOT THE GAMES THEY DON'T LIKE, BUT HOW YOU PLAY THEM.
WHAT DO YOU MEAN?
YOUR GAMING HAS BEEN KIND OF . . . INTENSE LATELY. I KNOW YOU'RE JUST HAVING FUN,
BUT YOU TEND TO TAKE OVER, AND THE KIDS BARELY GET TO PLAY.
WHAT? THAT'S ABSURD!

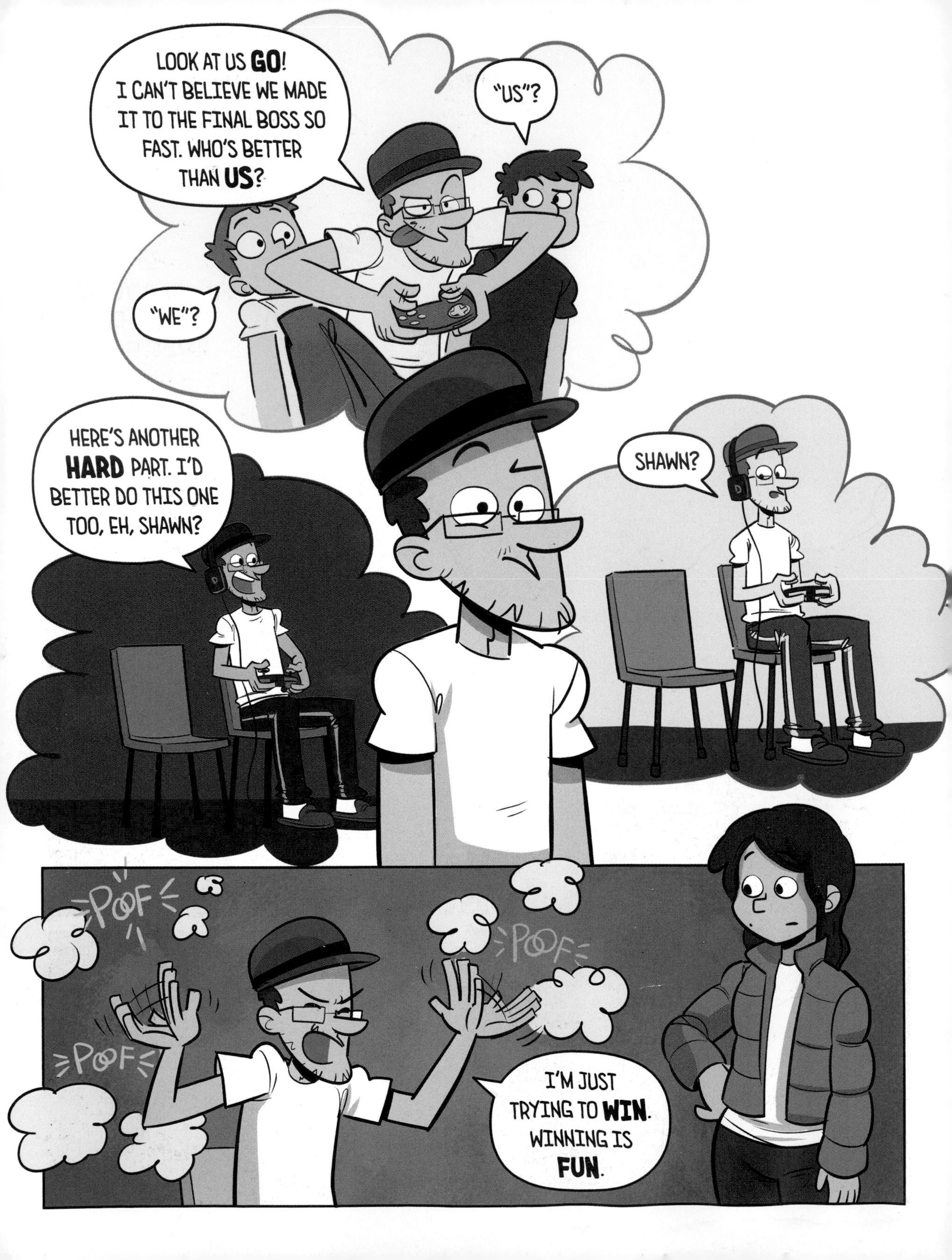
LOOK AT US **GO**! I CAN'T BELIEVE WE MADE IT TO THE FINAL BOSS SO FAST. WHO'S BETTER THAN **US**?
"US"?
"WE"?
HERE'S ANOTHER **HARD** PART. I'D BETTER DO THIS ONE TOO, EH, SHAWN?
SHAWN?
POOF
POOF
POOF
I'M JUST TRYING TO **WIN**. WINNING IS **FUN**.

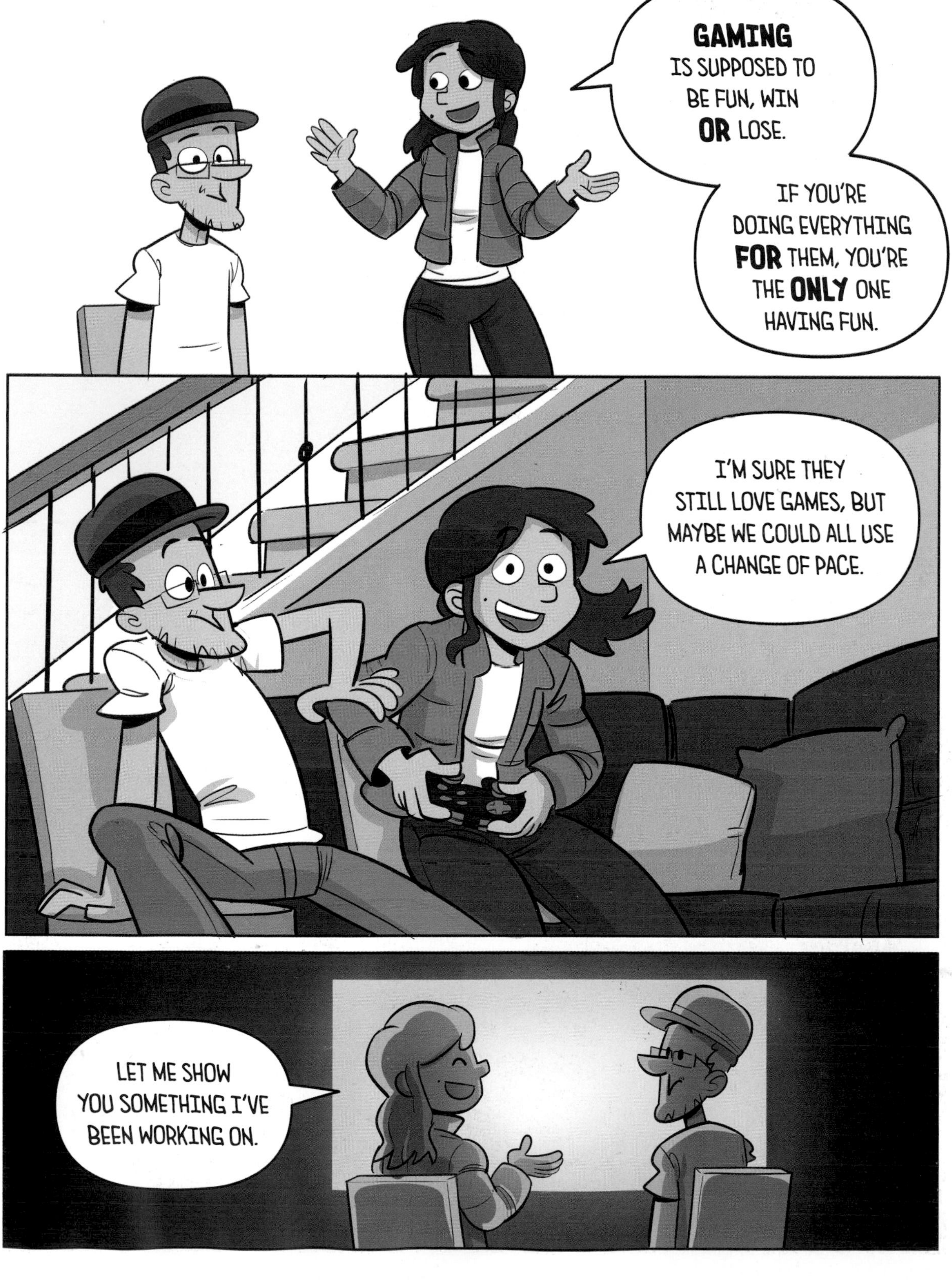
GAMING IS SUPPOSED TO BE FUN, WIN OR LOSE.
IF YOU'RE DOING EVERYTHING FOR THEM, YOU'RE THE ONLY ONE HAVING FUN.
I'M SURE THEY STILL LOVE GAMES, BUT MAYBE WE COULD ALL USE A CHANGE OF PACE.
LET ME SHOW YOU SOMETHING I'VE BEEN WORKING ON.

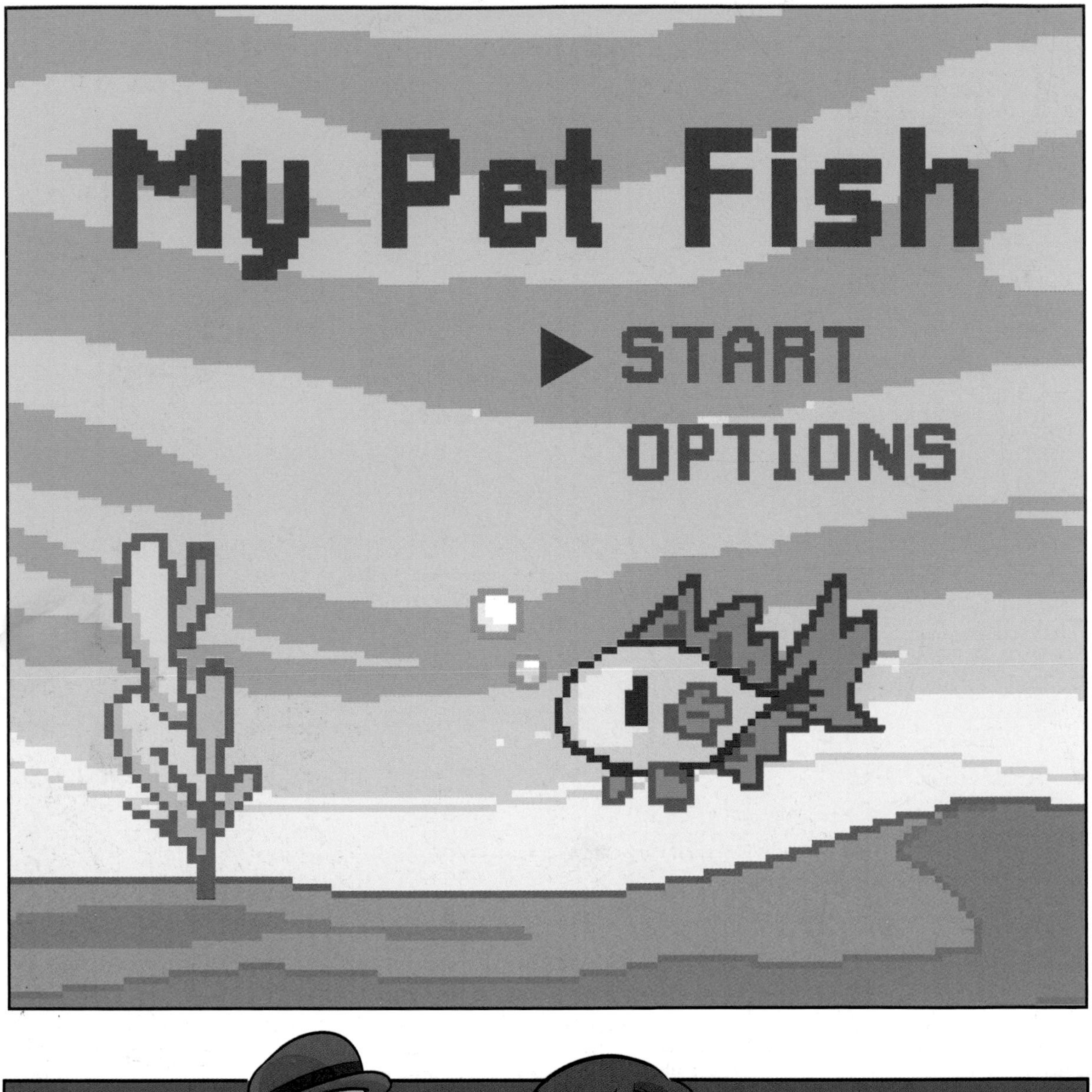
My Pet Fish
▶ START
OPTIONS

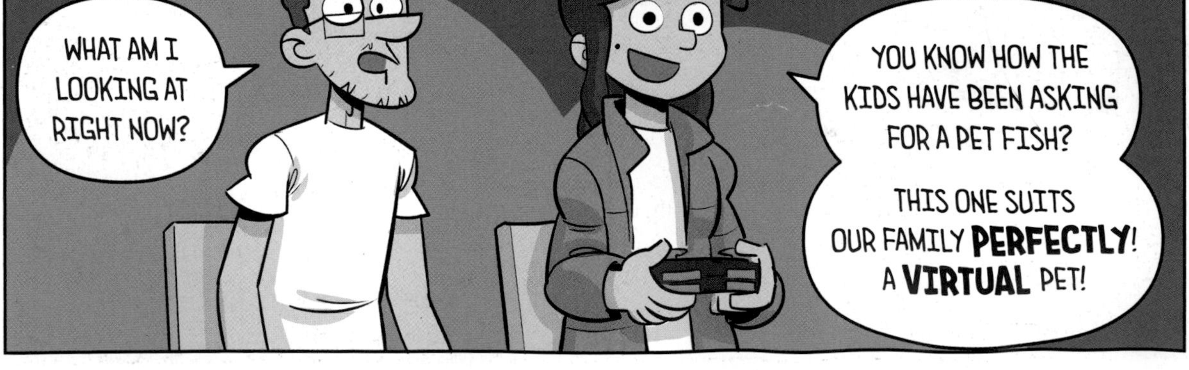
WHAT AM I LOOKING AT RIGHT NOW?
YOU KNOW HOW THE KIDS HAVE BEEN ASKING FOR A PET FISH?
THIS ONE SUITS OUR FAMILY PERFECTLY! A VIRTUAL PET!

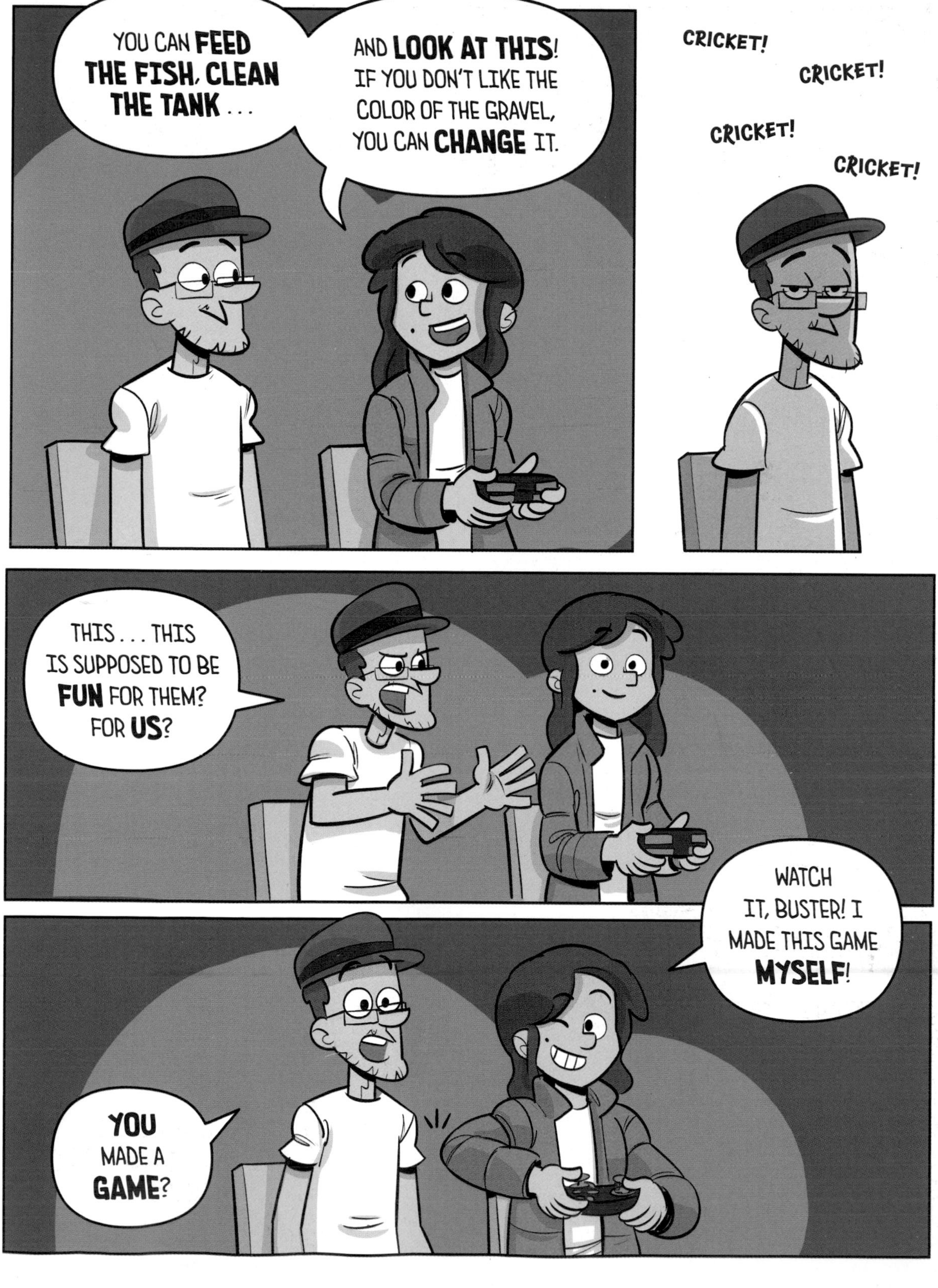
YOU CAN FEED THE FISH, CLEAN THE TANK . . .
AND LOOK AT THIS! IF YOU DON'T LIKE THE COLOR OF THE GRAVEL, YOU CAN CHANGE IT.
CRICKET!
CRICKET!
CRICKET!
CRICKET!
THIS . . . THIS IS SUPPOSED TO BE FUN FOR THEM? FOR US?
WATCH IT, BUSTER! I MADE THIS GAME MYSELF!
YOU MADE A GAME?

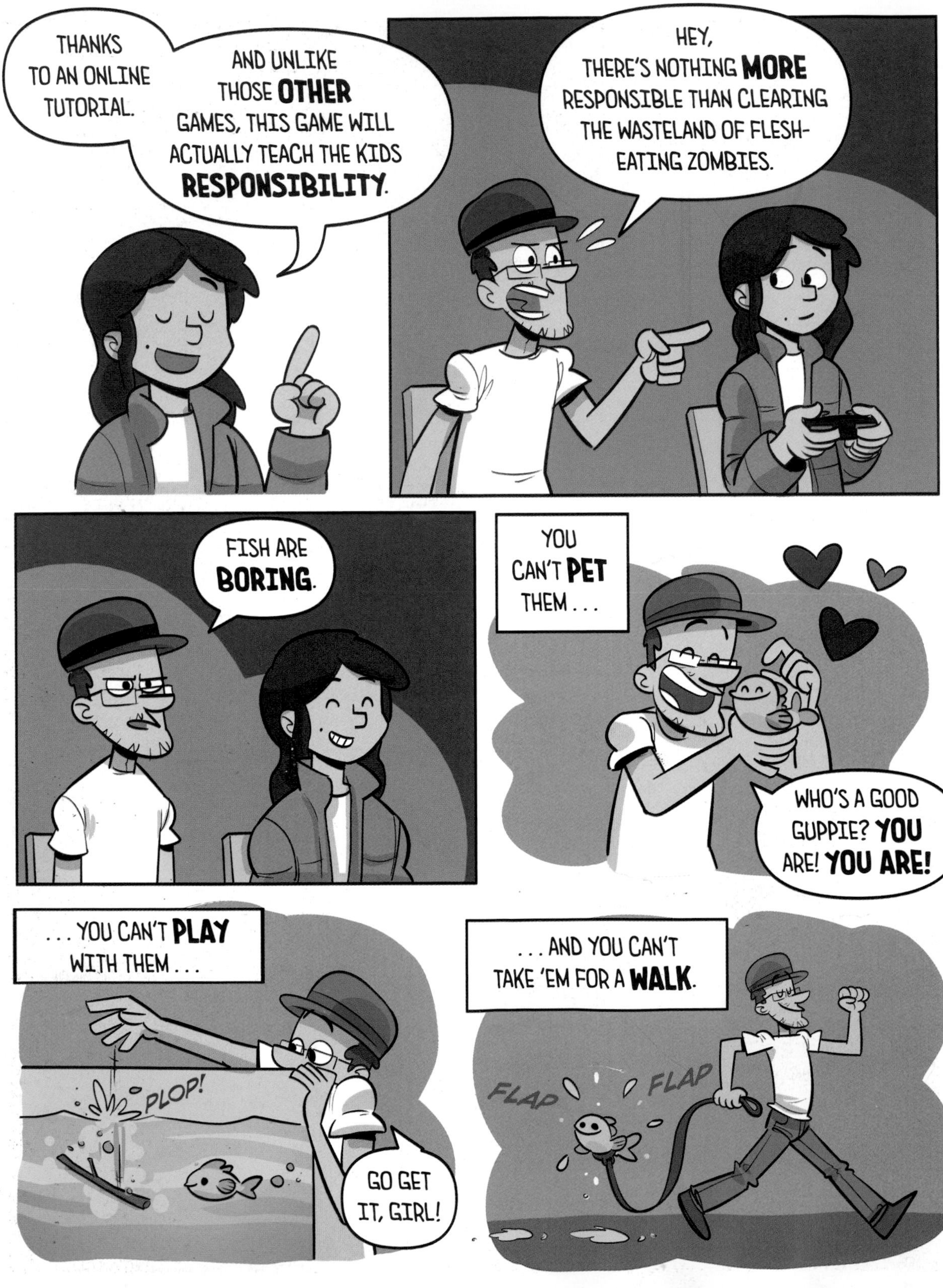
THANKS TO AN ONLINE TUTORIAL.
AND UNLIKE THOSE **OTHER** GAMES, THIS GAME WILL ACTUALLY TEACH THE KIDS **RESPONSIBILITY**.
HEY, THERE'S NOTHING **MORE** RESPONSIBLE THAN CLEARING THE WASTELAND OF FLESH-EATING ZOMBIES.
FISH ARE **BORING**.
YOU CAN'T **PET** THEM . . .
WHO'S A GOOD GUPPIE? **YOU** ARE! **YOU ARE!**
. . . YOU CAN'T **PLAY** WITH THEM . . .
PLOP!
GO GET IT, GIRL!
. . . AND YOU CAN'T TAKE 'EM FOR A **WALK**.
FLAP
FLAP

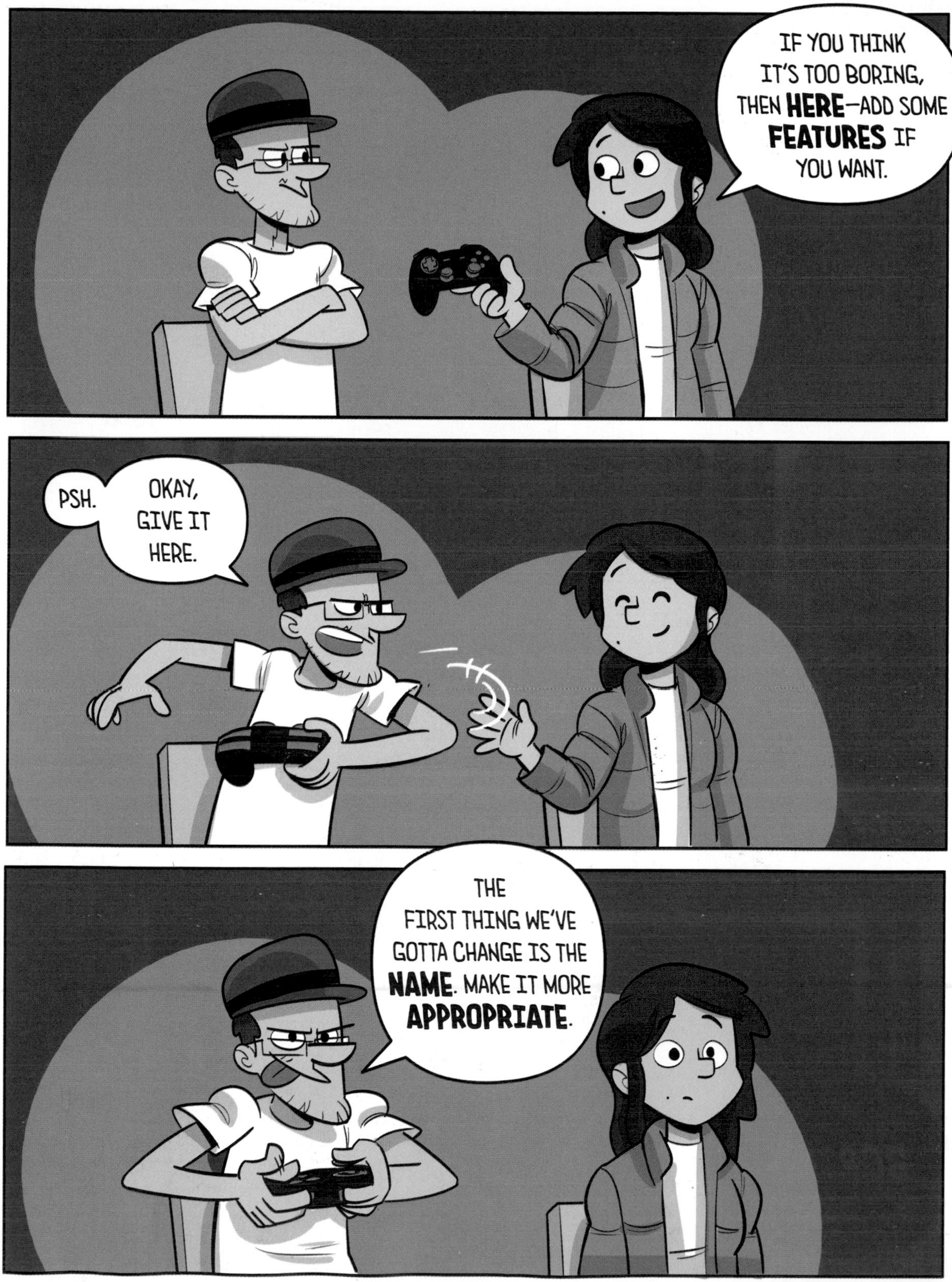
IF YOU THINK IT'S TOO BORING, THEN **HERE**—ADD SOME **FEATURES** IF YOU WANT.
PSH.
OKAY, GIVE IT HERE.
THE FIRST THING WE'VE GOTTA CHANGE IS THE **NAME**. MAKE IT MORE **APPROPRIATE**.

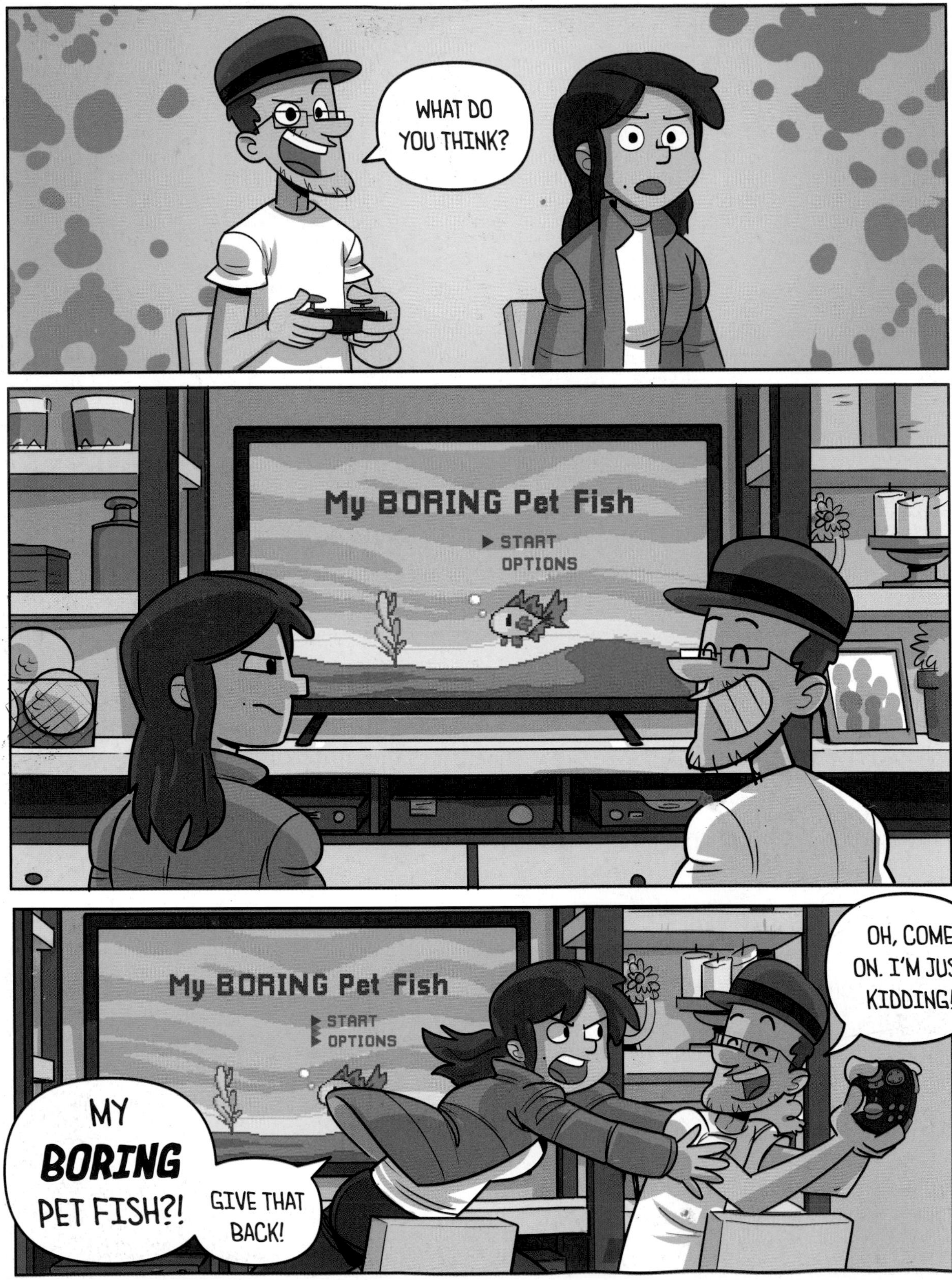
WHAT DO YOU THINK?
My BORING Pet Fish
START
OPTIONS
My BORING Pet Fish
START
OPTIONS
OH, COME ON. I'M JUST KIDDING!
MY BORING PET FISH?!
GIVE THAT BACK!

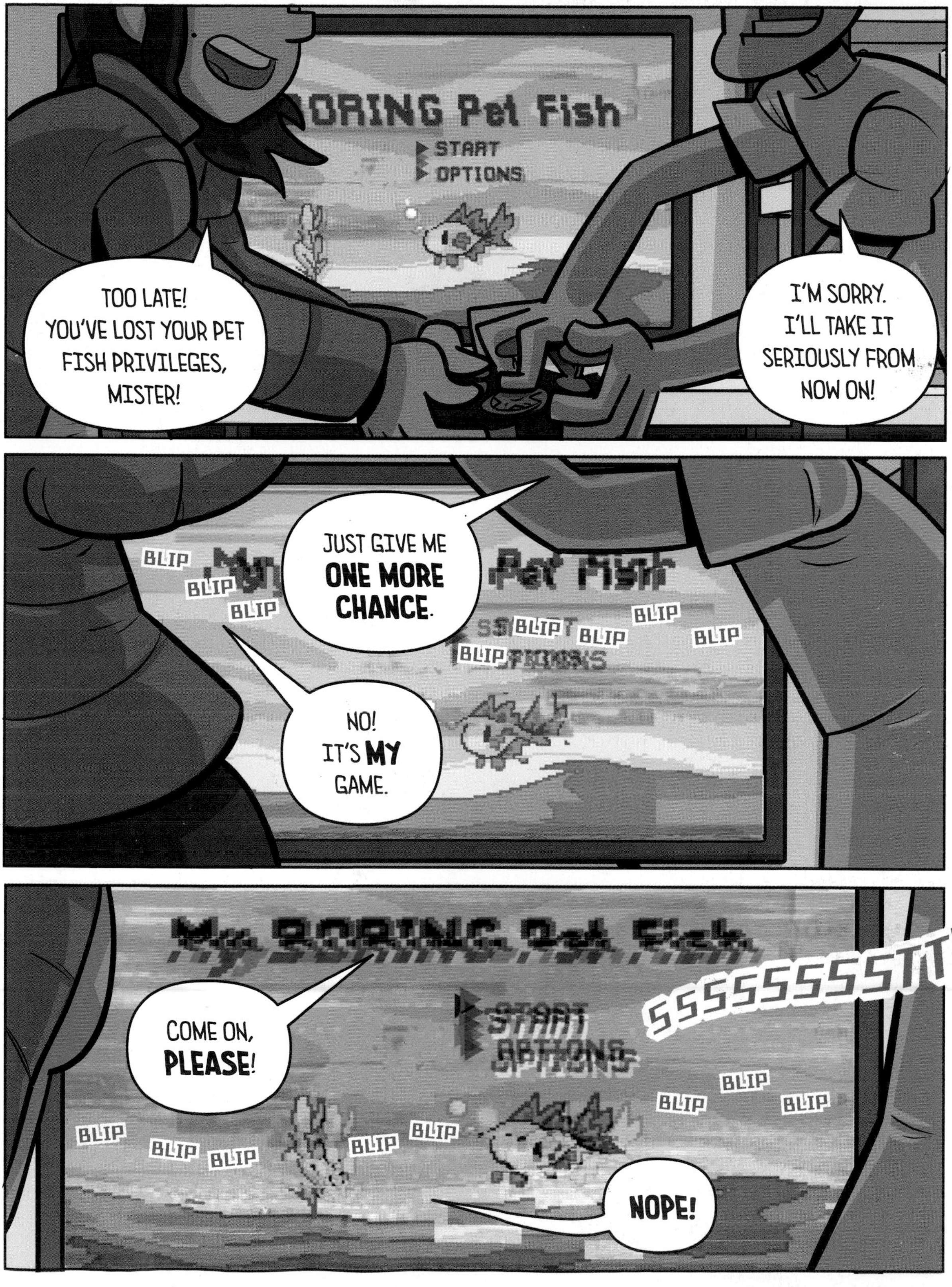
BORING Pet Fish
START
OPTIONS
TOO LATE! YOU'VE LOST YOUR PET FISH PRIVILEGES, MISTER!
I'M SORRY. I'LL TAKE IT SERIOUSLY FROM NOW ON!
JUST GIVE ME **ONE MORE CHANCE**.
BLIP BLIP BLIP
NO! IT'S **MY** GAME.
BLIP BLIP BLIP BLIP BLIP BLIP
My BORING Pet Fish
COME ON, **PLEASE**!
START
OPTIONS
SSSSSSSSTT!
BLIP BLIP BLIP BLIP BLIP BLIP BLIP BLIP BLIP
NOPE!

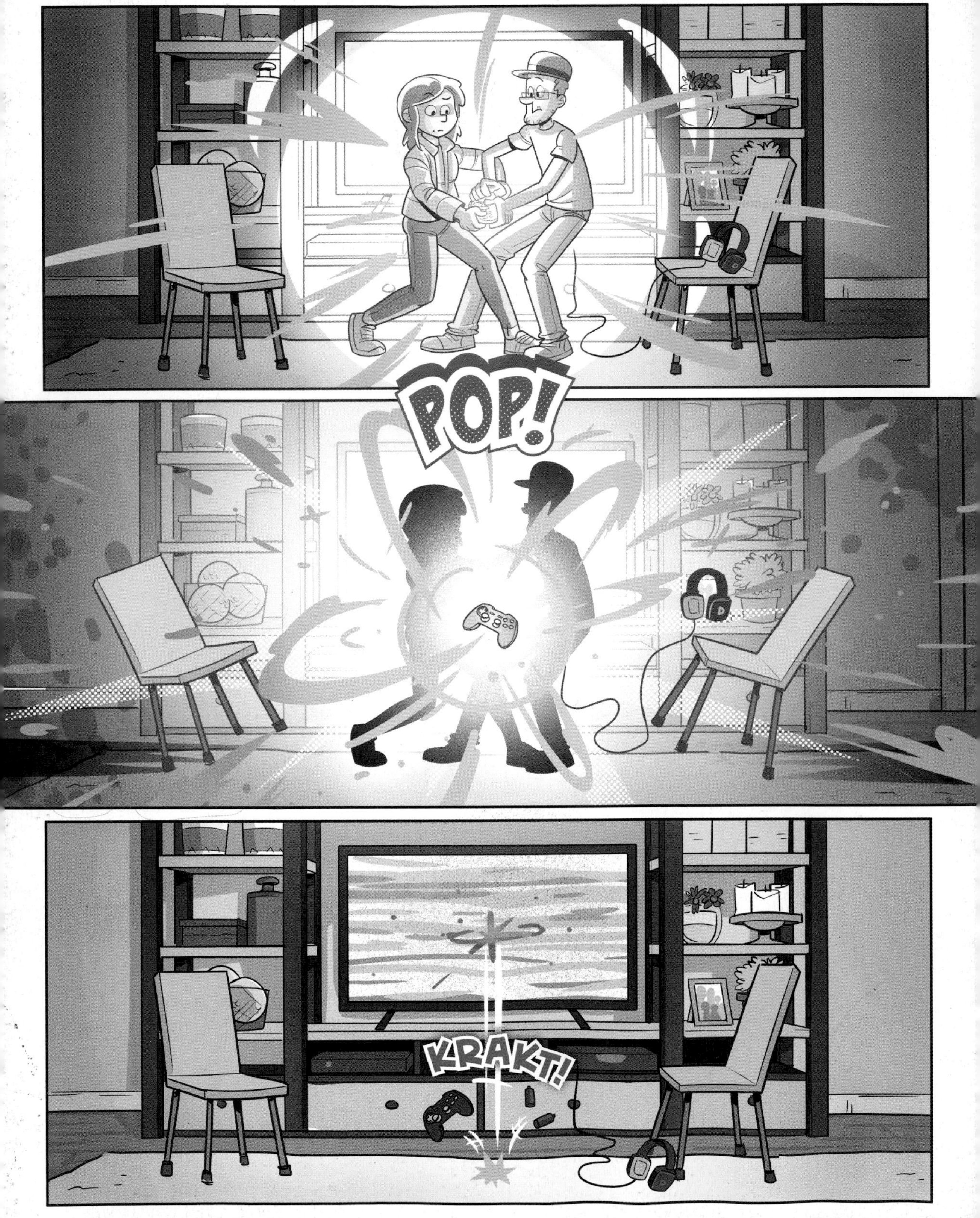
POP!
KRAKT!

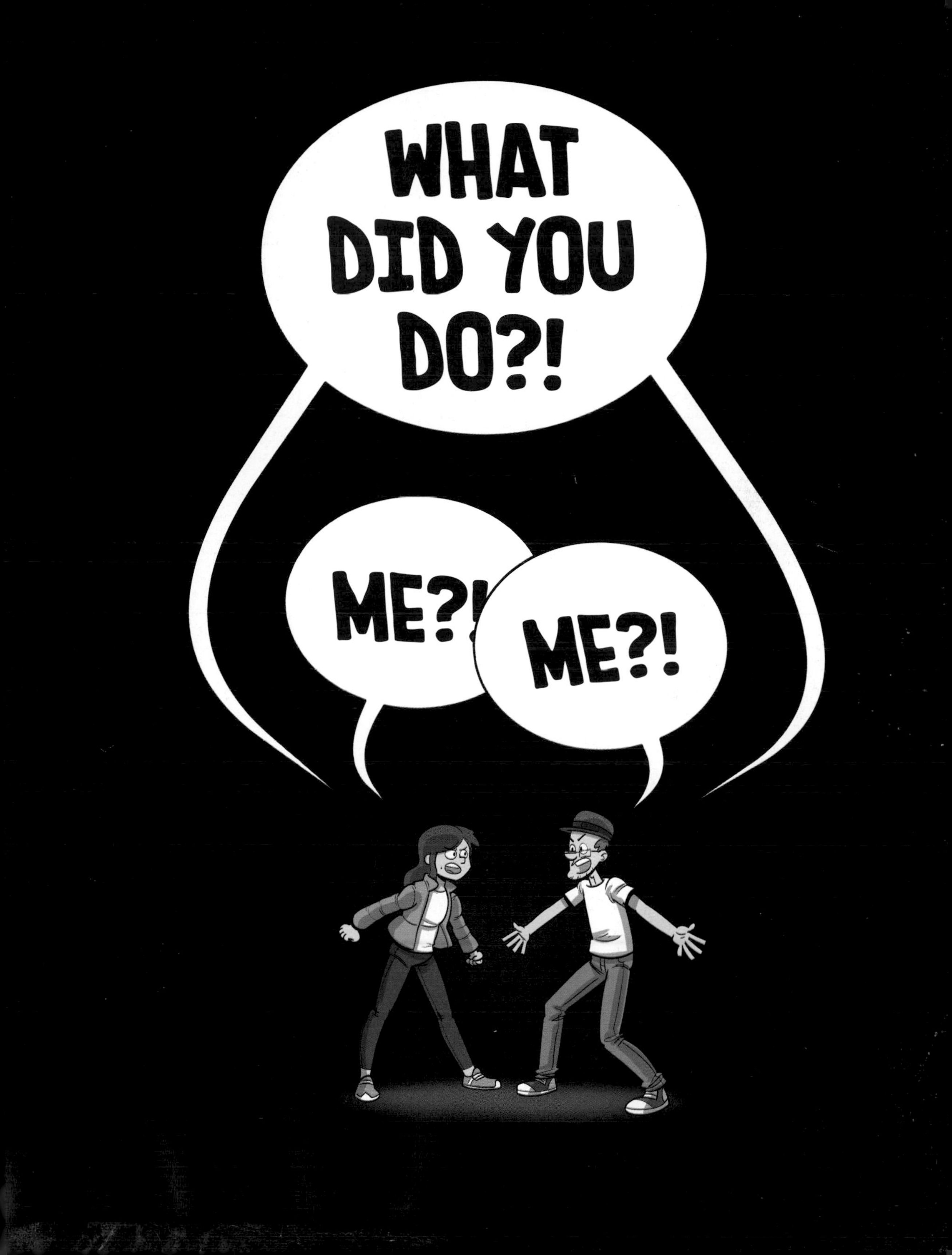
WHAT DID YOU DO?!
ME?!
ME?!

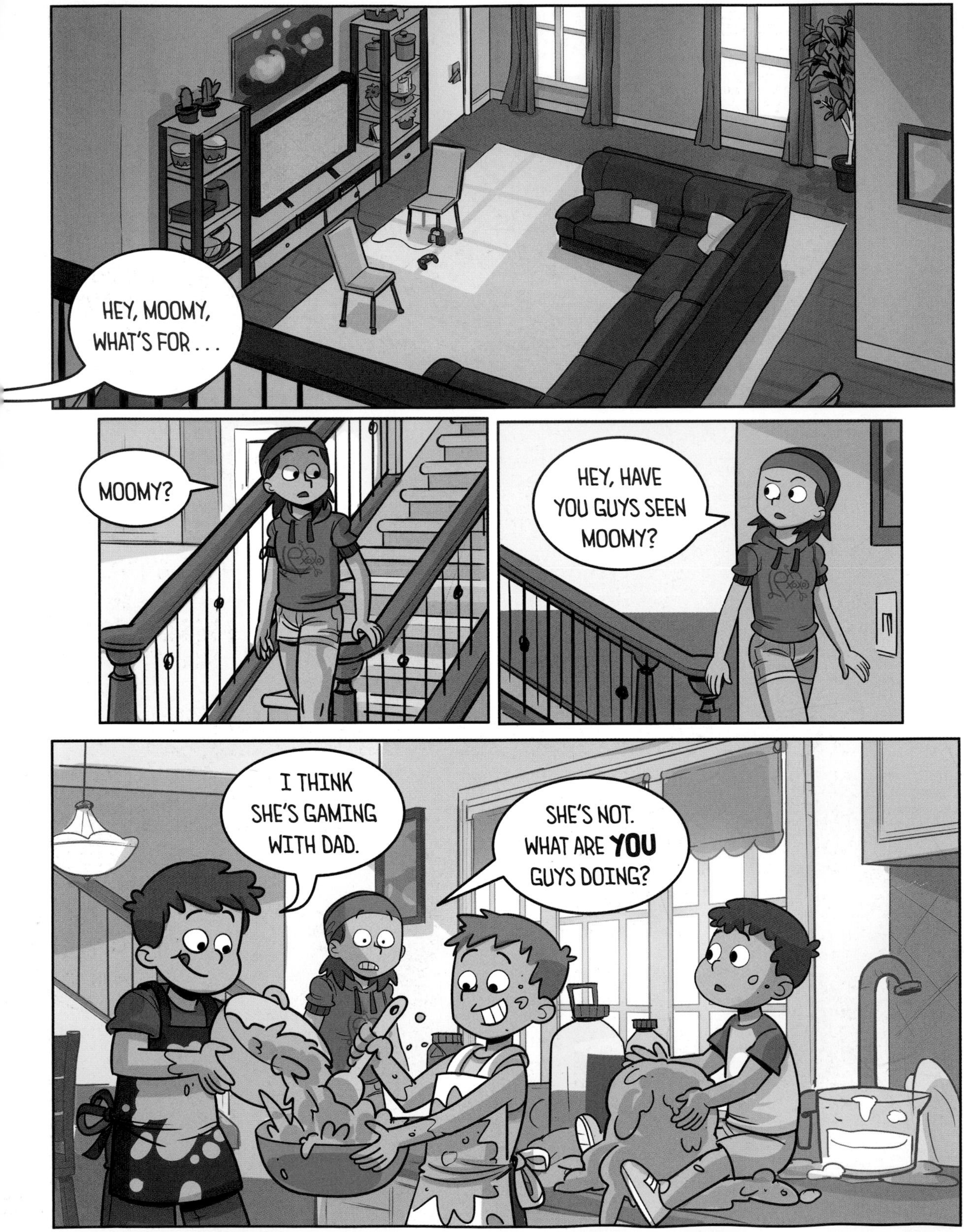
HEY, MOOMY, WHAT'S FOR . . .
MOOMY?
HEY, HAVE YOU GUYS SEEN MOOMY?
I THINK SHE'S GAMING WITH DAD.
SHE'S NOT. WHAT ARE **YOU** GUYS DOING?

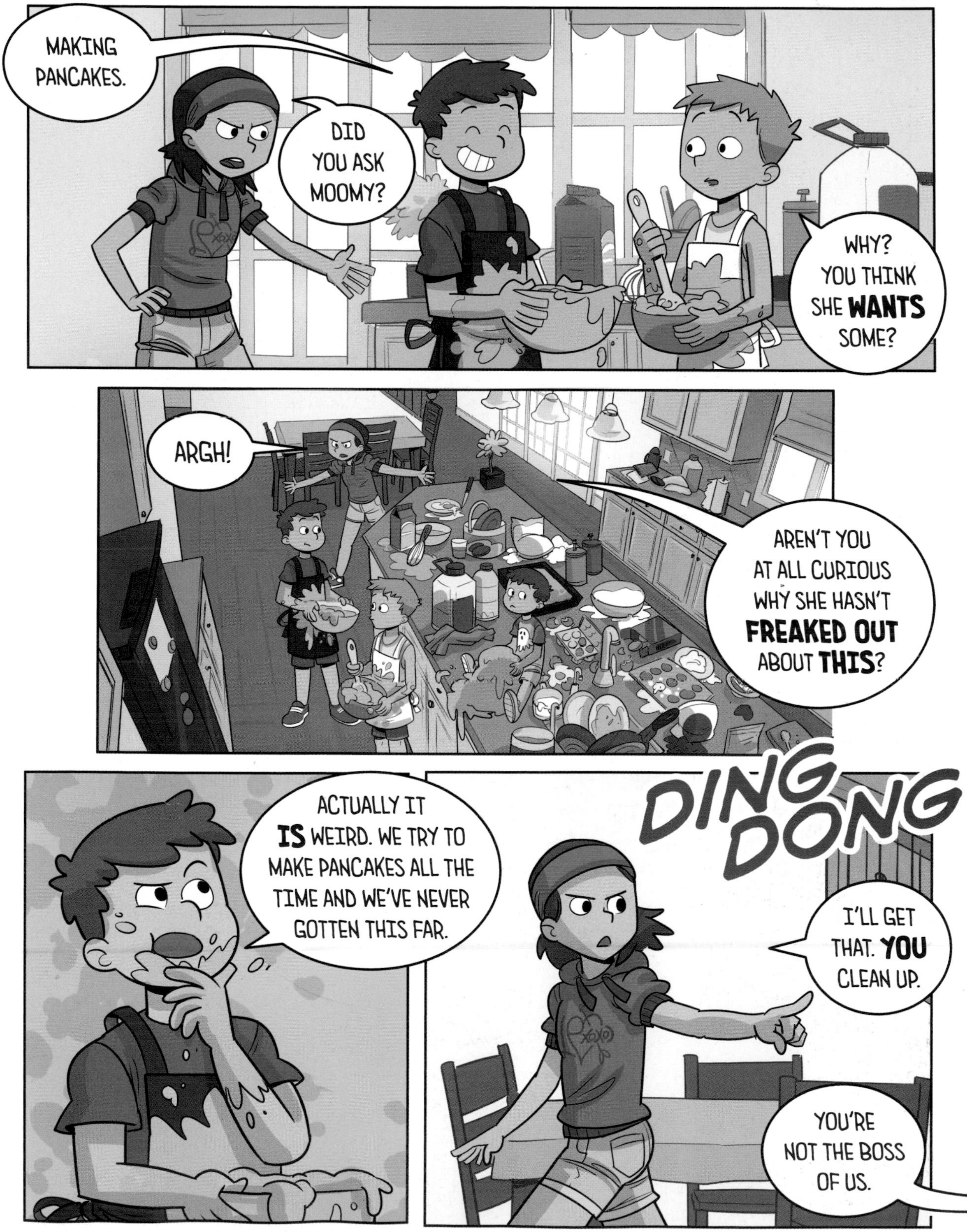
MAKING PANCAKES.
DID YOU ASK MOOMY?
WHY? YOU THINK SHE **WANTS** SOME?
ARGH!
AREN'T YOU AT ALL CURIOUS WHY SHE HASN'T **FREAKED OUT** ABOUT **THIS**?
ACTUALLY IT **IS** WEIRD. WE TRY TO MAKE PANCAKES ALL THE TIME AND WE'VE NEVER GOTTEN THIS FAR.
DING DONG
I'LL GET THAT. **YOU** CLEAN UP.
YOU'RE NOT THE BOSS OF US.

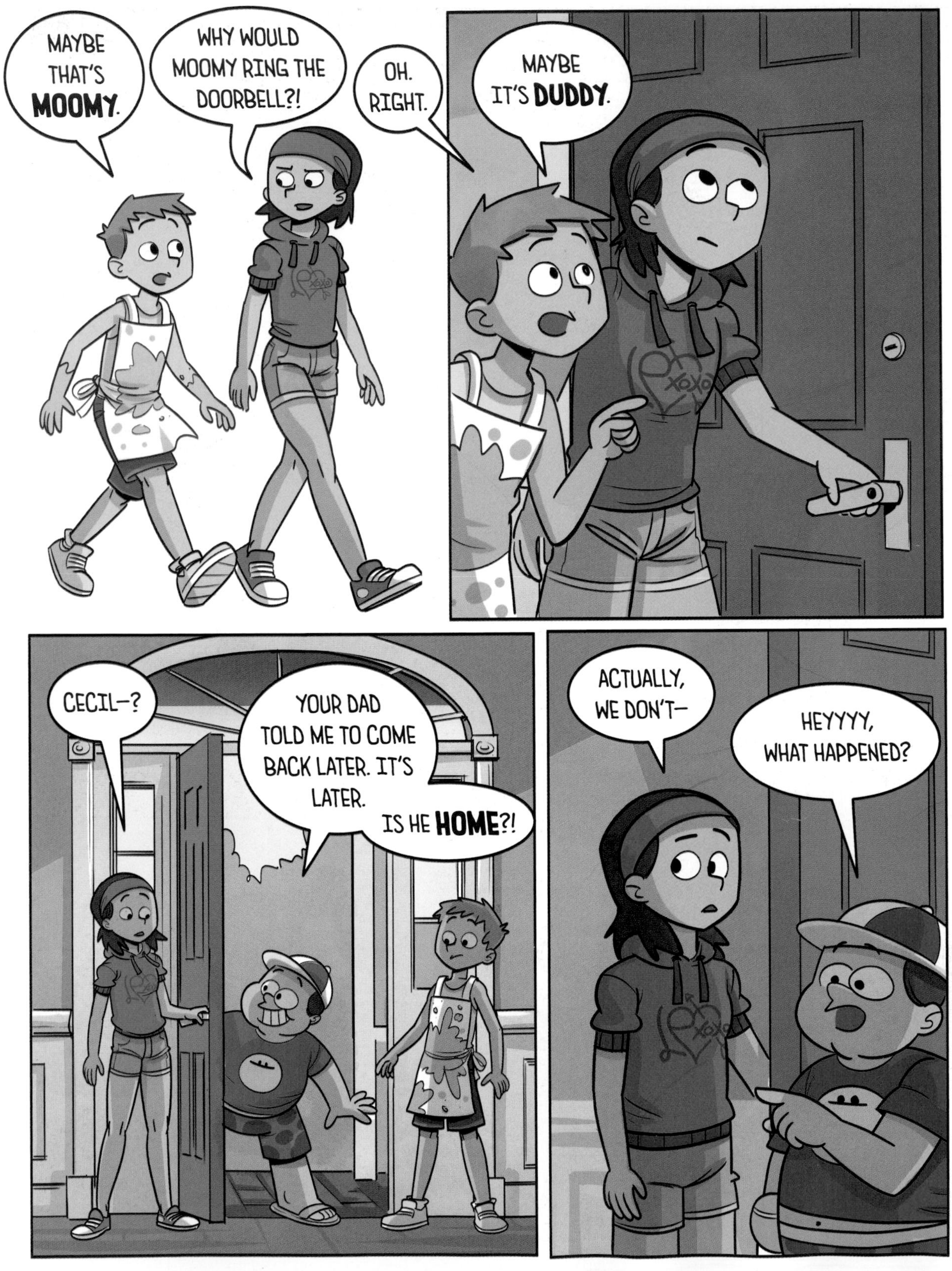
MAYBE THAT'S **MOOMY**.
WHY WOULD MOOMY RING THE DOORBELL?!
OH. RIGHT.
MAYBE IT'S **DUDDY**.
CECIL—?
YOUR DAD TOLD ME TO COME BACK LATER. IT'S LATER.
IS HE **HOME**?!
ACTUALLY, WE DON'T—
HEYYYY, WHAT HAPPENED?

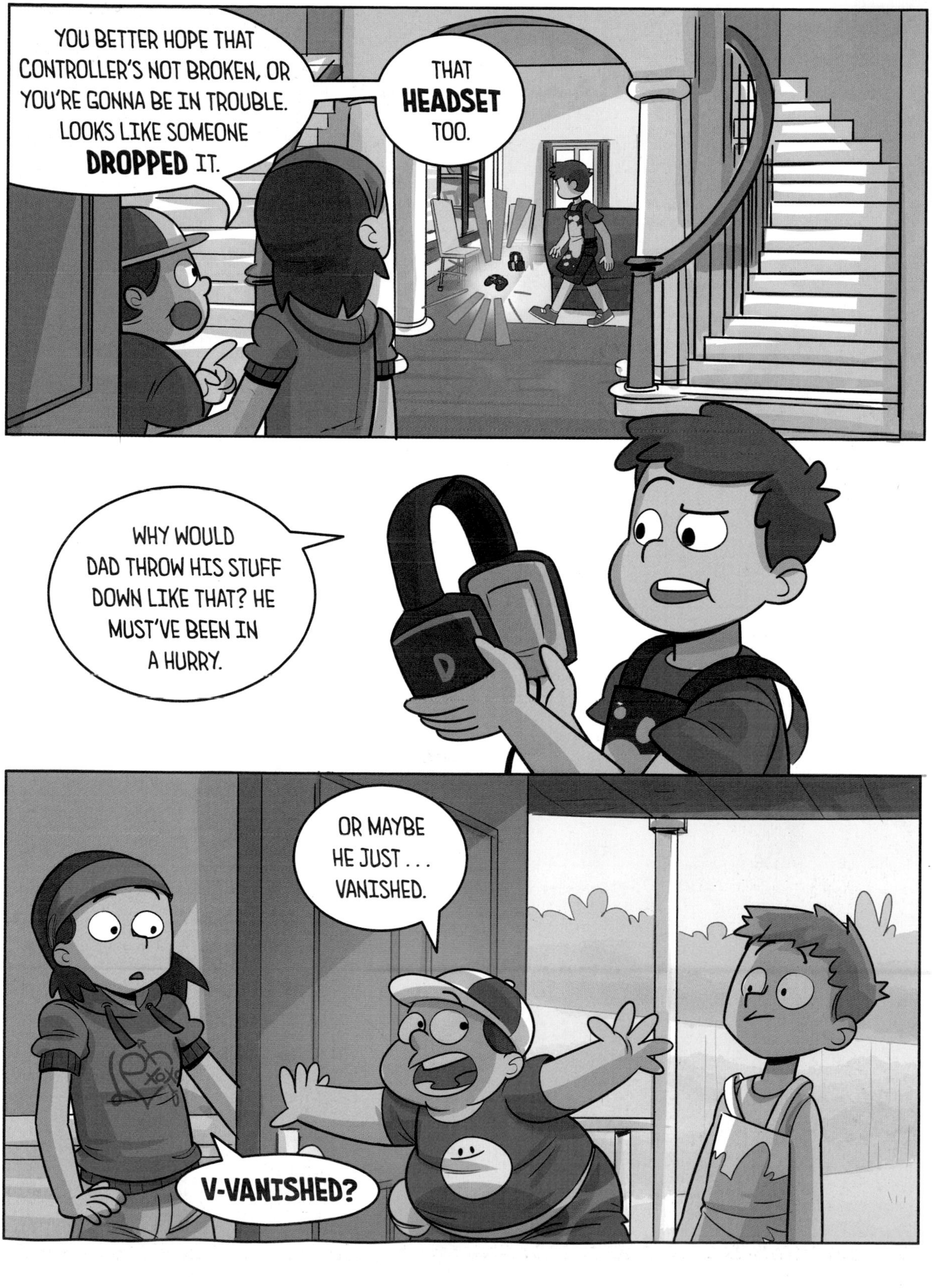
YOU BETTER HOPE THAT CONTROLLER'S NOT BROKEN, OR YOU'RE GONNA BE IN TROUBLE. LOOKS LIKE SOMEONE **DROPPED** IT.
THAT **HEADSET** TOO.
WHY WOULD DAD THROW HIS STUFF DOWN LIKE THAT? HE MUST'VE BEEN IN A HURRY.
OR MAYBE HE JUST . . . VANISHED.
V-VANISHED?

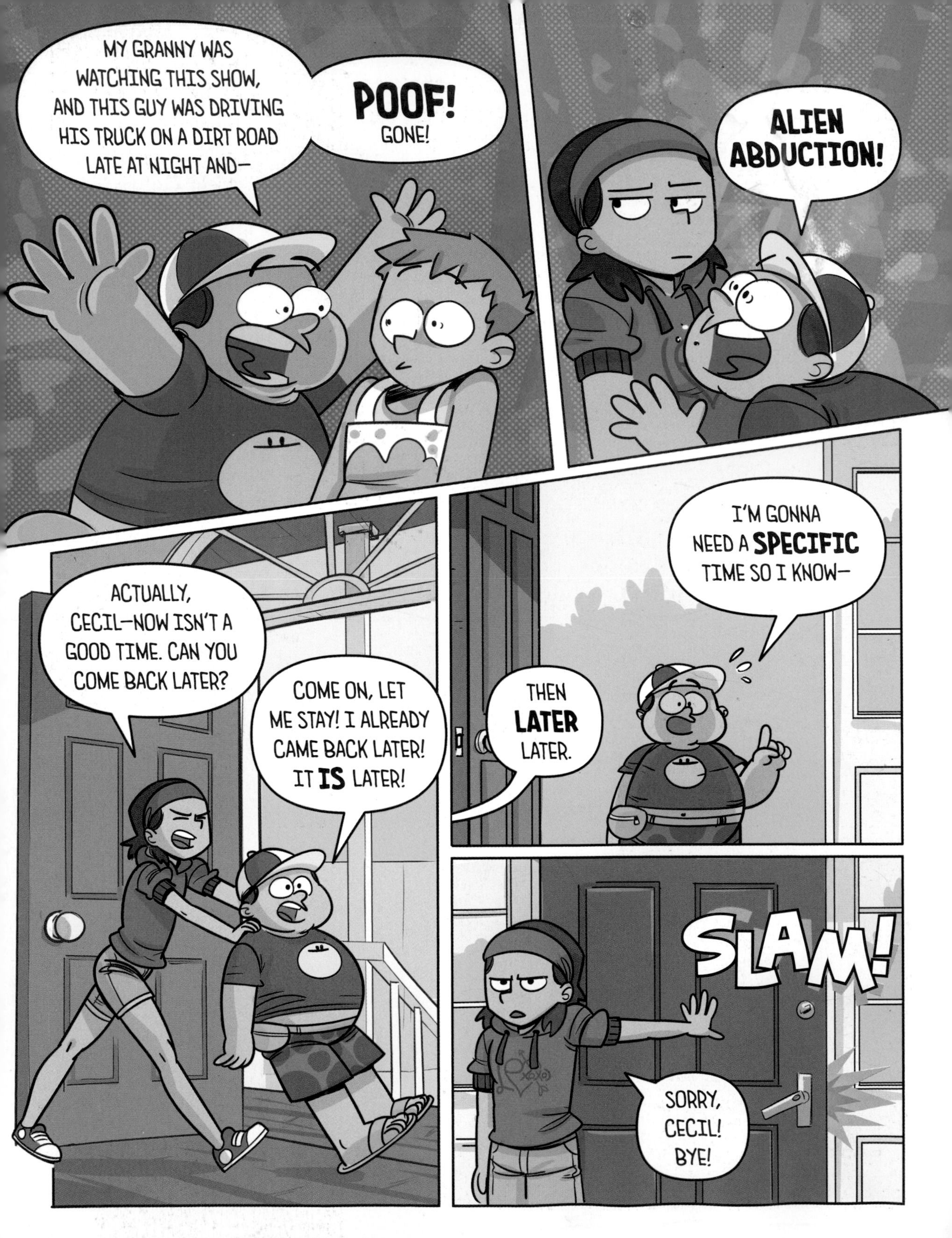
MY GRANNY WAS WATCHING THIS SHOW, AND THIS GUY WAS DRIVING HIS TRUCK ON A DIRT ROAD LATE AT NIGHT AND—
POOF! GONE!
ALIEN ABDUCTION!
ACTUALLY, CECIL—NOW ISN'T A GOOD TIME. CAN YOU COME BACK LATER?
COME ON, LET ME STAY! I ALREADY CAME BACK LATER! IT IS LATER!
I'M GONNA NEED A SPECIFIC TIME SO I KNOW—
THEN LATER LATER.
SLAM!
SORRY, CECIL! BYE!

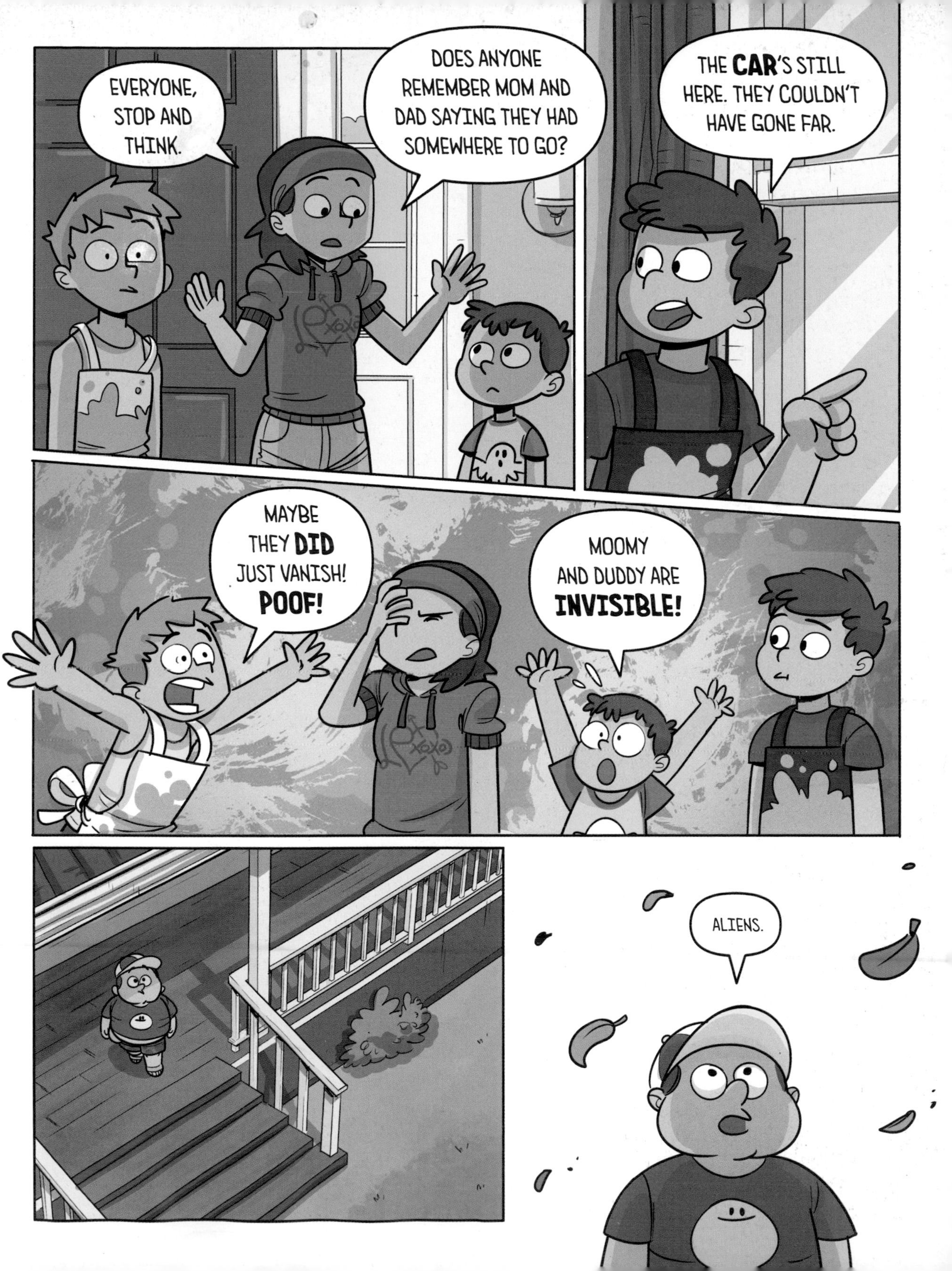
EVERYONE, STOP AND THINK.
DOES ANYONE REMEMBER MOM AND DAD SAYING THEY HAD SOMEWHERE TO GO?
THE CAR'S STILL HERE. THEY COULDN'T HAVE GONE FAR.
MAYBE THEY DID JUST VANISH! POOF!
MOOMY AND DUDDY ARE INVISIBLE!
ALIENS.

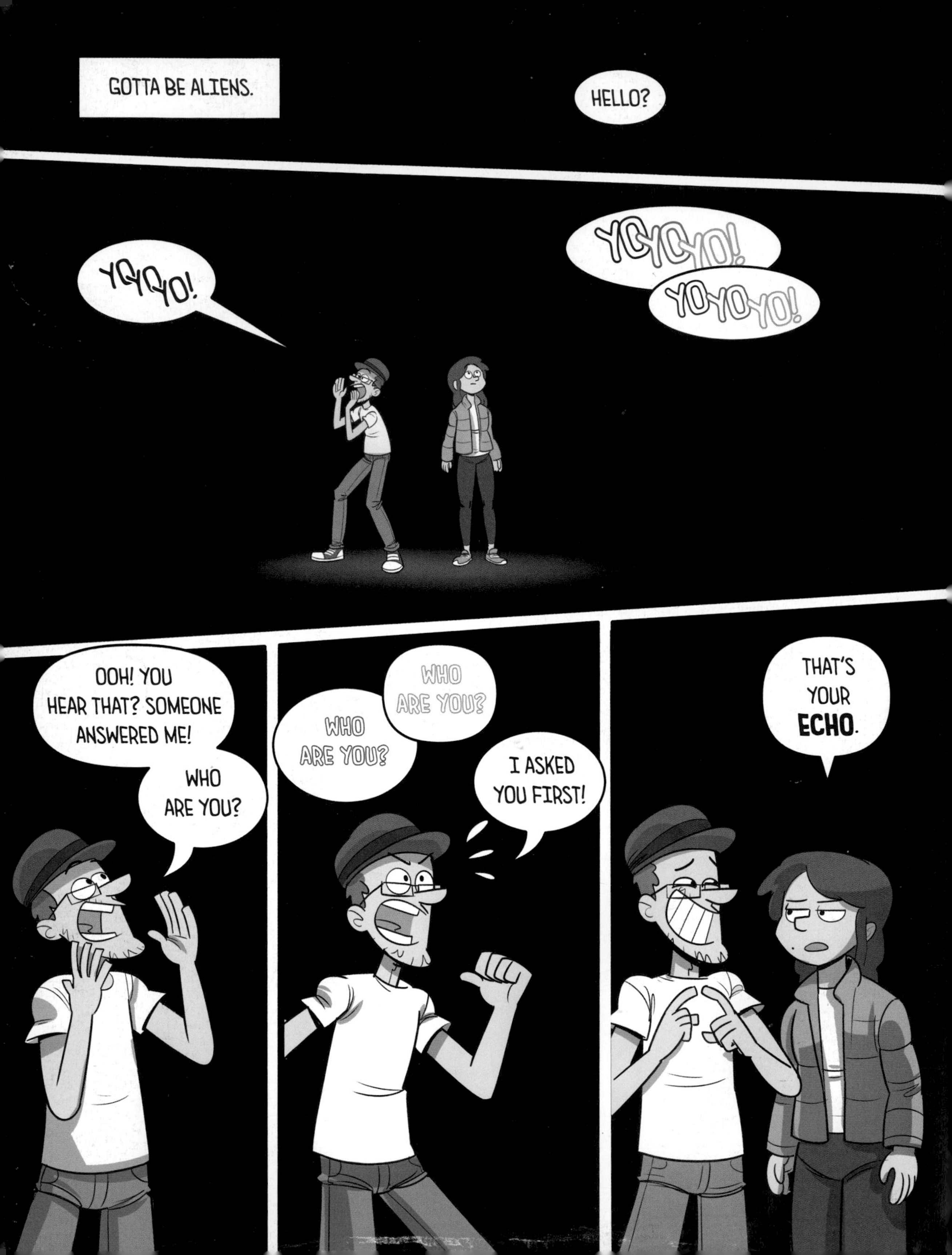
GOTTA BE ALIENS.
HELLO?
YOYOYO!
YOYOYO!
YOYOYO!
OOH! YOU HEAR THAT? SOMEONE ANSWERED ME!
WHO ARE YOU?
WHO ARE YOU?
WHO ARE YOU?
I ASKED YOU FIRST!
THAT'S YOUR **ECHO**.

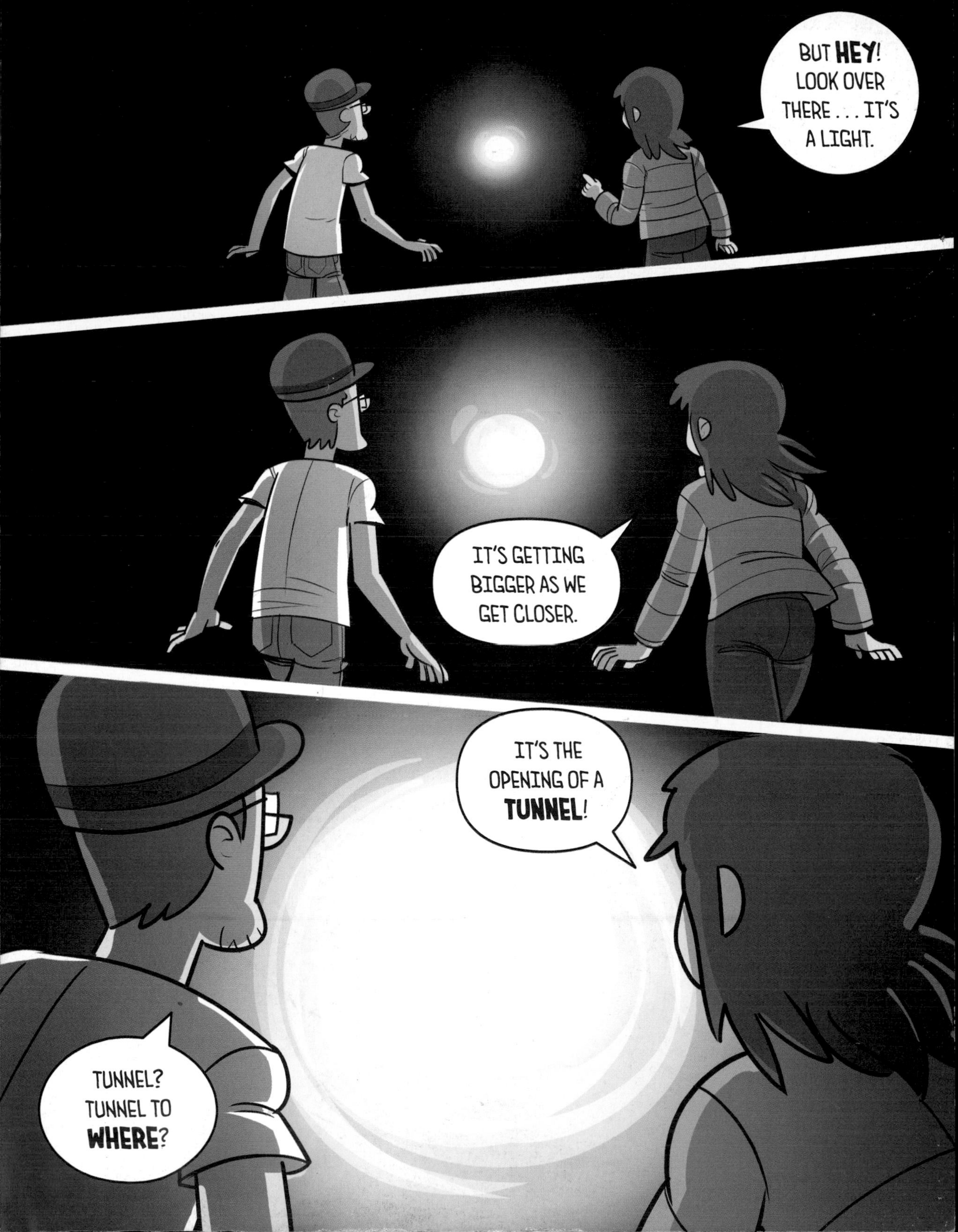
BUT HEY! LOOK OVER THERE . . . IT'S A LIGHT.
IT'S GETTING BIGGER AS WE GET CLOSER.
IT'S THE OPENING OF A TUNNEL!
TUNNEL? TUNNEL TO WHERE?

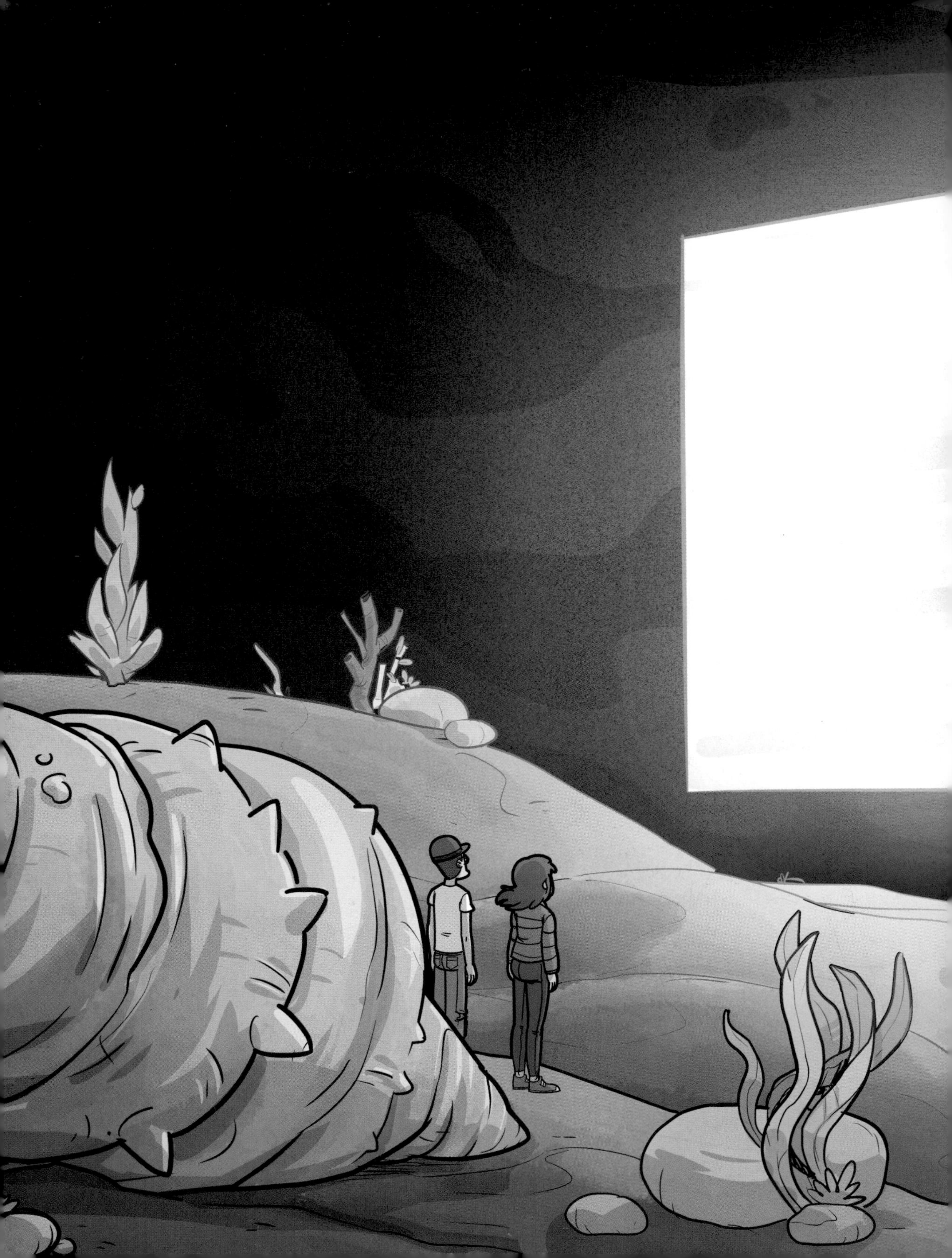

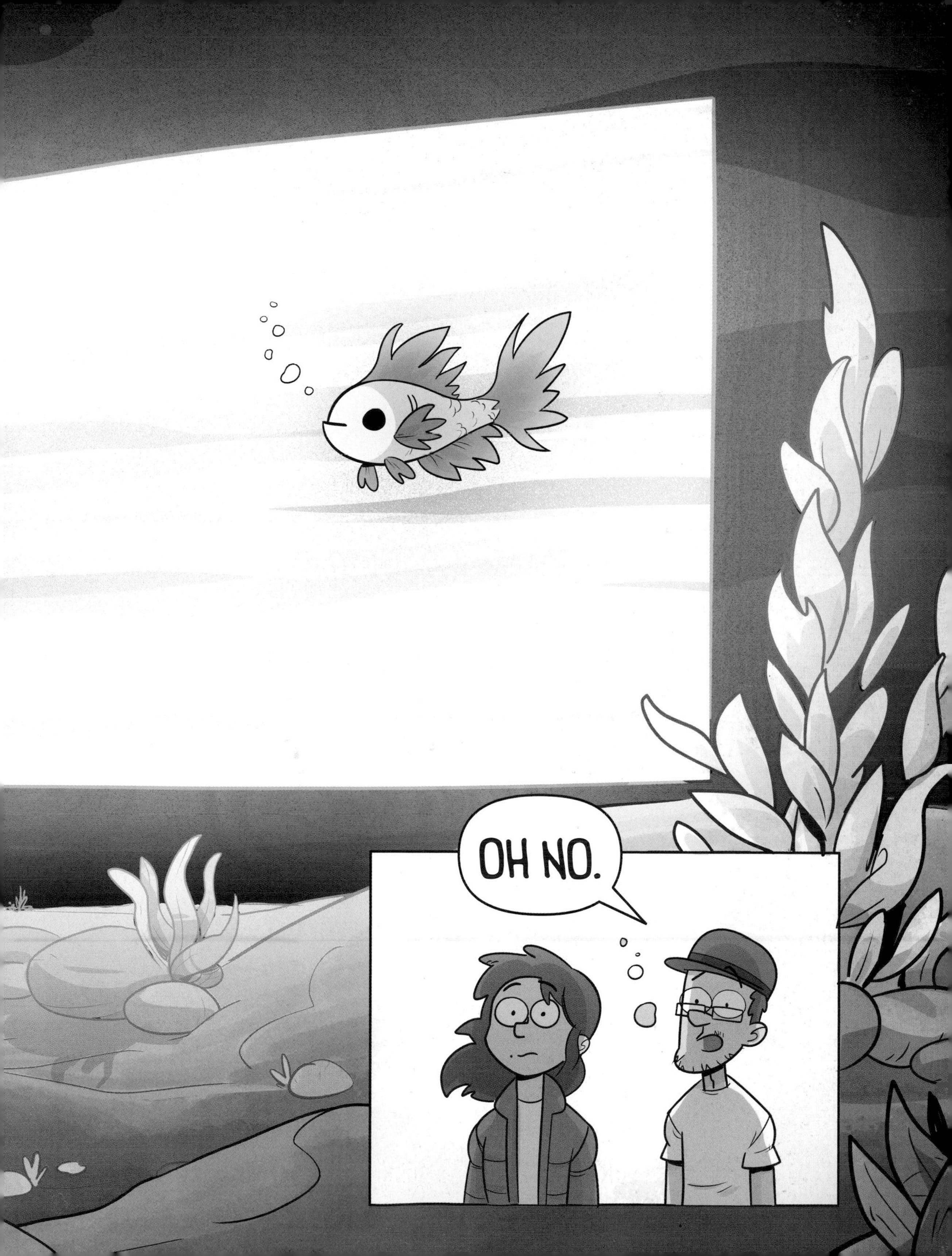
OH NO.

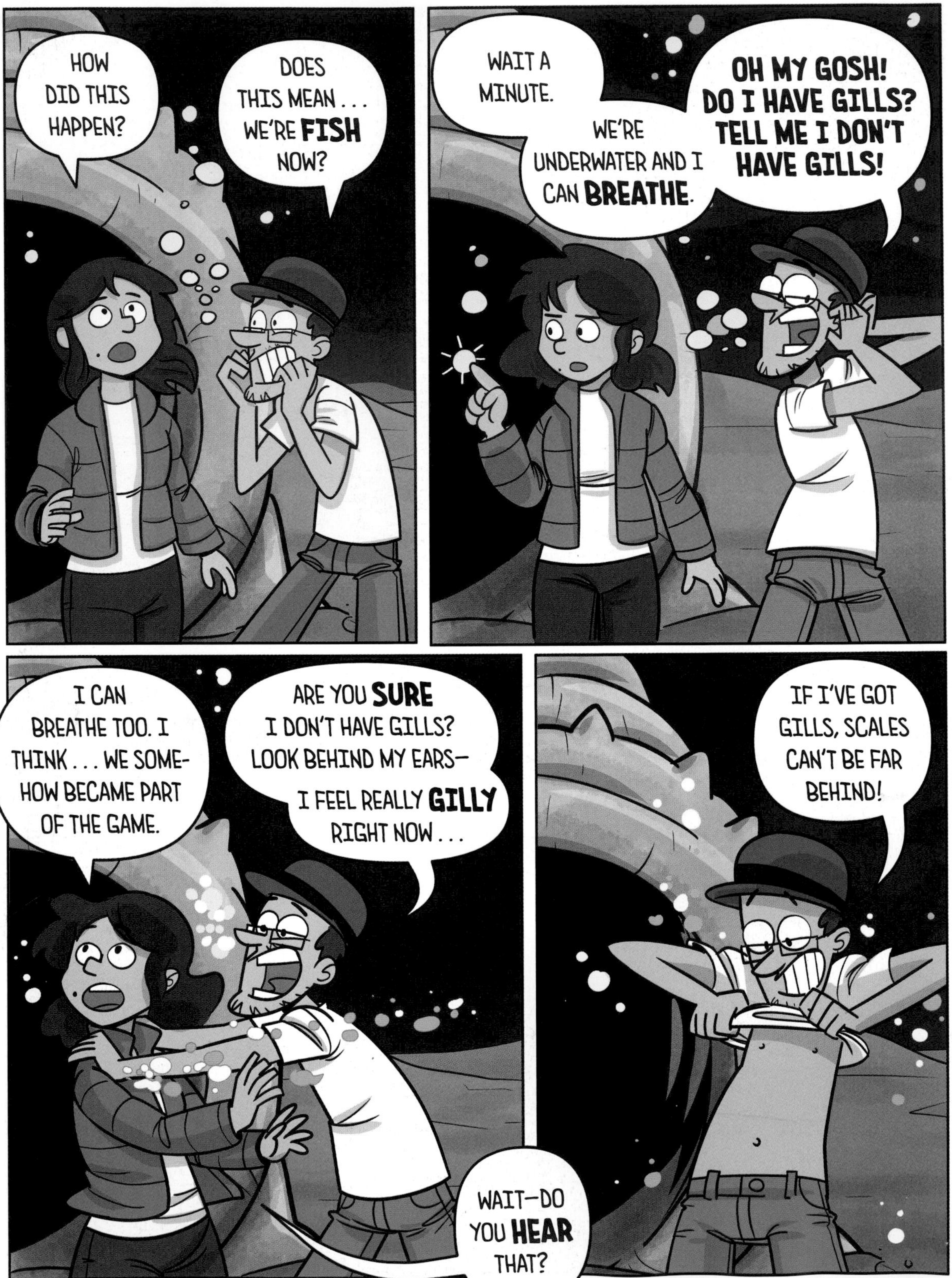
HOW DID THIS HAPPEN?
DOES THIS MEAN . . . WE'RE **FISH** NOW?
WAIT A MINUTE.
WE'RE UNDERWATER AND I CAN **BREATHE**.
OH MY GOSH! DO I HAVE GILLS? TELL ME I DON'T HAVE GILLS!
I CAN BREATHE TOO. I THINK . . . WE SOMEHOW BECAME PART OF THE GAME.
ARE YOU **SURE** I DON'T HAVE GILLS? LOOK BEHIND MY EARS—
I FEEL REALLY **GILLY** RIGHT NOW . . .
WAIT—DO YOU **HEAR** THAT?
IF I'VE GOT GILLS, SCALES CAN'T BE FAR BEHIND!

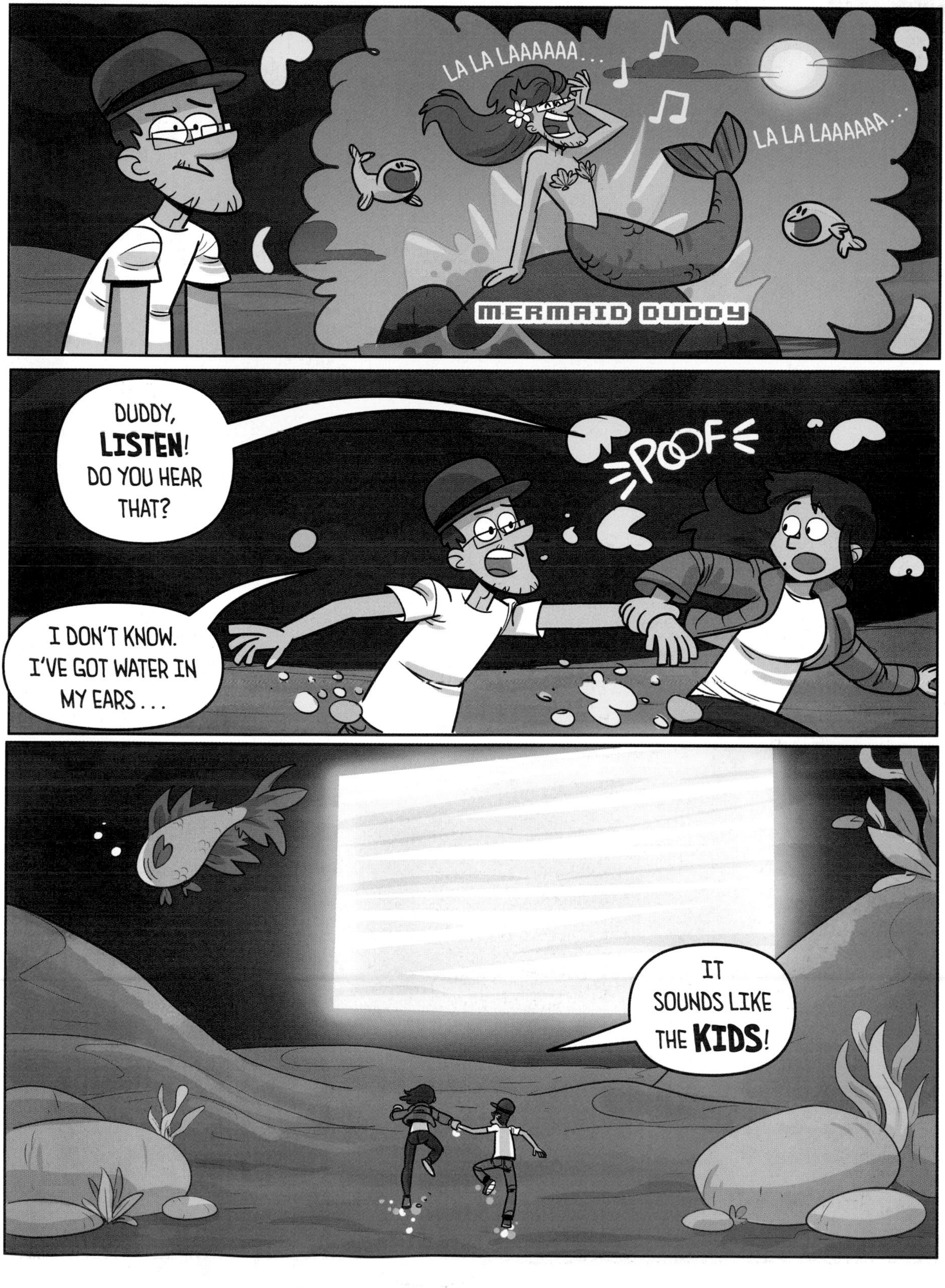
LA LA LAAAAAA . . .
LA LA LAAAAAA . . .
MERMAID DUDDY
DUDDY, LISTEN! DO YOU HEAR THAT?
POOF
I DON'T KNOW. I'VE GOT WATER IN MY EARS . . .
IT SOUNDS LIKE THE KIDS!

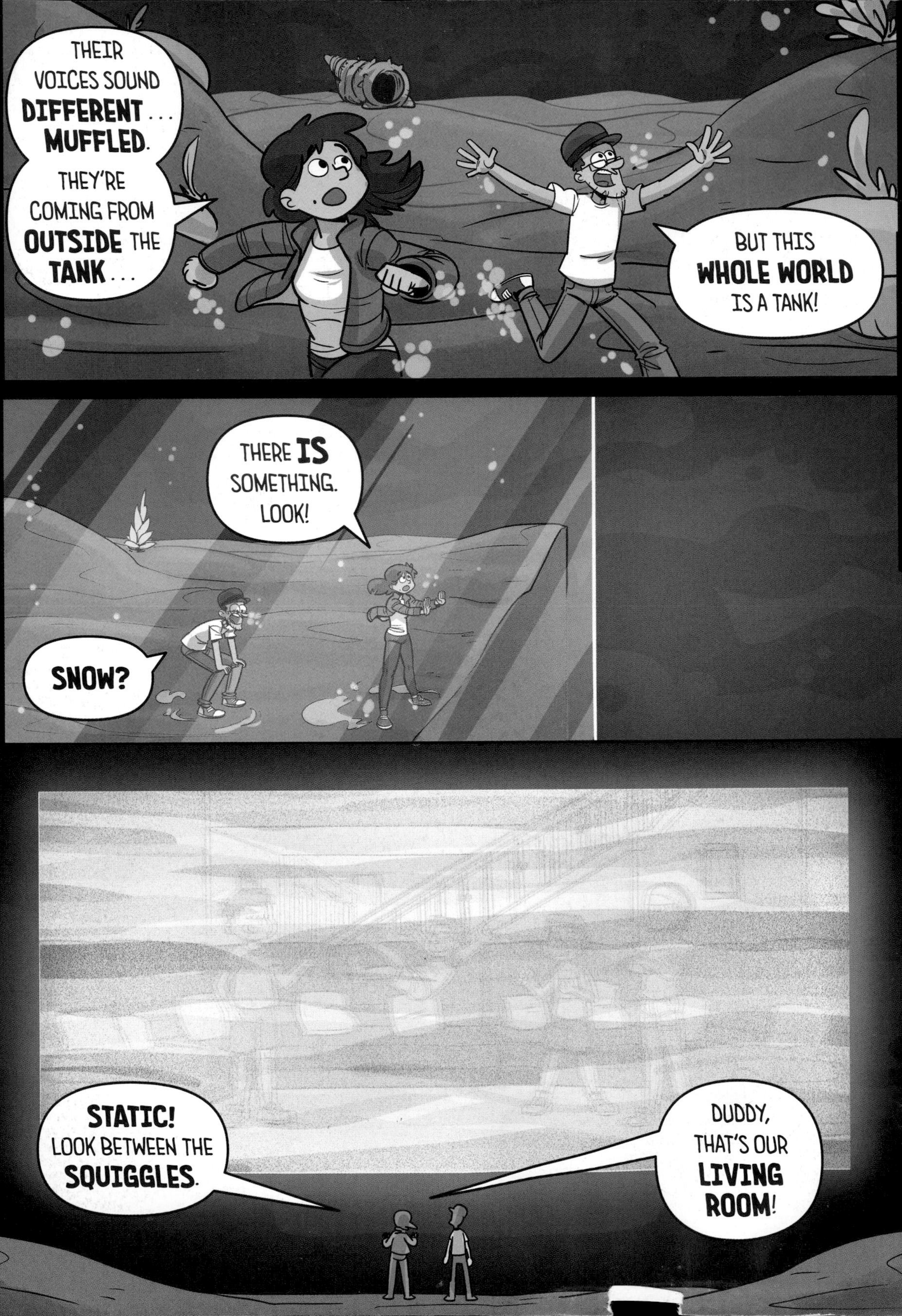
THEIR VOICES SOUND DIFFERENT . . . MUFFLED.
THEY'RE COMING FROM OUTSIDE THE TANK . . .
BUT THIS WHOLE WORLD IS A TANK!
THERE IS SOMETHING. LOOK!
SNOW?
STATIC! LOOK BETWEEN THE SQUIGGLES.
DUDDY, THAT'S OUR LIVING ROOM!

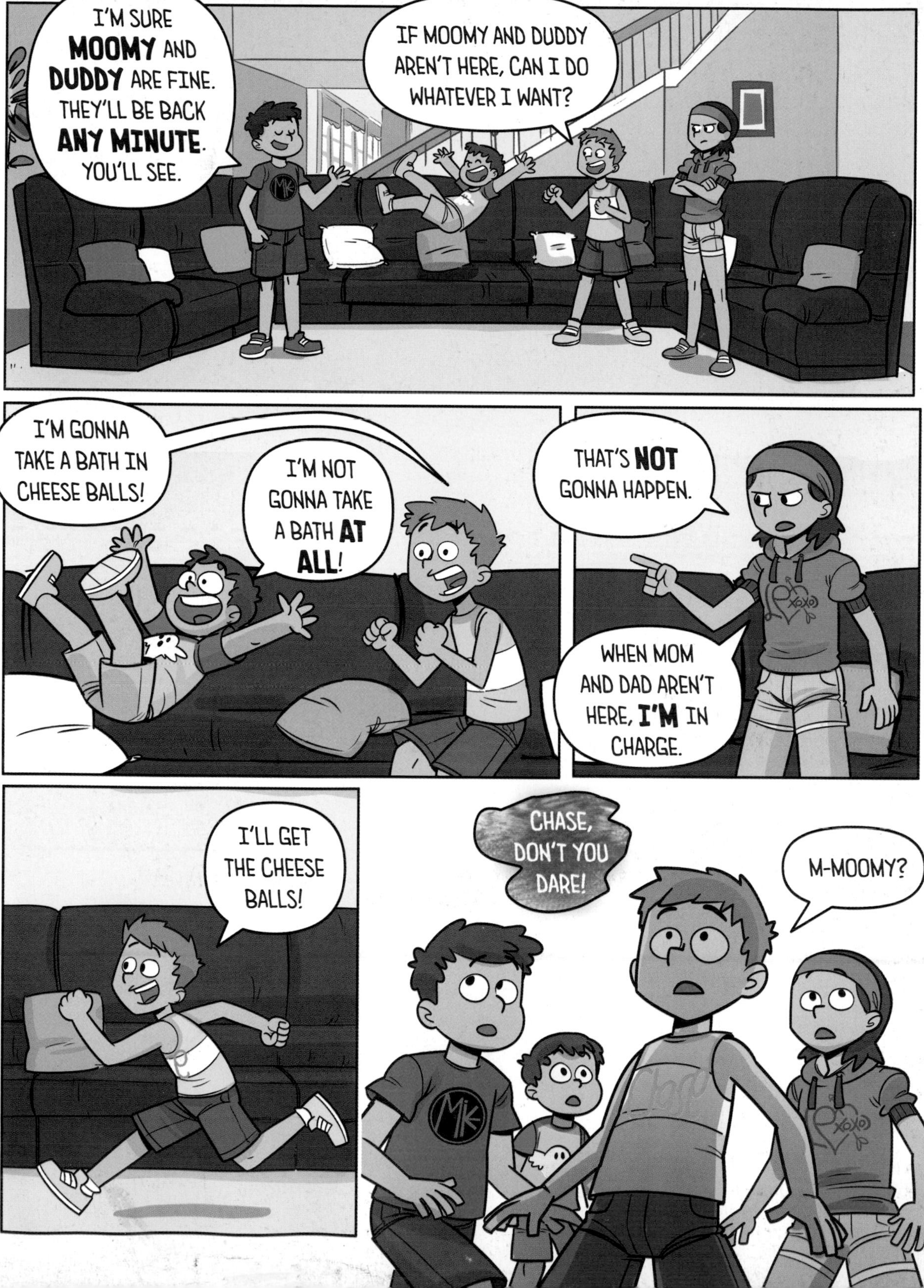
I'M SURE MOOMY AND DUDDY ARE FINE. THEY'LL BE BACK ANY MINUTE. YOU'LL SEE.
IF MOOMY AND DUDDY AREN'T HERE, CAN I DO WHATEVER I WANT?
I'M GONNA TAKE A BATH IN CHEESE BALLS!
I'M NOT GONNA TAKE A BATH AT ALL!
THAT'S NOT GONNA HAPPEN.
WHEN MOM AND DAD AREN'T HERE, I'M IN CHARGE.
I'LL GET THE CHEESE BALLS!
CHASE, DON'T YOU DARE!
M-MOOMY?

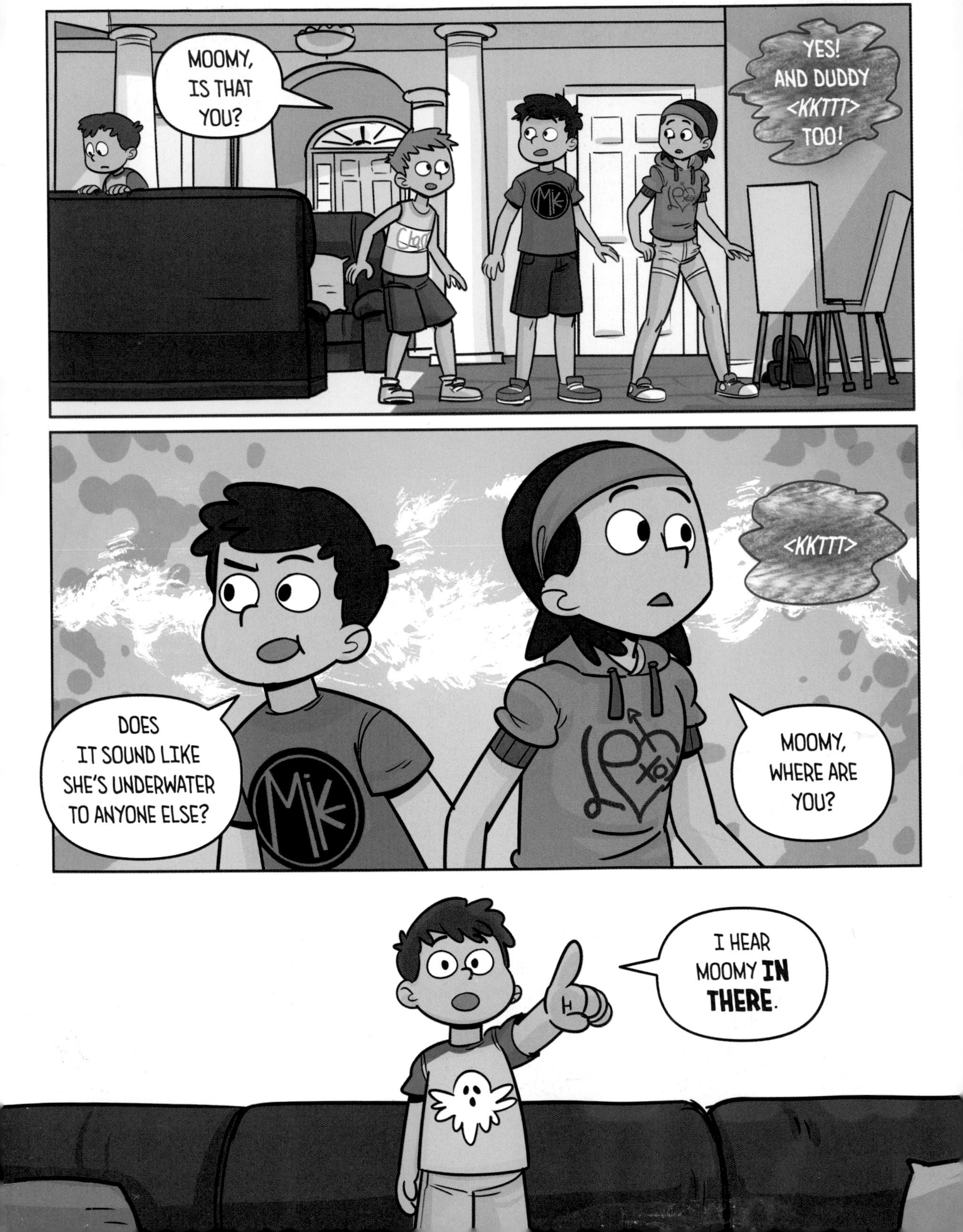
MOOMY, IS THAT YOU?
YES! AND DUDDY <KKTTT> TOO!
<KKTTT>
DOES IT SOUND LIKE SHE'S UNDERWATER TO ANYONE ELSE?
MOOMY, WHERE ARE YOU?
I HEAR MOOMY **IN THERE**.

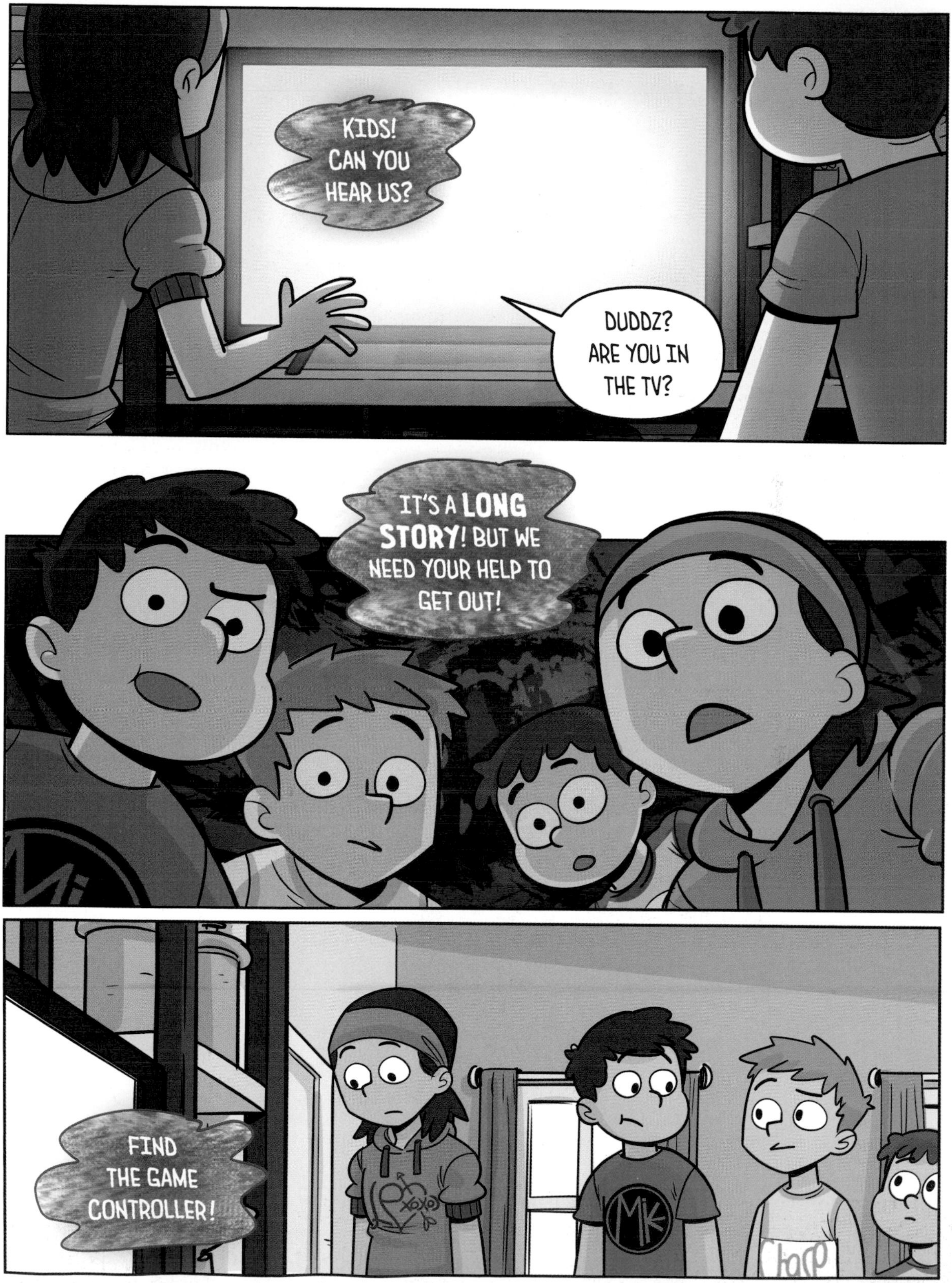
KIDS! CAN YOU HEAR US?
DUDDZ? ARE YOU IN THE TV?
IT'S A **LONG STORY**! BUT WE NEED YOUR HELP TO GET OUT!
FIND THE GAME CONTROLLER!

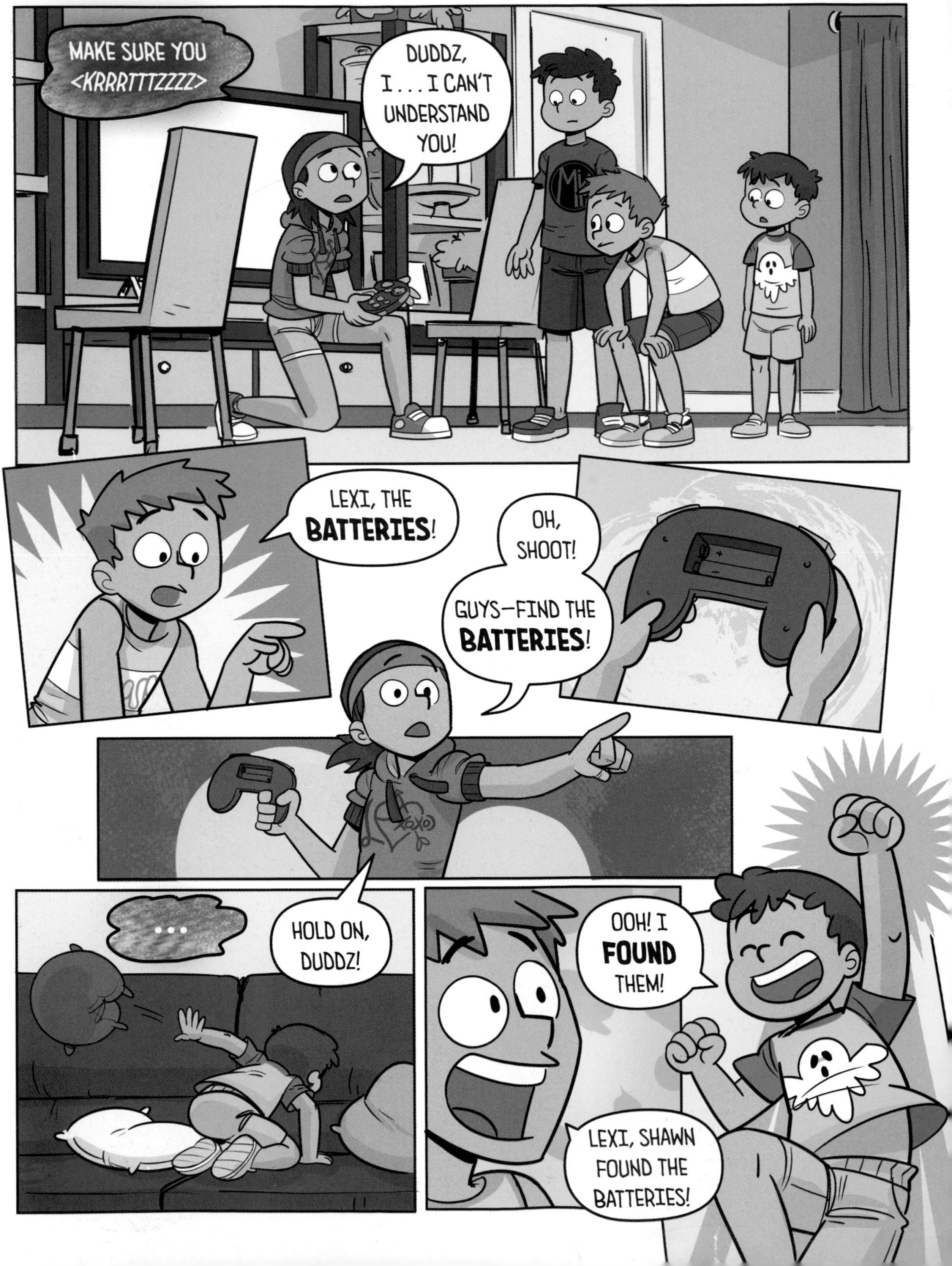
MAKE SURE YOU <KRRRTTTZZZZZ>
DUDDZ, I . . . I CAN'T UNDERSTAND YOU!
LEXI, THE **BATTERIES**!
OH, SHOOT!
GUYS—FIND THE **BATTERIES**!
HOLD ON, DUDDZ!
. . .
OOH! I **FOUND** THEM!
LEXI, SHAWN FOUND THE BATTERIES!

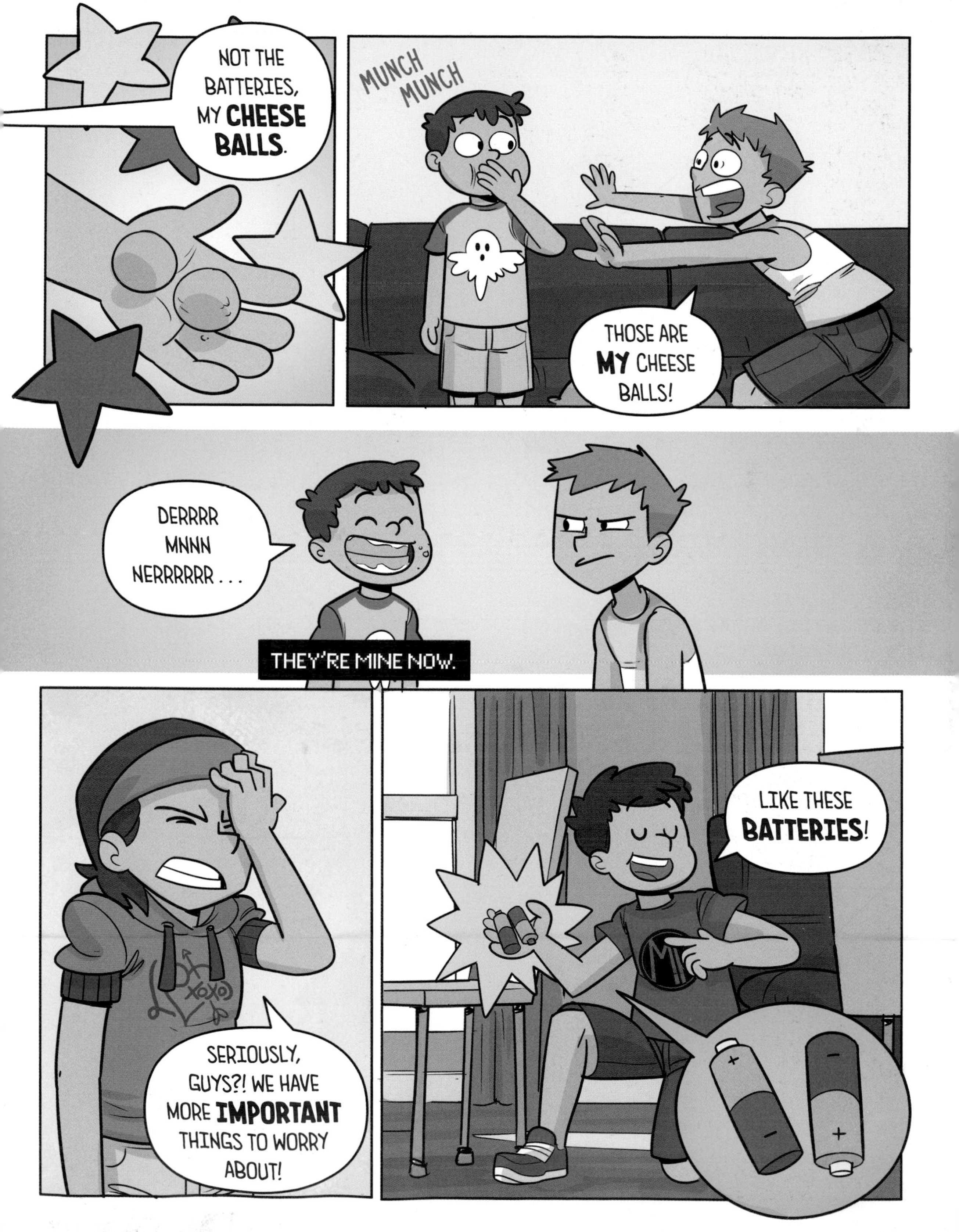
NOT THE BATTERIES, MY CHEESE BALLS.
MUNCH MUNCH
THOSE ARE MY CHEESE BALLS!
DERRRR MNNN NERRRRRR . . .
THEY'RE MINE NOW.
SERIOUSLY, GUYS?! WE HAVE MORE IMPORTANT THINGS TO WORRY ABOUT!
LIKE THESE BATTERIES!

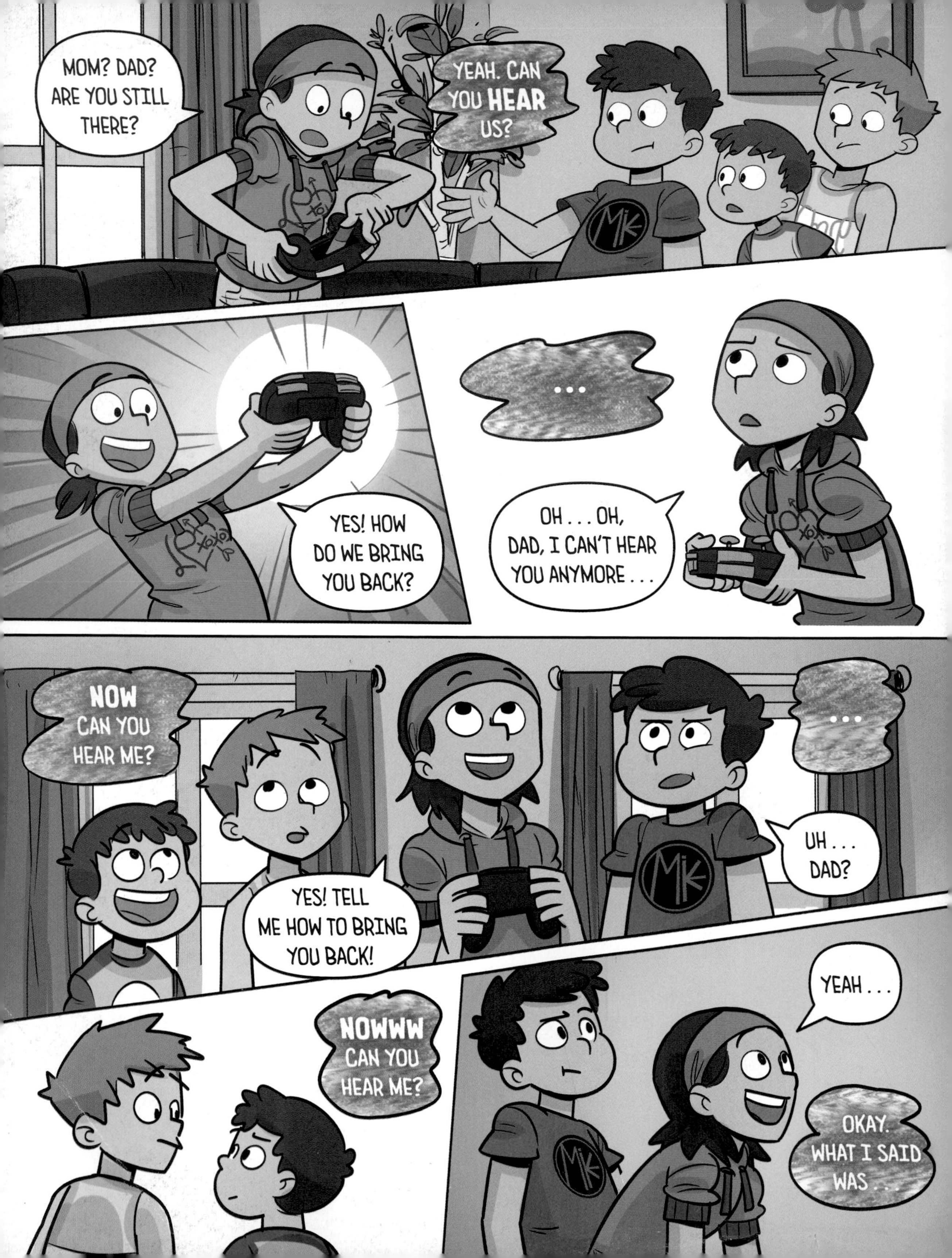
MOM? DAD? ARE YOU STILL THERE?
YEAH. CAN YOU HEAR US?
YES! HOW DO WE BRING YOU BACK?
...
OH . . . OH, DAD, I CAN'T HEAR YOU ANYMORE . . .
NOW CAN YOU HEAR ME?
YES! TELL ME HOW TO BRING YOU BACK!
...
UH . . . DAD?
NOWWW CAN YOU HEAR ME?
YEAH . . .
OKAY. WHAT I SAID WAS . . .

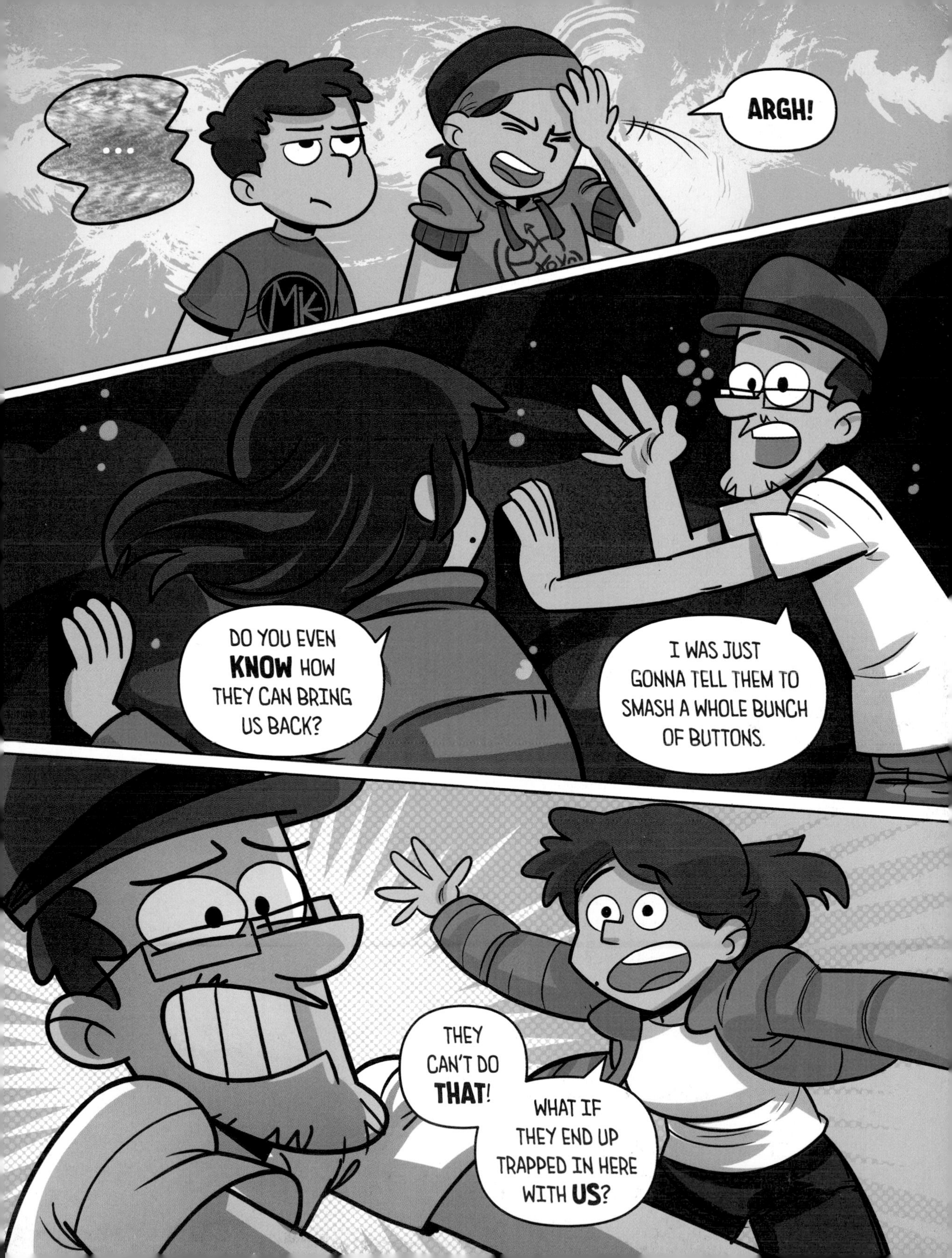

...
ARGH!
DO YOU EVEN **KNOW** HOW THEY CAN BRING US BACK?
I WAS JUST GONNA TELL THEM TO SMASH A WHOLE BUNCH OF BUTTONS.
THEY CAN'T DO **THAT**!
WHAT IF THEY END UP TRAPPED IN HERE WITH **US**?

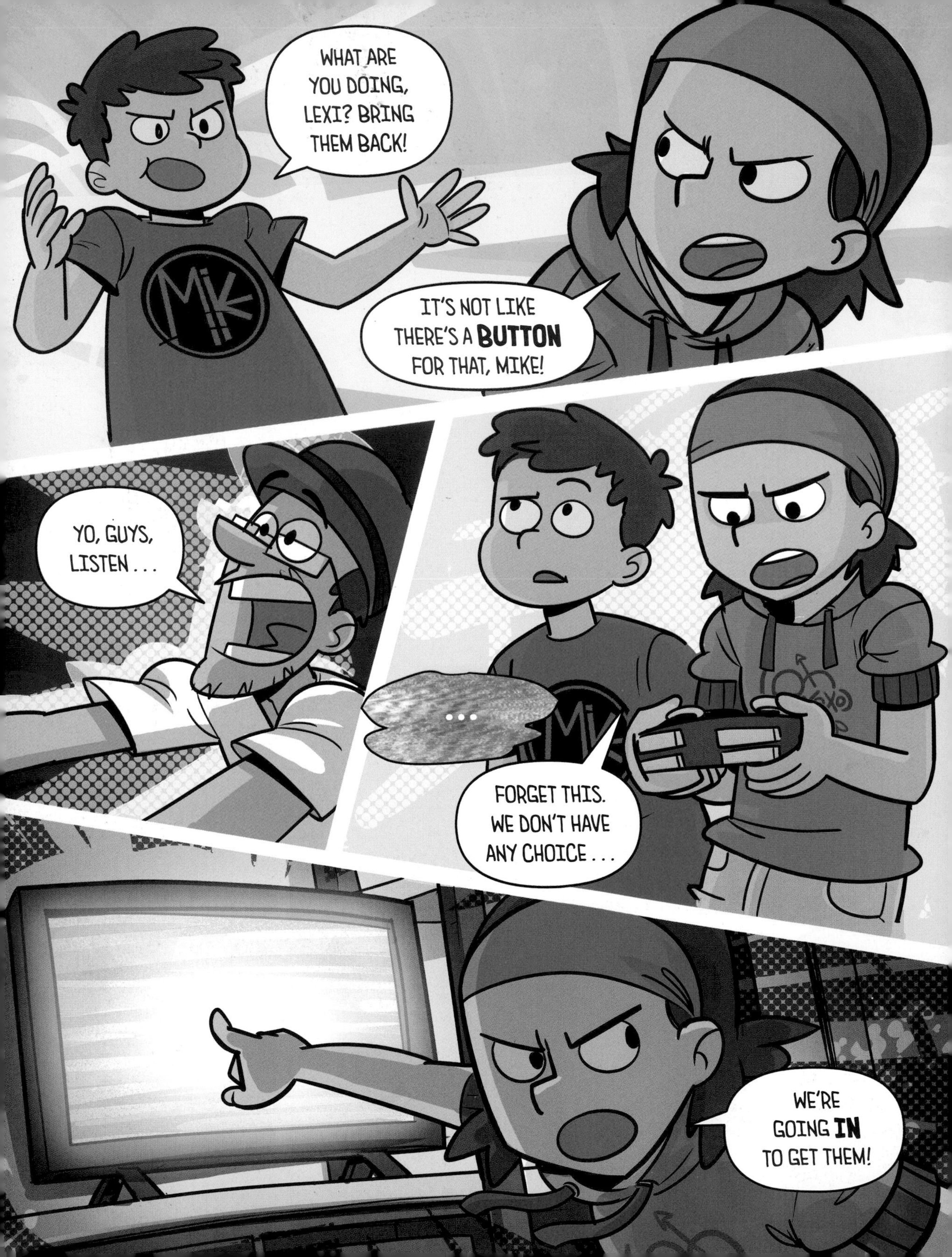
WHAT ARE YOU DOING, LEXI? BRING THEM BACK!
IT'S NOT LIKE THERE'S A **BUTTON** FOR THAT, MIKE!
YO, GUYS, LISTEN . . .
...
FORGET THIS. WE DON'T HAVE ANY CHOICE . . .
WE'RE GOING **IN** TO GET THEM!

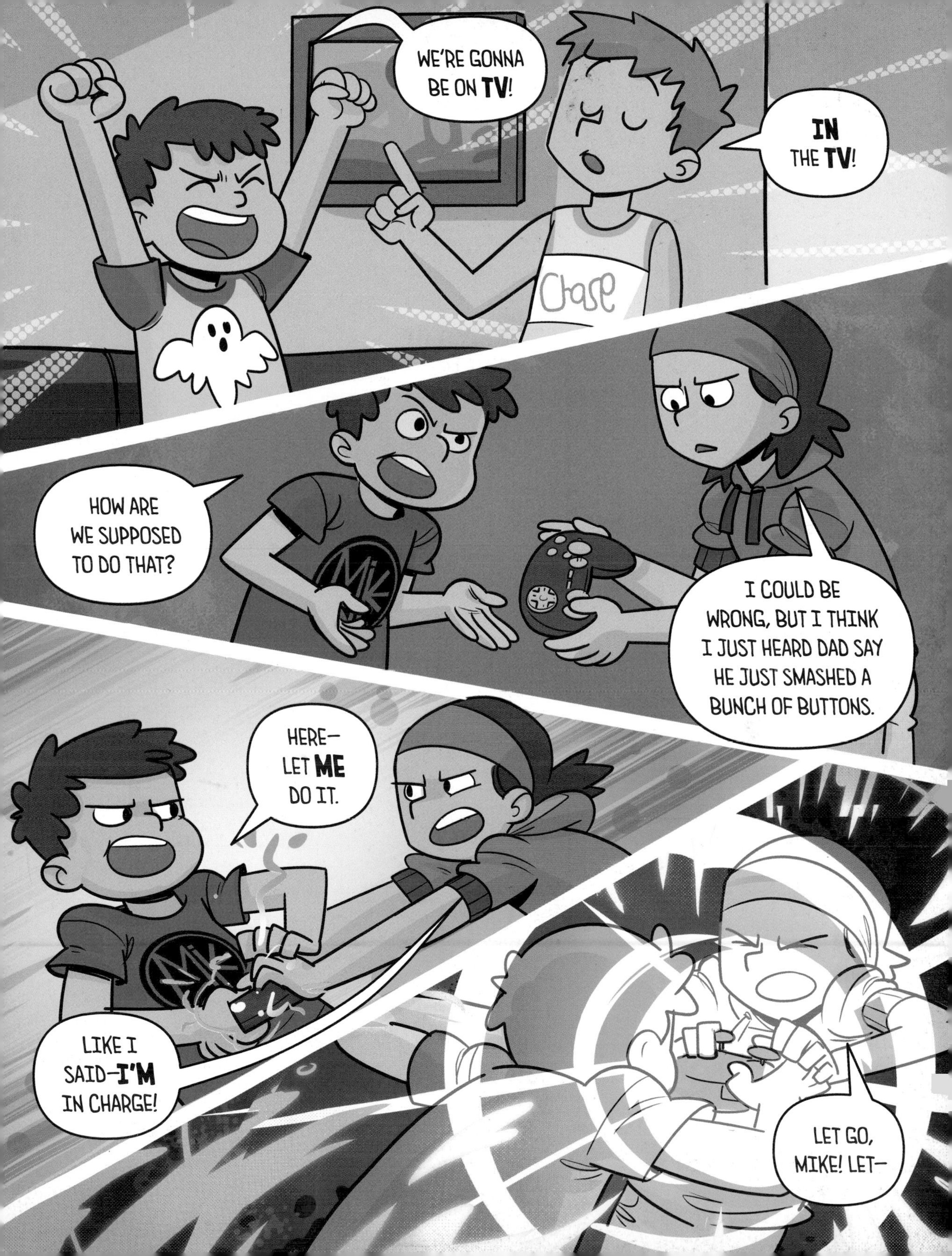
WE'RE GONNA BE ON **TV**!
IN THE **TV**!
Chase
HOW ARE WE SUPPOSED TO DO THAT?
I COULD BE WRONG, BUT I THINK I JUST HEARD DAD SAY HE JUST SMASHED A BUNCH OF BUTTONS.
HERE— LET **ME** DO IT.
LIKE I SAID—**I'M** IN CHARGE!
LET GO, MIKE! LET—

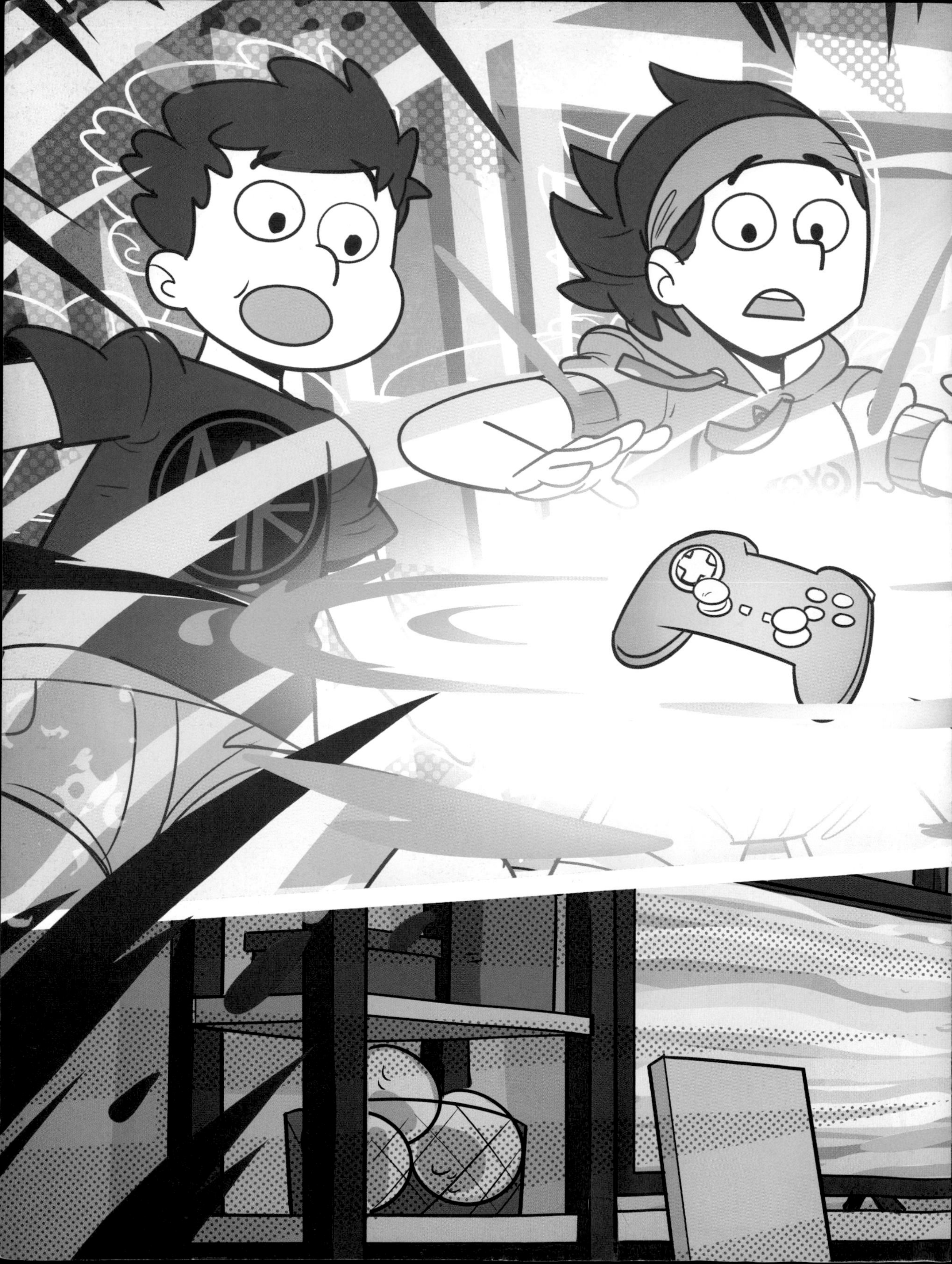

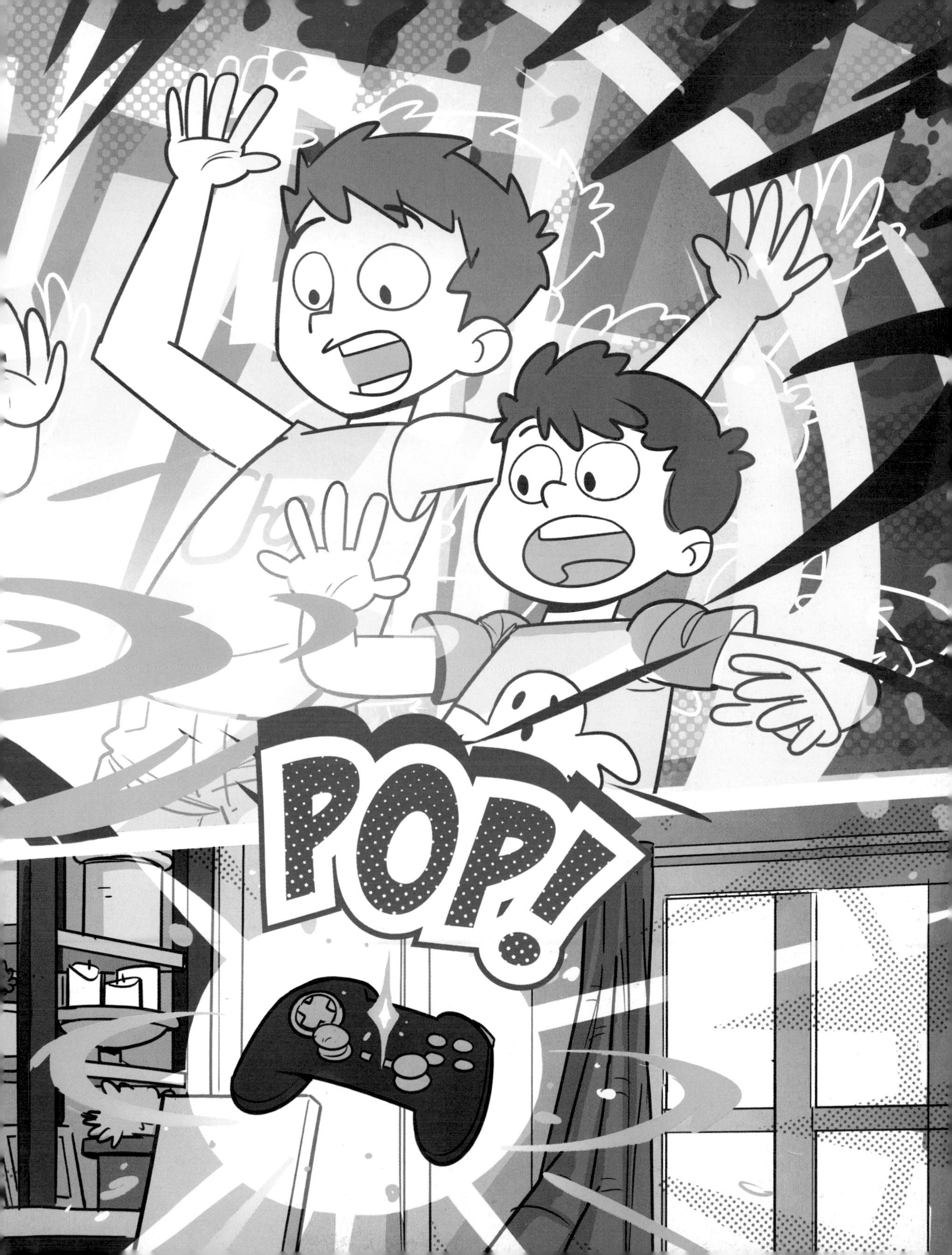
POP!

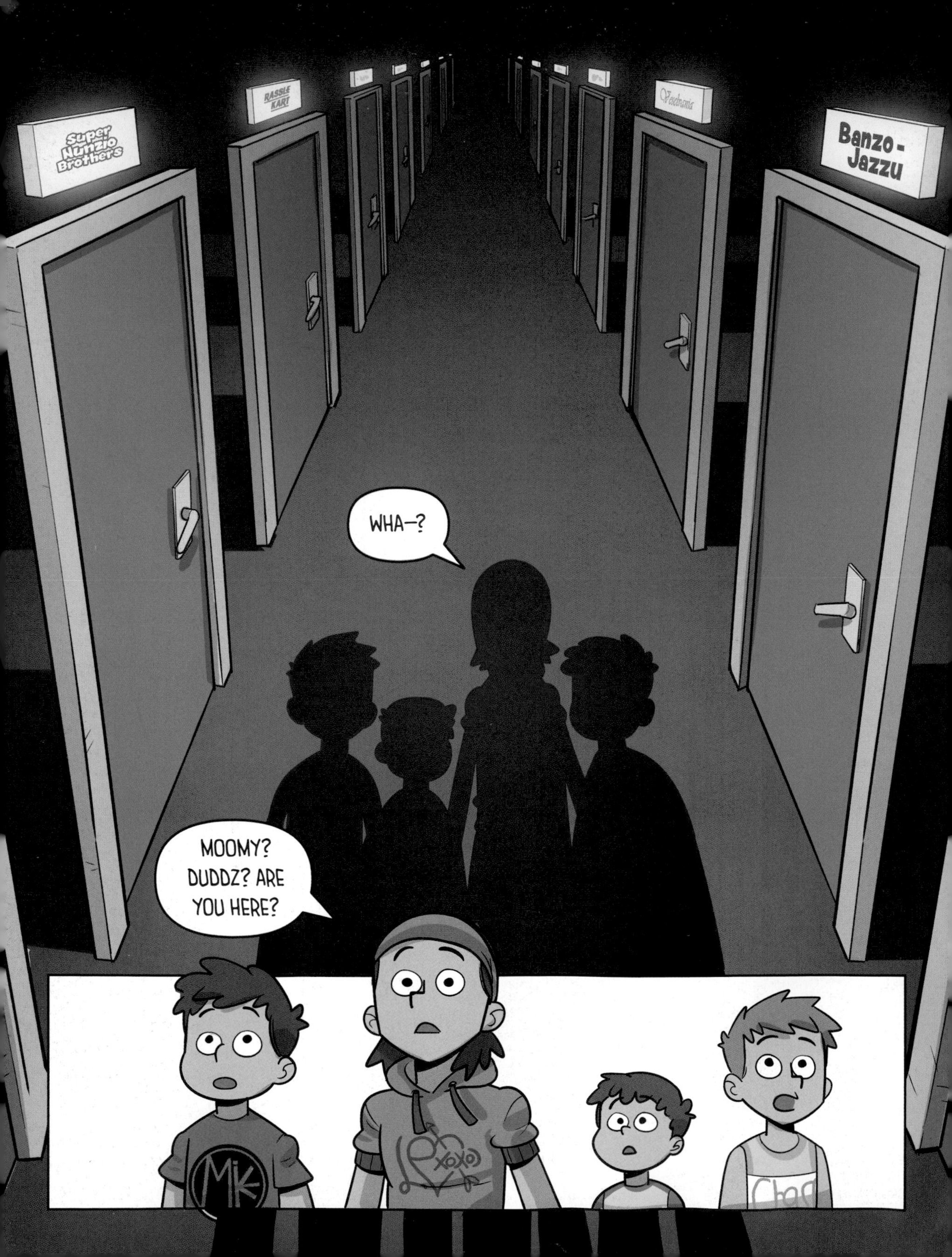

Super Nunzio Brothers
RASSLE KART
Vesebrania
Banzo-Jazzu
WHA—?
MOOMY? DUDDZ? ARE YOU HERE?

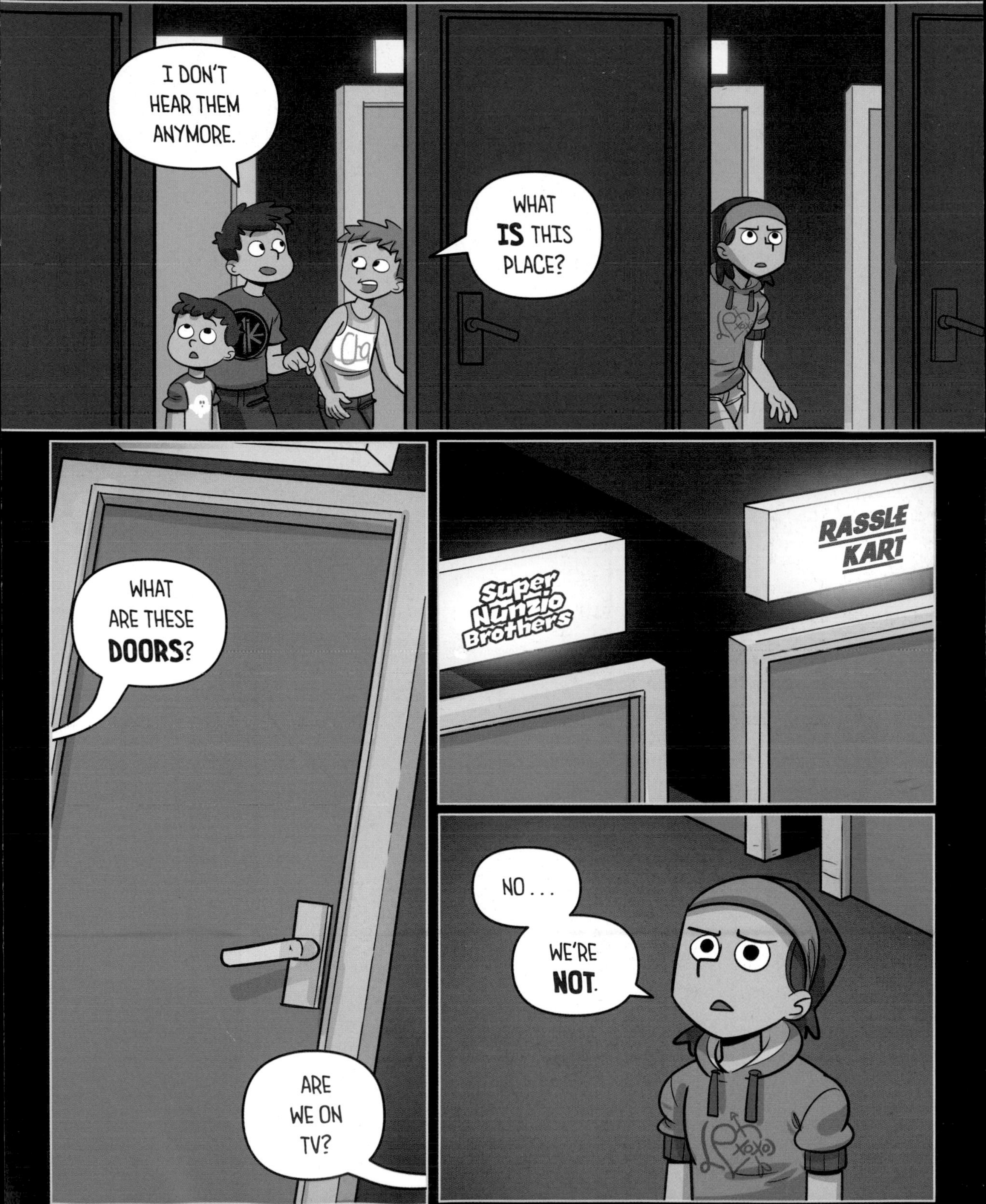
I DON'T HEAR THEM ANYMORE.
WHAT **IS** THIS PLACE?
WHAT ARE THESE **DOORS**?
Super Nunzio Brothers
RASSLE KART
ARE WE ON TV?
NO . . .
WE'RE **NOT**.

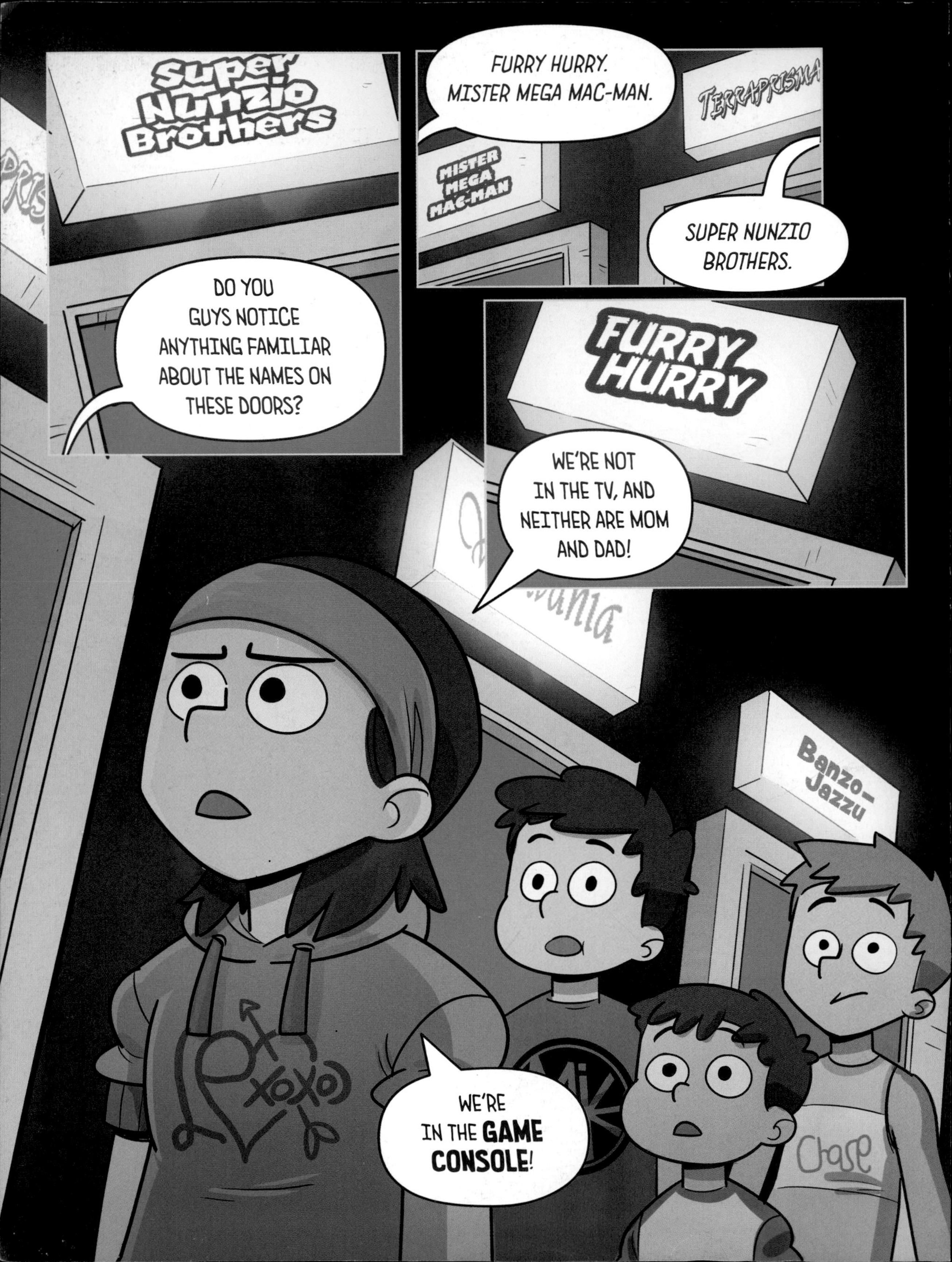
Super Nunzio Brothers
DO YOU GUYS NOTICE ANYTHING FAMILIAR ABOUT THE NAMES ON THESE DOORS?
FURRY HURRY. MISTER MEGA MAC-MAN.
TERRAPRISMA
MISTER MEGA MAC-MAN
SUPER NUNZIO BROTHERS.
FURRY HURRY
WE'RE NOT IN THE TV, AND NEITHER ARE MOM AND DAD!
Banzo-Jazzu
WE'RE IN THE **GAME CONSOLE**!
XOXO
Chase

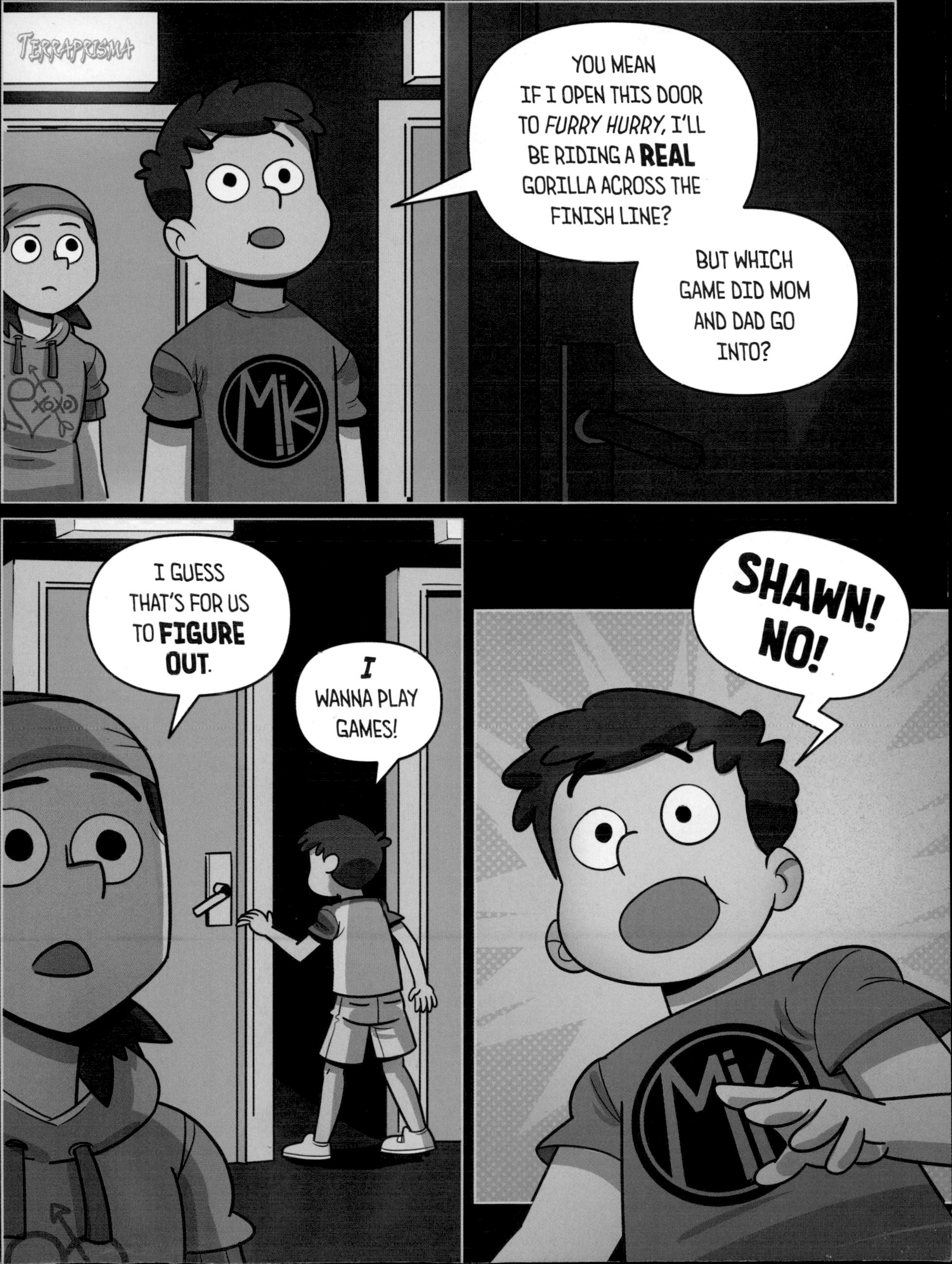
TERRAPRISMA
YOU MEAN IF I OPEN THIS DOOR TO *FURRY HURRY*, I'LL BE RIDING A **REAL** GORILLA ACROSS THE FINISH LINE?
BUT WHICH GAME DID MOM AND DAD GO INTO?
I GUESS THAT'S FOR US TO **FIGURE OUT**.
I WANNA PLAY GAMES!
SHAWN! NO!

SPOOKADILLY MANOR

BOOM

NOT **THIS** ONE!

BUT WHAT IF MOOMY AND DUDDY ARE IN THERE?

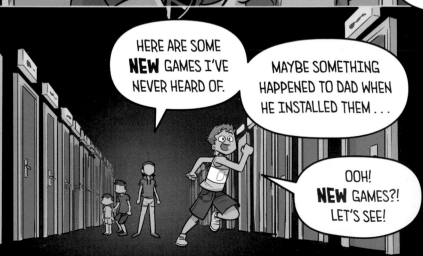

HERE ARE SOME **NEW** GAMES I'VE NEVER HEARD OF.

MAYBE SOMETHING HAPPENED TO DAD WHEN HE INSTALLED THEM . . .

OOH! **NEW** GAMES?! LET'S SEE!

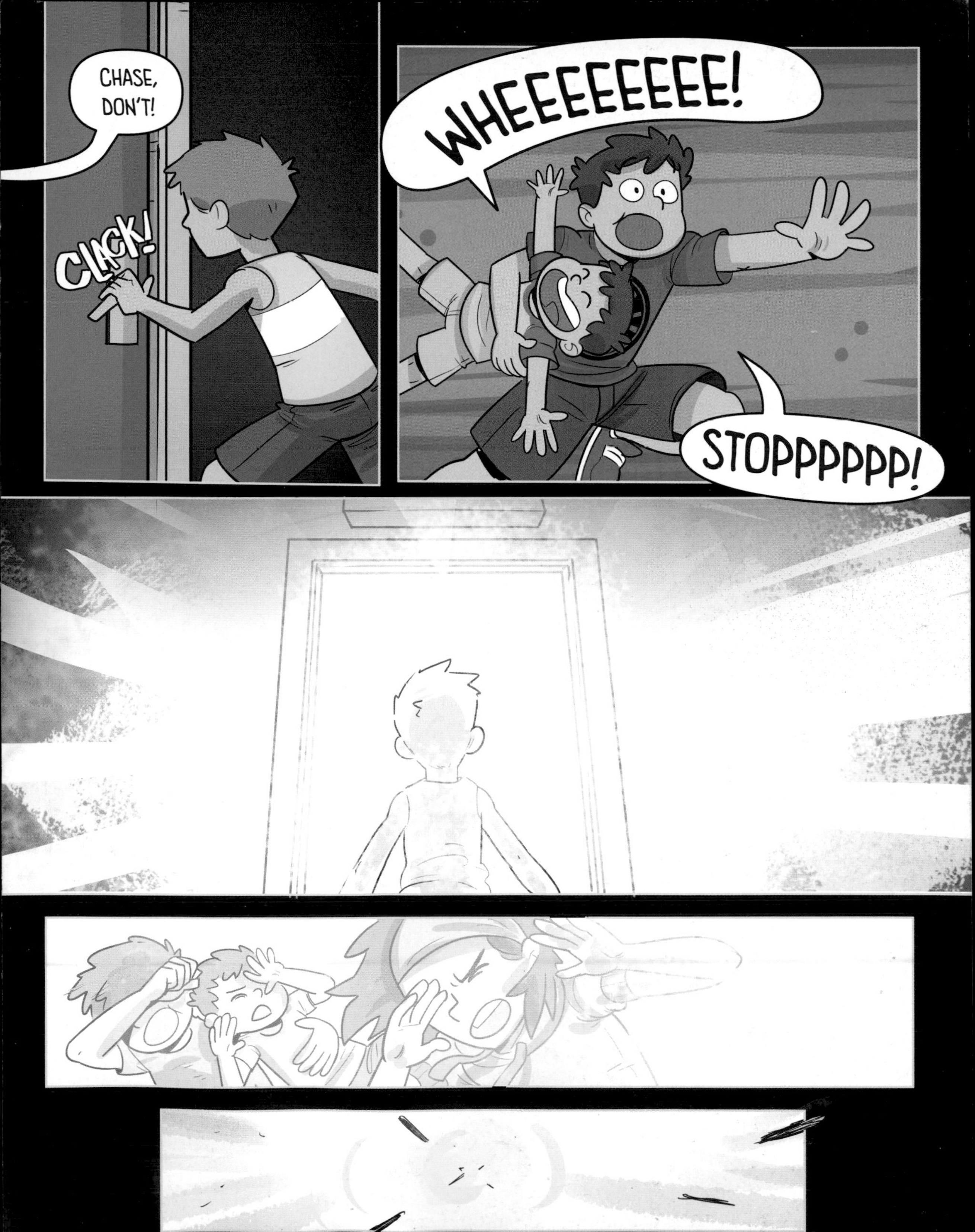

CHASE, DON'T!
CLACK!
WHEEEEEEEEE!
STOPPPPPP!

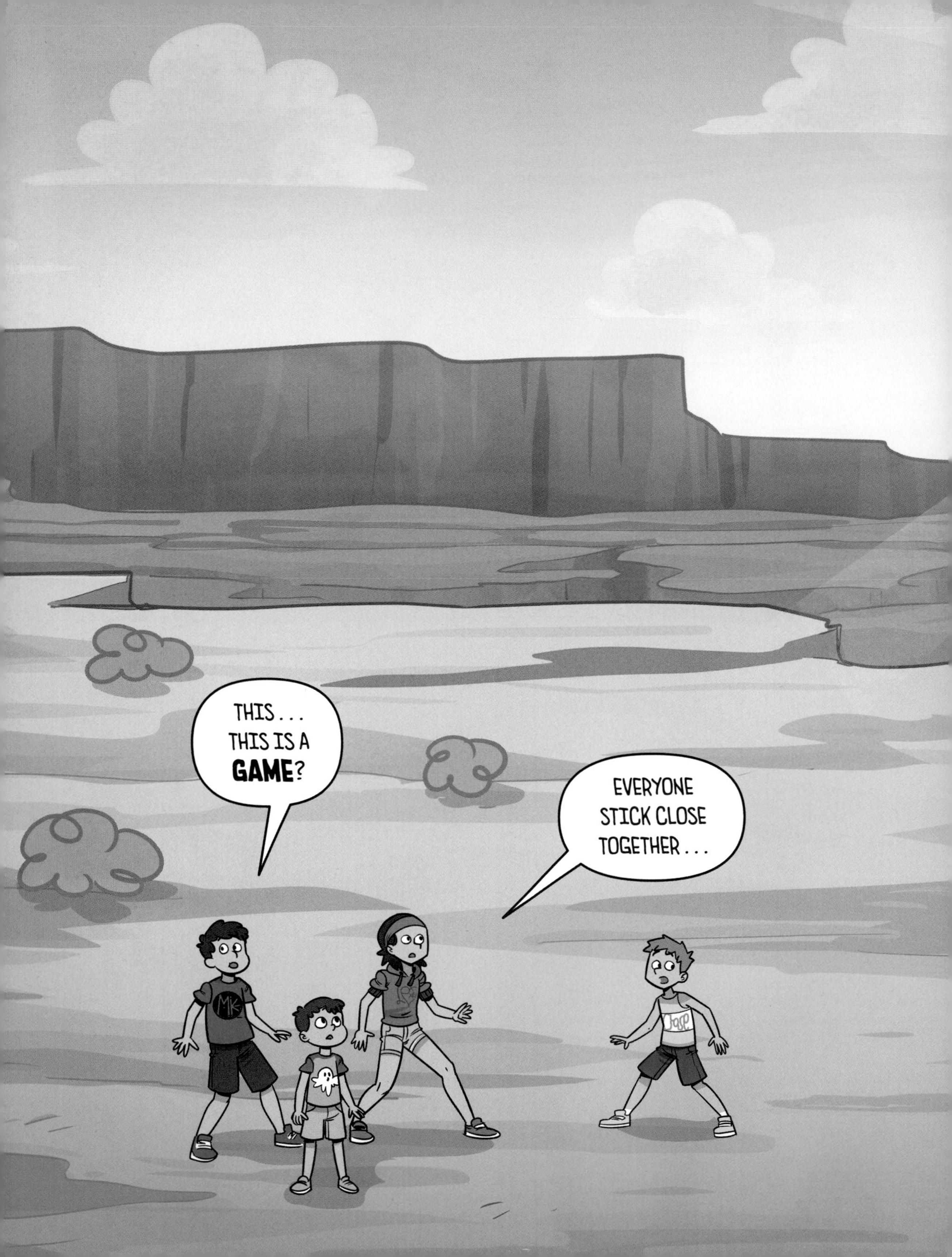
THIS . . . THIS IS A GAME?
EVERYONE STICK CLOSE TOGETHER . . .

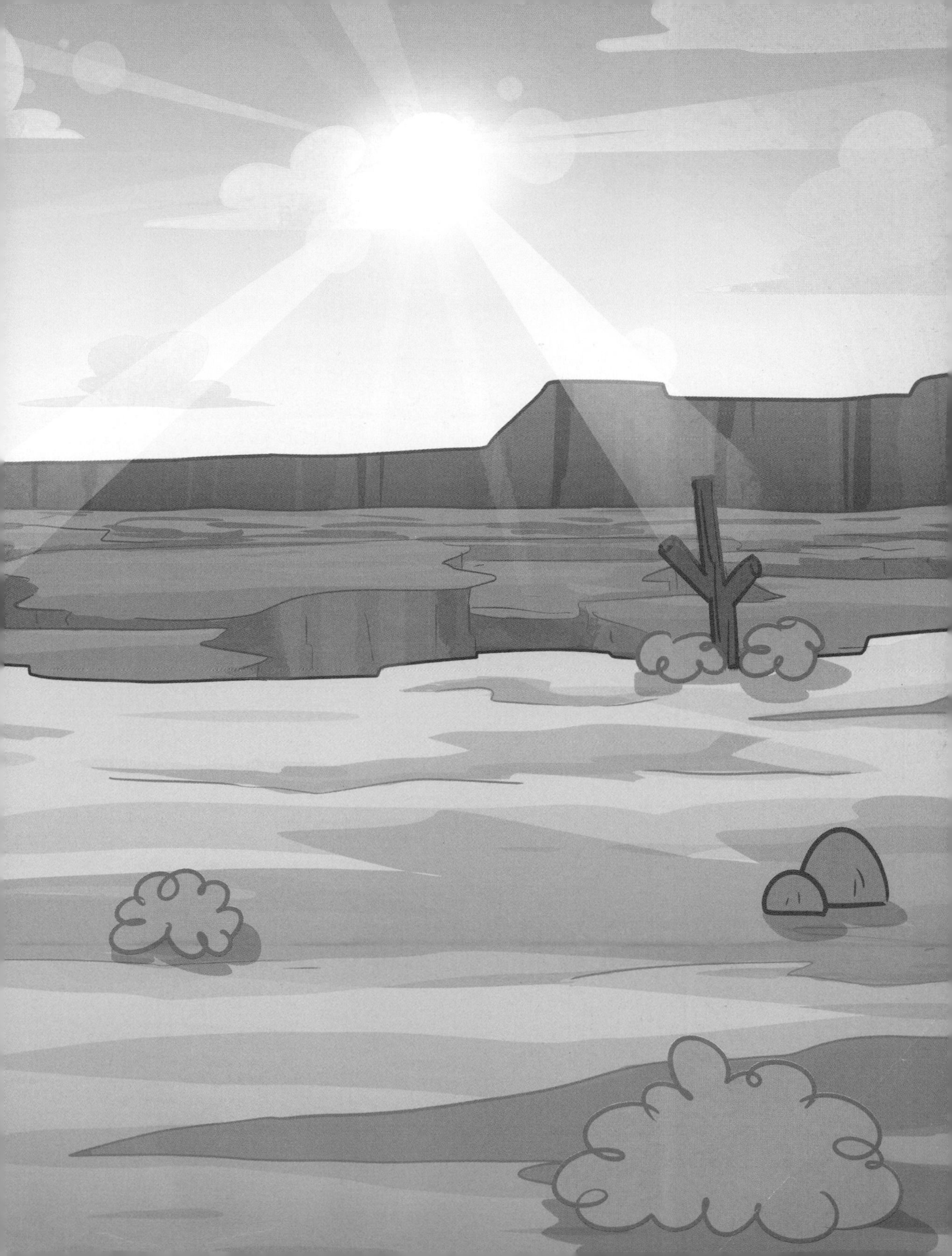

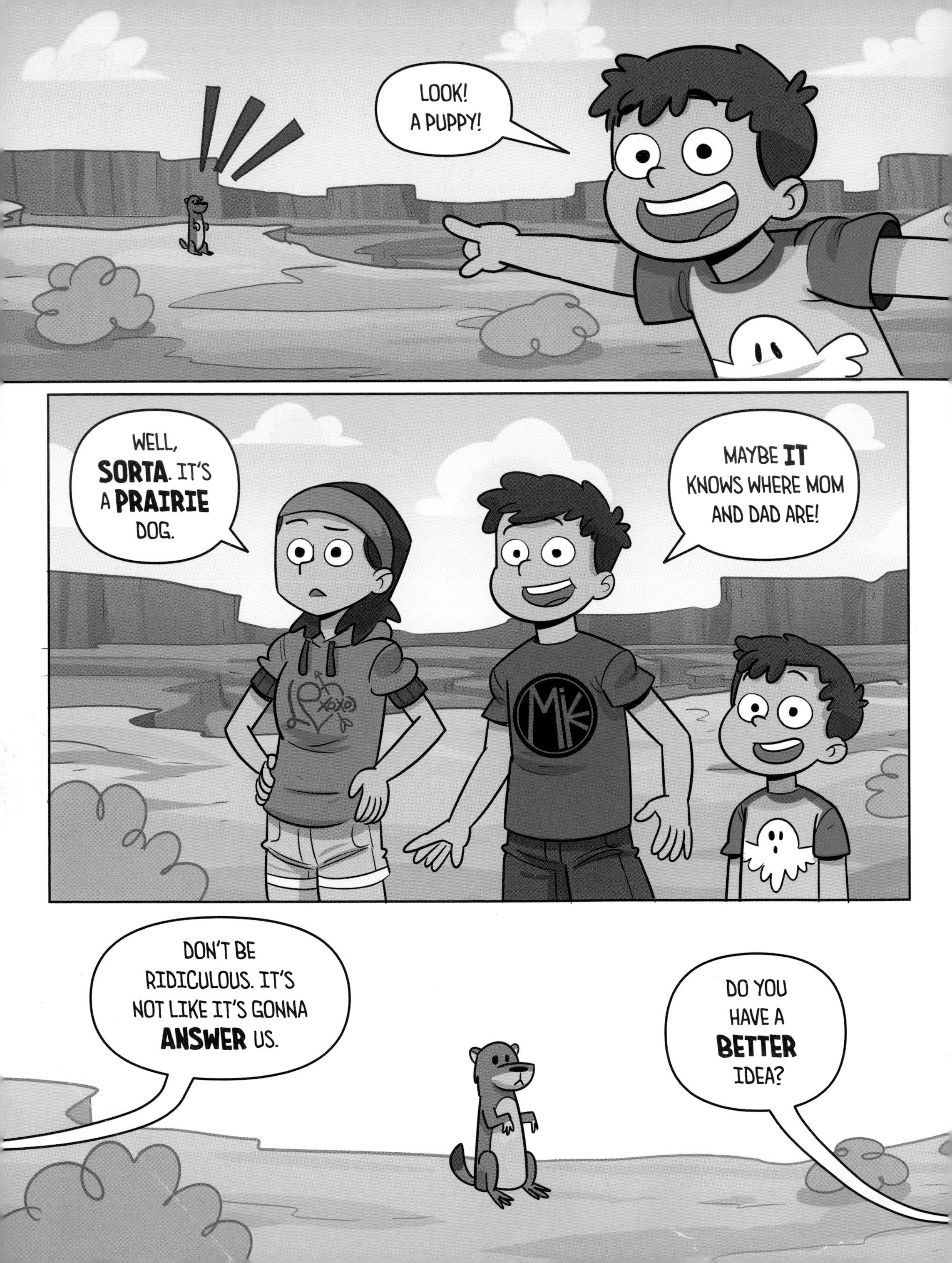
LOOK! A PUPPY!
WELL, SORTA. IT'S A PRAIRIE DOG.
MAYBE IT KNOWS WHERE MOM AND DAD ARE!
DON'T BE RIDICULOUS. IT'S NOT LIKE IT'S GONNA ANSWER US.
DO YOU HAVE A BETTER IDEA?

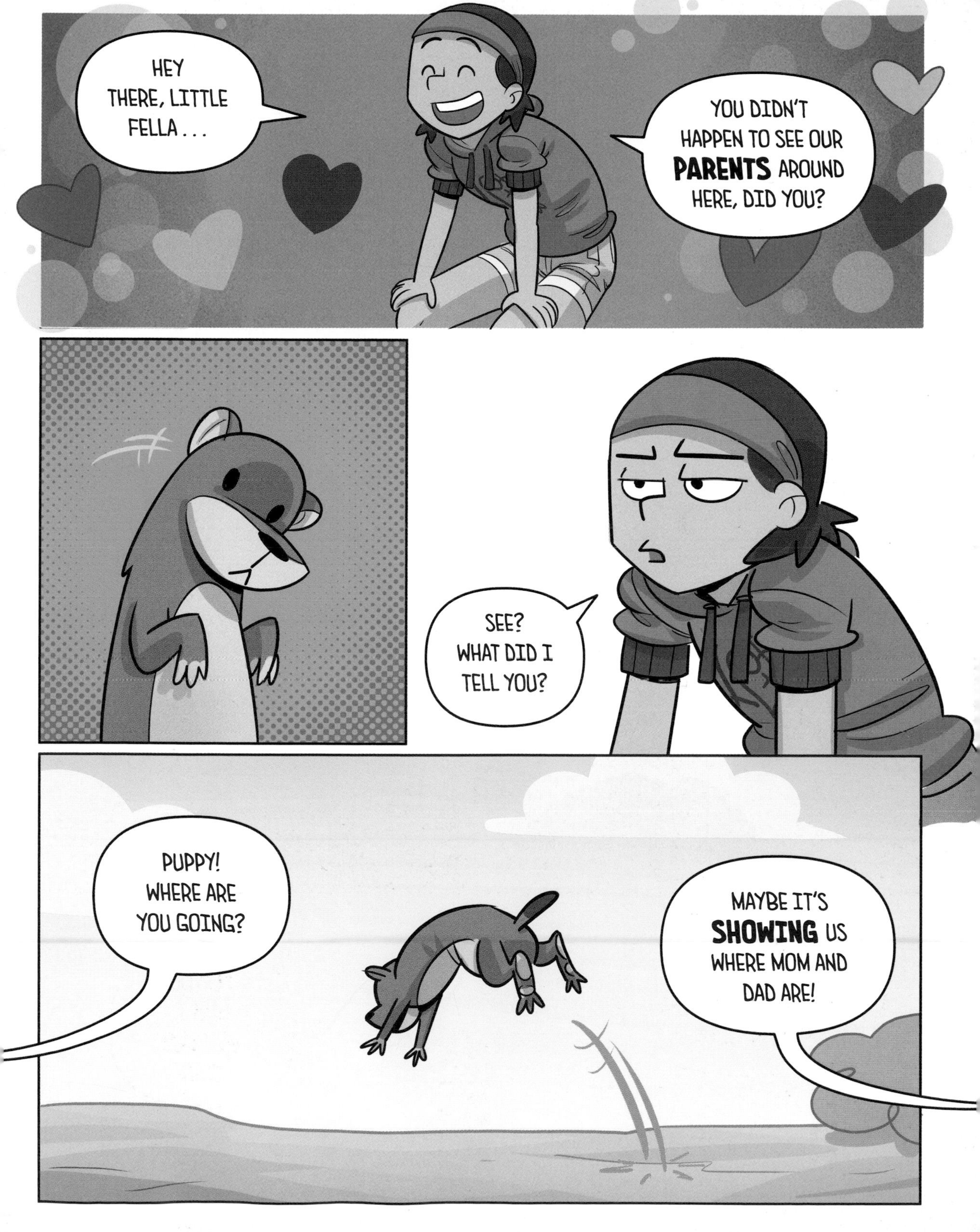
HEY THERE, LITTLE FELLA . . .
YOU DIDN'T HAPPEN TO SEE OUR **PARENTS** AROUND HERE, DID YOU?
SEE? WHAT DID I TELL YOU?
PUPPY! WHERE ARE YOU GOING?
MAYBE IT'S **SHOWING** US WHERE MOM AND DAD ARE!

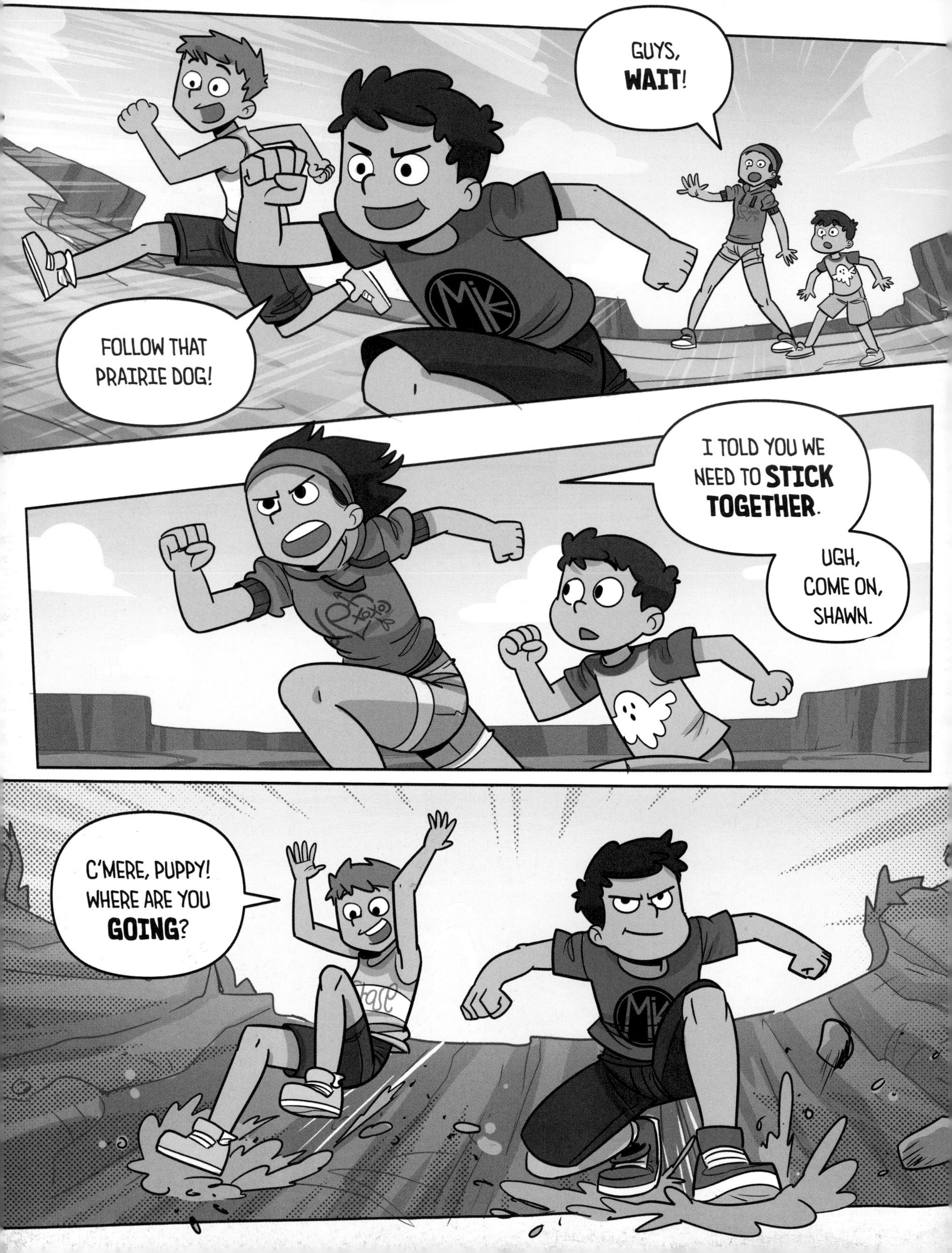
GUYS, WAIT!
FOLLOW THAT PRAIRIE DOG!
I TOLD YOU WE NEED TO STICK TOGETHER.
UGH, COME ON, SHAWN.
C'MERE, PUPPY! WHERE ARE YOU GOING?

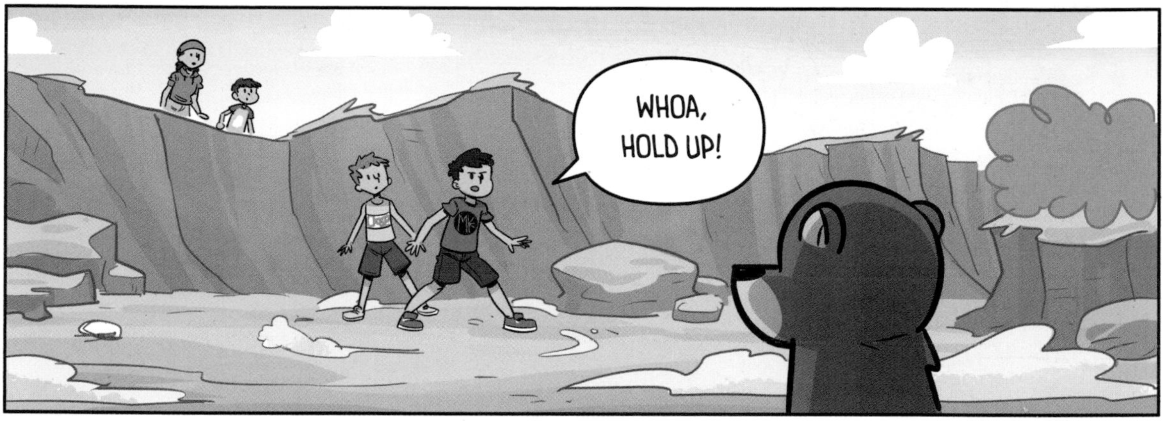
WHOA, HOLD UP!

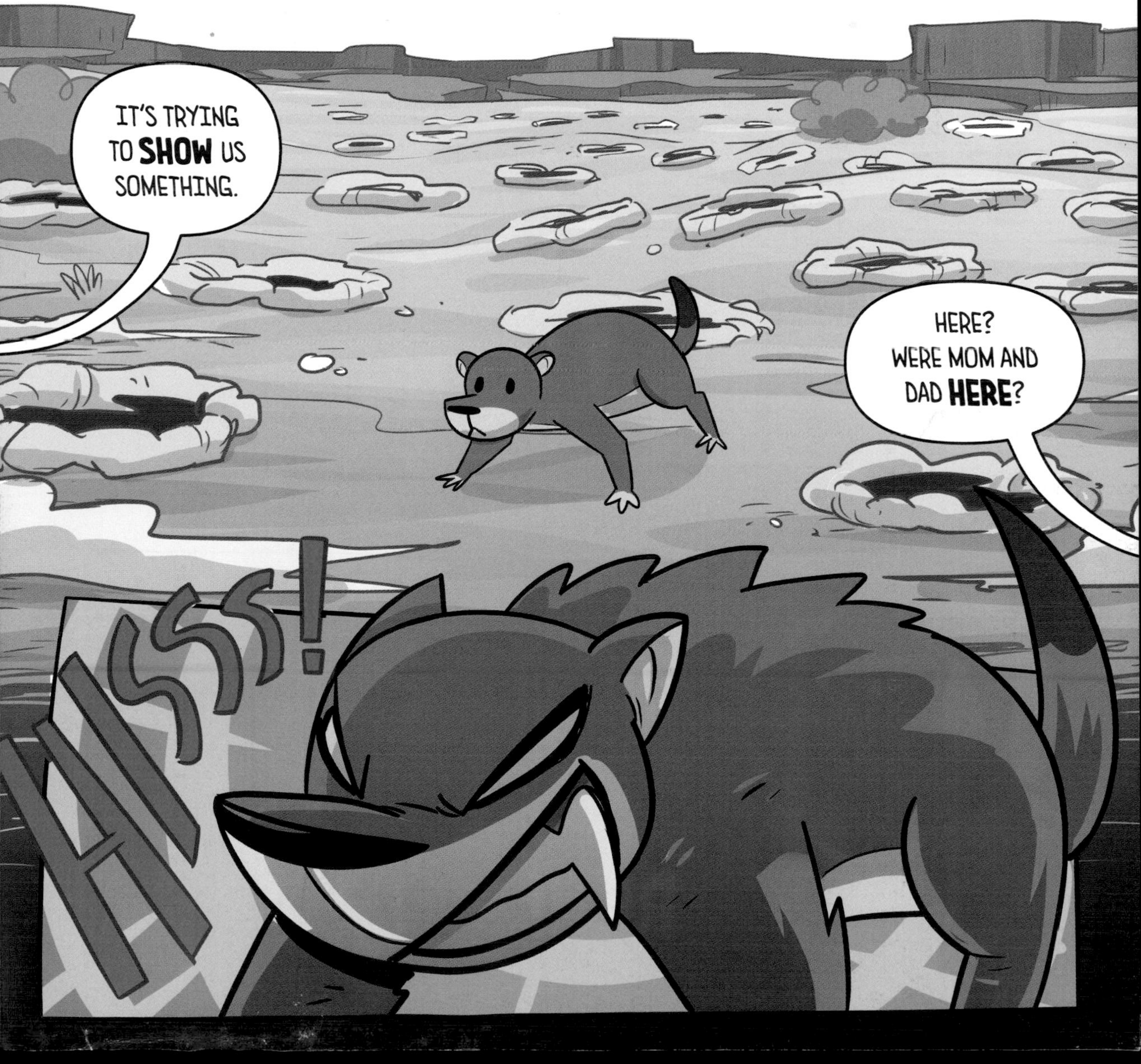
IT'S TRYING TO **SHOW** US SOMETHING.
HERE? WERE MOM AND DAD **HERE**?
HSSS!

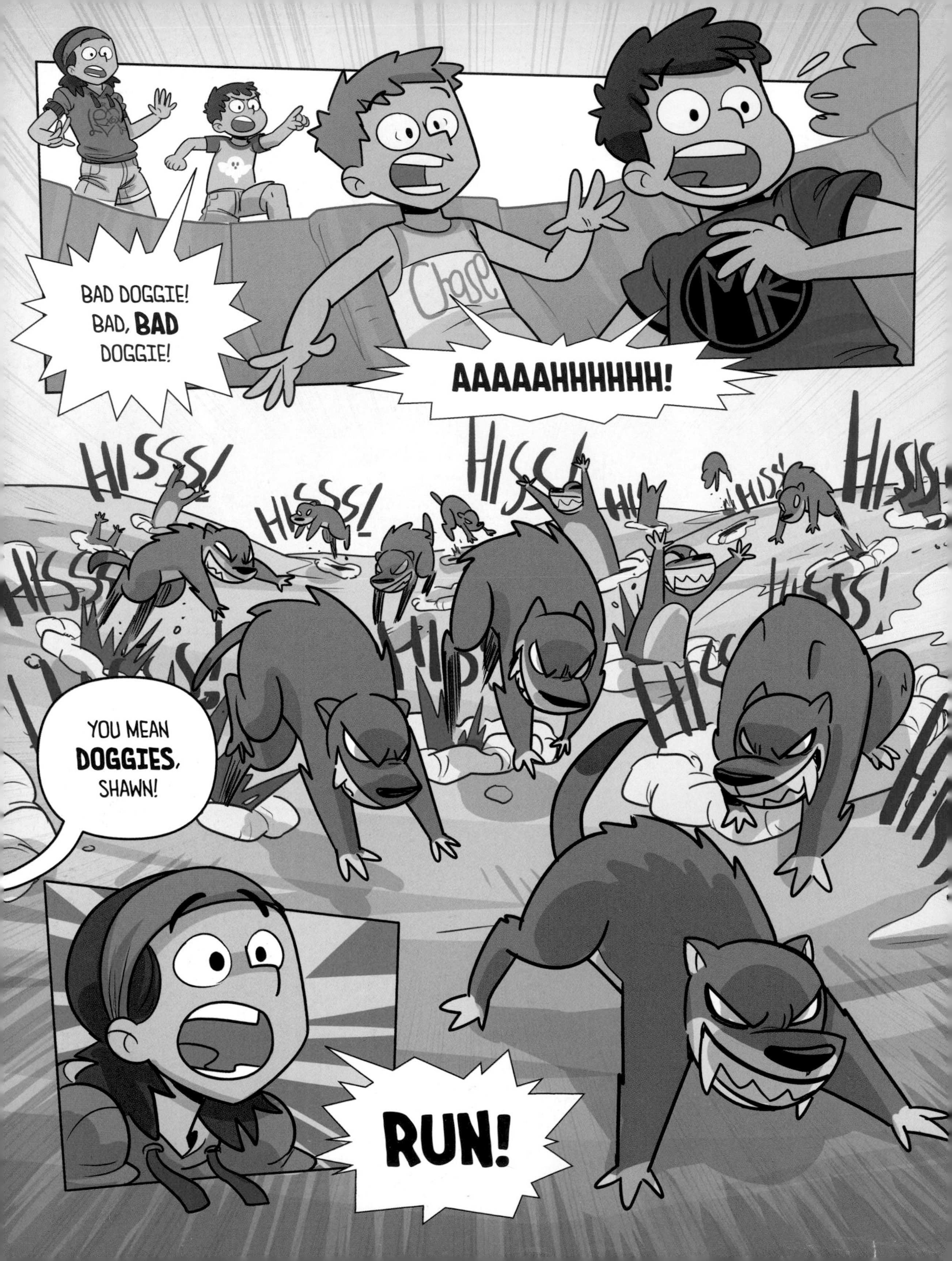
BAD DOGGIE! BAD, BAD DOGGIE!
AAAAAHHHHHH!
HISSS!
HISSS!
HISSS!
HISS!
YOU MEAN DOGGIES, SHAWN!
RUN!

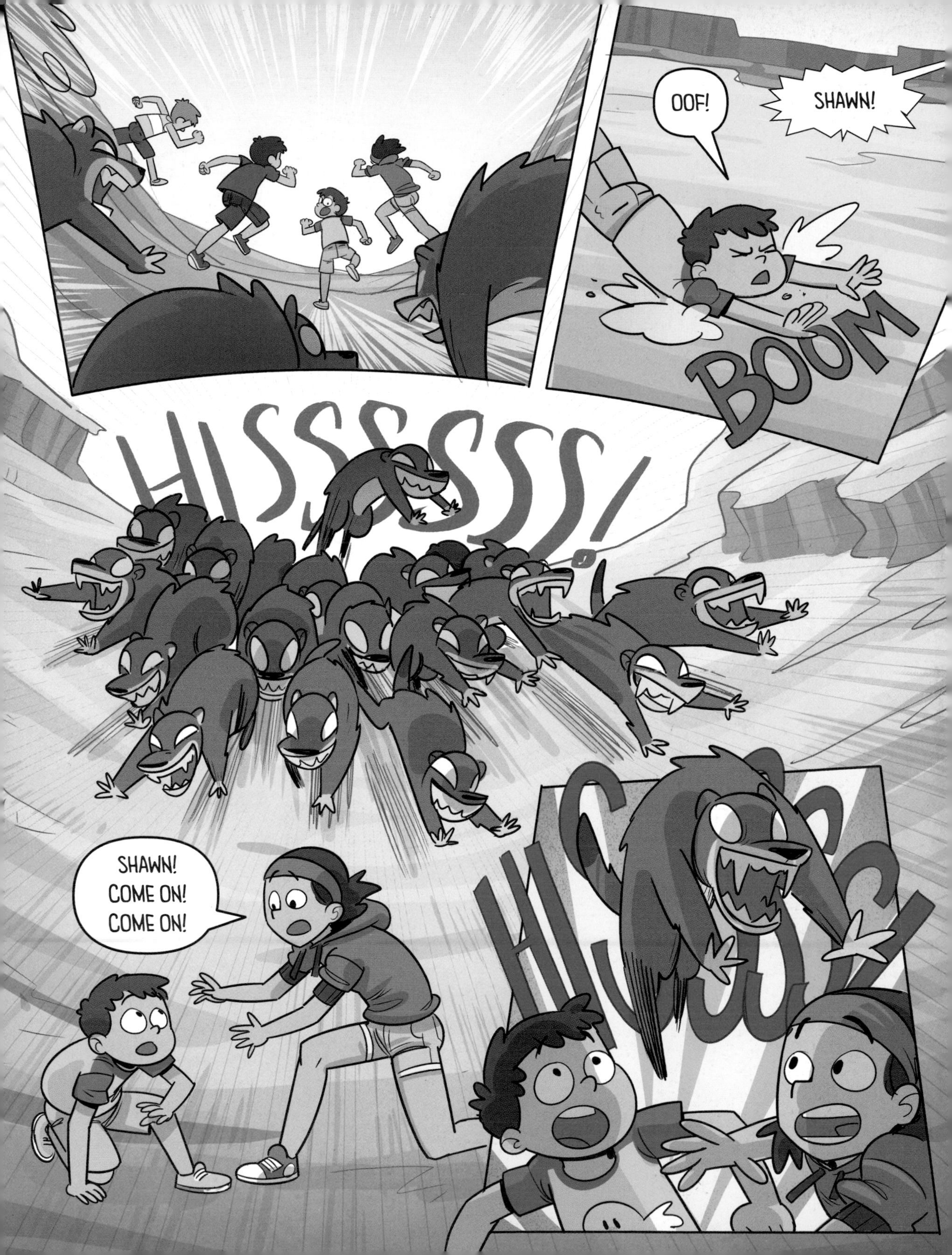
OOF!
SHAWN!
BOOM
HISSSSS!
SHAWN!
COME ON!
COME ON!
HISSSS!

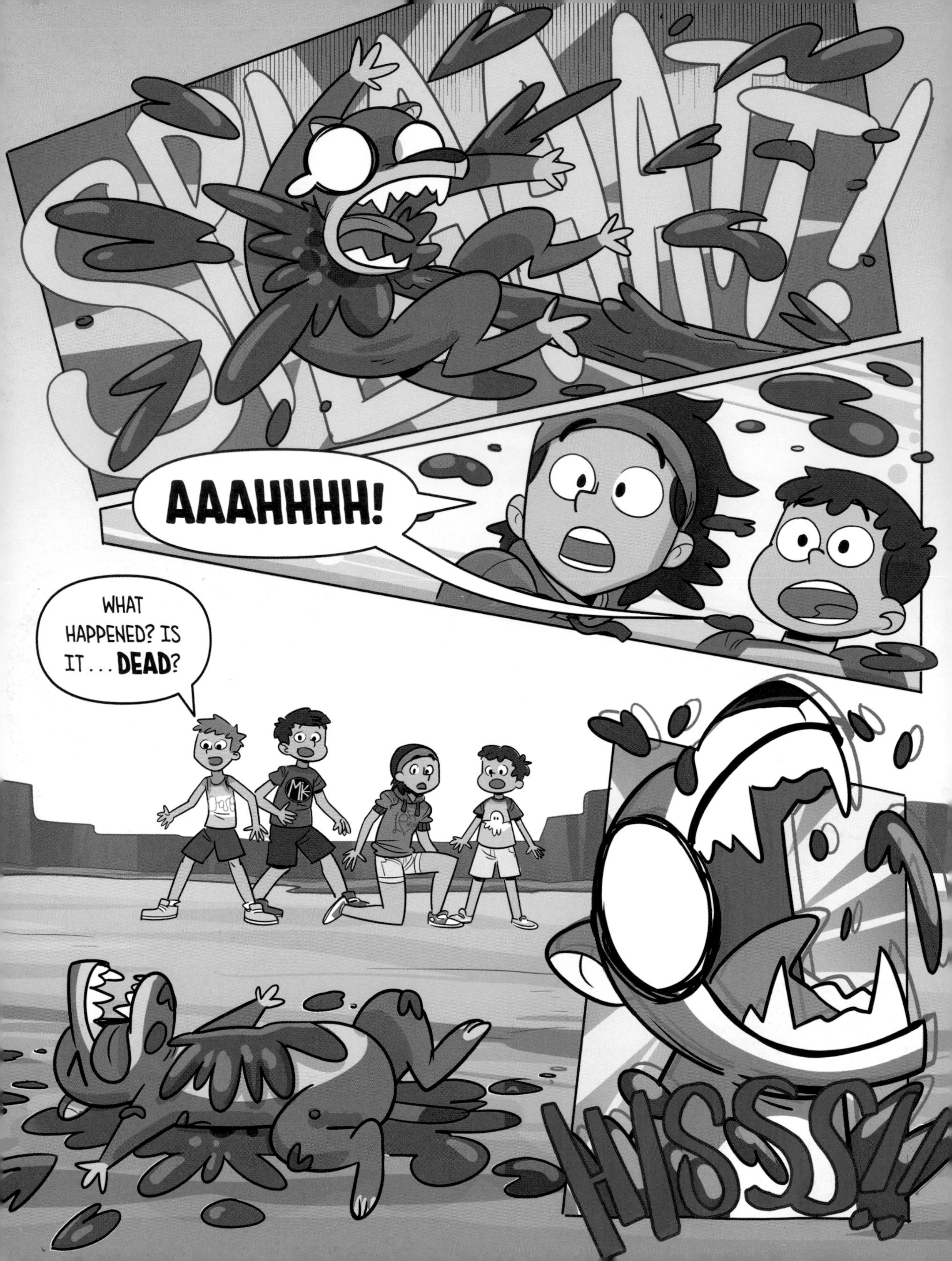
AAAHHHH!
WHAT HAPPENED? IS IT . . . **DEAD**?
HISSS!

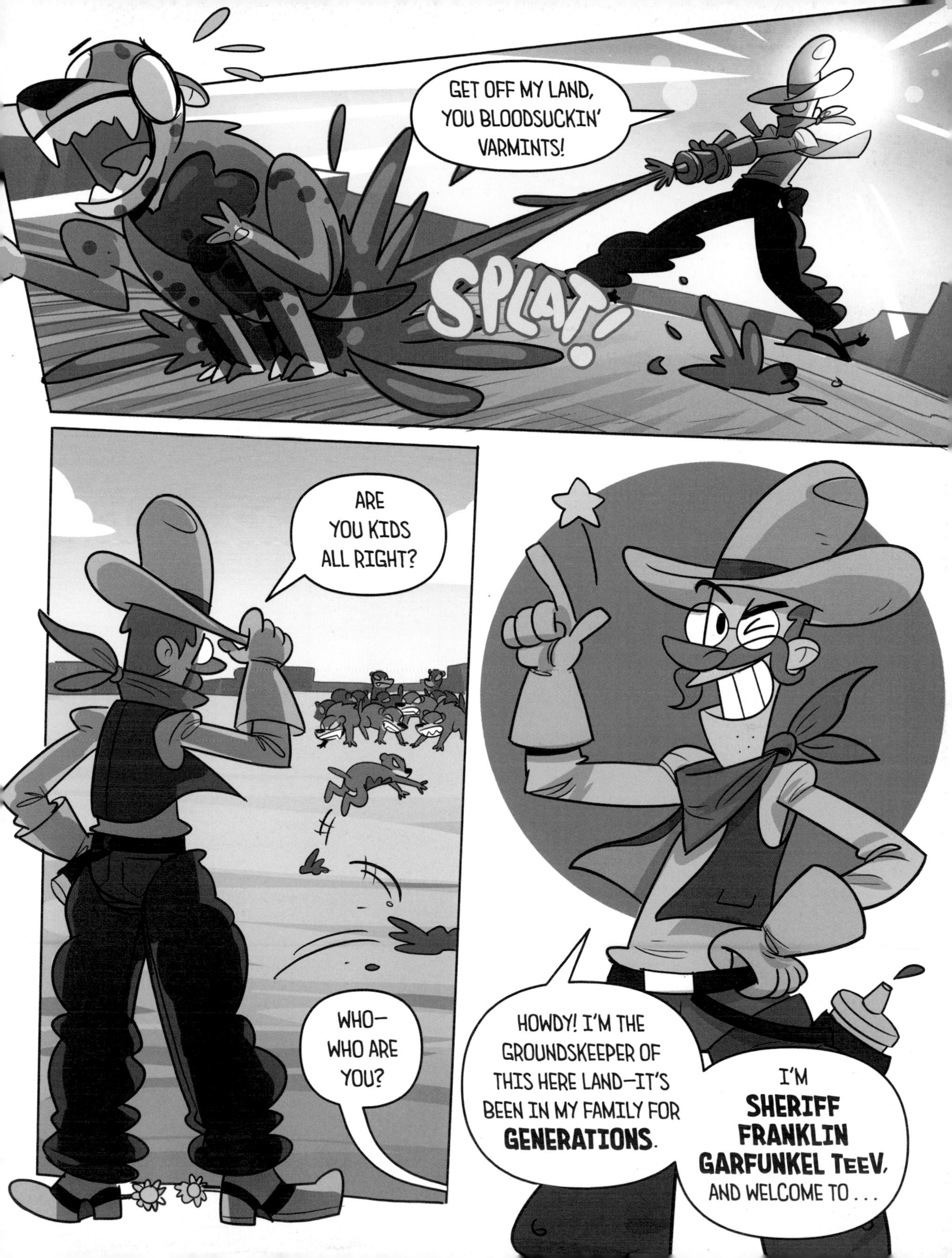
GET OFF MY LAND, YOU BLOODSUCKIN' VARMINTS!
SPLAT!
ARE YOU KIDS ALL RIGHT?
WHO— WHO ARE YOU?
HOWDY! I'M THE GROUNDSKEEPER OF THIS HERE LAND—IT'S BEEN IN MY FAMILY FOR GENERATIONS.
I'M SHERIFF FRANKLIN GARFUNKEL TEEV, AND WELCOME TO . . .

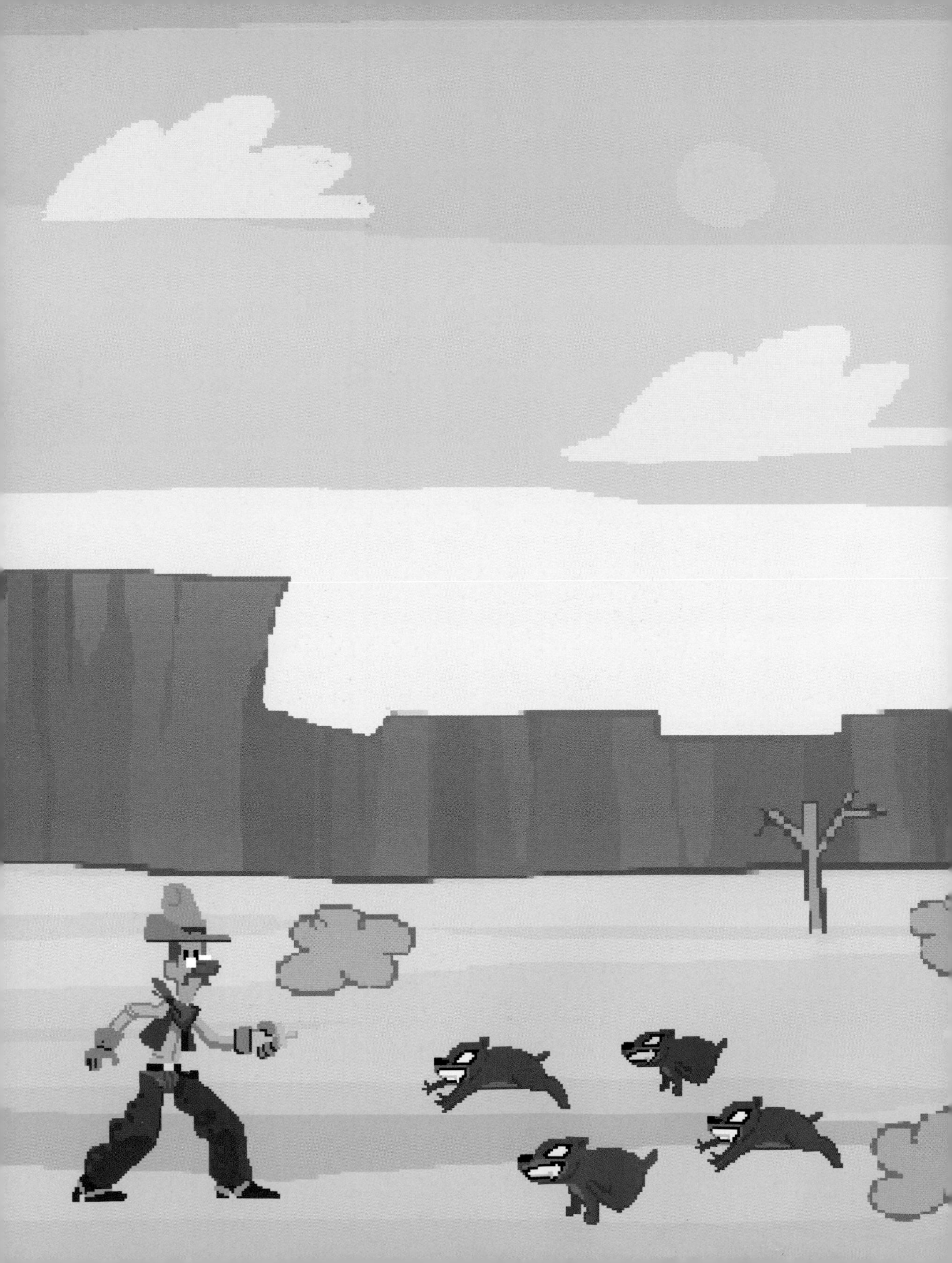

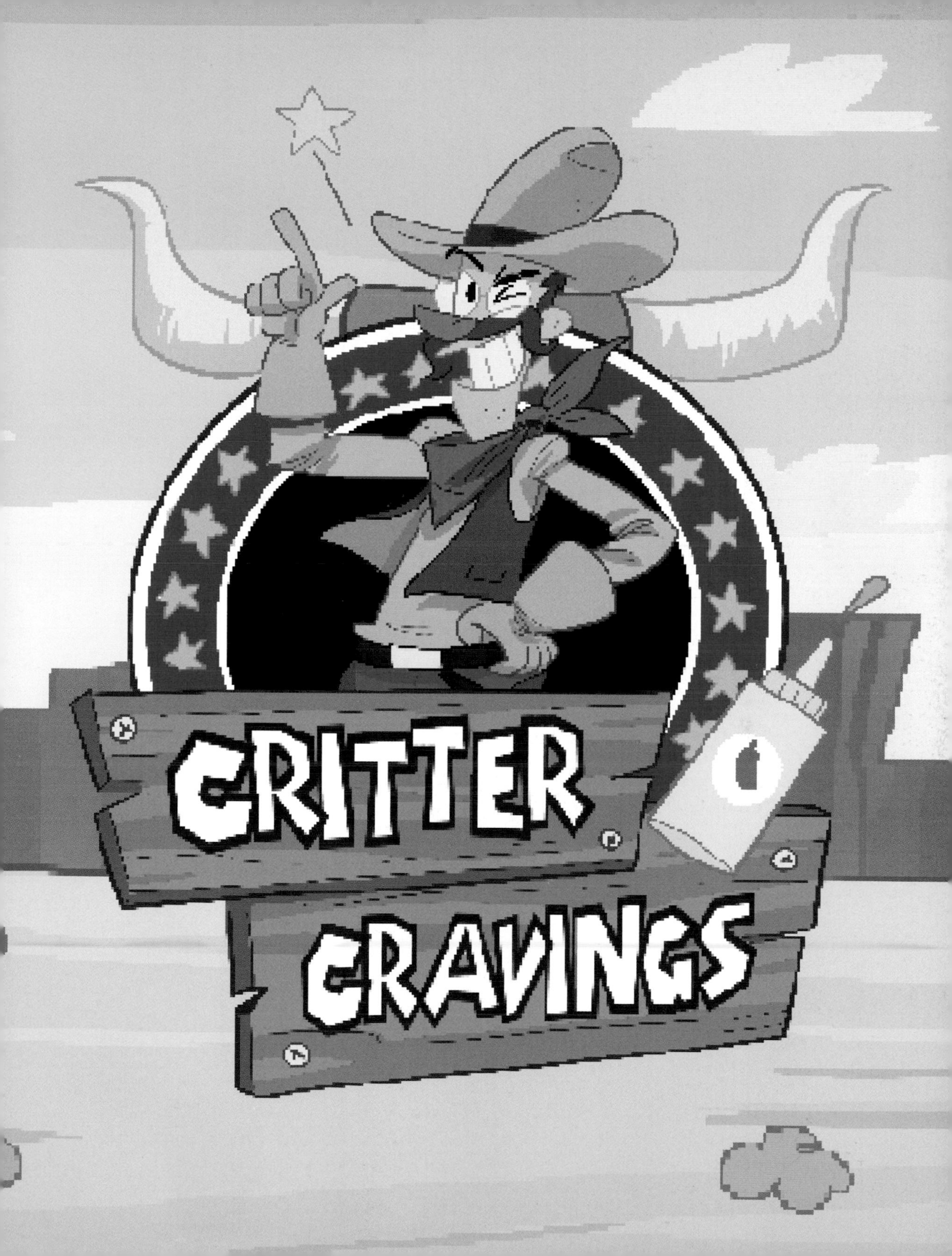
CRITTER
CRAVINGS

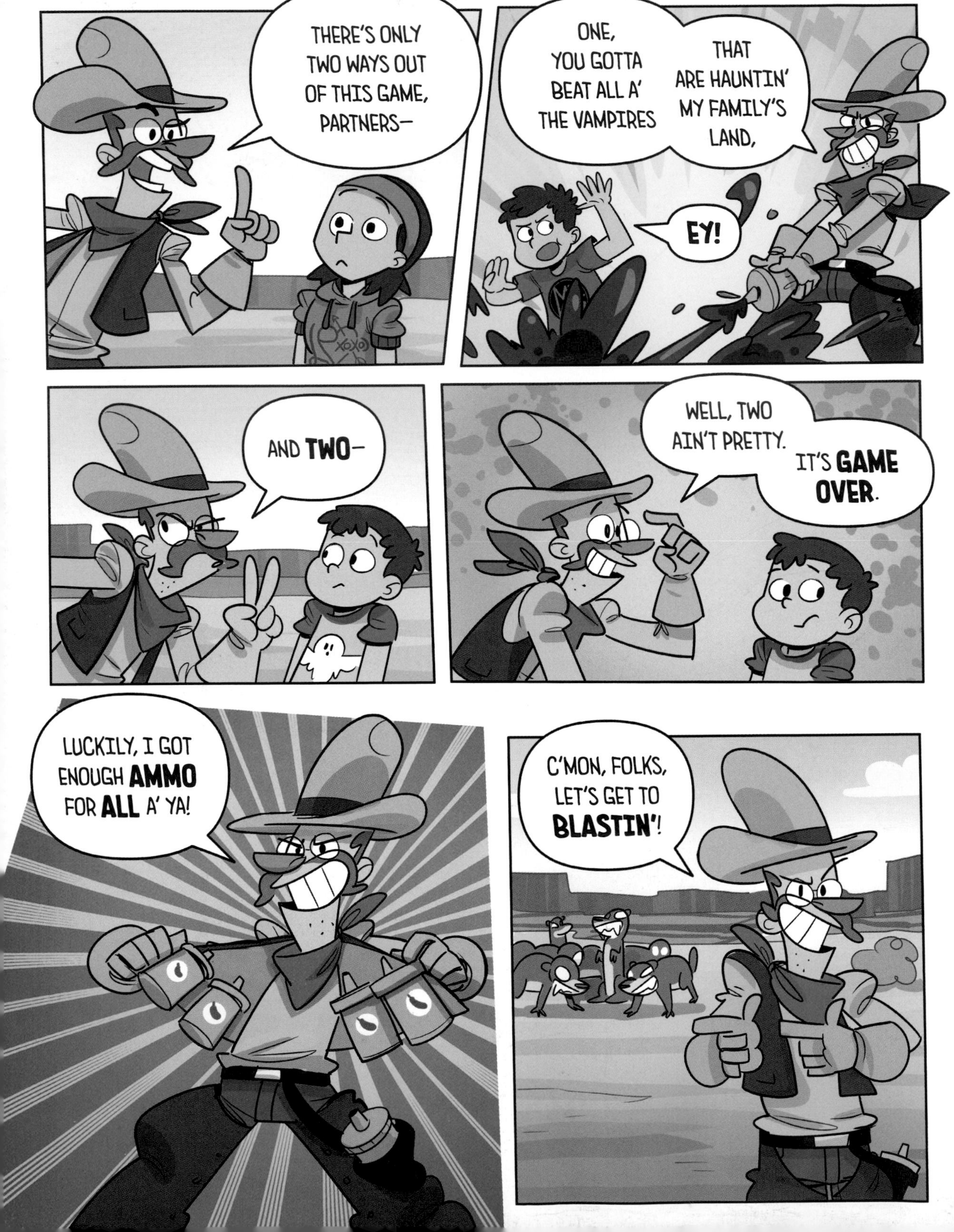
THERE'S ONLY TWO WAYS OUT OF THIS GAME, PARTNERS—
ONE, YOU GOTTA BEAT ALL A' THE VAMPIRES
THAT ARE HAUNTIN' MY FAMILY'S LAND,
EY!
AND TWO—
WELL, TWO AIN'T PRETTY.
IT'S GAME OVER.
LUCKILY, I GOT ENOUGH AMMO FOR ALL A' YA!
C'MON, FOLKS, LET'S GET TO BLASTIN'!

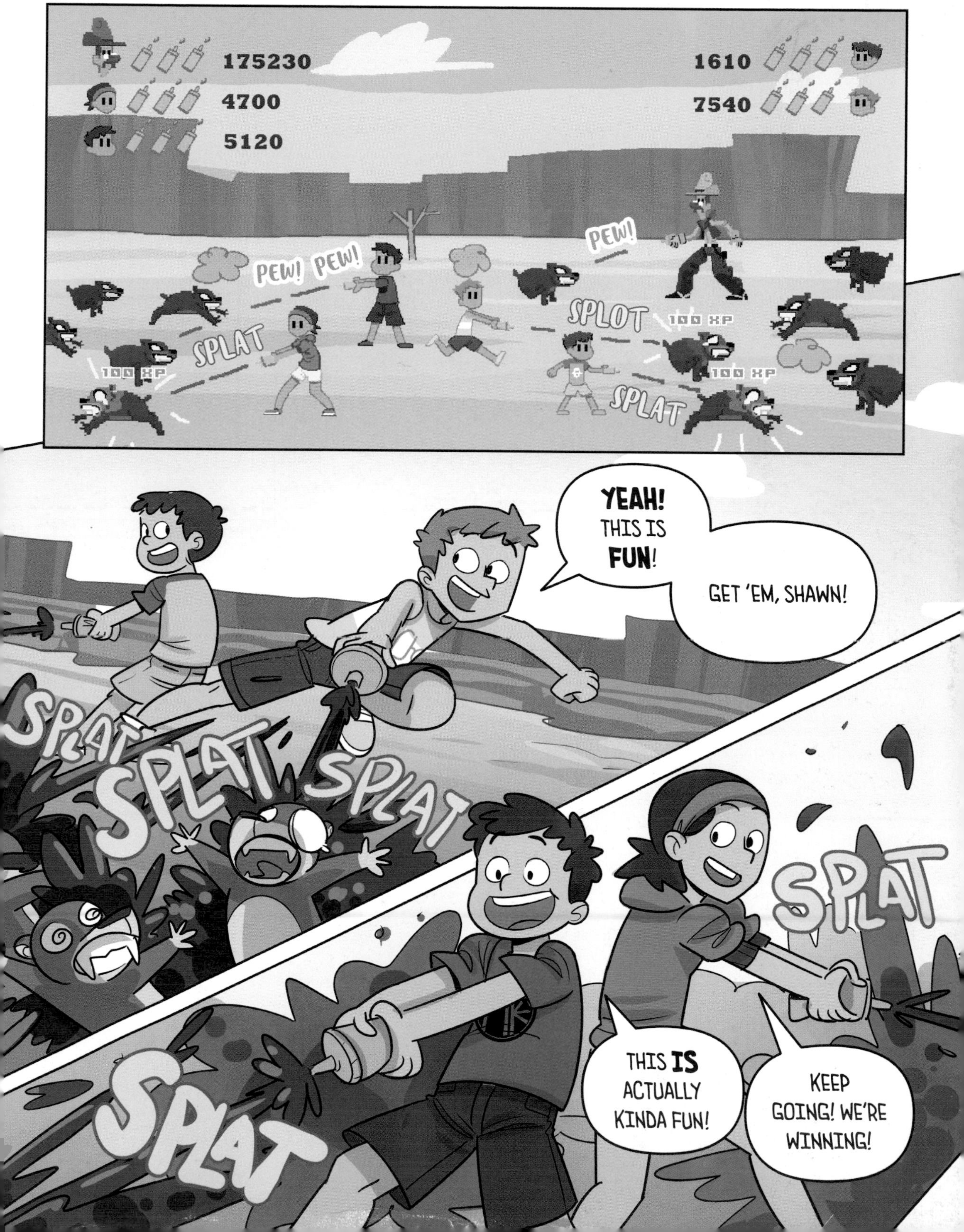

175230
4700
5120
1610
7540
PEW! PEW!
PEW!
SPLAT
100 XP
SPLOT
100 XP
100 XP
SPLAT
YEAH! THIS IS FUN!
GET 'EM, SHAWN!
SPLAT SPLAT SPLAT SPLAT
SPLAT
SPLAT
THIS IS ACTUALLY KINDA FUN!
KEEP GOING! WE'RE WINNING!

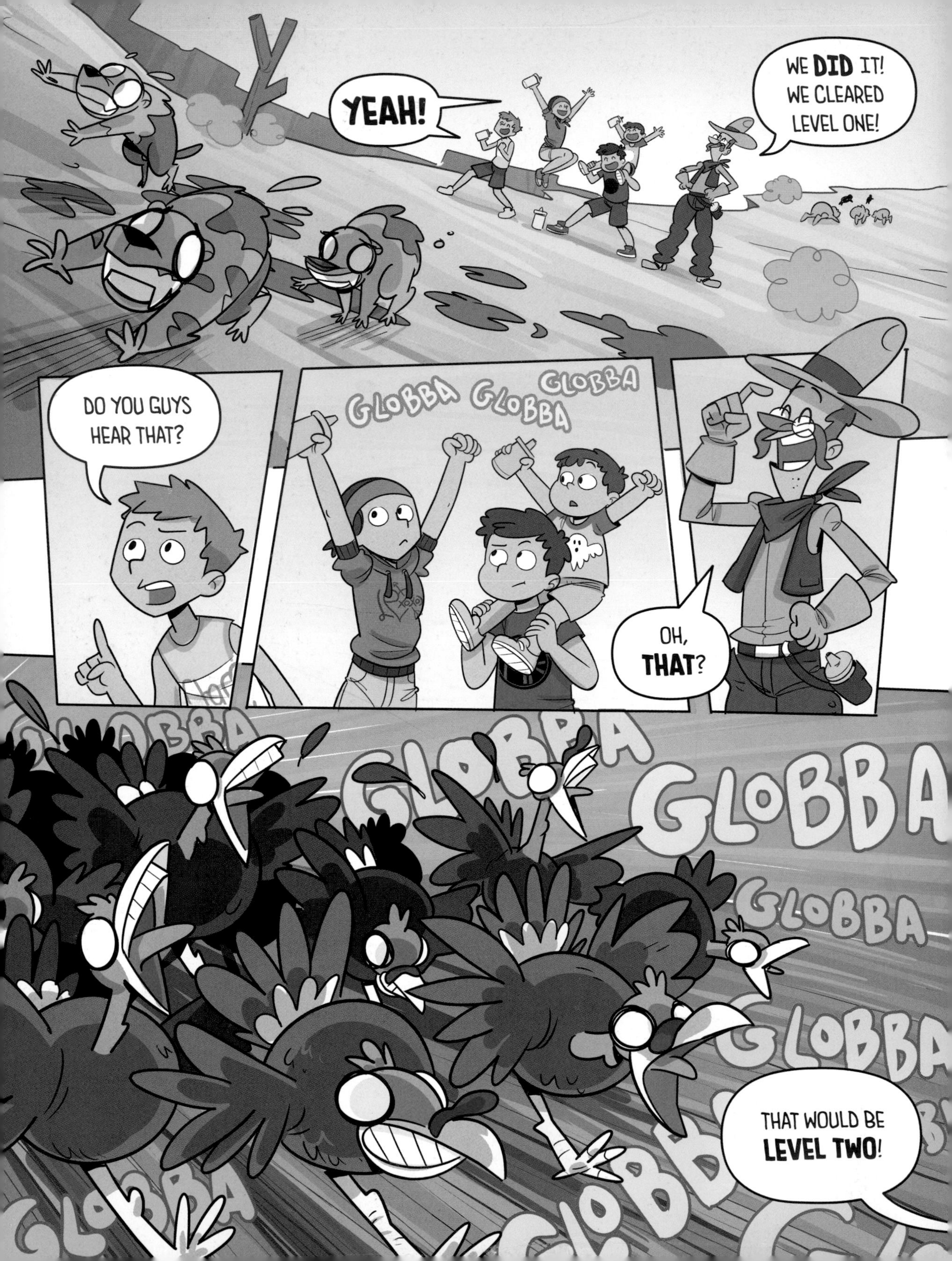
YEAH!
WE DID IT! WE CLEARED LEVEL ONE!
DO YOU GUYS HEAR THAT?
GLOBBA GLOBBA GLOBBA
OH, THAT?
GLOBBA GLOBBA GLOBBA GLOBBA GLOBBA
THAT WOULD BE LEVEL TWO!

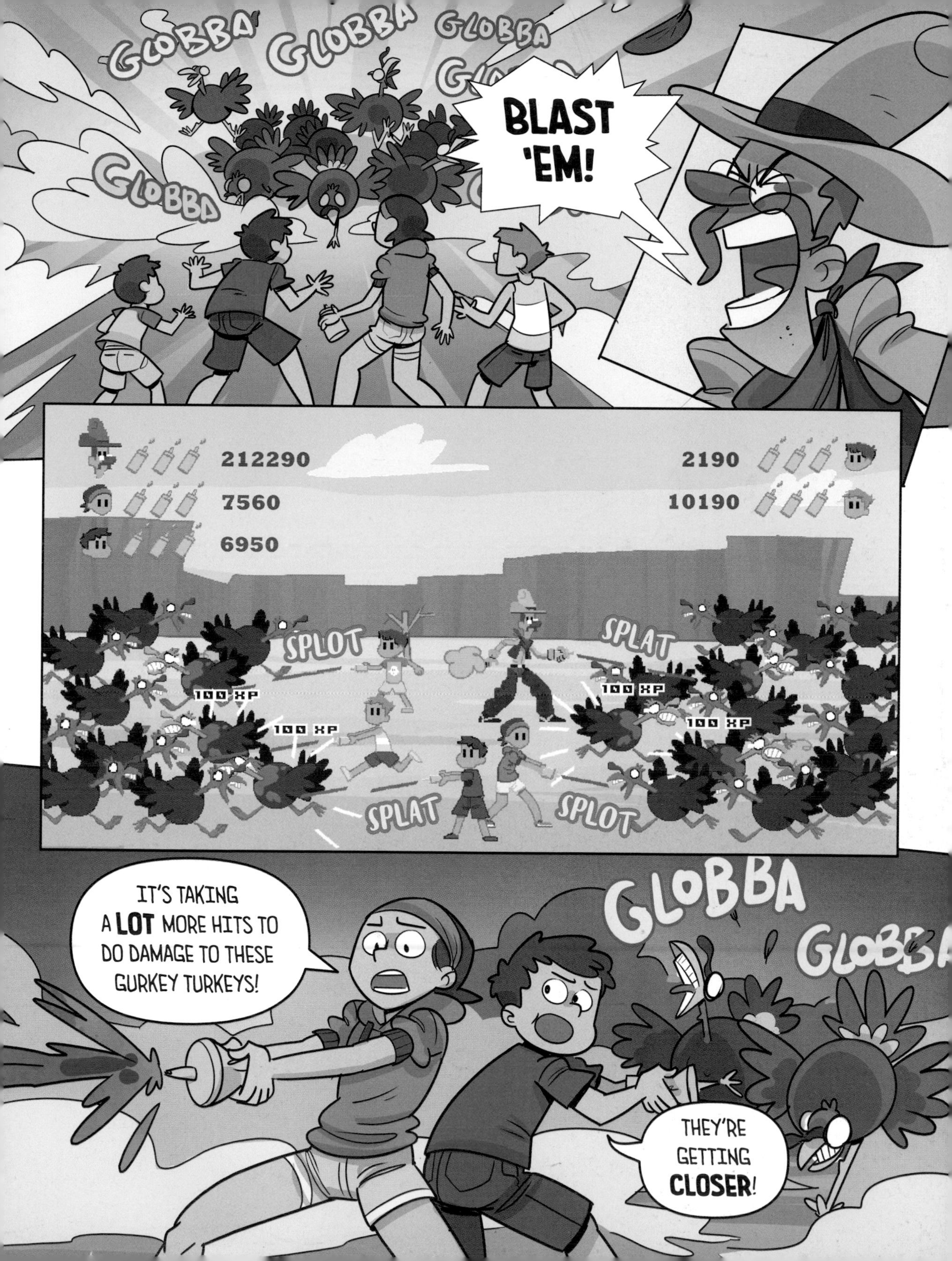
GLOBBA GLOBBA GLOBBA
GLOBBA
BLAST 'EM!
212290
7560
6950
2190
10190
SPLOT
SPLAT
100 XP
100 XP
100 XP
100 XP
SPLAT
SPLOT
GLOBBA
GLOBBA
IT'S TAKING A **LOT** MORE HITS TO DO DAMAGE TO THESE GURKEY TURKEYS!
THEY'RE GETTING **CLOSER**!

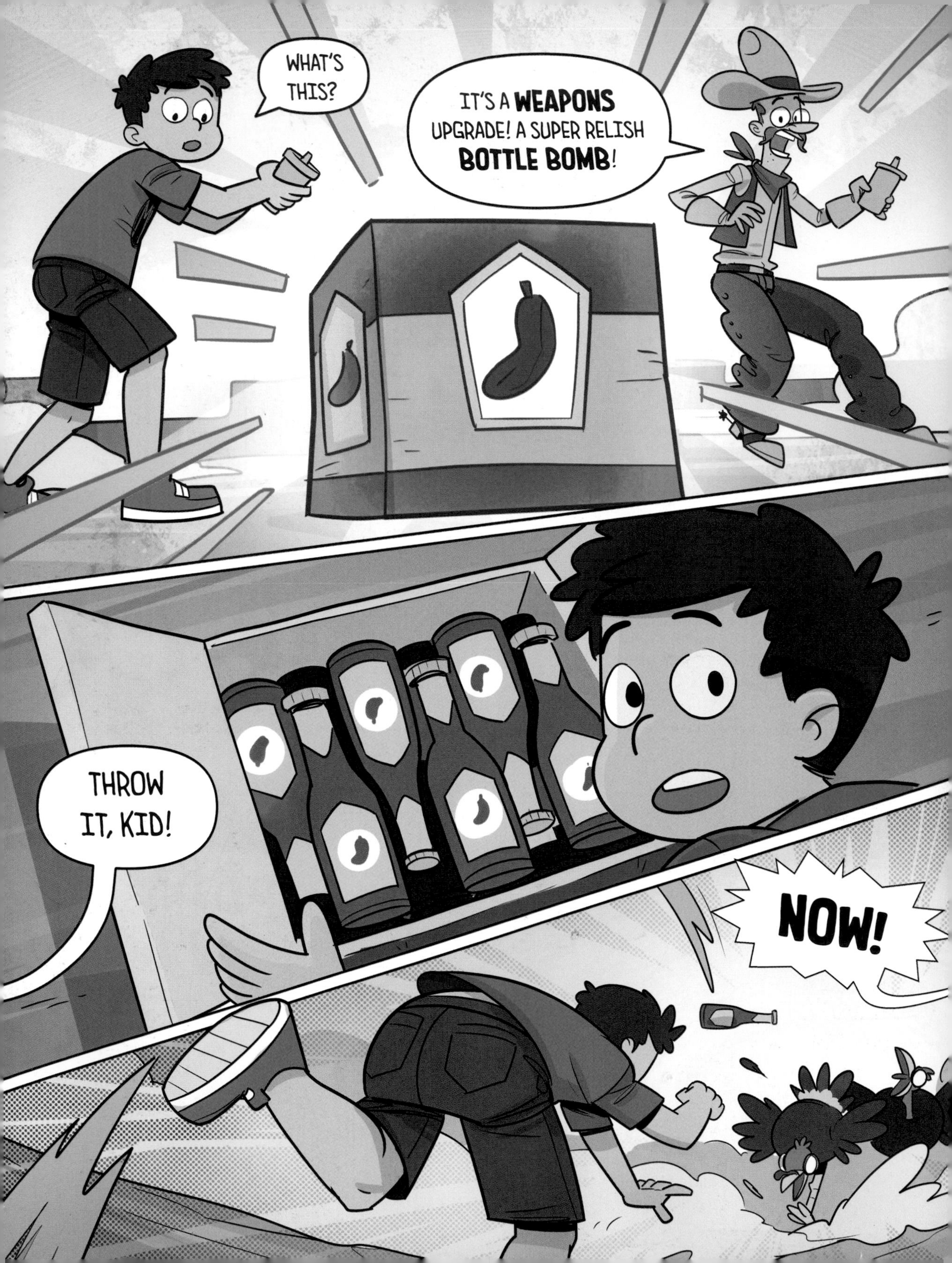
WHAT'S THIS?
IT'S A **WEAPONS** UPGRADE! A SUPER RELISH **BOTTLE BOMB**!
THROW IT, KID!
NOW!

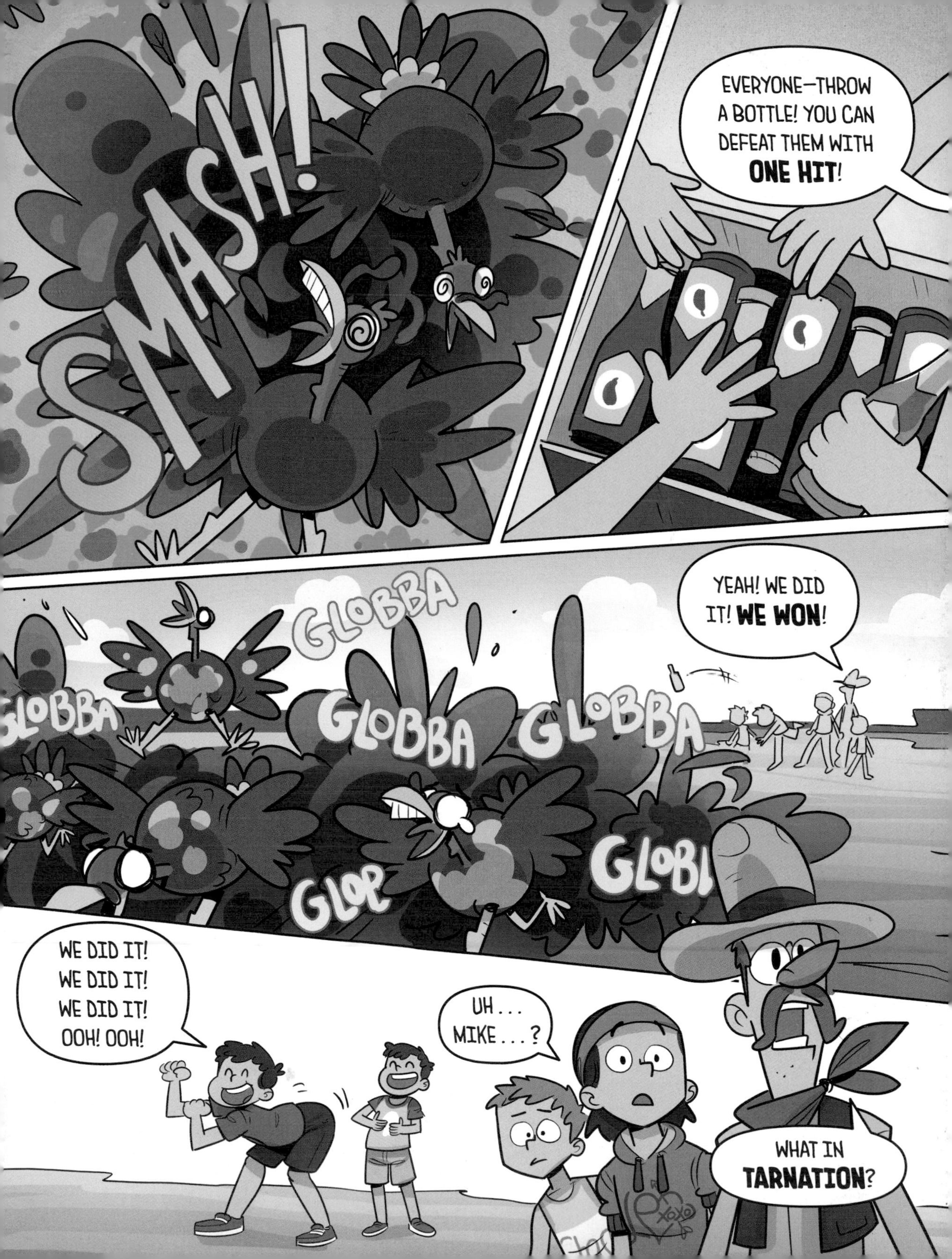
SMASH!
EVERYONE—THROW A BOTTLE! YOU CAN DEFEAT THEM WITH **ONE HIT**!
GLOBBA
GLOBBA
GLOBBA
GLOBBA
YEAH! WE DID IT! **WE WON**!
GLOP
GLOBI
WE DID IT! WE DID IT! WE DID IT! OOH! OOH!
UH . . . MIKE . . . ?
WHAT IN **TARNATION**?

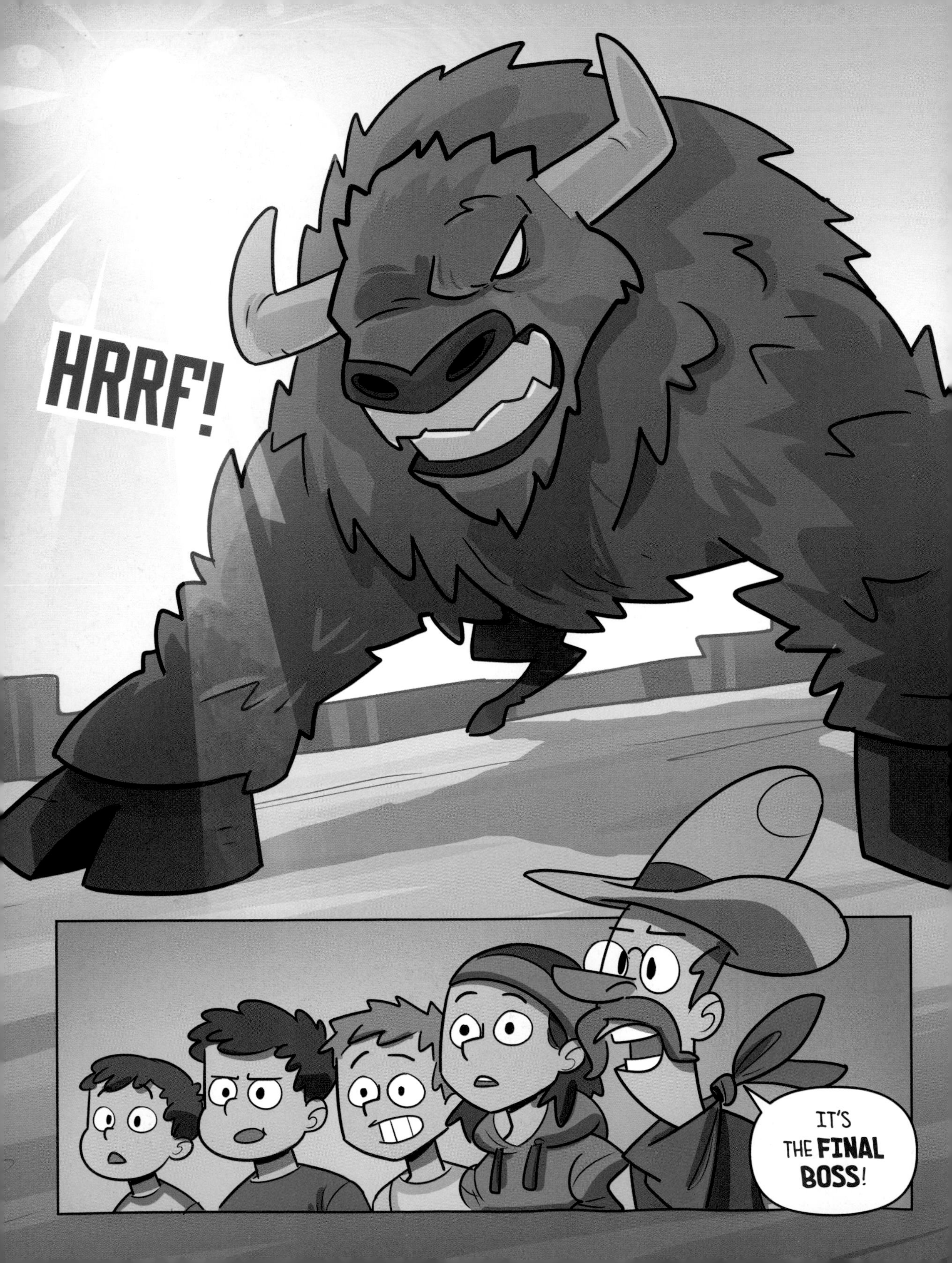
HRRF!
IT'S THE FINAL BOSS!

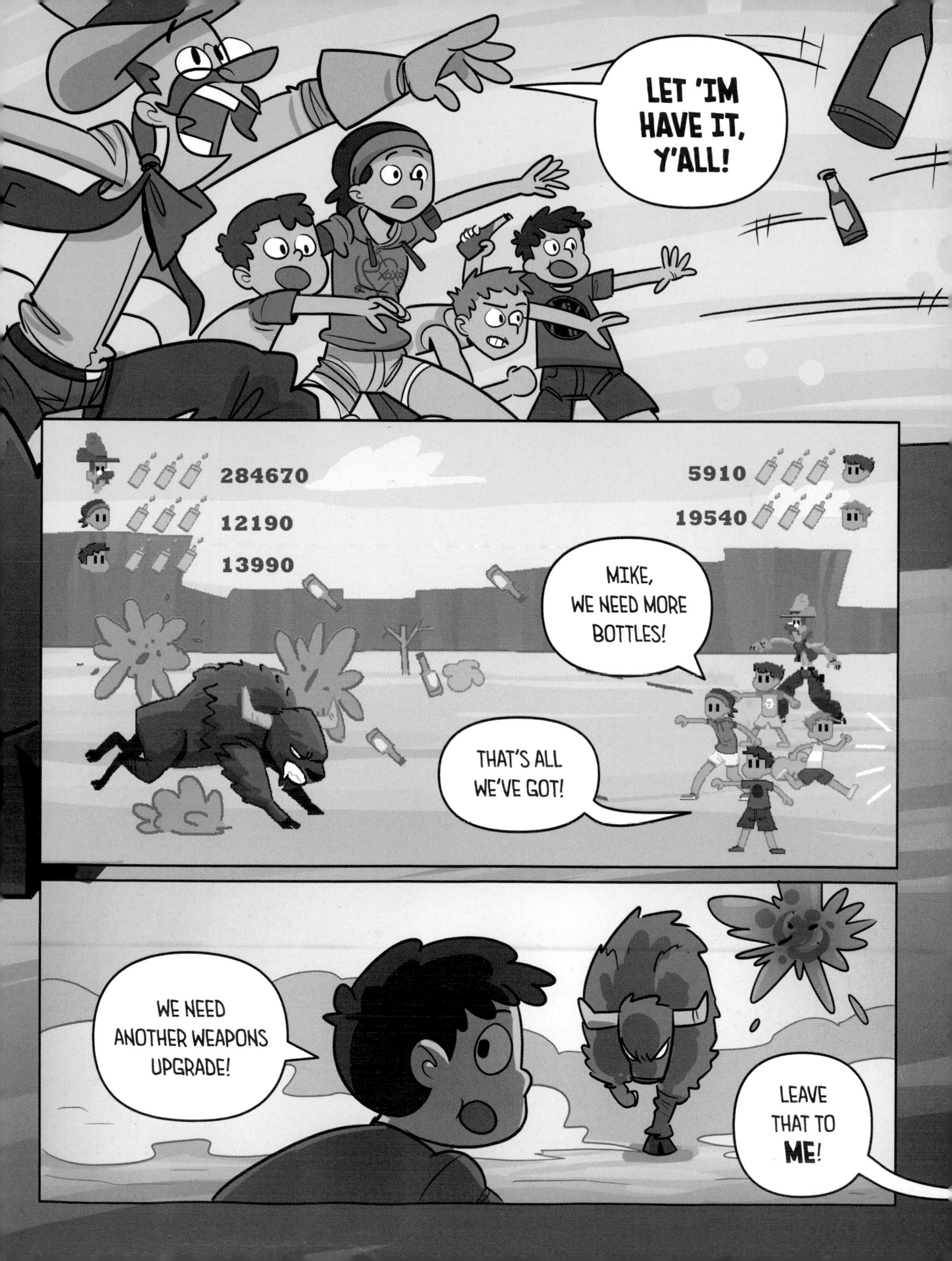
LET 'IM HAVE IT, Y'ALL!
284670
12190
13990
5910
19540
MIKE, WE NEED MORE BOTTLES!
THAT'S ALL WE'VE GOT!
WE NEED ANOTHER WEAPONS UPGRADE!
LEAVE THAT TO **ME**!

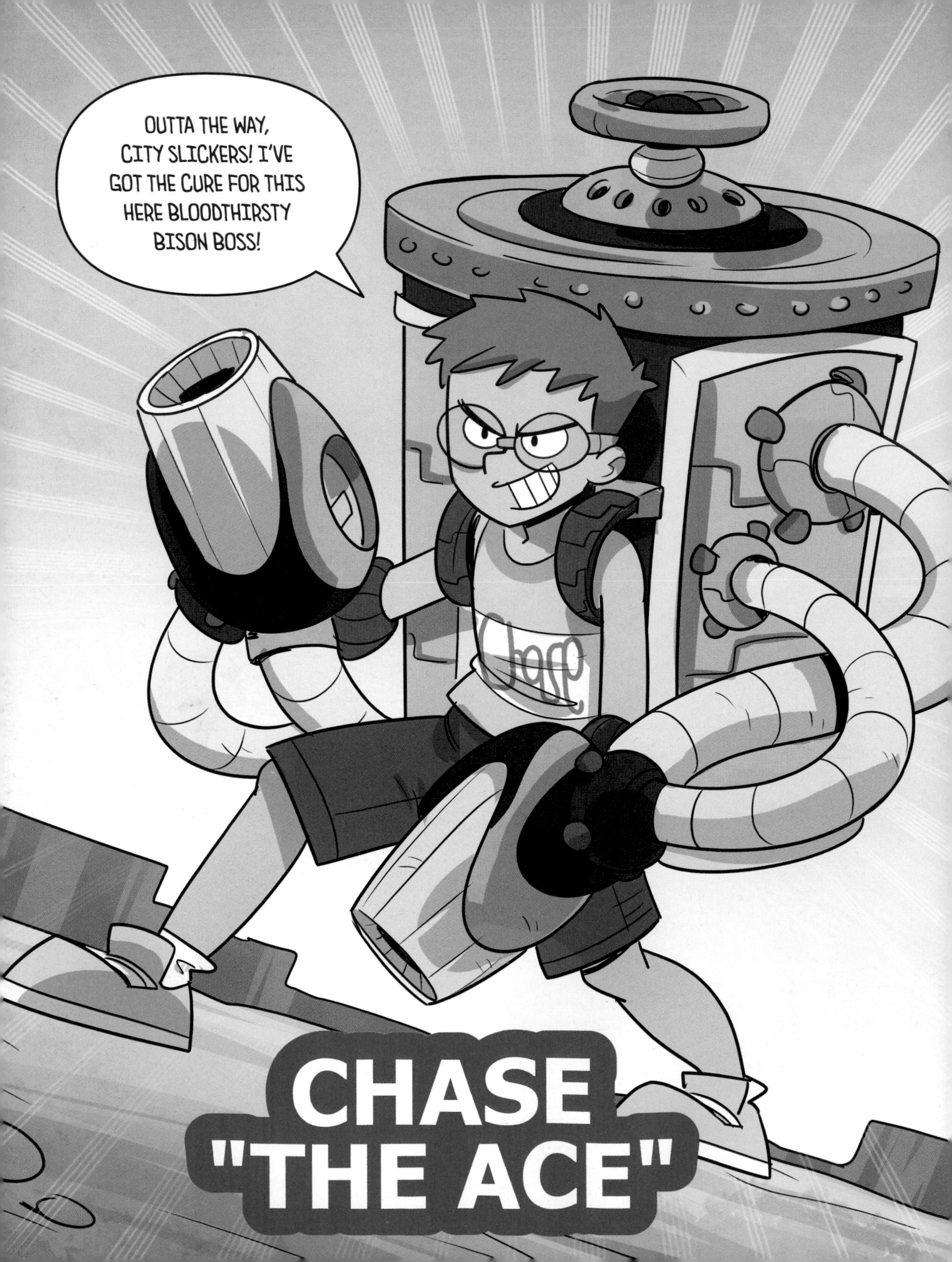
OUTTA THE WAY, CITY SLICKERS! I'VE GOT THE CURE FOR THIS HERE BLOODTHIRSTY BISON BOSS!
Chase
CHASE "THE ACE"

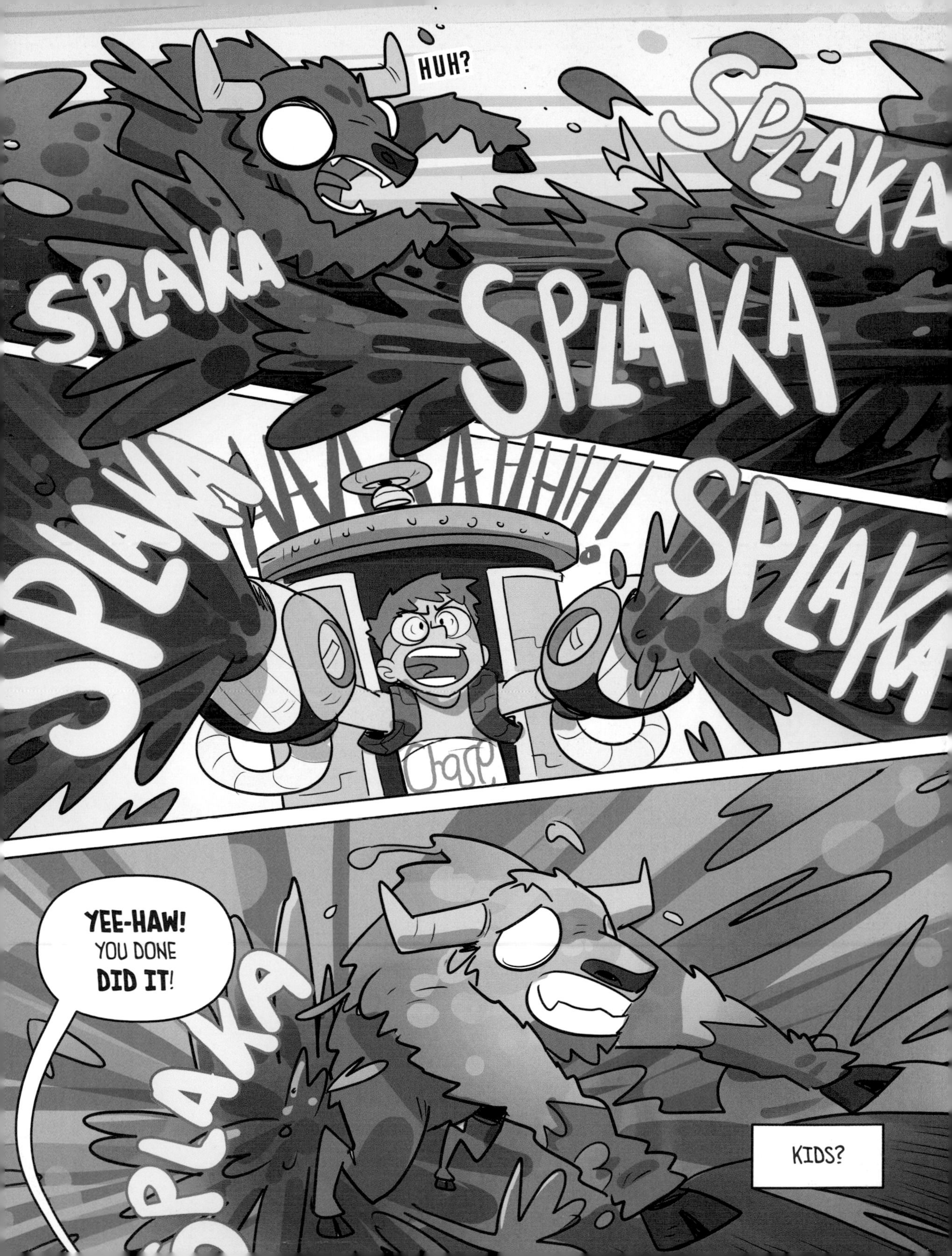
HUH?
SPLAKA
SPLAKA
SPLAKA
SPLAKA
AAAAHHHH!
SPLAKA
Chase
YEE-HAW! YOU DONE DID IT!
SPLAKA
KIDS?

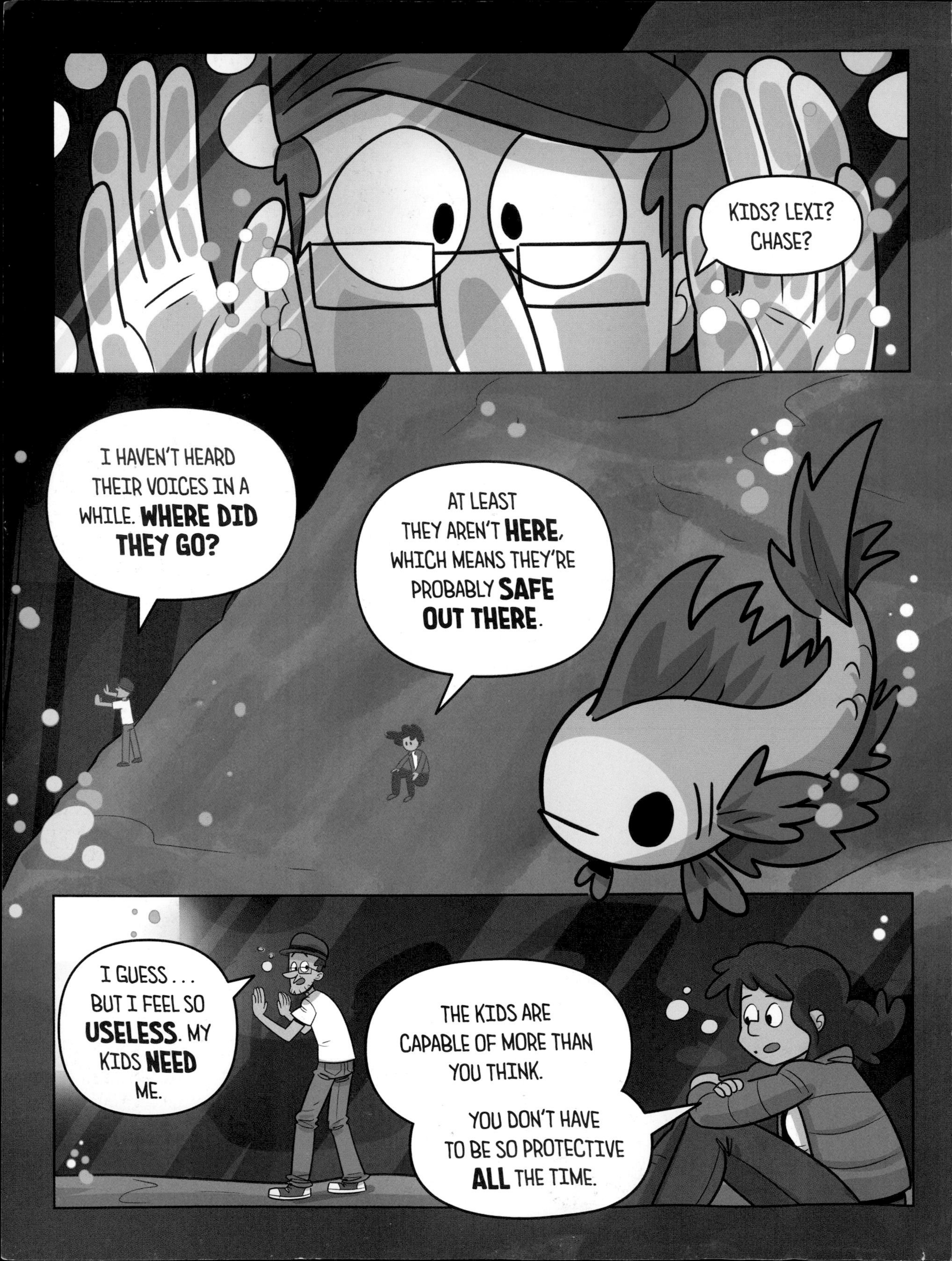
KIDS? LEXI? CHASE?
I HAVEN'T HEARD THEIR VOICES IN A WHILE. WHERE DID THEY GO?
AT LEAST THEY AREN'T HERE, WHICH MEANS THEY'RE PROBABLY SAFE OUT THERE.
I GUESS . . . BUT I FEEL SO USELESS. MY KIDS NEED ME.
THE KIDS ARE CAPABLE OF MORE THAN YOU THINK.
YOU DON'T HAVE TO BE SO PROTECTIVE ALL THE TIME.

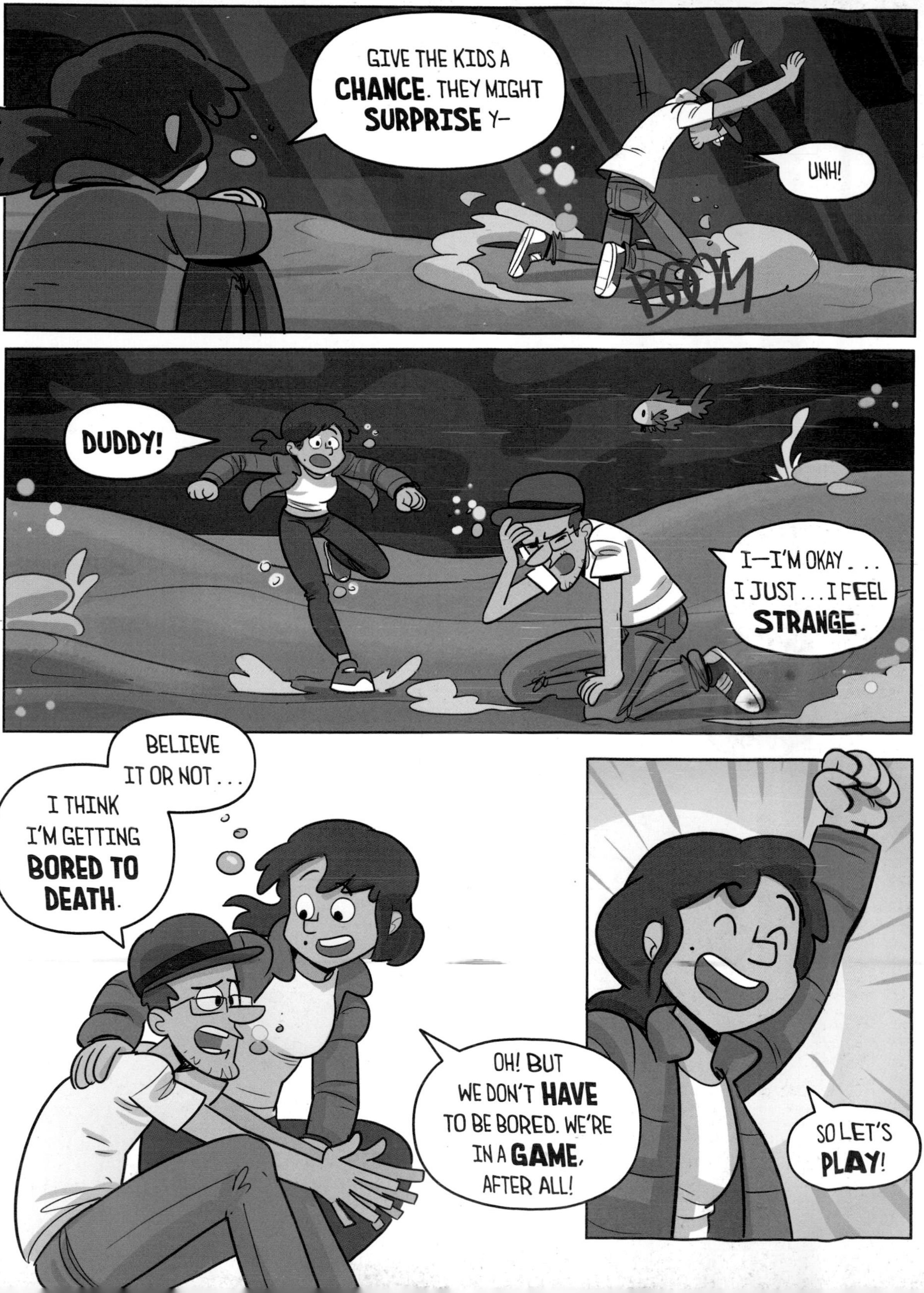
GIVE THE KIDS A **CHANCE**. THEY MIGHT **SURPRISE** Y—
UNH!
BOOM
DUDDY!
I—I'M OKAY . . . I JUST . . . I FEEL **STRANGE**.
BELIEVE IT OR NOT . . .
I THINK I'M GETTING **BORED TO DEATH**.
OH! BUT WE DON'T **HAVE** TO BE BORED. WE'RE IN A **GAME**, AFTER ALL!
SO LET'S **PLAY**!

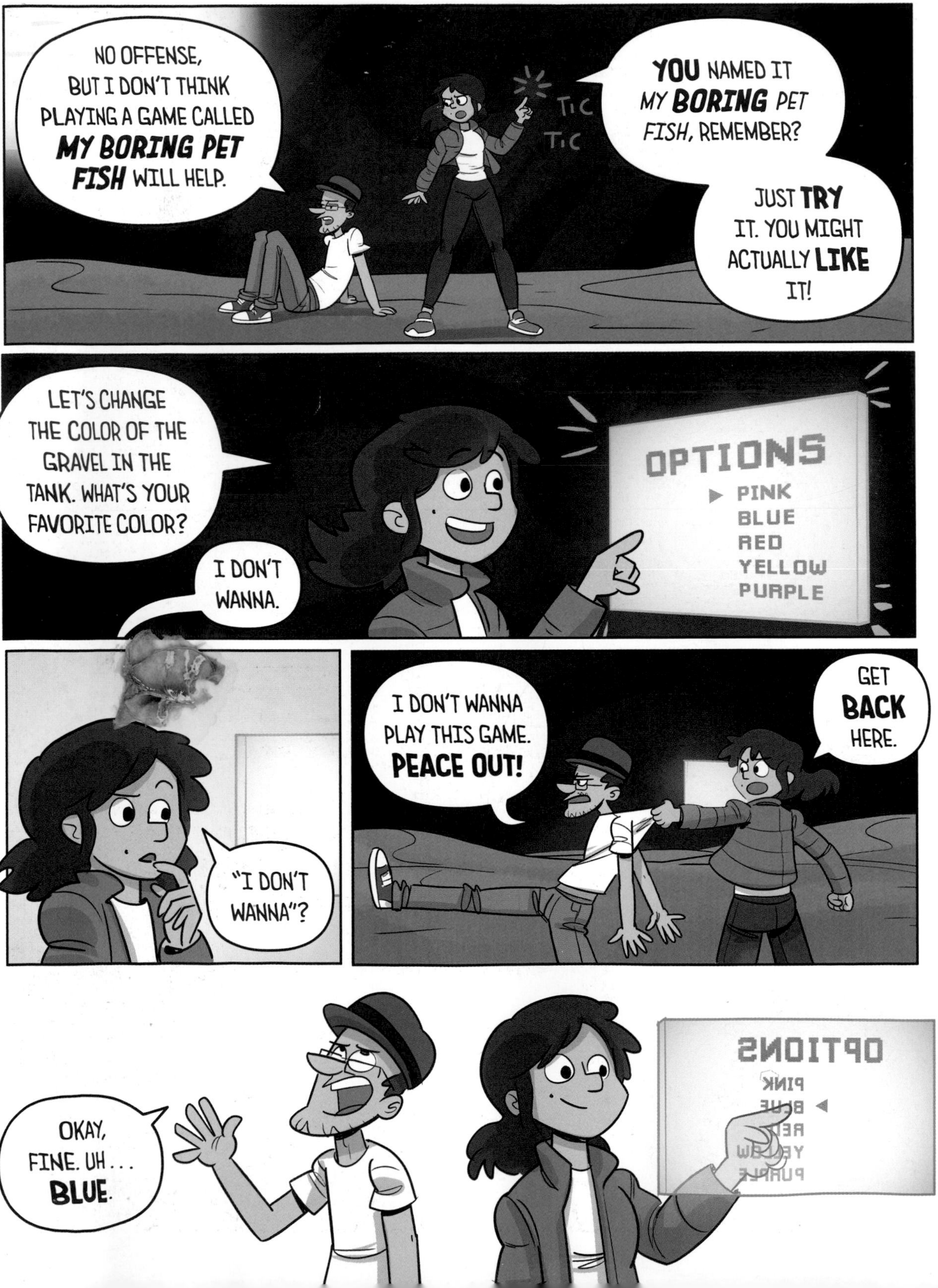

NO OFFENSE, BUT I DON'T THINK PLAYING A GAME CALLED **MY BORING PET FISH** WILL HELP.
TIC TIC
YOU NAMED IT MY **BORING** PET FISH, REMEMBER?
JUST **TRY** IT. YOU MIGHT ACTUALLY **LIKE** IT!
LET'S CHANGE THE COLOR OF THE GRAVEL IN THE TANK. WHAT'S YOUR FAVORITE COLOR?
OPTIONS
PINK
BLUE
RED
YELLOW
PURPLE
I DON'T WANNA.
"I DON'T WANNA"?
I DON'T WANNA PLAY THIS GAME. **PEACE OUT!**
GET **BACK** HERE.
OKAY, FINE. UH . . . **BLUE**.

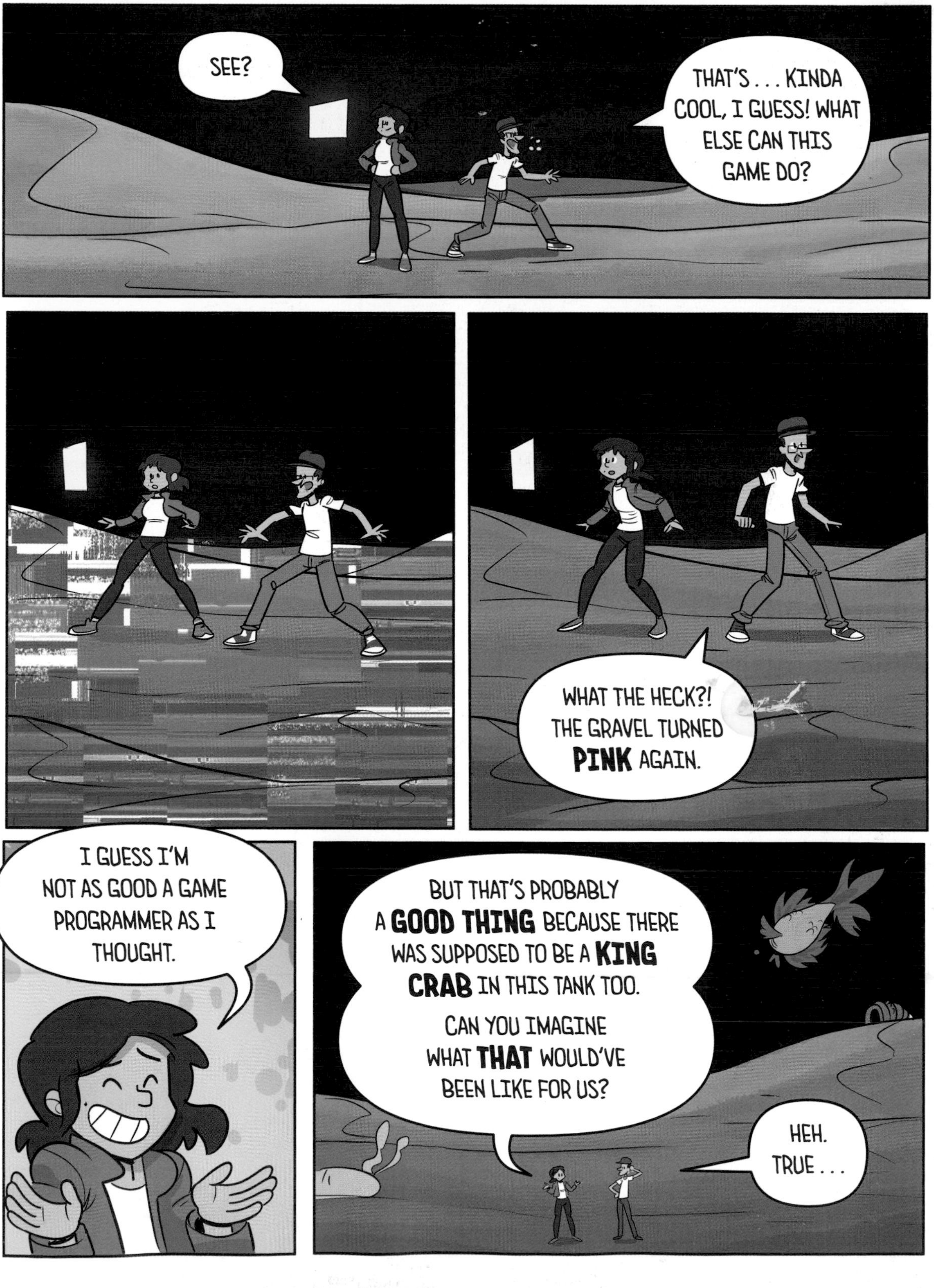
SEE?
THAT'S . . . KINDA COOL, I GUESS! WHAT ELSE CAN THIS GAME DO?
WHAT THE HECK?! THE GRAVEL TURNED PINK AGAIN.
I GUESS I'M NOT AS GOOD A GAME PROGRAMMER AS I THOUGHT.
BUT THAT'S PROBABLY A GOOD THING BECAUSE THERE WAS SUPPOSED TO BE A KING CRAB IN THIS TANK TOO.
CAN YOU IMAGINE WHAT THAT WOULD'VE BEEN LIKE FOR US?
HEH. TRUE . . .

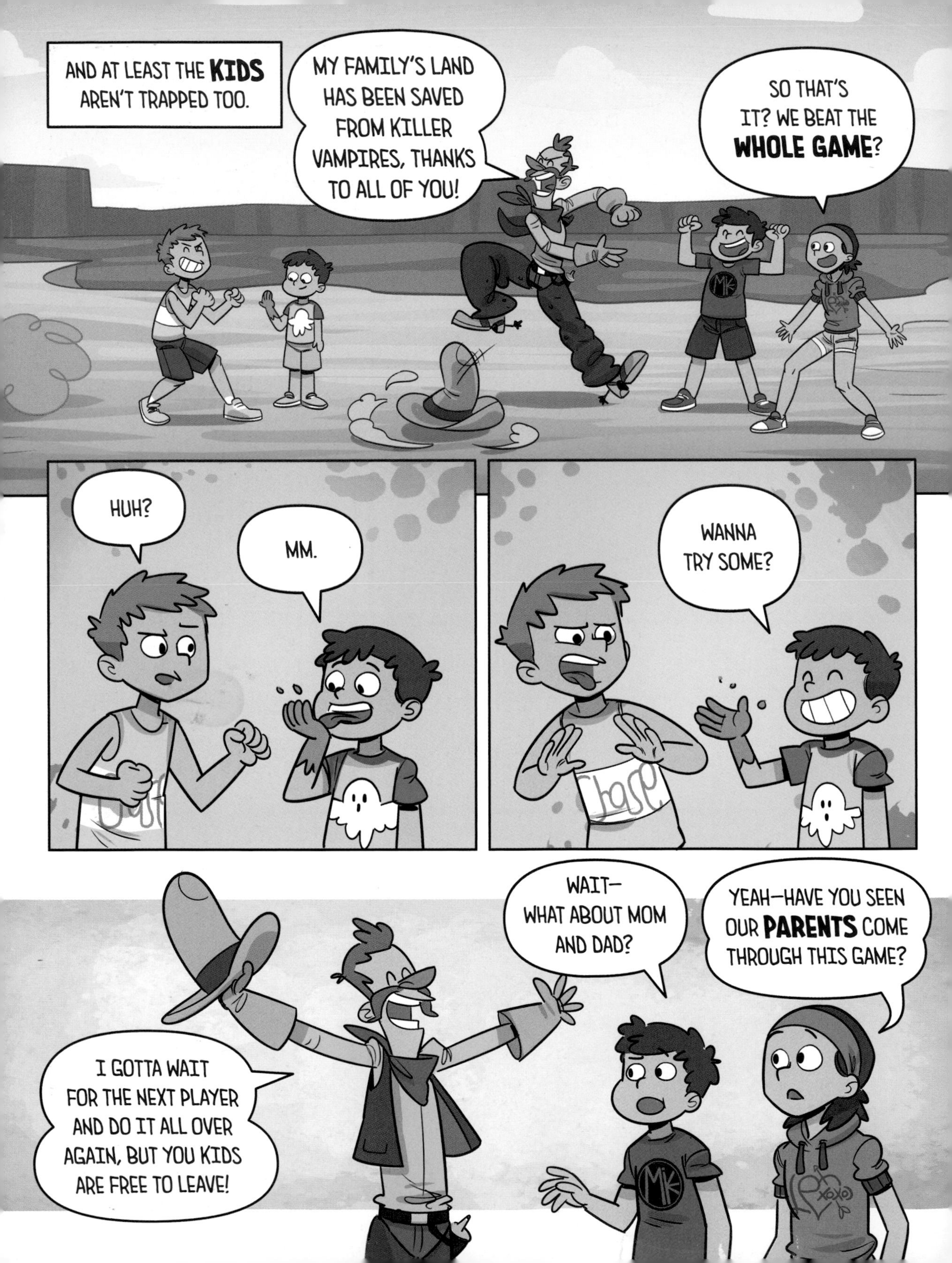
AND AT LEAST THE **KIDS** AREN'T TRAPPED TOO.
MY FAMILY'S LAND HAS BEEN SAVED FROM KILLER VAMPIRES, THANKS TO ALL OF YOU!
SO THAT'S IT? WE BEAT THE **WHOLE GAME**?
HUH?
MM.
WANNA TRY SOME?
Chase
WAIT— WHAT ABOUT MOM AND DAD?
YEAH—HAVE YOU SEEN OUR **PARENTS** COME THROUGH THIS GAME?
I GOTTA WAIT FOR THE NEXT PLAYER AND DO IT ALL OVER AGAIN, BUT YOU KIDS ARE FREE TO LEAVE!

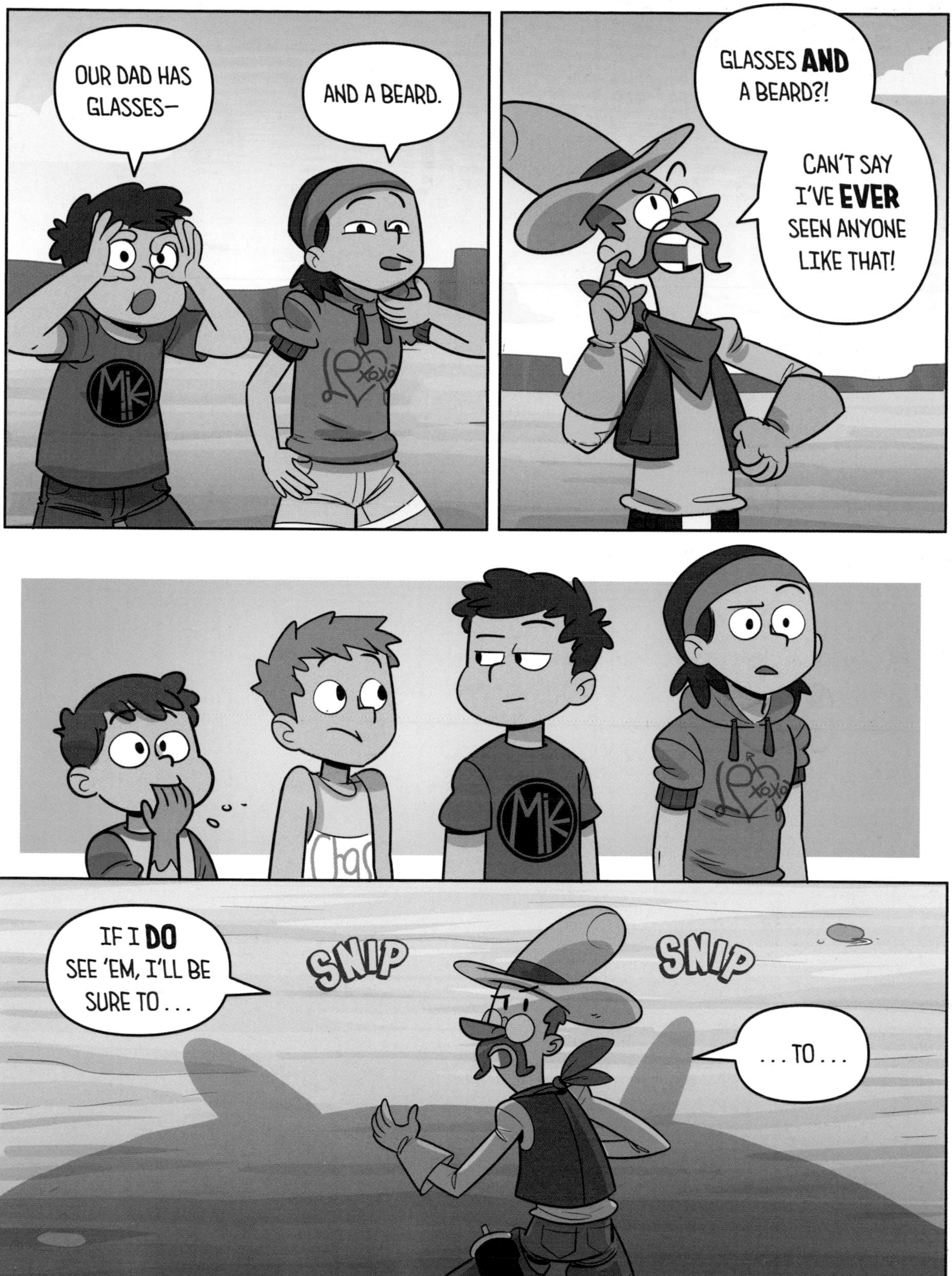
OUR DAD HAS GLASSES—
AND A BEARD.
GLASSES **AND** A BEARD?!
CAN'T SAY I'VE **EVER** SEEN ANYONE LIKE THAT!
IF I **DO** SEE 'EM, I'LL BE SURE TO . . .
SNIP
SNIP
. . . TO . . .

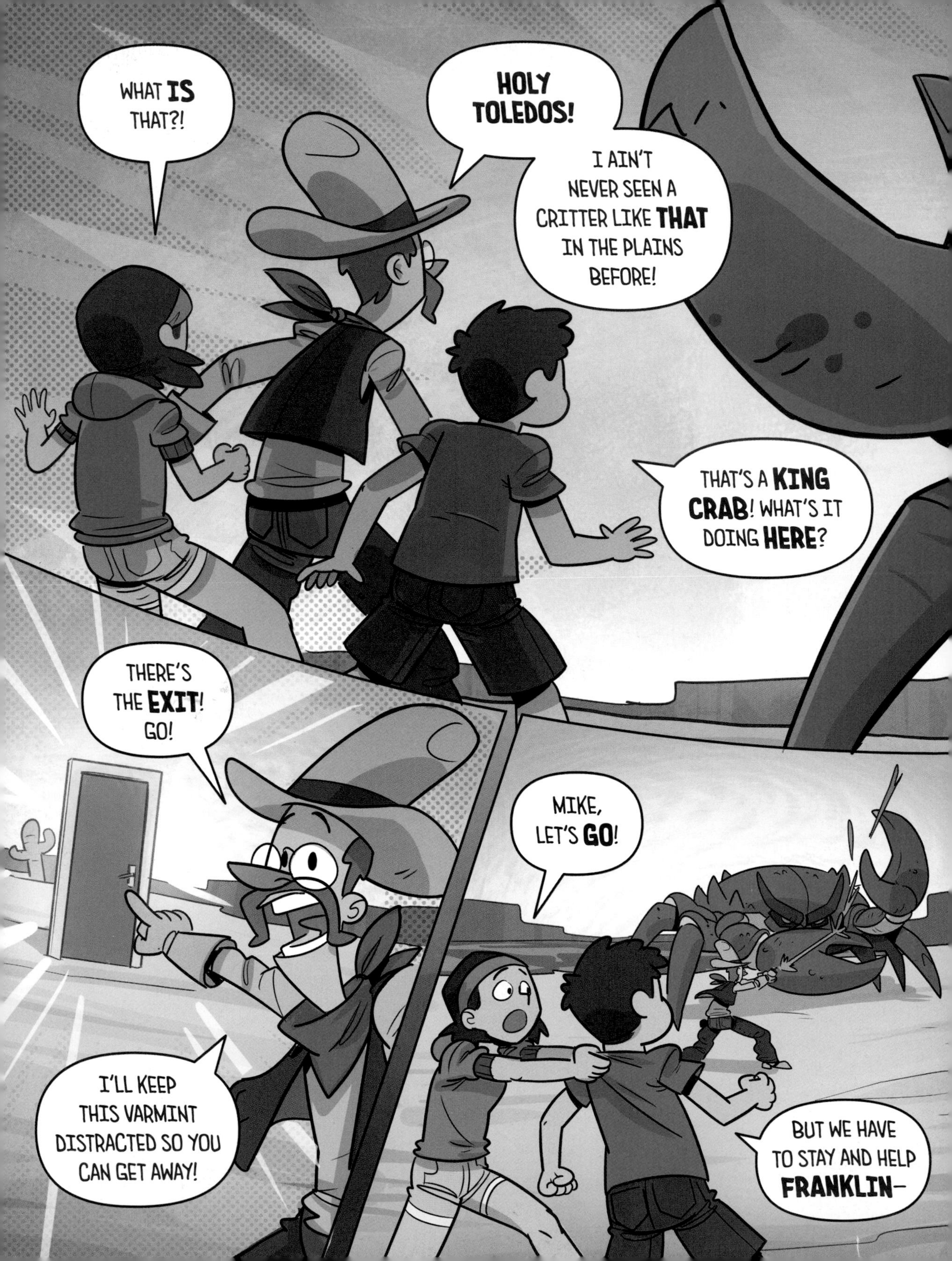
WHAT IS THAT?!
HOLY TOLEDOS!
I AIN'T NEVER SEEN A CRITTER LIKE THAT IN THE PLAINS BEFORE!
THAT'S A KING CRAB! WHAT'S IT DOING HERE?
THERE'S THE EXIT! GO!
I'LL KEEP THIS VARMINT DISTRACTED SO YOU CAN GET AWAY!
MIKE, LET'S GO!
BUT WE HAVE TO STAY AND HELP FRANKLIN–

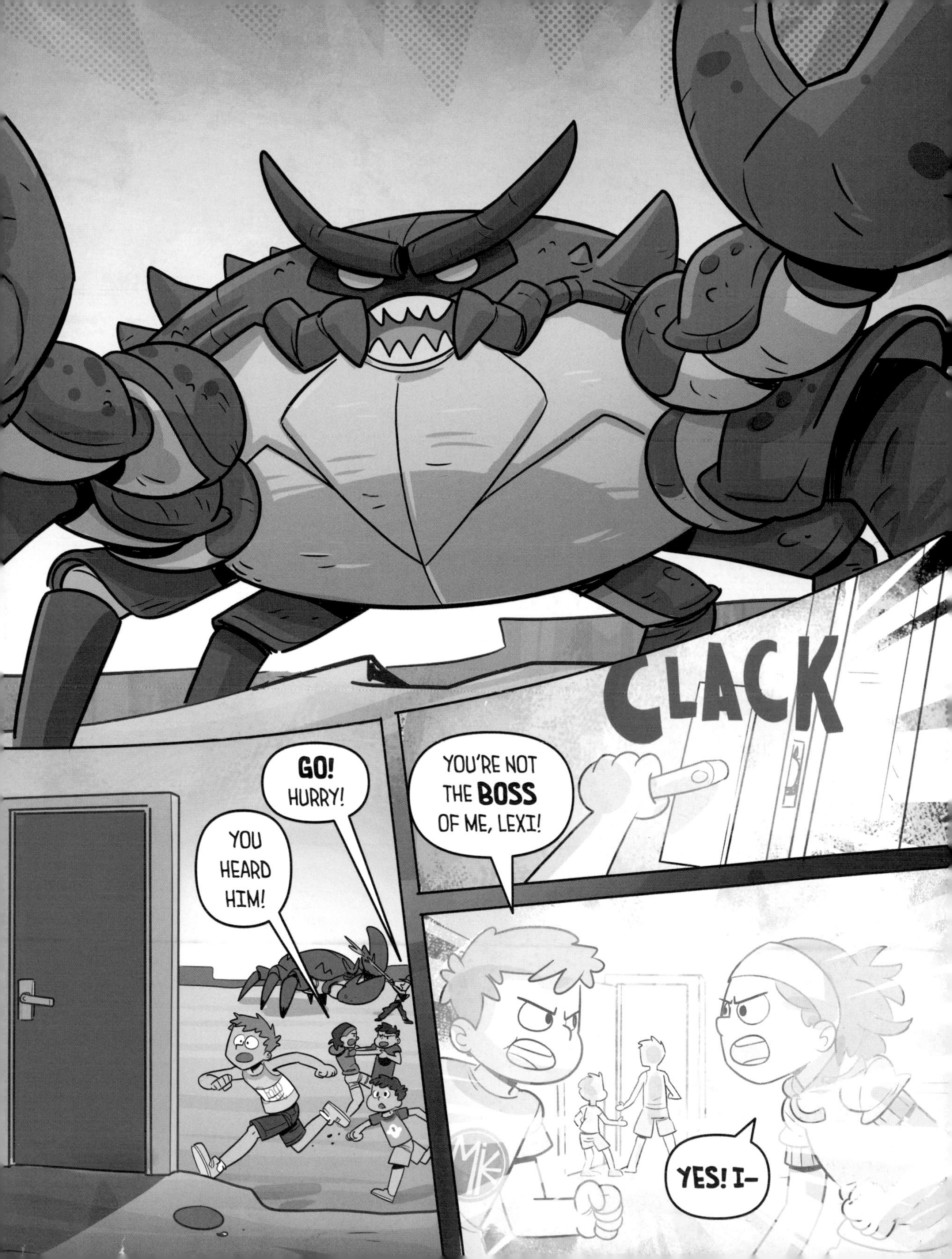
CLACK
YOU HEARD HIM!
GO! HURRY!
YOU'RE NOT THE BOSS OF ME, LEXI!
YES! I—

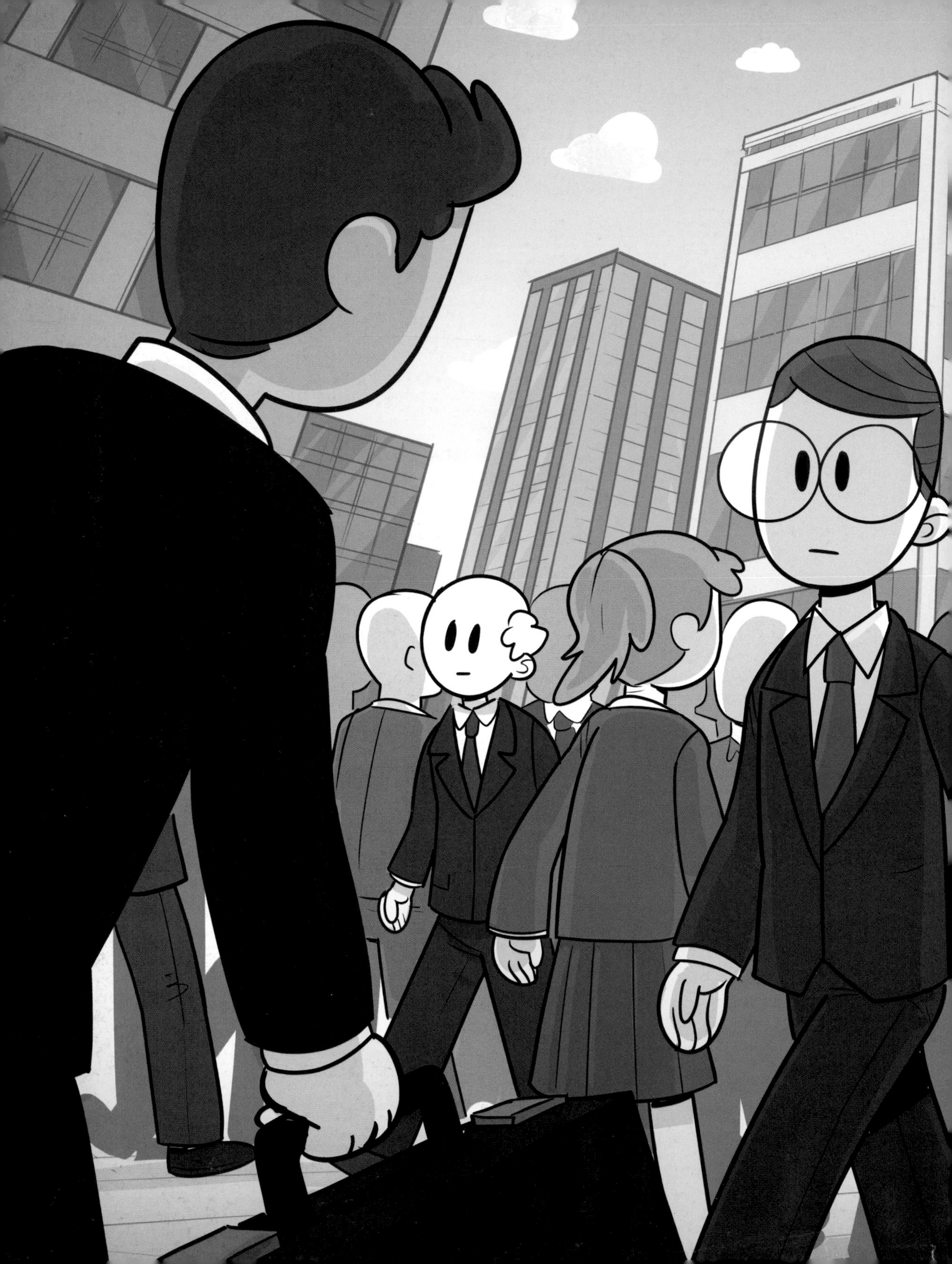

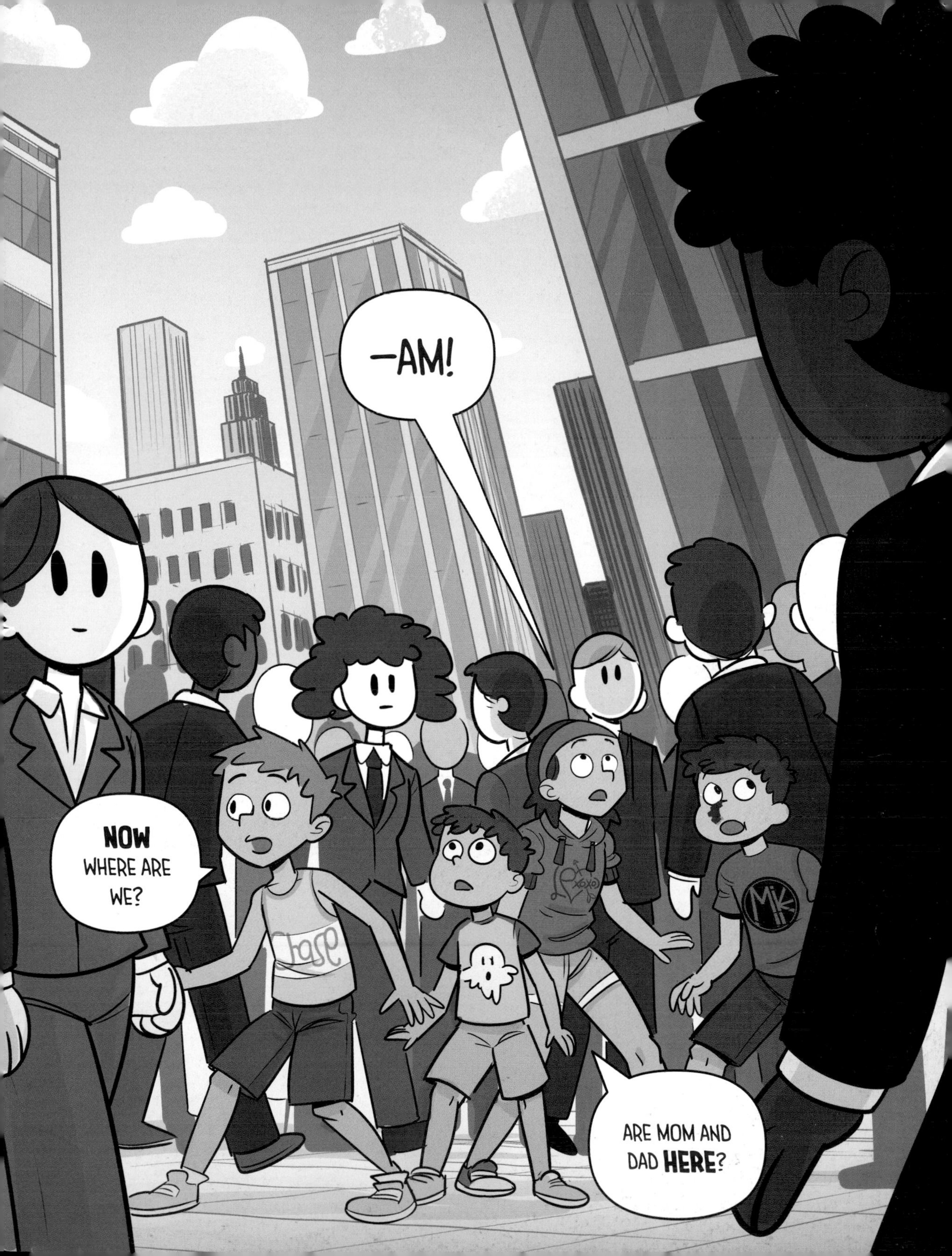
—AM!
NOW WHERE ARE WE?
ARE MOM AND DAD HERE?

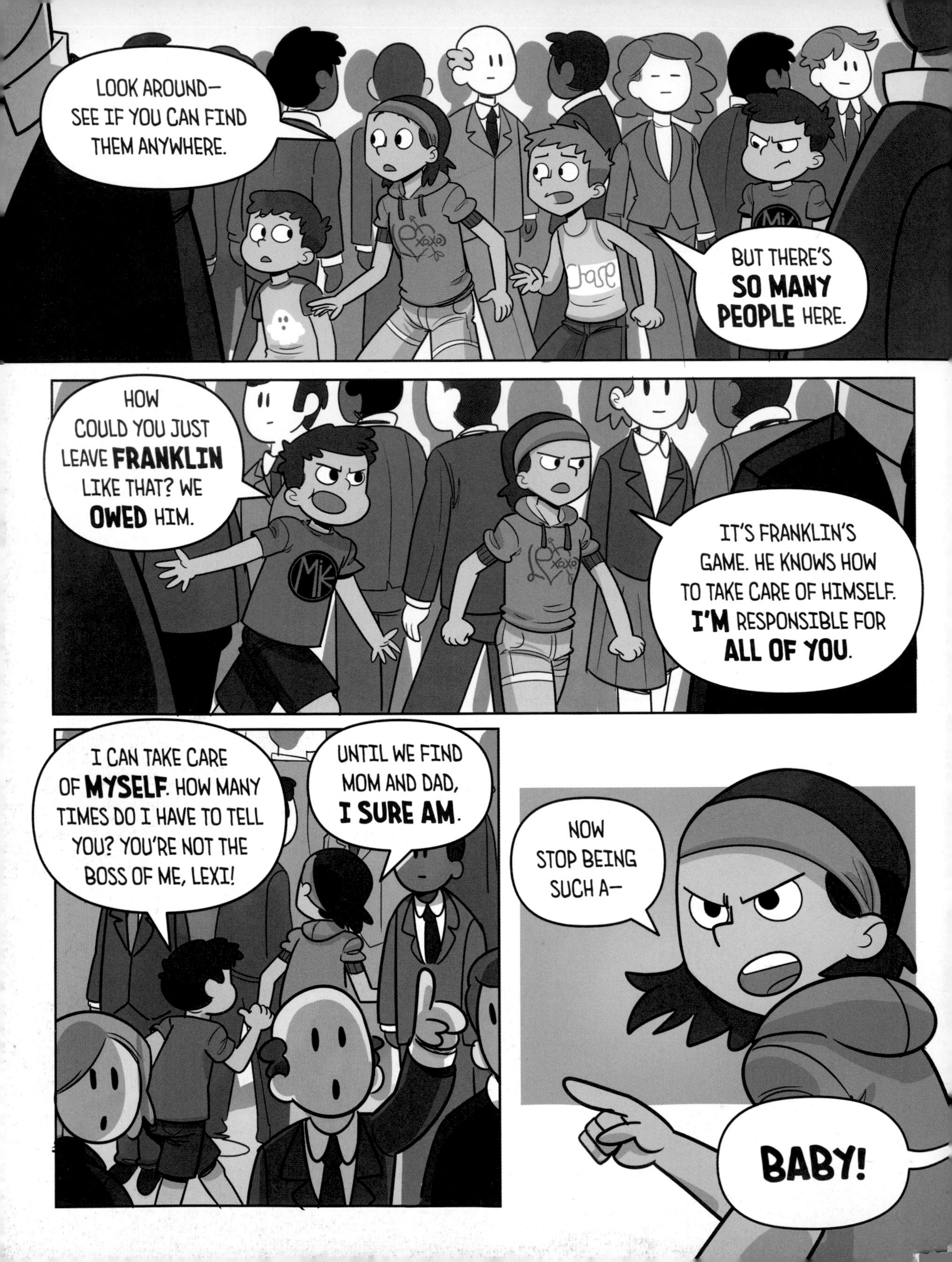
LOOK AROUND— SEE IF YOU CAN FIND THEM ANYWHERE.
BUT THERE'S **SO MANY PEOPLE** HERE.
HOW COULD YOU JUST LEAVE **FRANKLIN** LIKE THAT? WE **OWED** HIM.
IT'S FRANKLIN'S GAME. HE KNOWS HOW TO TAKE CARE OF HIMSELF. **I'M** RESPONSIBLE FOR **ALL OF YOU**.
I CAN TAKE CARE OF **MYSELF**. HOW MANY TIMES DO I HAVE TO TELL YOU? YOU'RE NOT THE BOSS OF ME, LEXI!
UNTIL WE FIND MOM AND DAD, **I SURE AM**.
NOW STOP BEING SUCH A—
BABY!

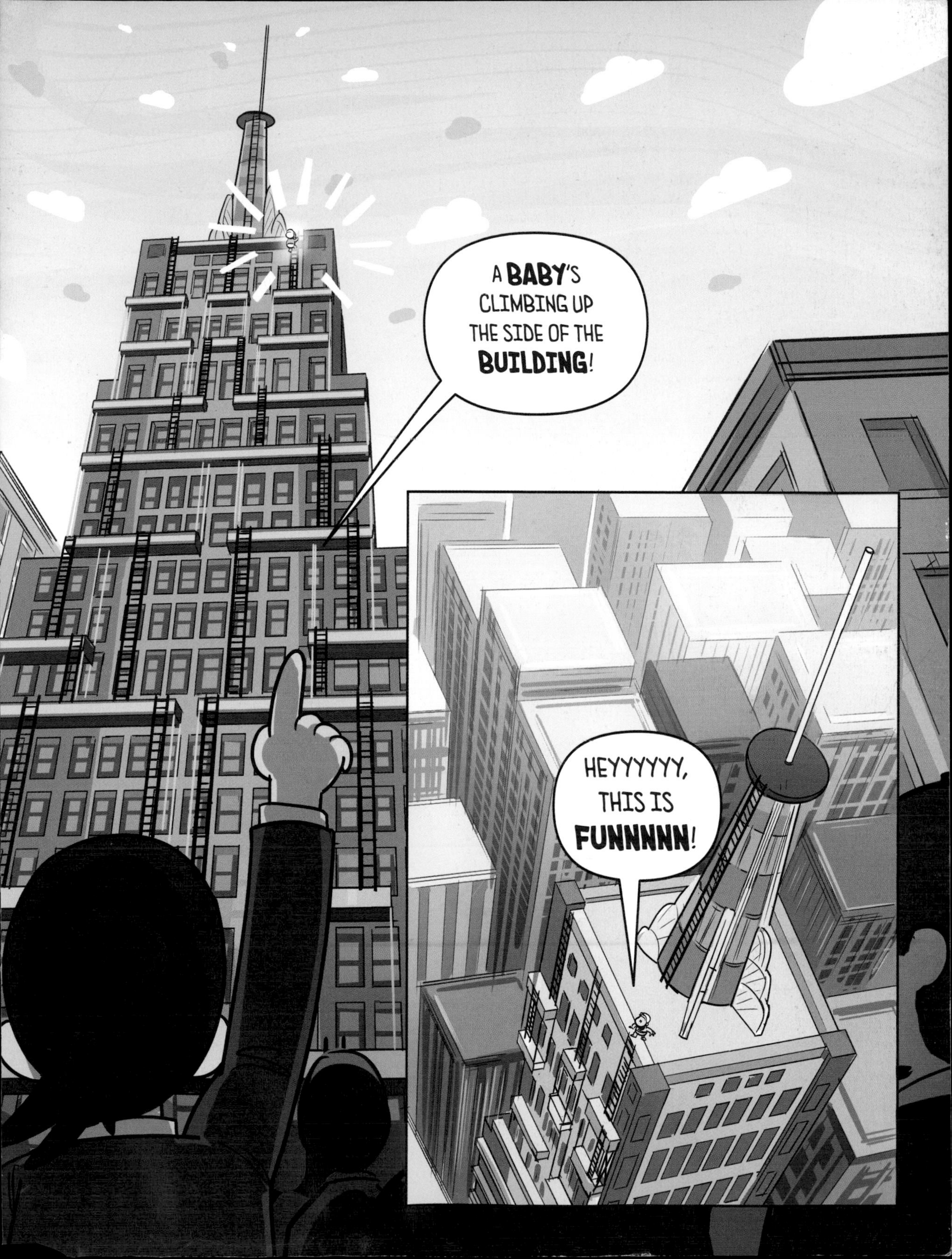
A BABY'S CLIMBING UP THE SIDE OF THE BUILDING!
HEYYYYYY, THIS IS FUNNNNN!

BIG BABY DIAPER DROP

Get to the baby before the baby reaches the top!

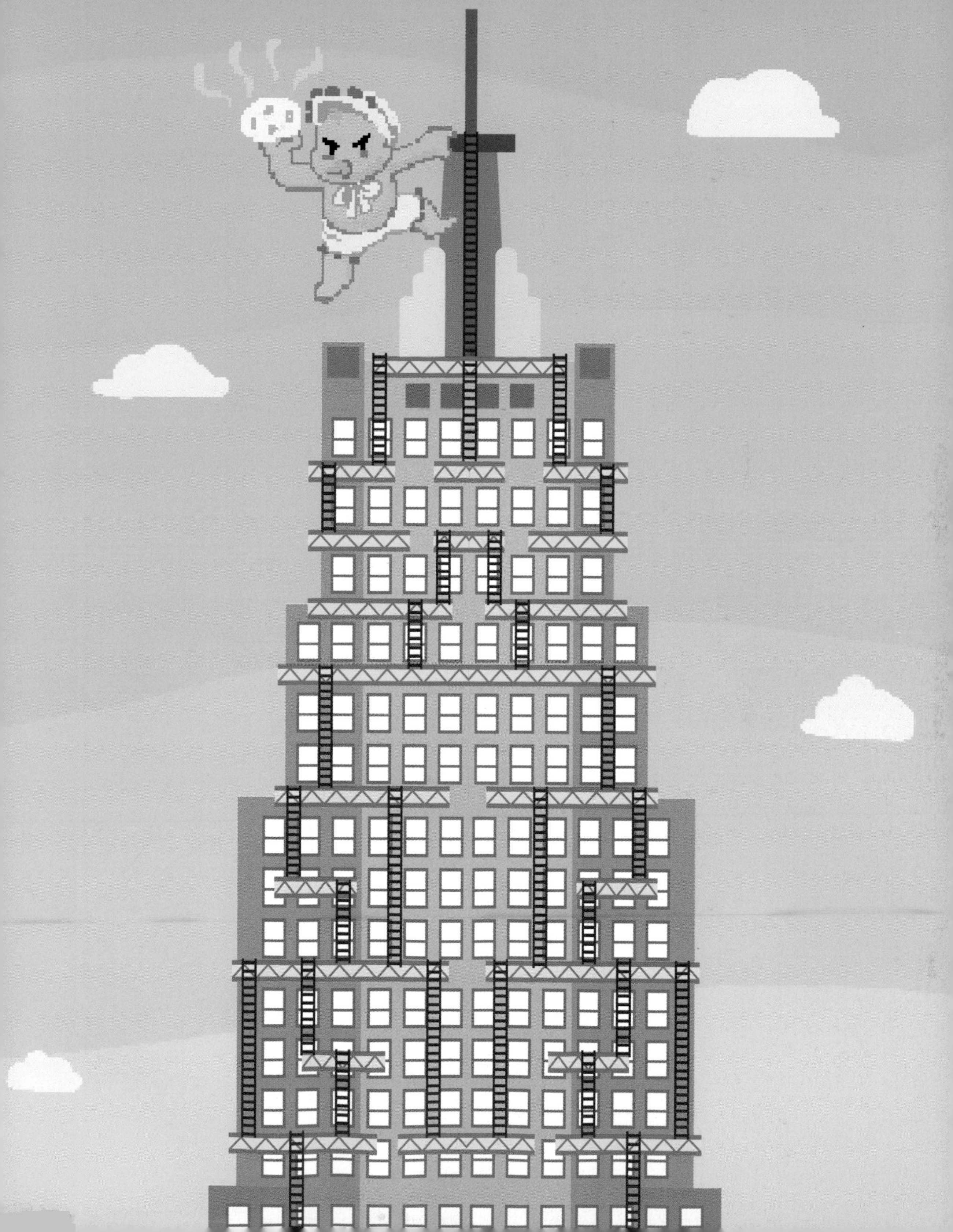

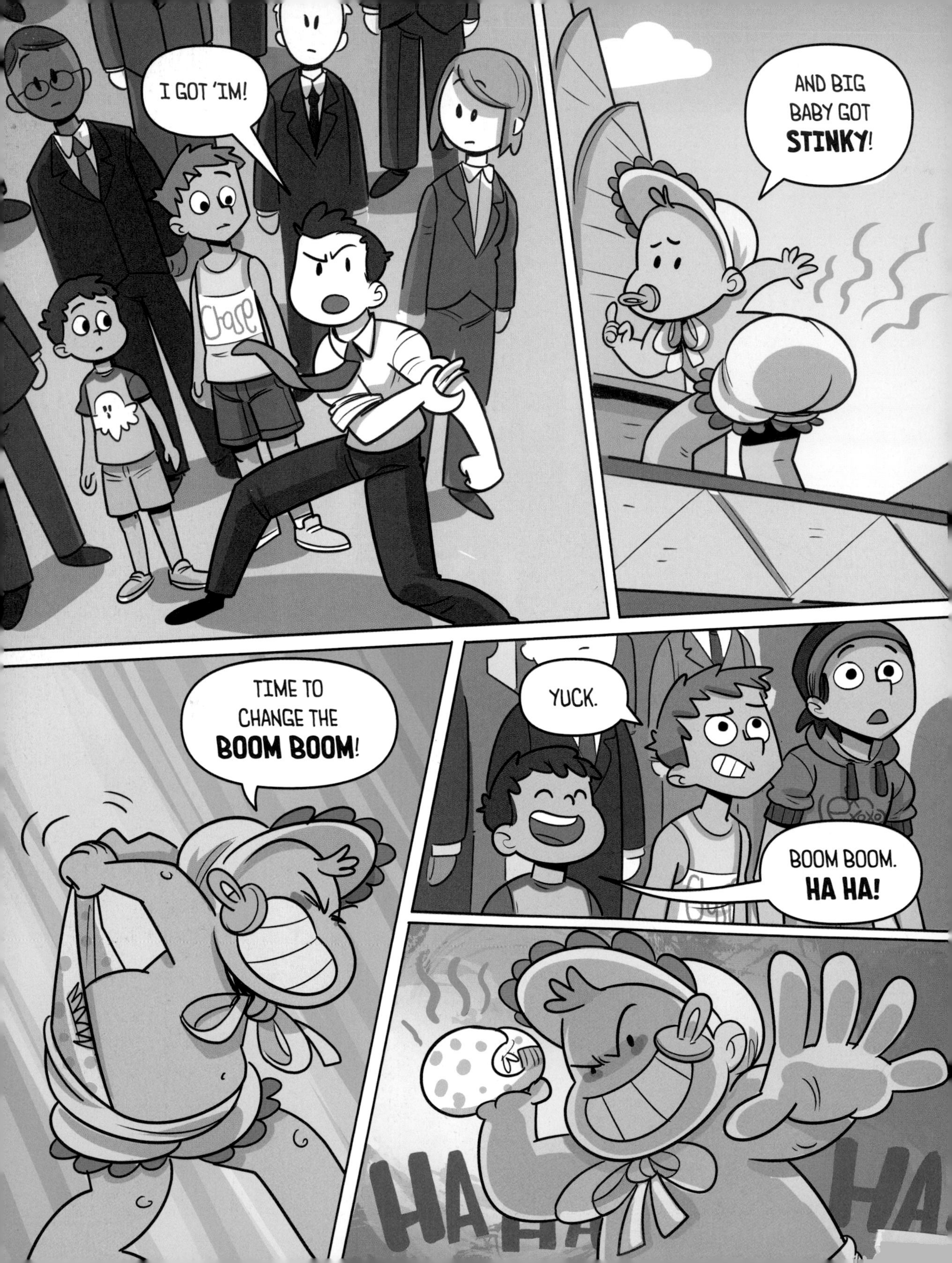
I GOT 'IM!
AND BIG BABY GOT STINKY!
TIME TO CHANGE THE BOOM BOOM!
YUCK.
BOOM BOOM. HA HA!
HA HA HA

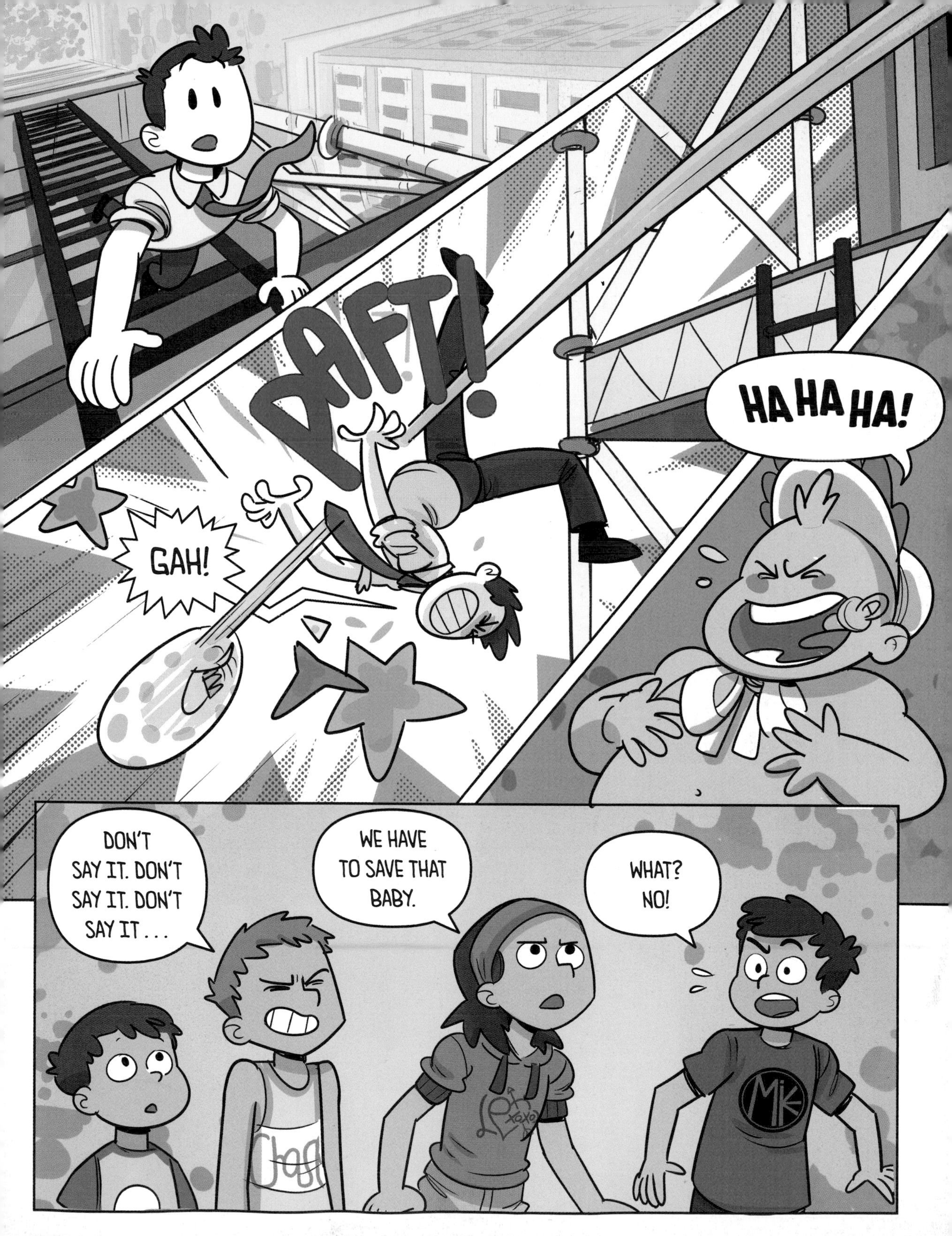
PAFT!
GAH!
HA HA HA!
DON'T SAY IT. DON'T SAY IT. DON'T SAY IT . . .
WE HAVE TO SAVE THAT BABY.
WHAT? NO!

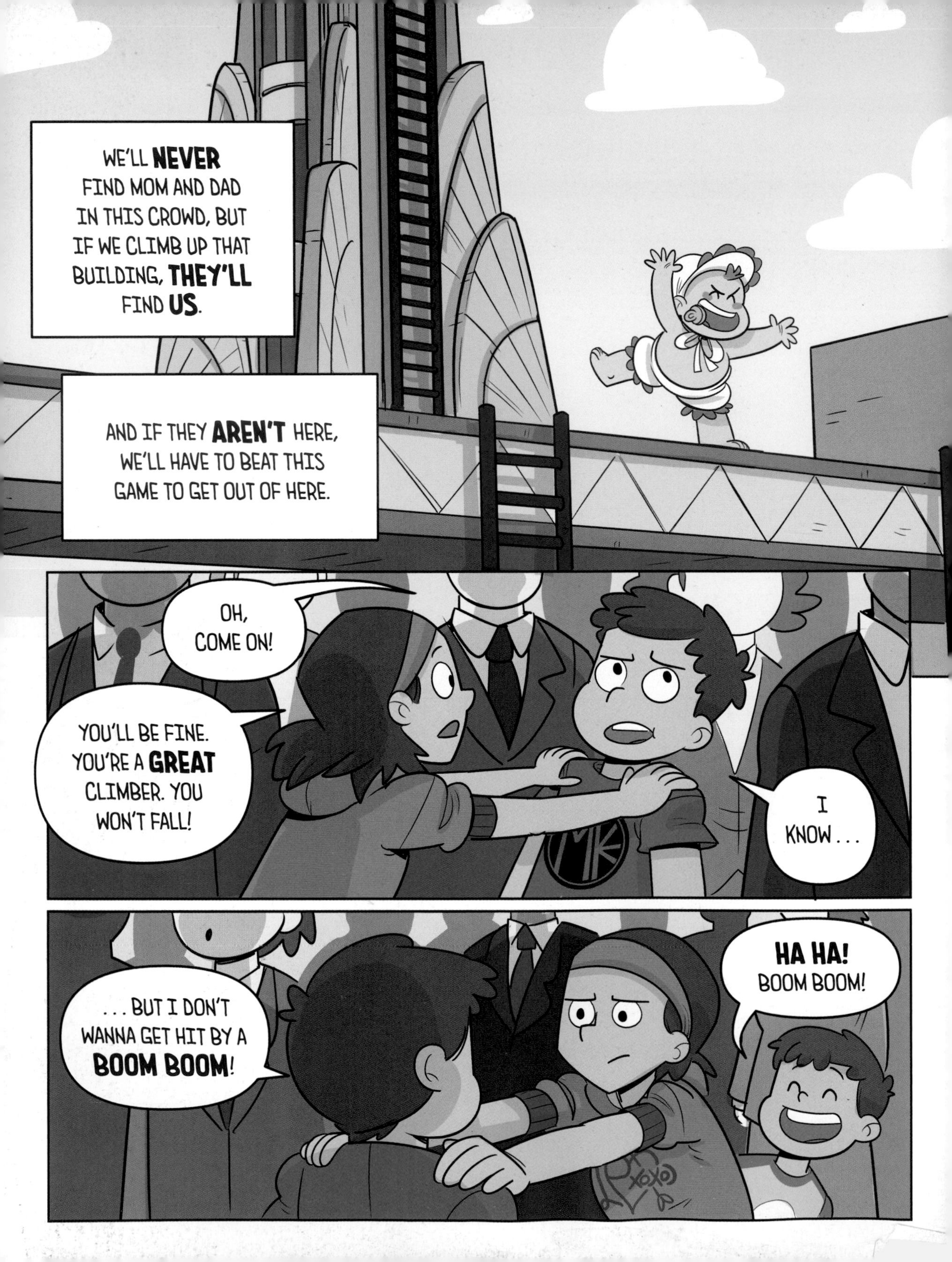

WE'LL **NEVER** FIND MOM AND DAD IN THIS CROWD, BUT IF WE CLIMB UP THAT BUILDING, **THEY'LL** FIND **US**.
AND IF THEY **AREN'T** HERE, WE'LL HAVE TO BEAT THIS GAME TO GET OUT OF HERE.
OH, COME ON!
YOU'LL BE FINE. YOU'RE A **GREAT** CLIMBER. YOU WON'T FALL!
I KNOW . . .
. . . BUT I DON'T WANNA GET HIT BY A **BOOM BOOM**!
HA HA! BOOM BOOM!

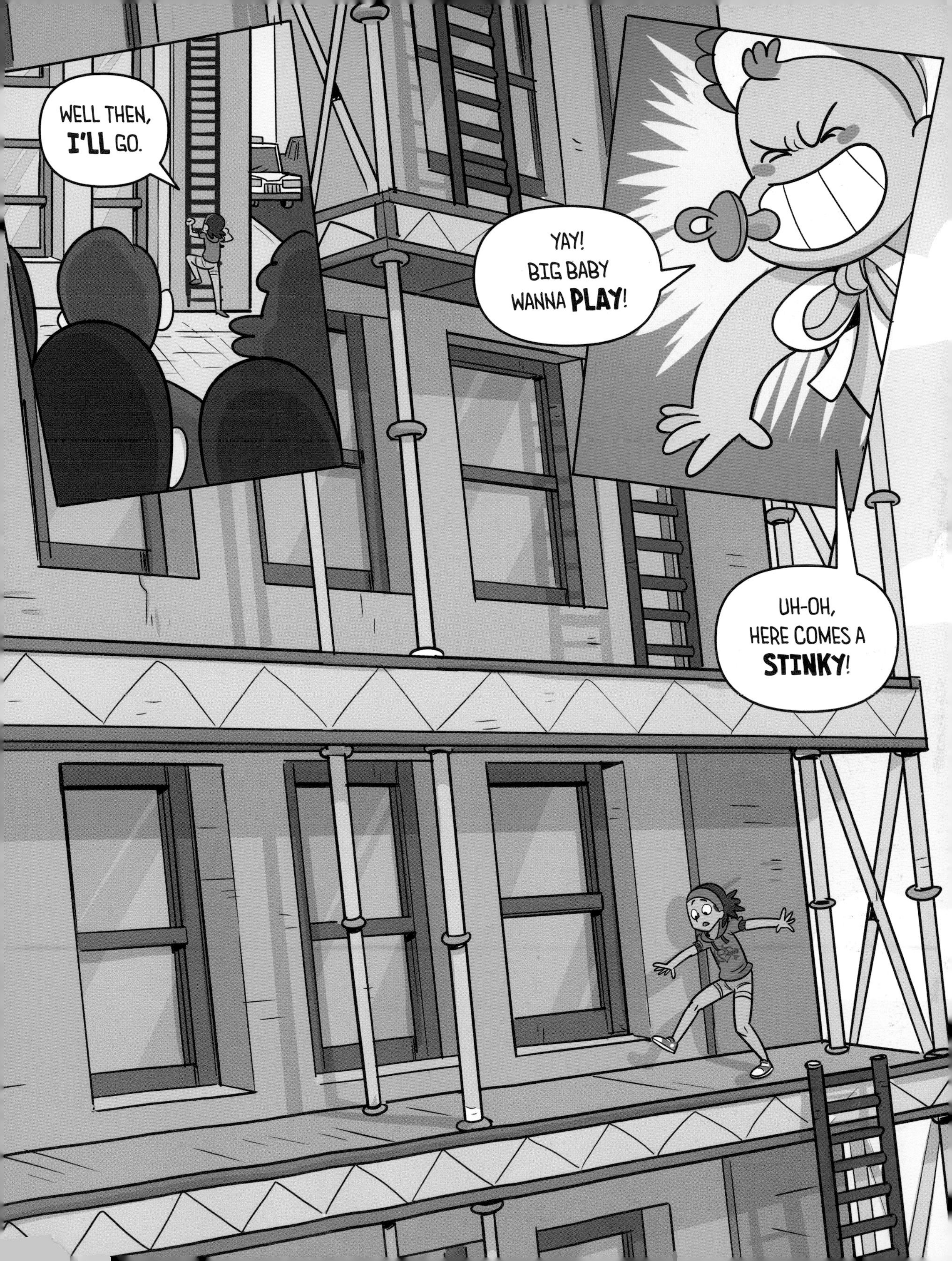
WELL THEN, **I'LL** GO.
YAY! BIG BABY WANNA **PLAY**!
UH-OH, HERE COMES A **STINKY**!

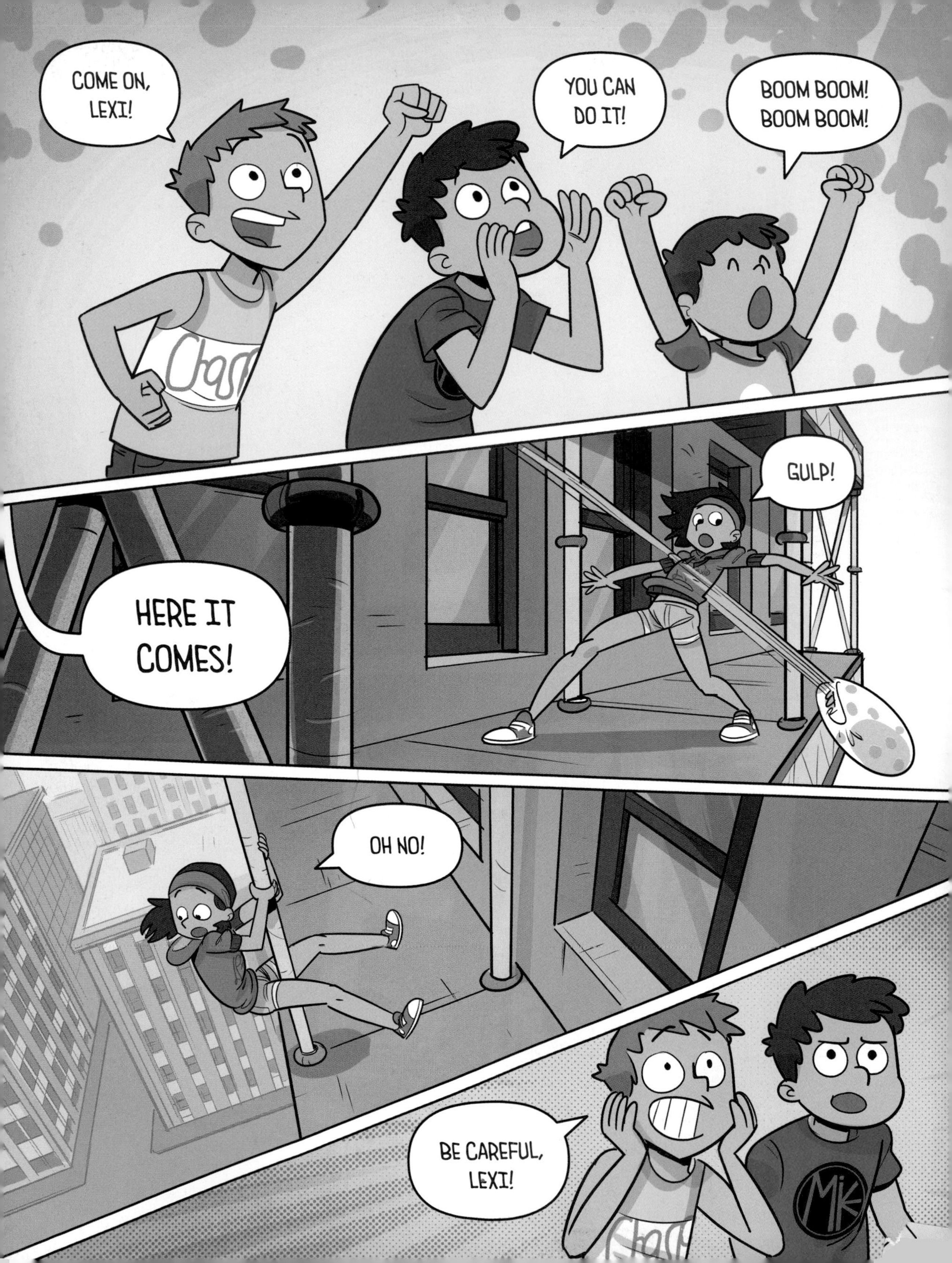

COME ON, LEXI!
YOU CAN DO IT!
BOOM BOOM! BOOM BOOM!
GULP!
HERE IT COMES!
OH NO!
BE CAREFUL, LEXI!

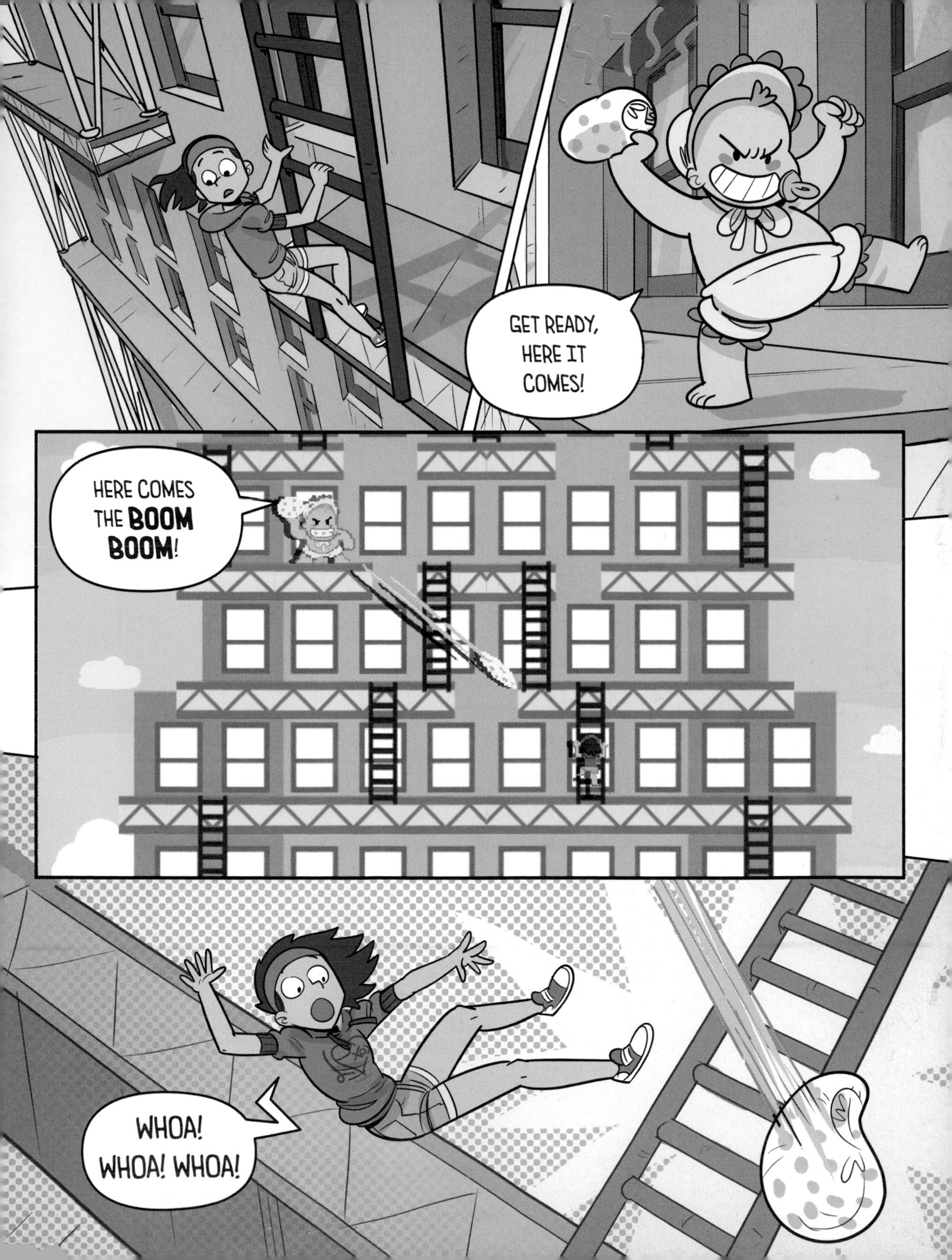
GET READY, HERE IT COMES!
HERE COMES THE **BOOM BOOM**!
WHOA! WHOA! WHOA!

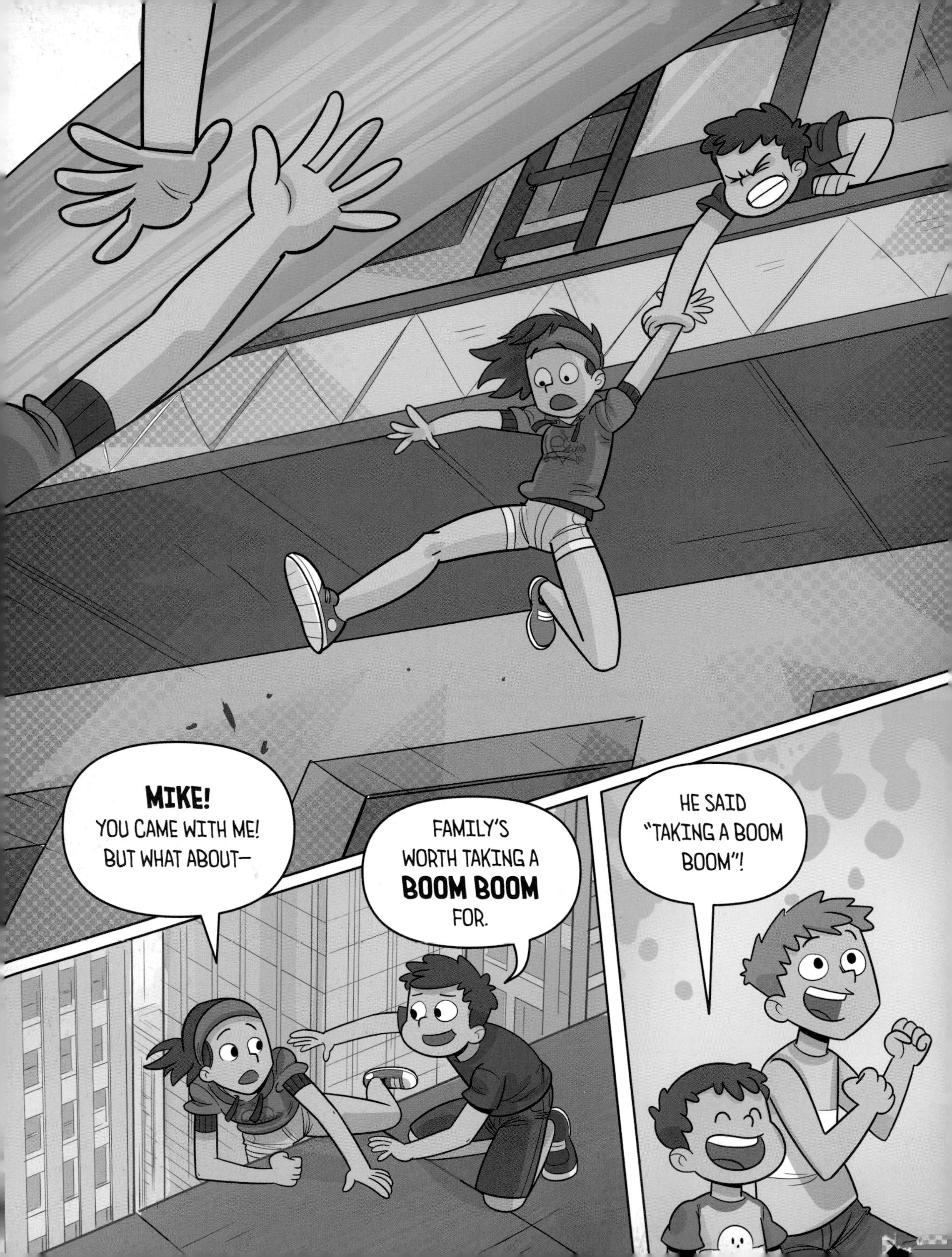

MIKE! YOU CAME WITH ME! BUT WHAT ABOUT—
FAMILY'S WORTH TAKING A BOOM BOOM FOR.
HE SAID "TAKING A BOOM BOOM"!

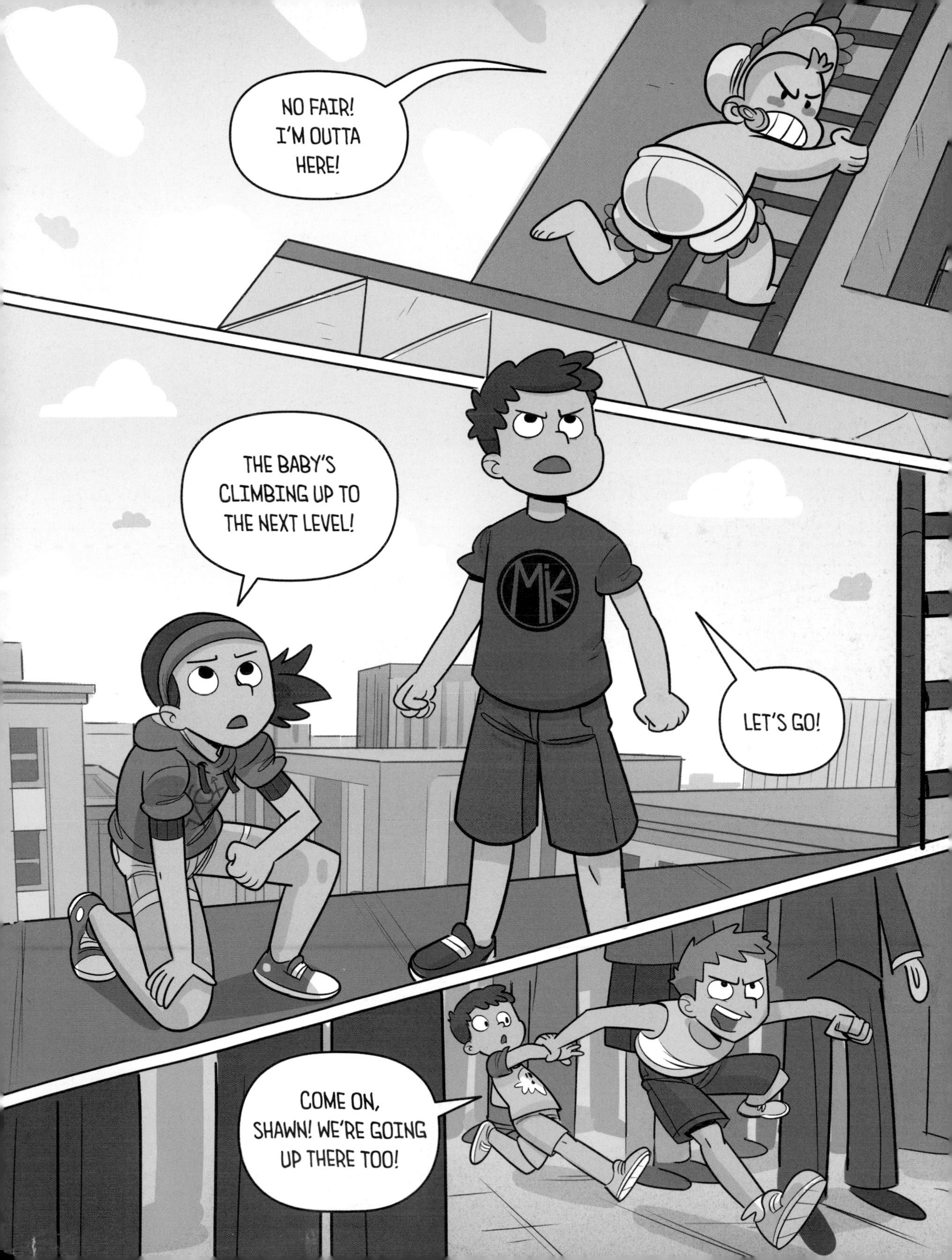
NO FAIR! I'M OUTTA HERE!
THE BABY'S CLIMBING UP TO THE NEXT LEVEL!
LET'S GO!
COME ON, SHAWN! WE'RE GOING UP THERE TOO!

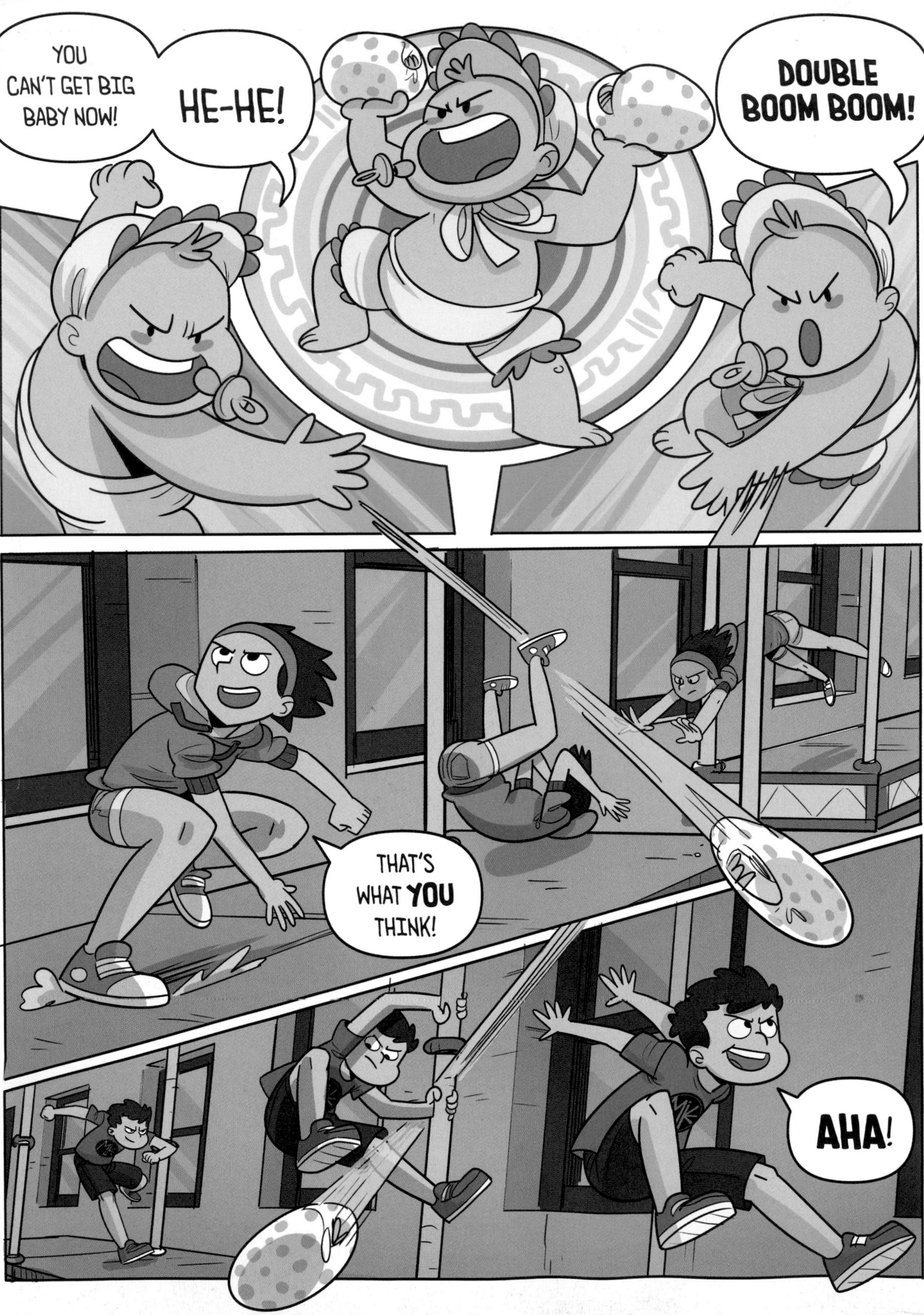
YOU CAN'T GET BIG BABY NOW!
HE-HE!
DOUBLE BOOM BOOM!
THAT'S WHAT YOU THINK!
AHA!

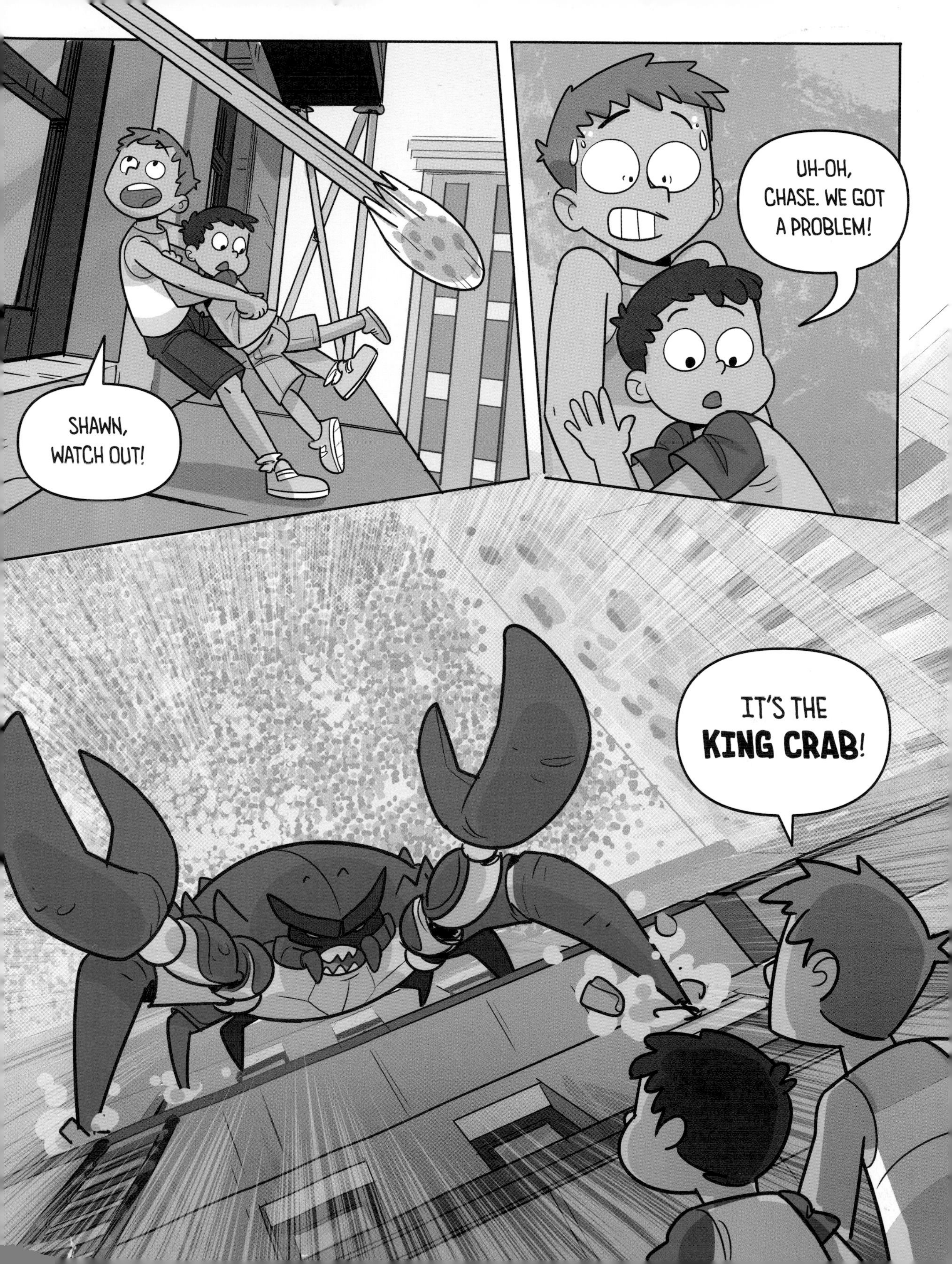
SHAWN, WATCH OUT!
UH-OH, CHASE. WE GOT A PROBLEM!
IT'S THE **KING CRAB**!

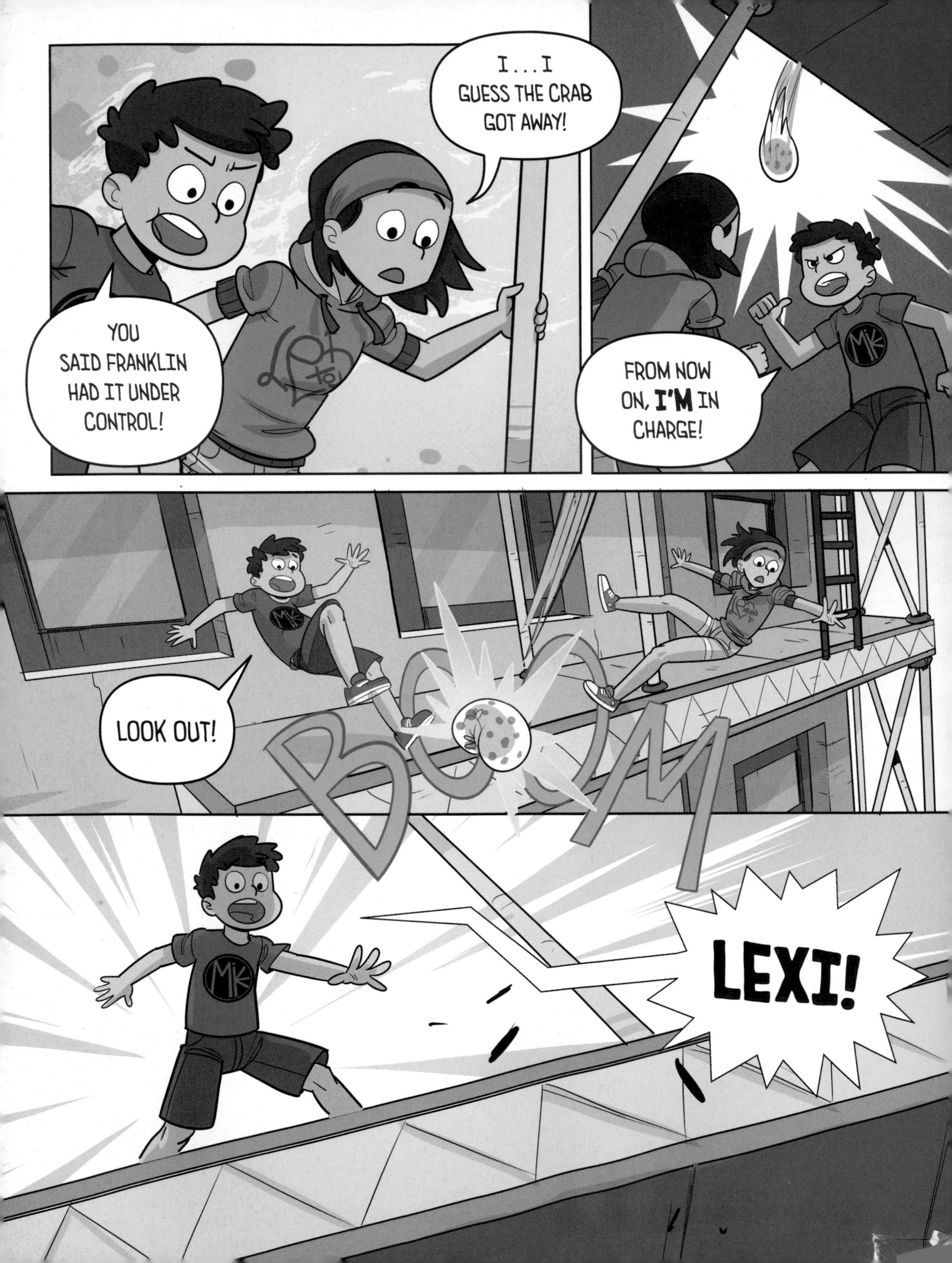
I...I GUESS THE CRAB GOT AWAY!
YOU SAID FRANKLIN HAD IT UNDER CONTROL!
FROM NOW ON, **I'M** IN CHARGE!
LOOK OUT!
BOOM
LEXI!

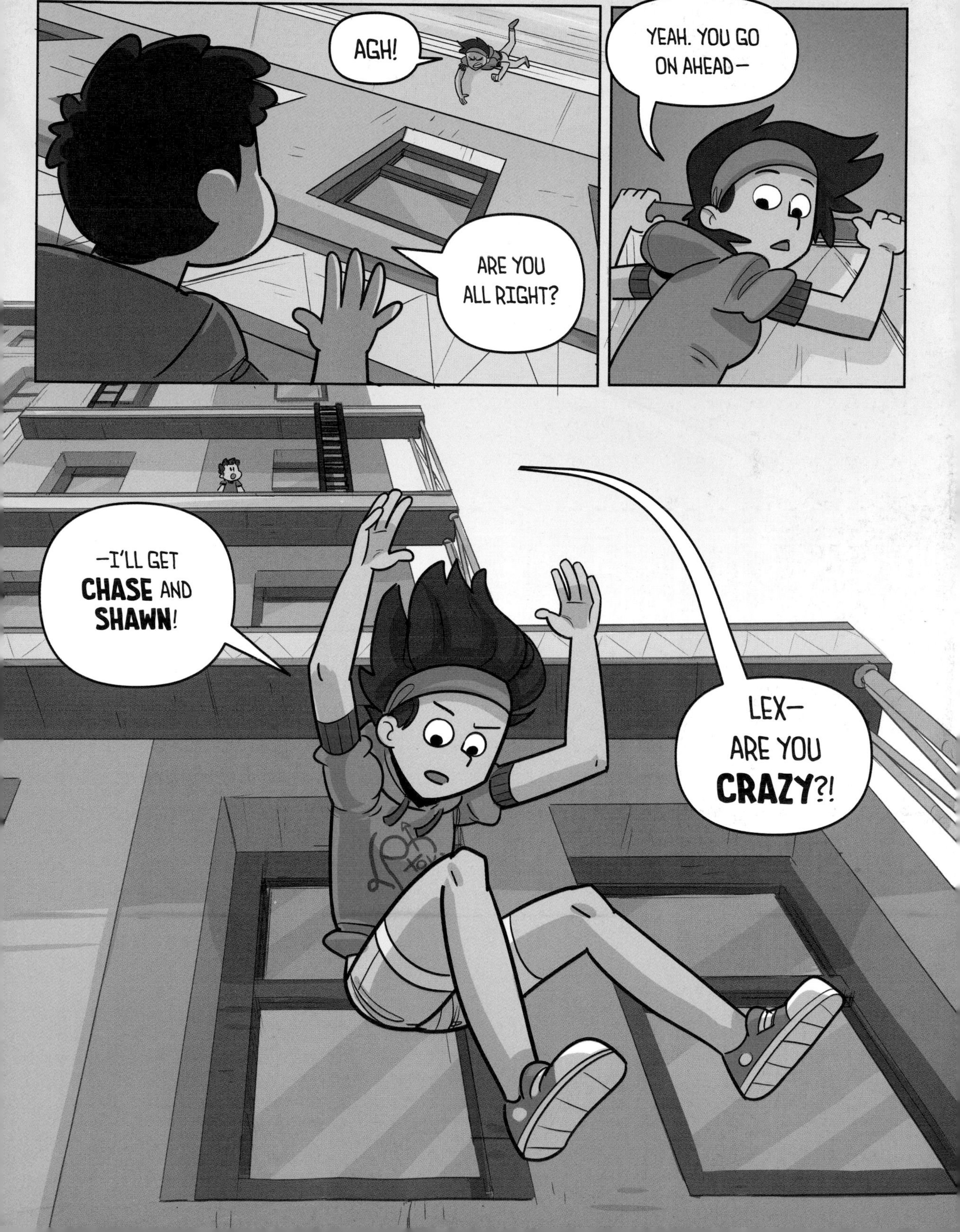
AGH!
ARE YOU ALL RIGHT?
YEAH. YOU GO ON AHEAD—
—I'LL GET **CHASE** AND **SHAWN**!
LEX— ARE YOU **CRAZY**?!

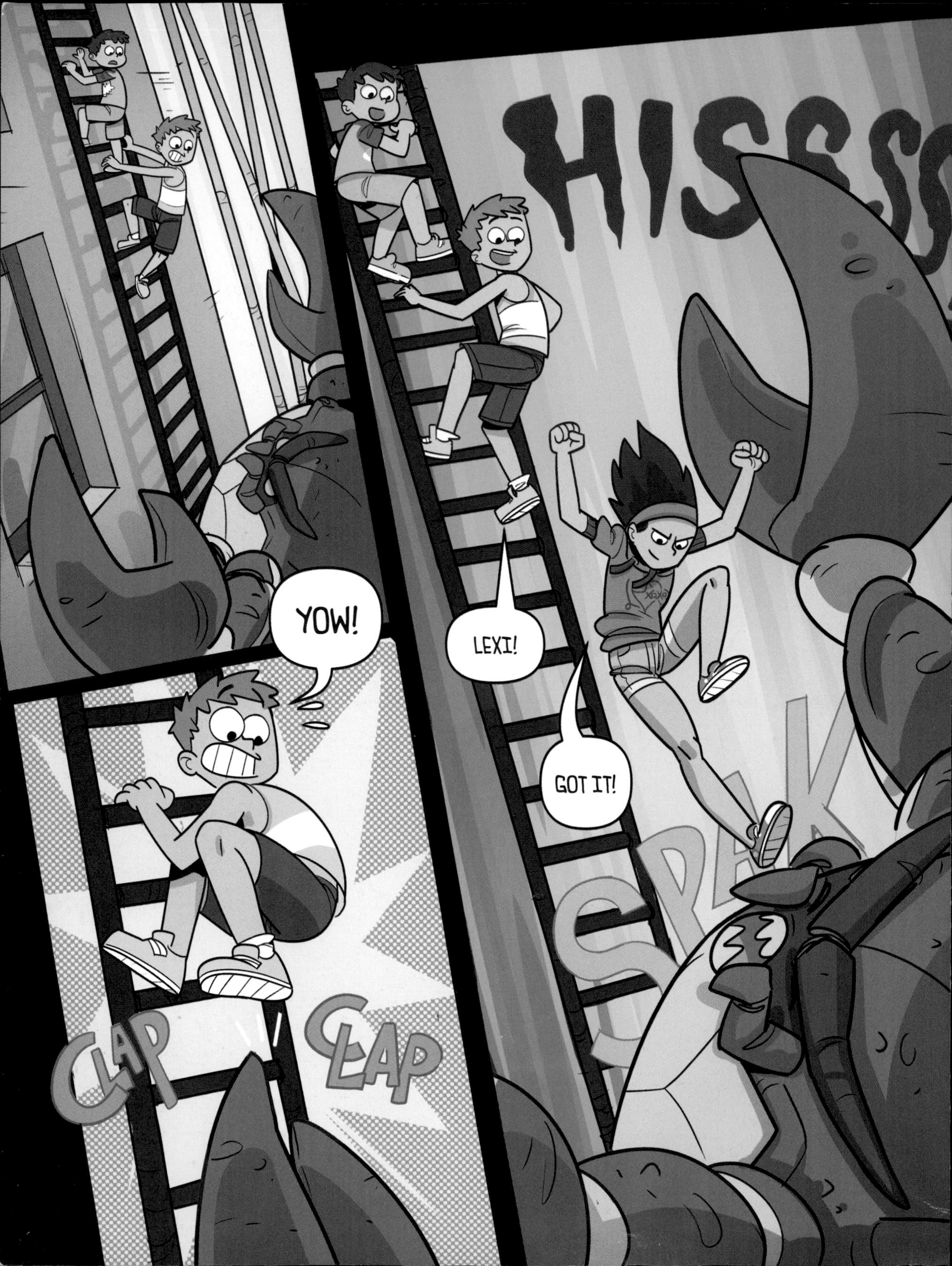
YOW!
CLAP
CLAP
HISSSS
LEXI!
GOT IT!
SPAK

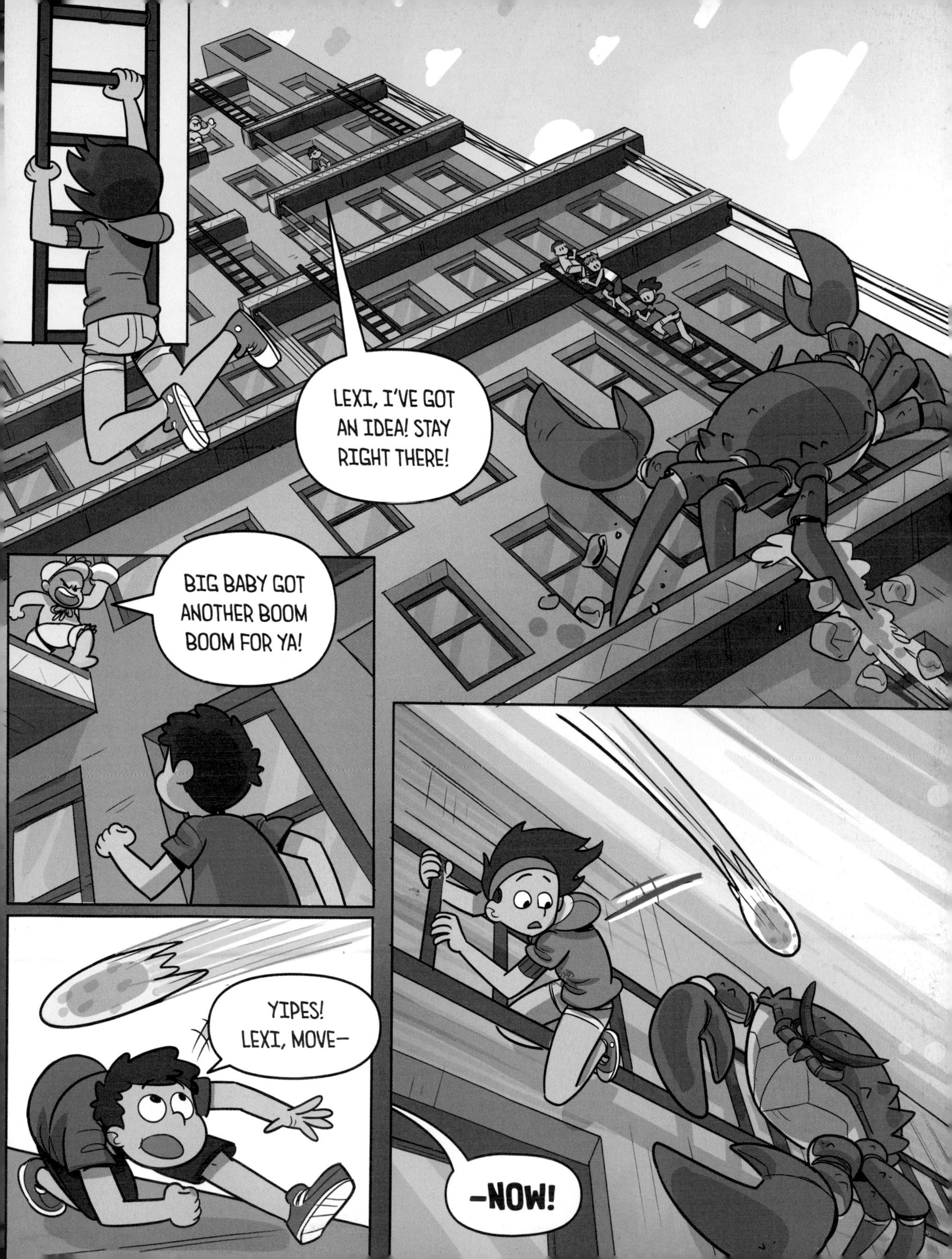
LEXI, I'VE GOT AN IDEA! STAY RIGHT THERE!
BIG BABY GOT ANOTHER BOOM BOOM FOR YA!
YIPES! LEXI, MOVE—
—NOW!

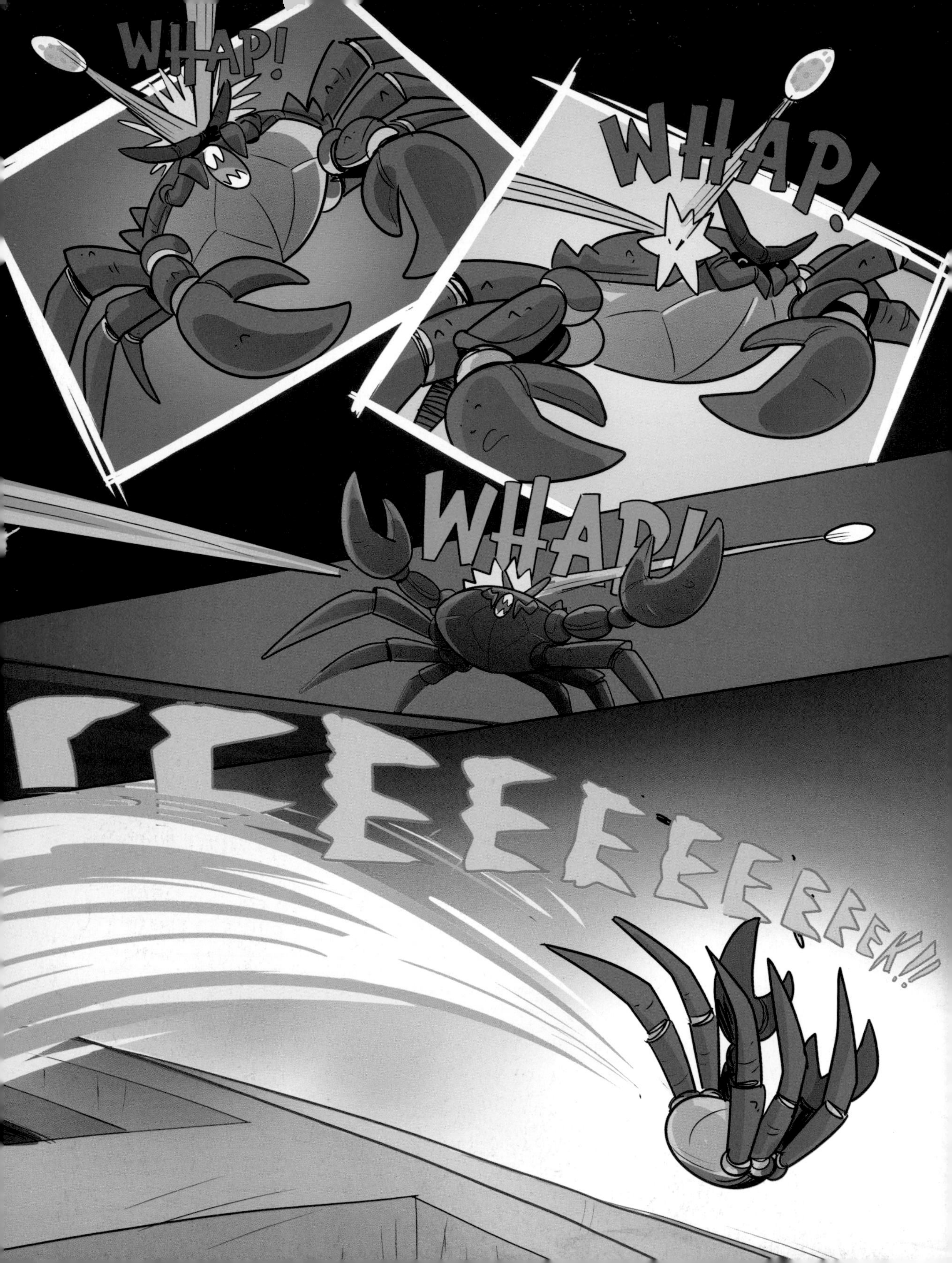
WHAP!
WHAP!
WHAP!
EEEEEEEEEEEEEEK!!

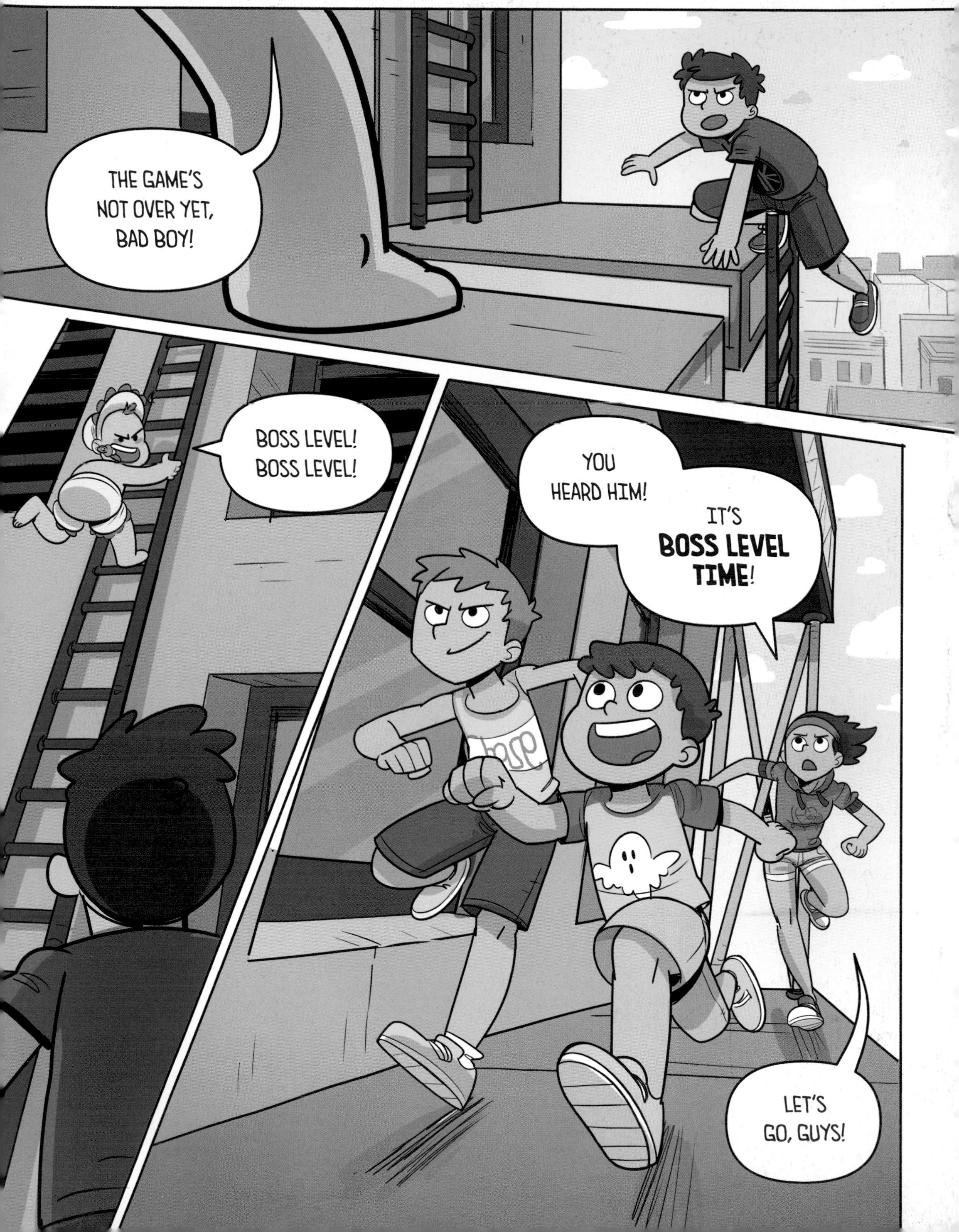
THE GAME'S NOT OVER YET, BAD BOY!
BOSS LEVEL! BOSS LEVEL!
YOU HEARD HIM!
IT'S **BOSS LEVEL TIME**!
LET'S GO, GUYS!

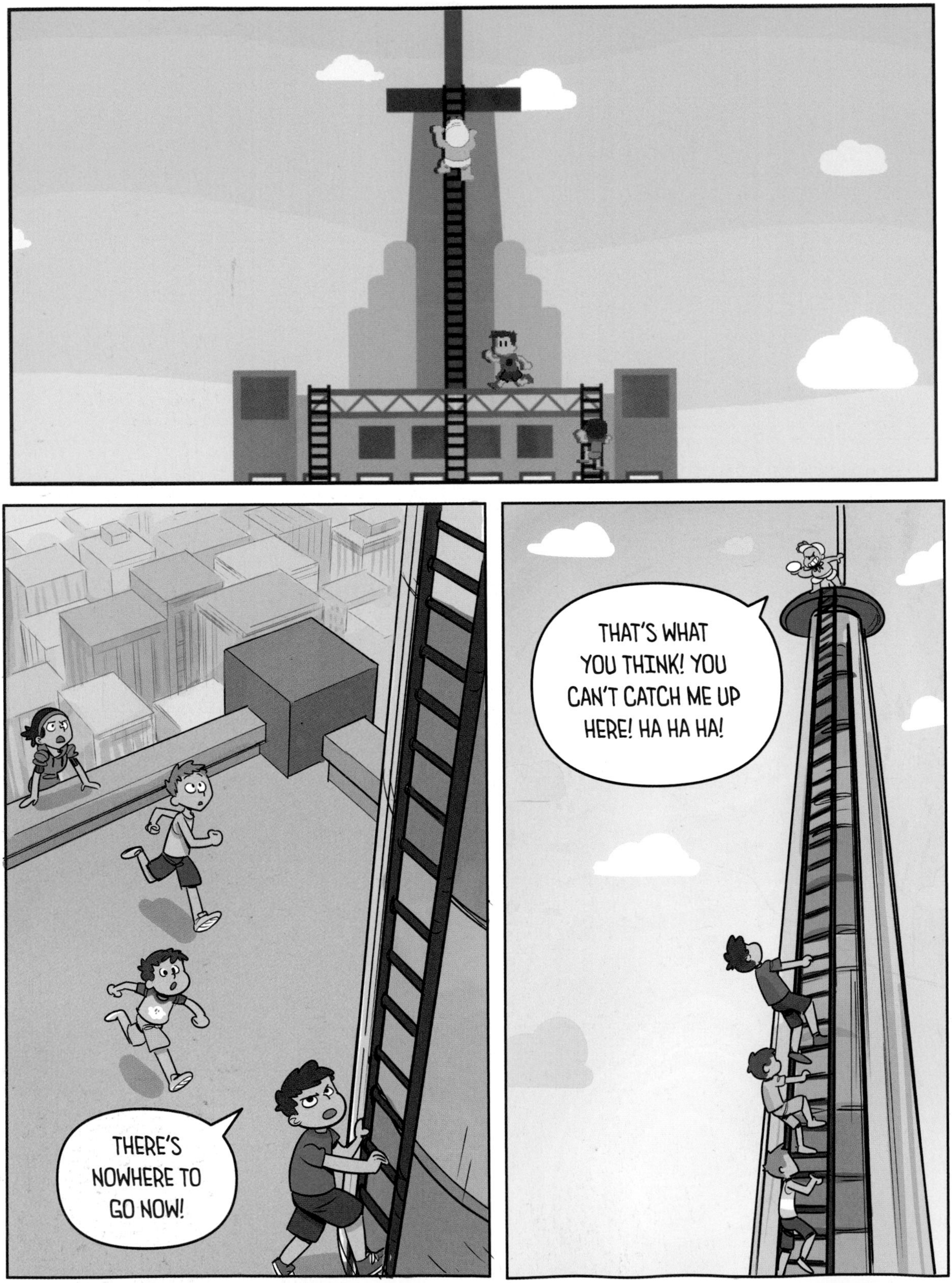
THERE'S NOWHERE TO GO NOW!
THAT'S WHAT YOU THINK! YOU CAN'T CATCH ME UP HERE! HA HA HA!

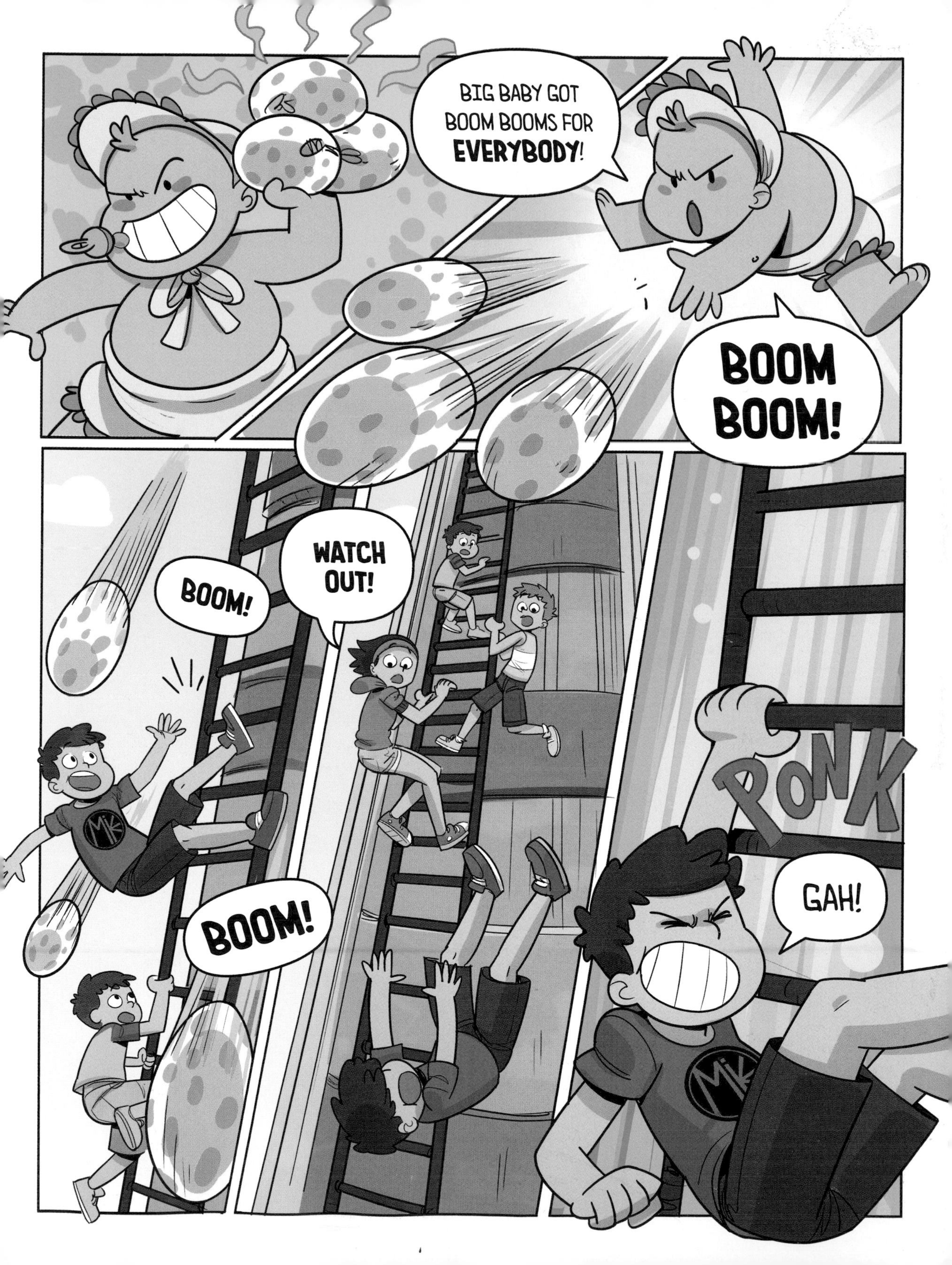
BIG BABY GOT BOOM BOOMS FOR **EVERYBODY**!
BOOM BOOM!
BOOM!
WATCH OUT!
BOOM!
PONK
GAH!

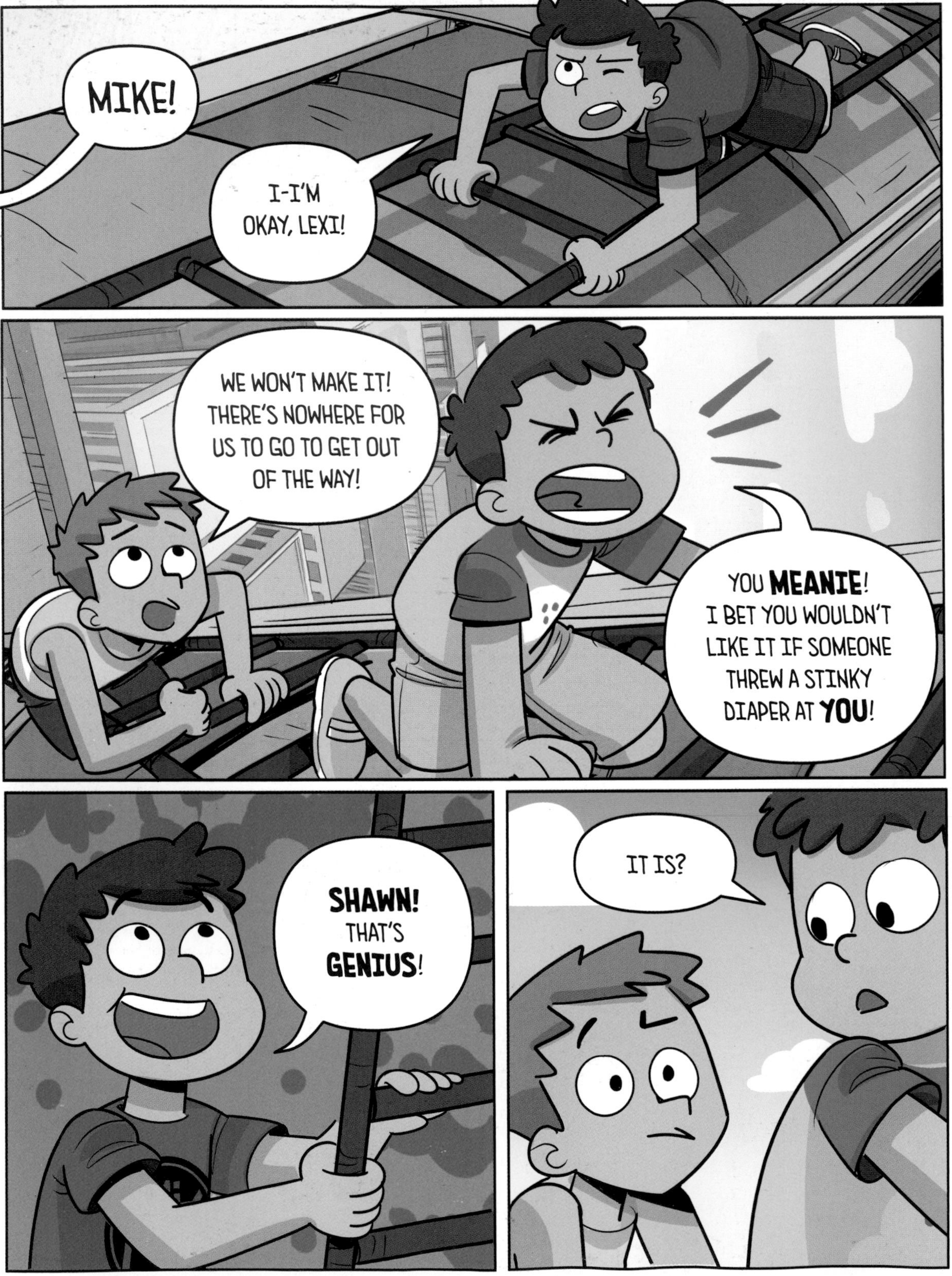
MIKE!
I-I'M OKAY, LEXI!
WE WON'T MAKE IT! THERE'S NOWHERE FOR US TO GO TO GET OUT OF THE WAY!
YOU **MEANIE**! I BET YOU WOULDN'T LIKE IT IF SOMEONE THREW A STINKY DIAPER AT **YOU**!
SHAWN! THAT'S **GENIUS**!
IT IS?

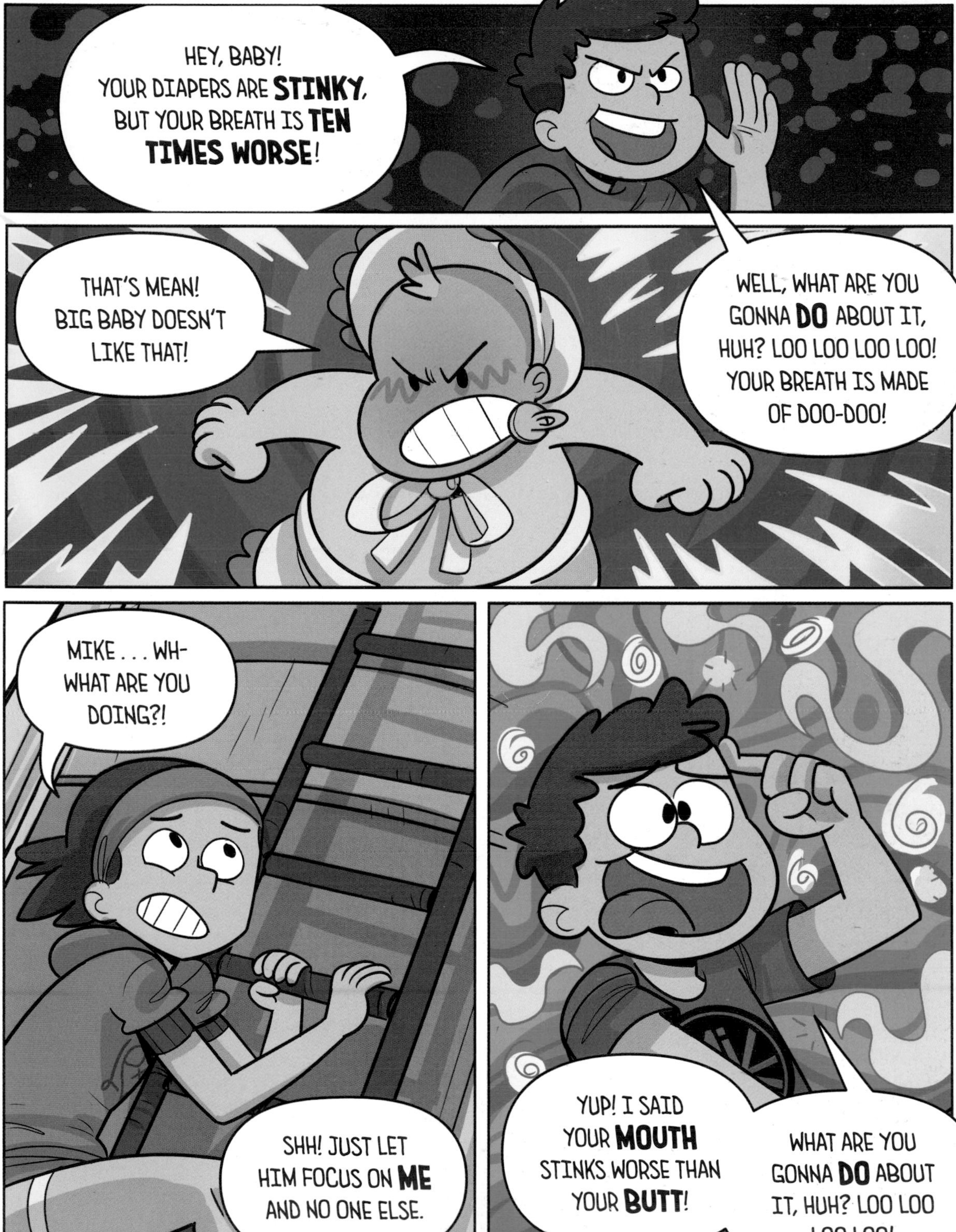
HEY, BABY! YOUR DIAPERS ARE **STINKY**, BUT YOUR BREATH IS **TEN TIMES WORSE**!
THAT'S MEAN! BIG BABY DOESN'T LIKE THAT!
WELL, WHAT ARE YOU GONNA **DO** ABOUT IT, HUH? LOO LOO LOO LOO! YOUR BREATH IS MADE OF DOO-DOO!
MIKE . . . WH- WHAT ARE YOU DOING?!
SHH! JUST LET HIM FOCUS ON **ME** AND NO ONE ELSE.
YUP! I SAID YOUR **MOUTH** STINKS WORSE THAN YOUR **BUTT**!
WHAT ARE YOU GONNA **DO** ABOUT IT, HUH? LOO LOO LOO LOO!

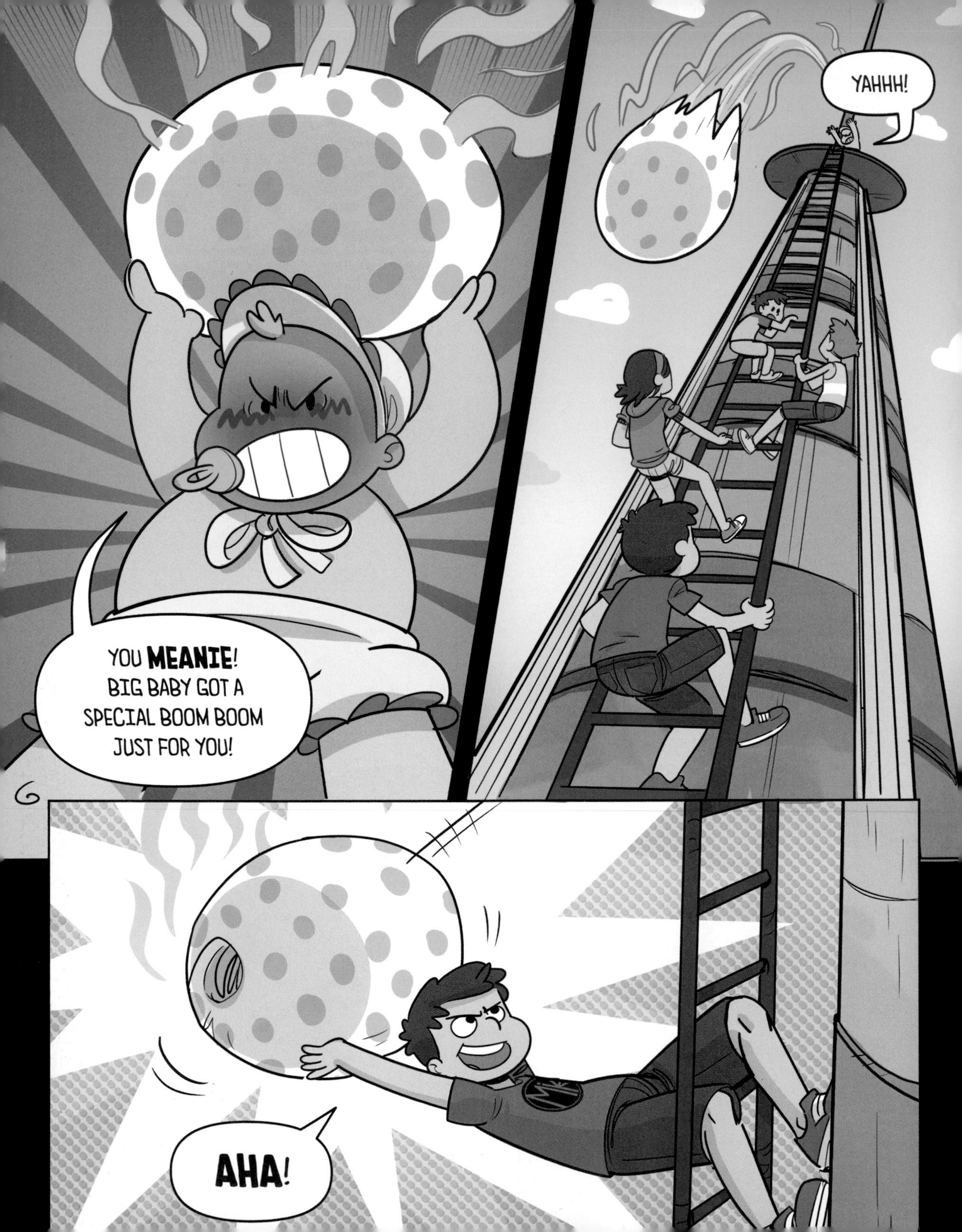
YOU **MEANIE**! BIG BABY GOT A SPECIAL BOOM BOOM JUST FOR YOU!
YAHHH!
AHA!

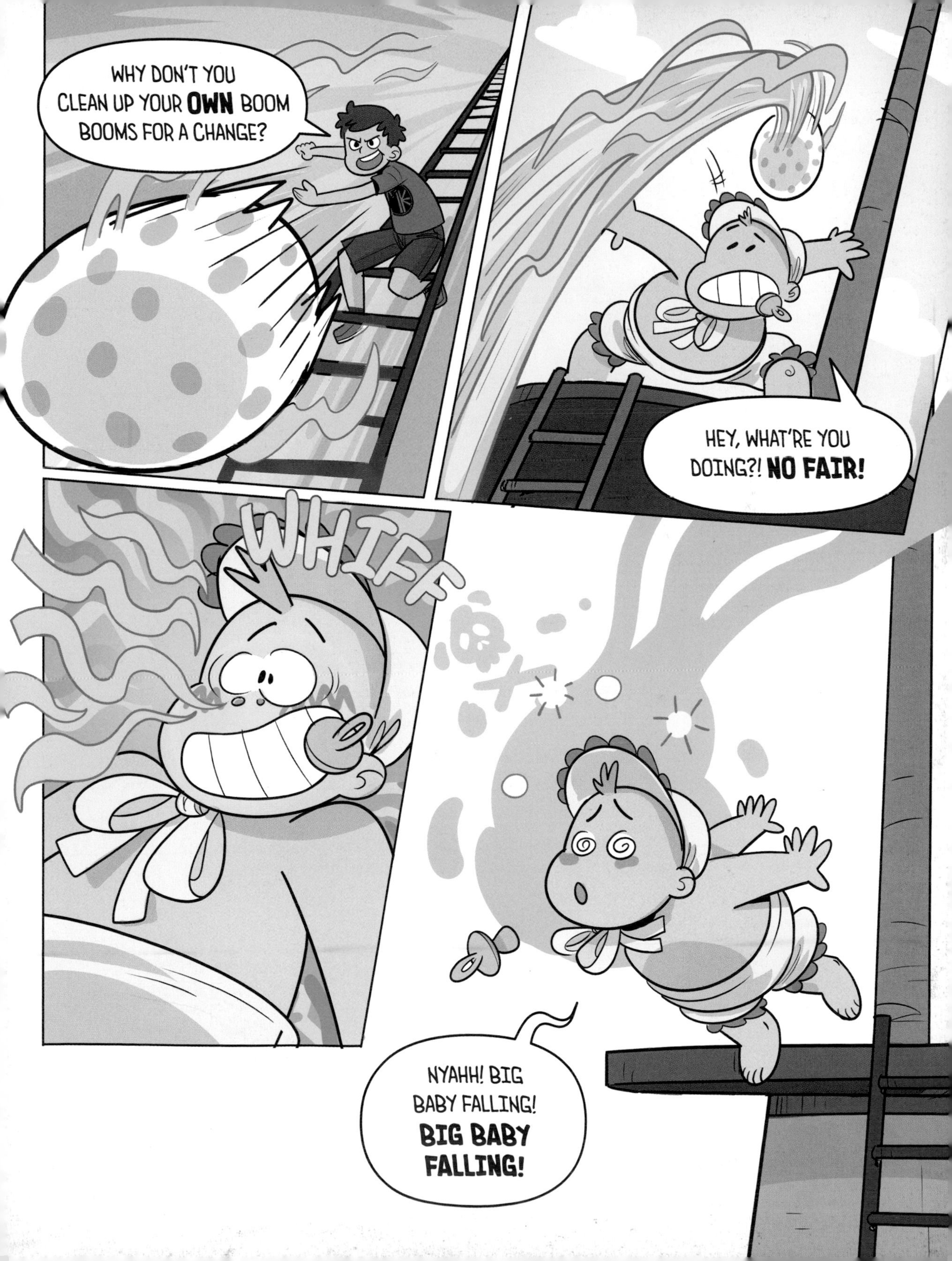
WHY DON'T YOU CLEAN UP YOUR OWN BOOM BOOMS FOR A CHANGE?
HEY, WHAT'RE YOU DOING?! NO FAIR!
WHIFF
NYAHH! BIG BABY FALLING! BIG BABY FALLING!

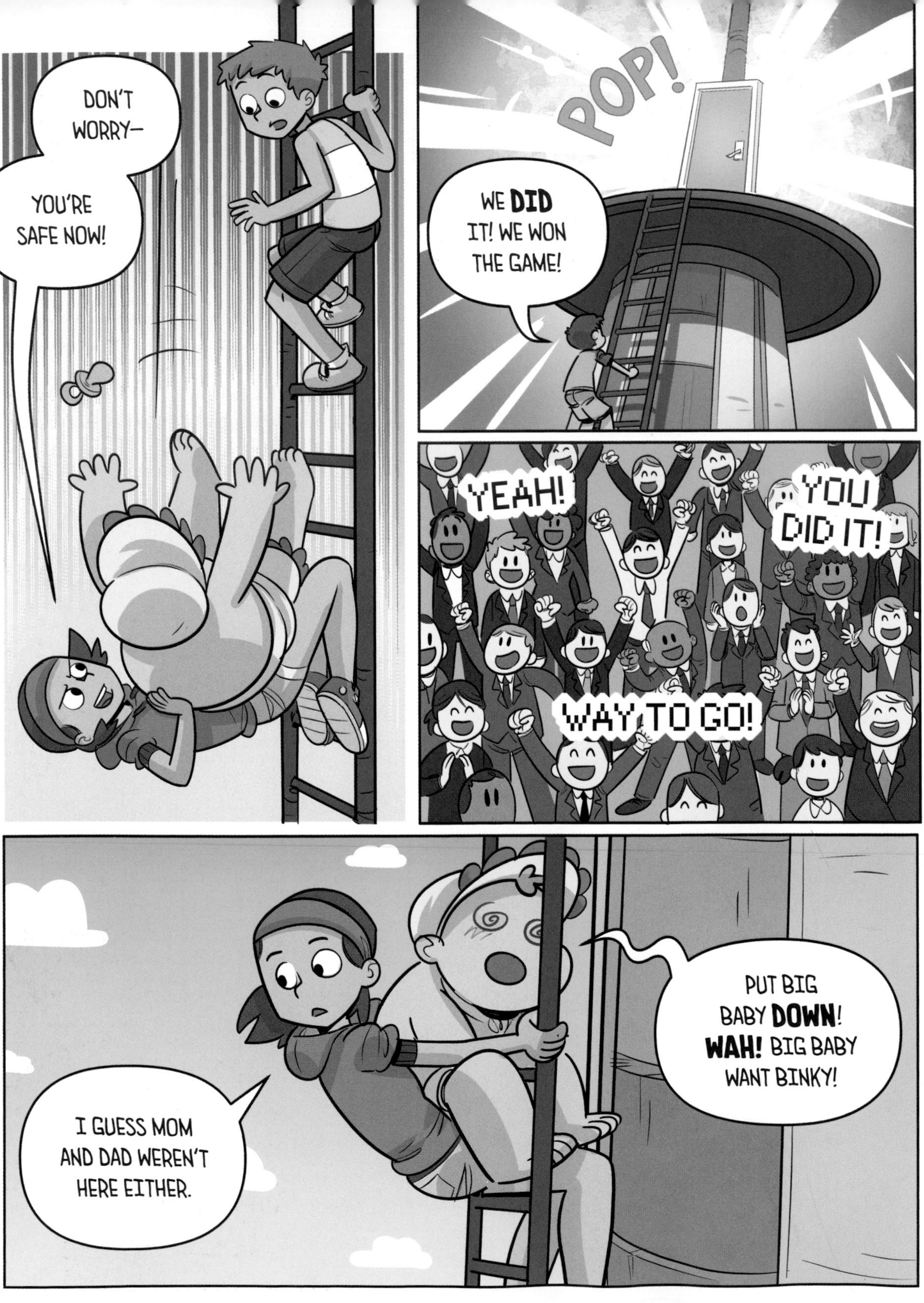
DON'T WORRY—
YOU'RE SAFE NOW!
POP!
WE **DID** IT! WE WON THE GAME!
YEAH!
YOU DID IT!
WAY TO GO!
I GUESS MOM AND DAD WEREN'T HERE EITHER.
PUT BIG BABY **DOWN**! **WAH!** BIG BABY WANT BINKY!

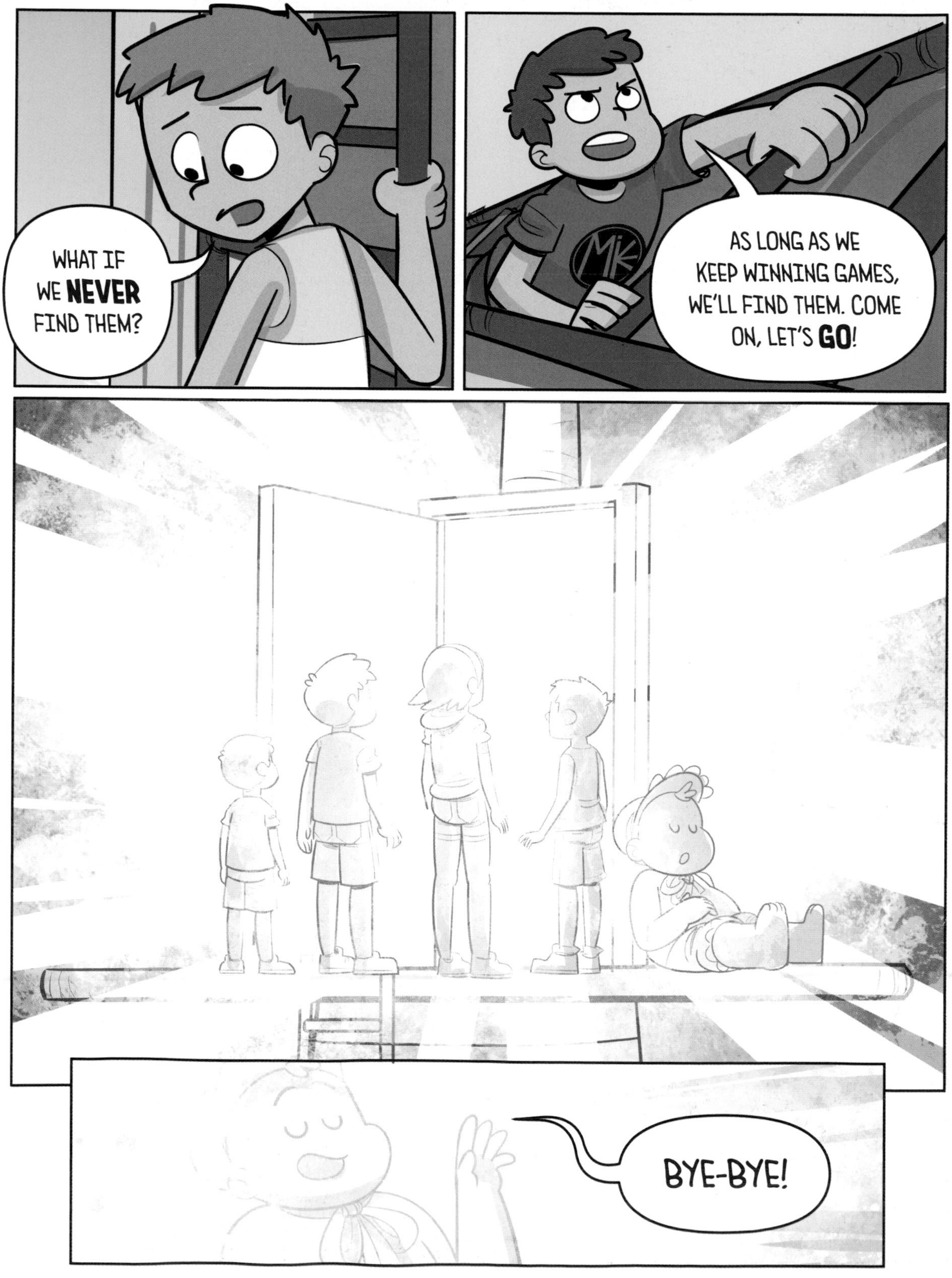
WHAT IF WE **NEVER** FIND THEM?
AS LONG AS WE KEEP WINNING GAMES, WE'LL FIND THEM. COME ON, LET'S **GO**!
BYE-BYE!

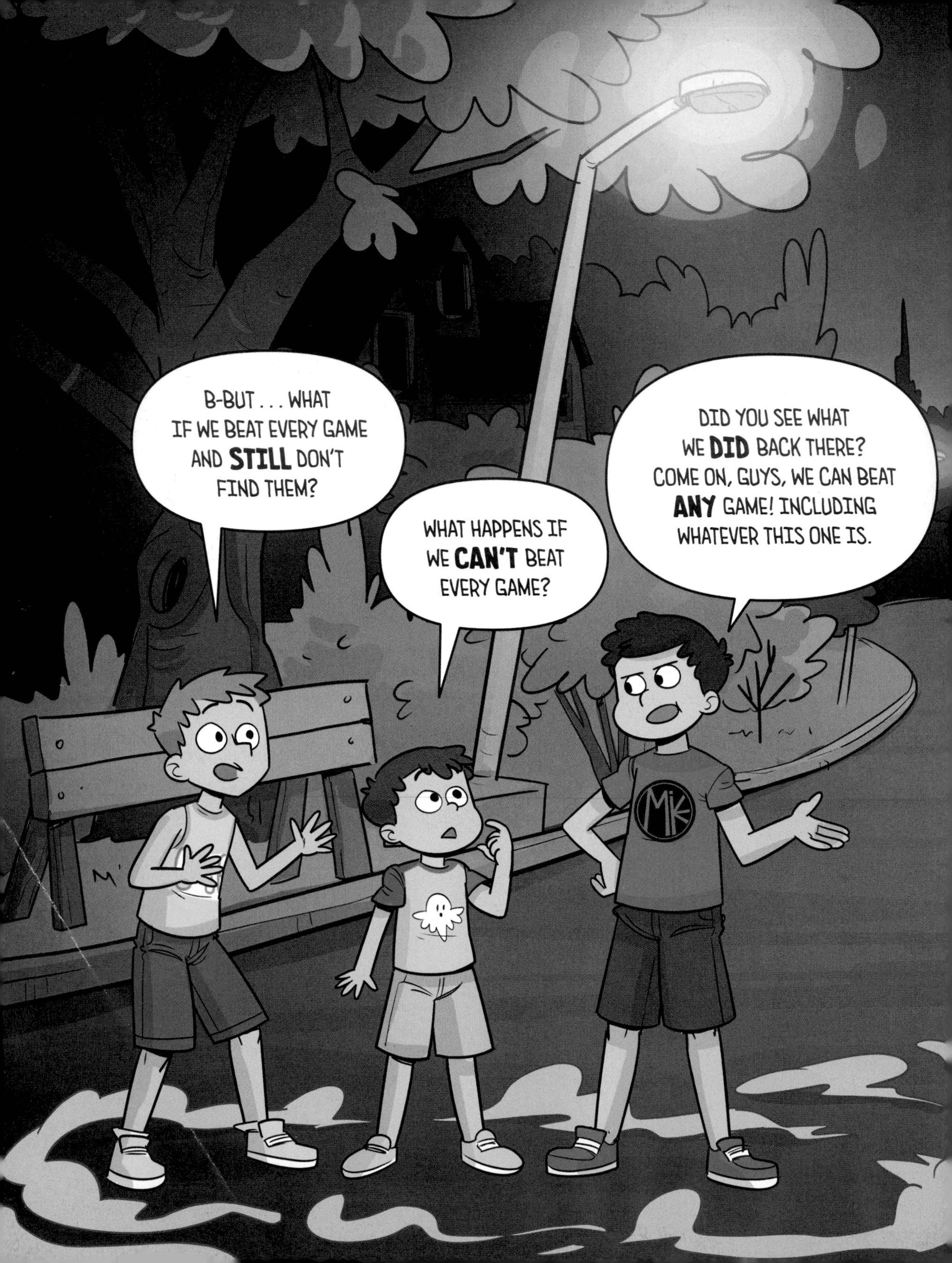
B-BUT . . . WHAT IF WE BEAT EVERY GAME AND STILL DON'T FIND THEM?
WHAT HAPPENS IF WE CAN'T BEAT EVERY GAME?
DID YOU SEE WHAT WE DID BACK THERE? COME ON, GUYS, WE CAN BEAT ANY GAME! INCLUDING WHATEVER THIS ONE IS.

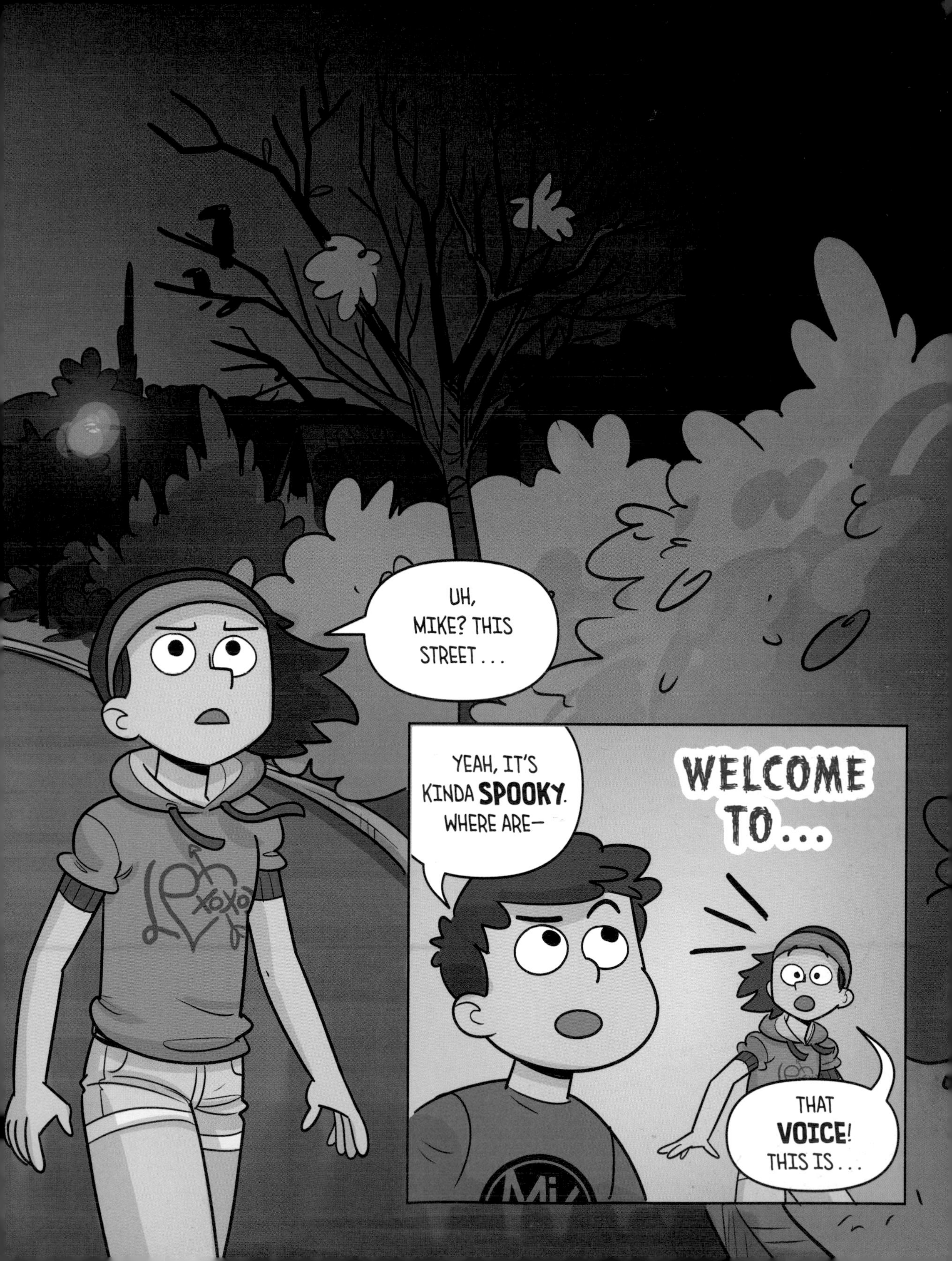
UH, MIKE? THIS STREET . . .
YEAH, IT'S KINDA **SPOOKY**. WHERE ARE—
WELCOME TO . . .
THAT **VOICE**! THIS IS . . .

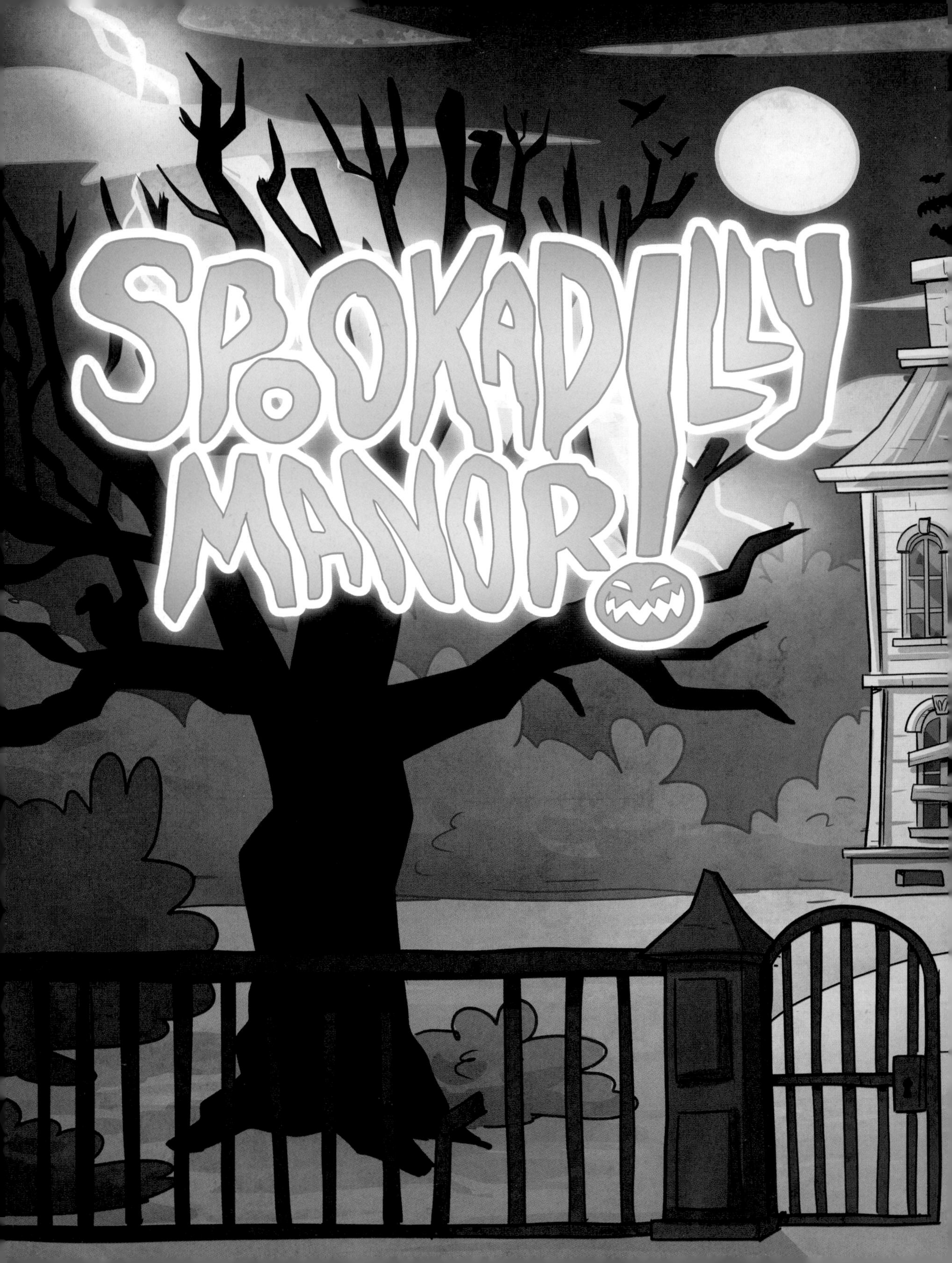
SPOOKADILLY MANOR!

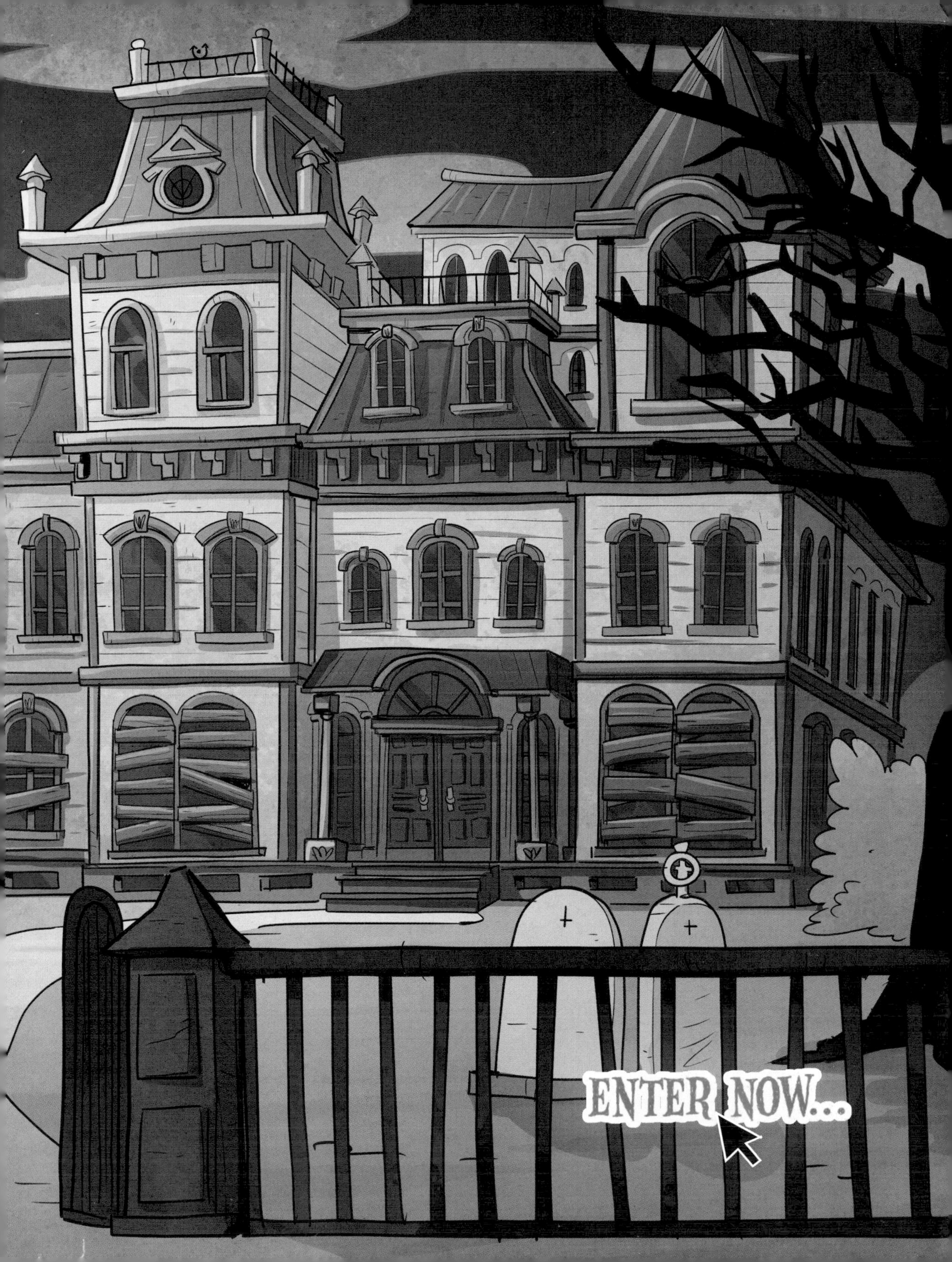
ENTER NOW...

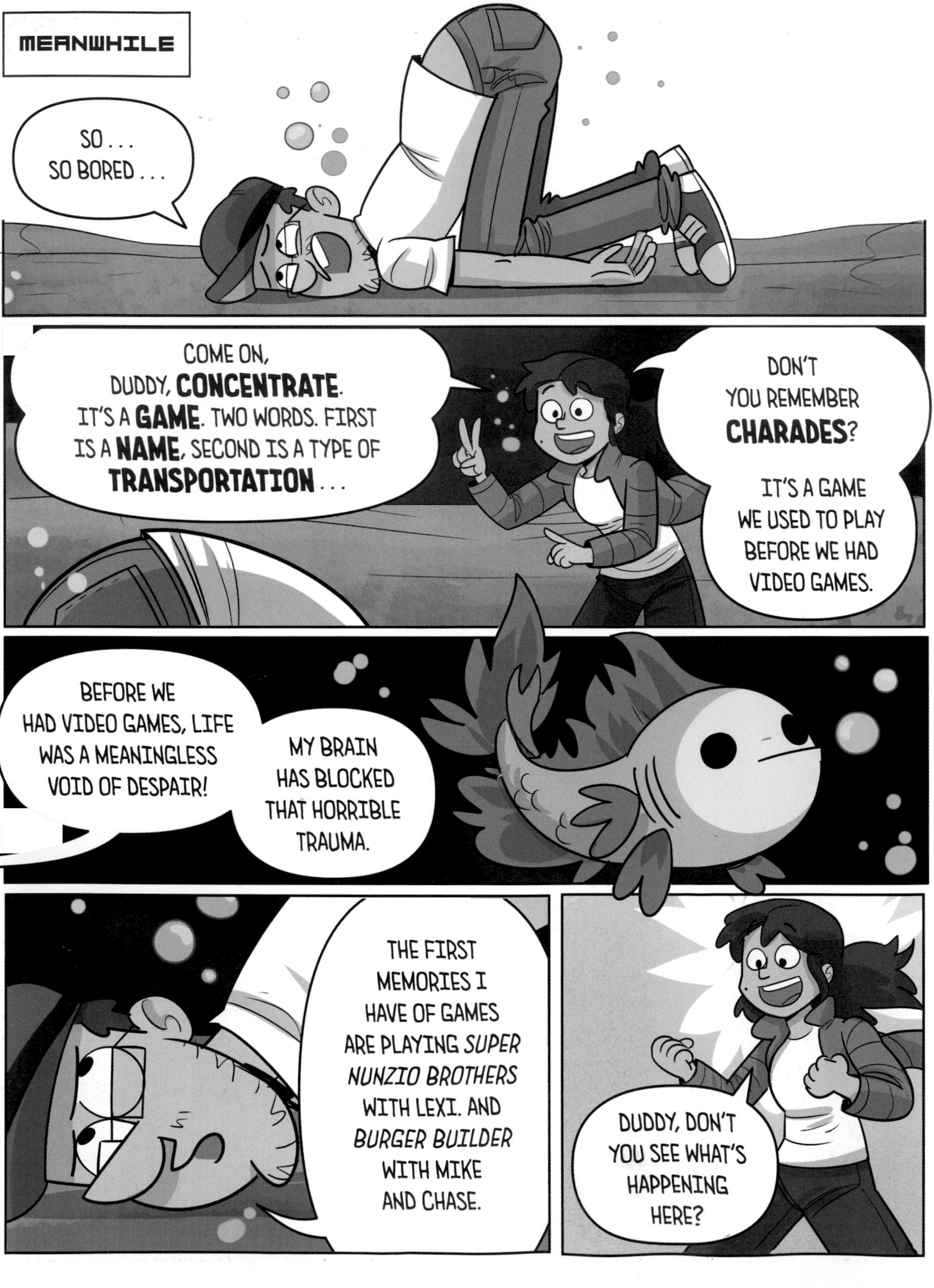
MEANWHILE
SO . . . SO BORED . . .
COME ON, DUDDY, CONCENTRATE. IT'S A GAME. TWO WORDS. FIRST IS A NAME, SECOND IS A TYPE OF TRANSPORTATION . . .
DON'T YOU REMEMBER CHARADES?
IT'S A GAME WE USED TO PLAY BEFORE WE HAD VIDEO GAMES.
BEFORE WE HAD VIDEO GAMES, LIFE WAS A MEANINGLESS VOID OF DESPAIR!
MY BRAIN HAS BLOCKED THAT HORRIBLE TRAUMA.
THE FIRST MEMORIES I HAVE OF GAMES ARE PLAYING SUPER NUNZIO BROTHERS WITH LEXI. AND BURGER BUILDER WITH MIKE AND CHASE.
DUDDY, DON'T YOU SEE WHAT'S HAPPENING HERE?

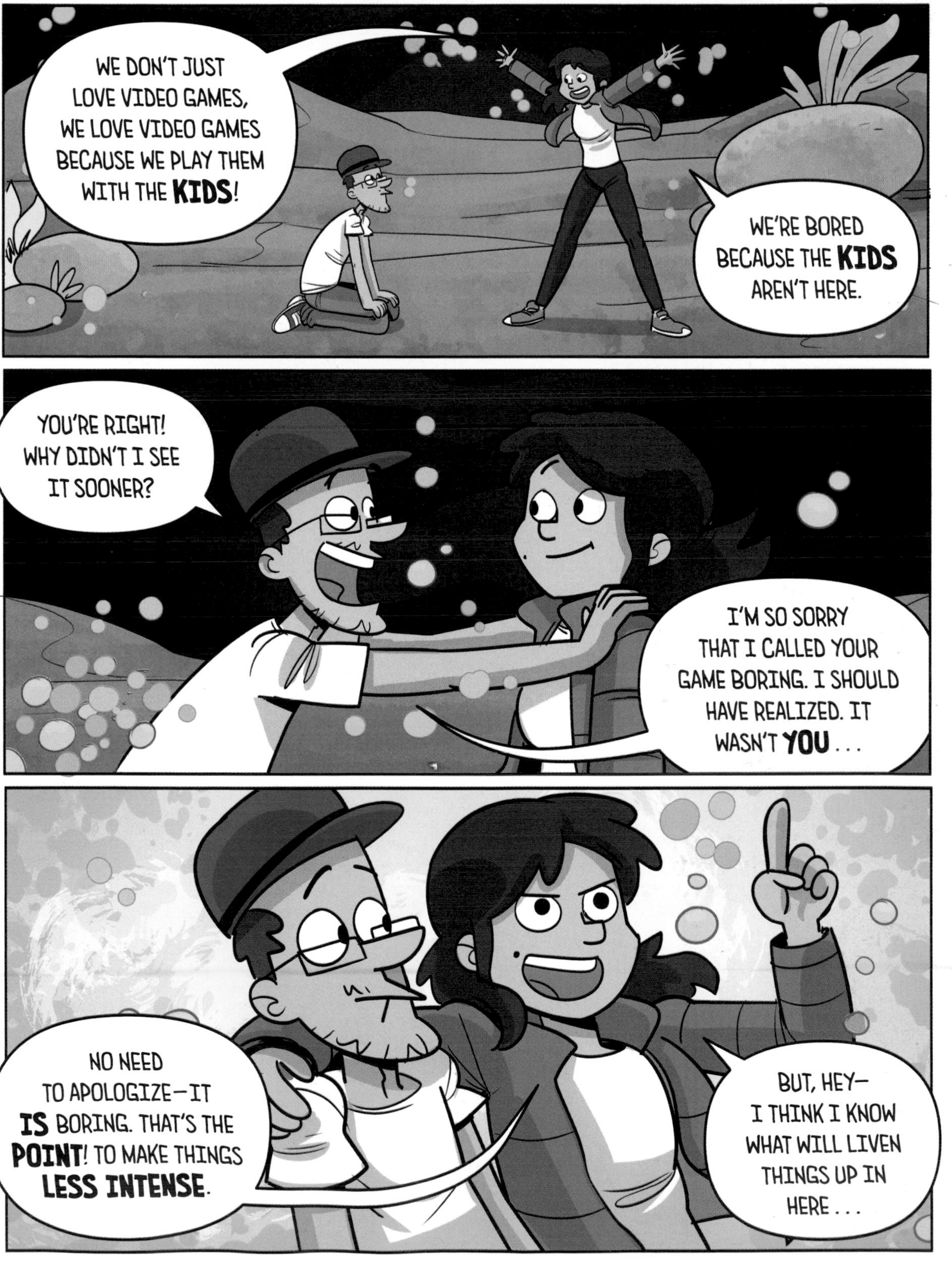
WE DON'T JUST LOVE VIDEO GAMES, WE LOVE VIDEO GAMES BECAUSE WE PLAY THEM WITH THE **KIDS**!
WE'RE BORED BECAUSE THE **KIDS** AREN'T HERE.
YOU'RE RIGHT! WHY DIDN'T I SEE IT SOONER?
I'M SO SORRY THAT I CALLED YOUR GAME BORING. I SHOULD HAVE REALIZED. IT WASN'T **YOU** . . .
NO NEED TO APOLOGIZE—IT **IS** BORING. THAT'S THE **POINT**! TO MAKE THINGS **LESS INTENSE**.
BUT, HEY— I THINK I KNOW WHAT WILL LIVEN THINGS UP IN HERE . . .

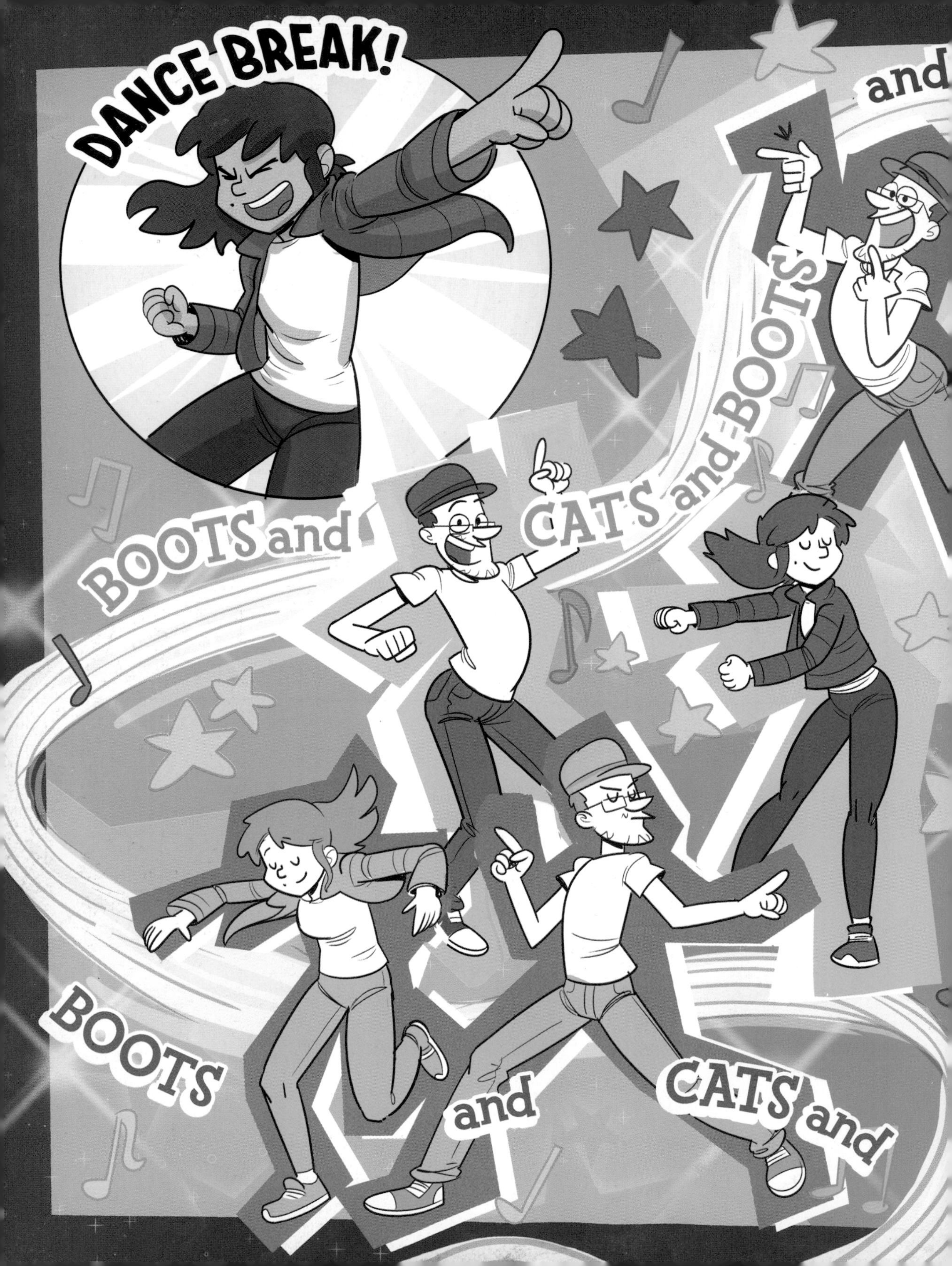

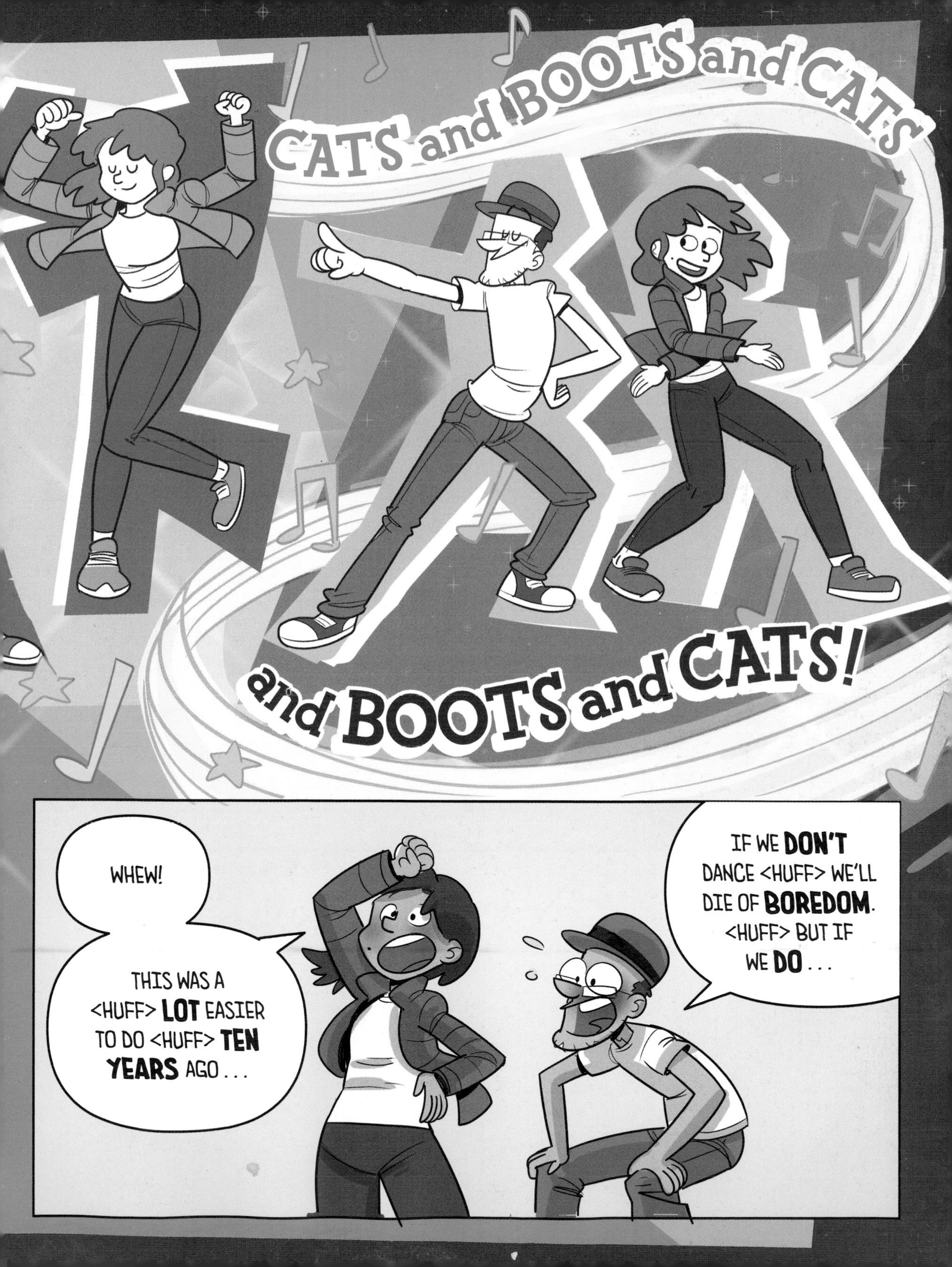
CATS and BOOTS and CATS
and BOOTS and CATS!
WHEW!
THIS WAS A <HUFF> **LOT** EASIER TO DO <HUFF> **TEN YEARS** AGO . . .
IF WE **DON'T** DANCE <HUFF> WE'LL DIE OF **BOREDOM**. <HUFF> BUT IF WE **DO** . . .

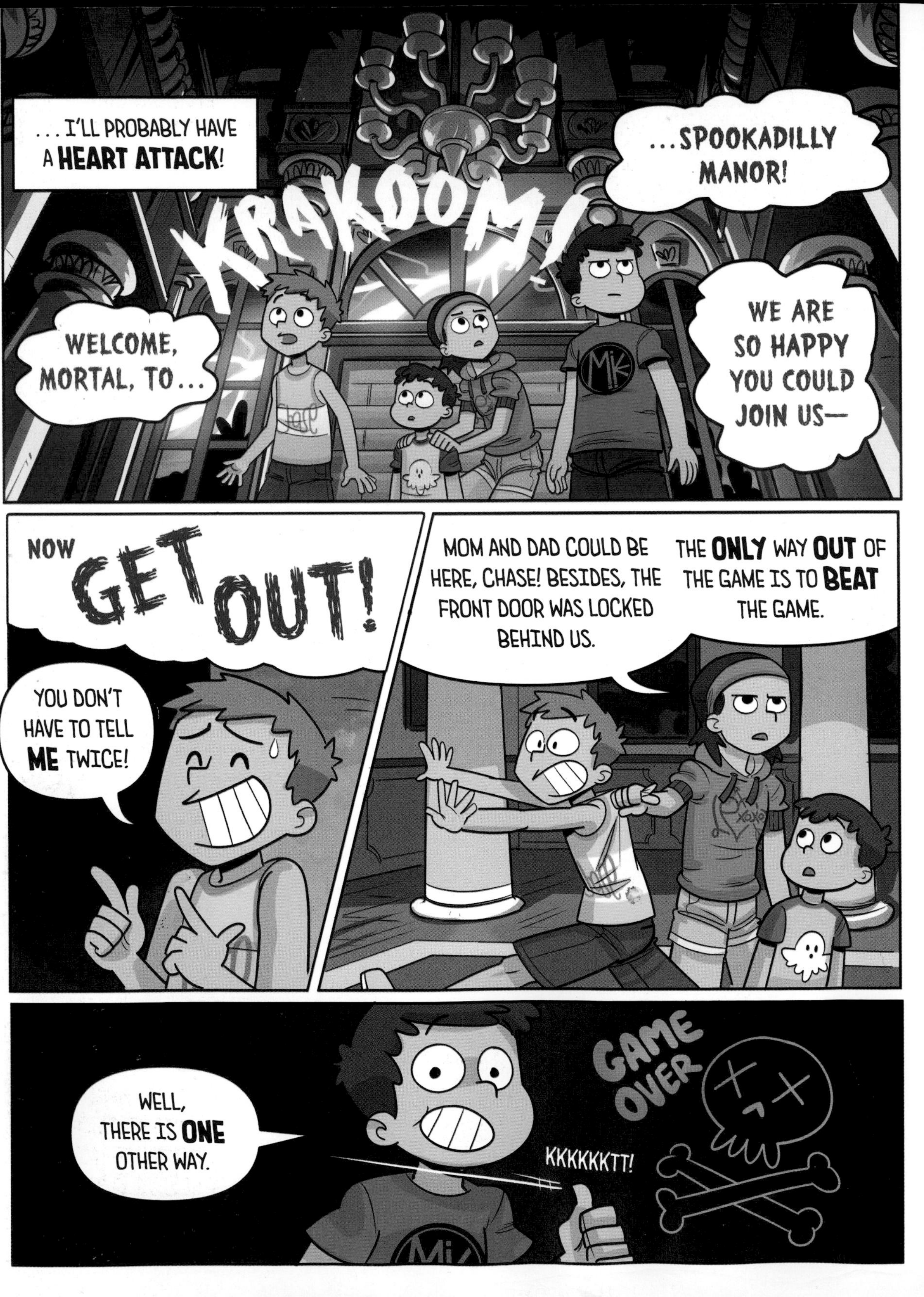

. . . I'LL PROBABLY HAVE A **HEART ATTACK**!
. . . SPOOKADILLY MANOR!
KRAKOOM!
WELCOME, MORTAL, TO . . .
WE ARE SO HAPPY YOU COULD JOIN US—
NOW GET OUT!
YOU DON'T HAVE TO TELL **ME** TWICE!
MOM AND DAD COULD BE HERE, CHASE! BESIDES, THE FRONT DOOR WAS LOCKED BEHIND US.
THE **ONLY** WAY **OUT** OF THE GAME IS TO **BEAT** THE GAME.
WELL, THERE IS **ONE** OTHER WAY.
KKKKKKTT!
GAME OVER

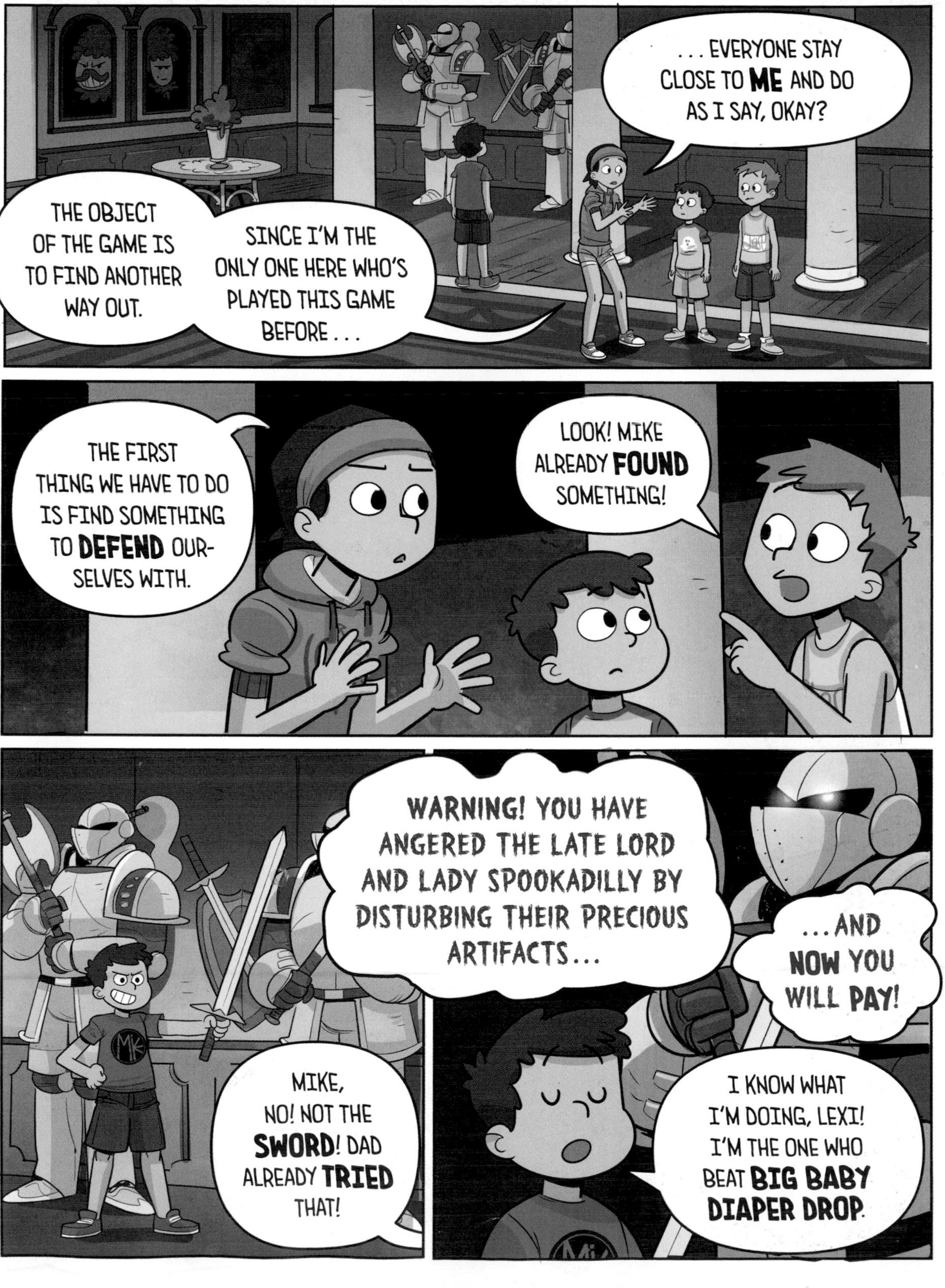
THE OBJECT OF THE GAME IS TO FIND ANOTHER WAY OUT.
SINCE I'M THE ONLY ONE HERE WHO'S PLAYED THIS GAME BEFORE . . .
. . . EVERYONE STAY CLOSE TO ME AND DO AS I SAY, OKAY?
THE FIRST THING WE HAVE TO DO IS FIND SOMETHING TO DEFEND OUR-SELVES WITH.
LOOK! MIKE ALREADY FOUND SOMETHING!
WARNING! YOU HAVE ANGERED THE LATE LORD AND LADY SPOOKADILLY BY DISTURBING THEIR PRECIOUS ARTIFACTS...
...AND NOW YOU WILL PAY!
MIKE, NO! NOT THE SWORD! DAD ALREADY TRIED THAT!
I KNOW WHAT I'M DOING, LEXI! I'M THE ONE WHO BEAT BIG BABY DIAPER DROP.

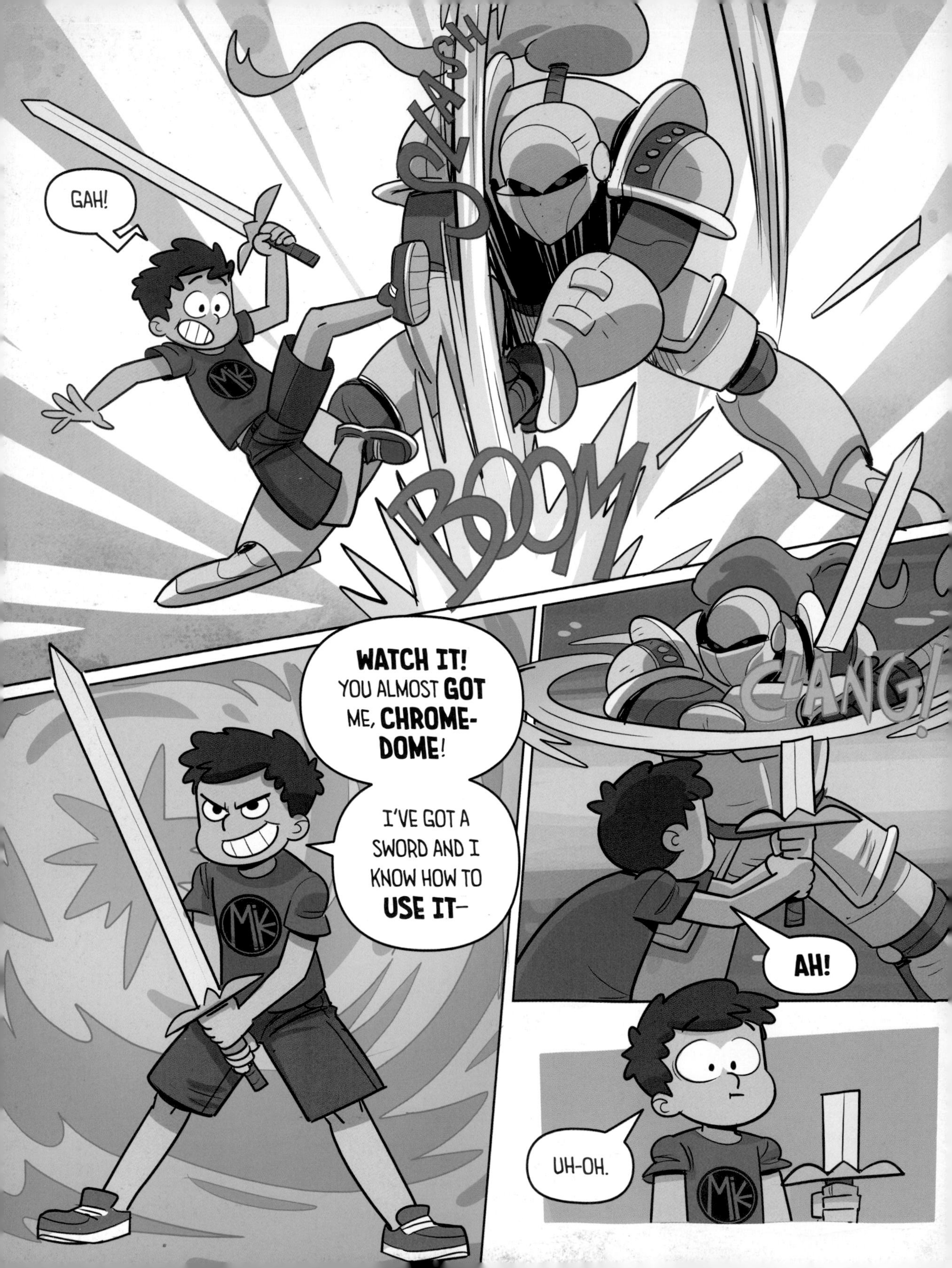
SLASH
GAH!
BOOM
WATCH IT! YOU ALMOST GOT ME, CHROME-DOME!
I'VE GOT A SWORD AND I KNOW HOW TO USE IT–
CLANG!
AH!
UH-OH.

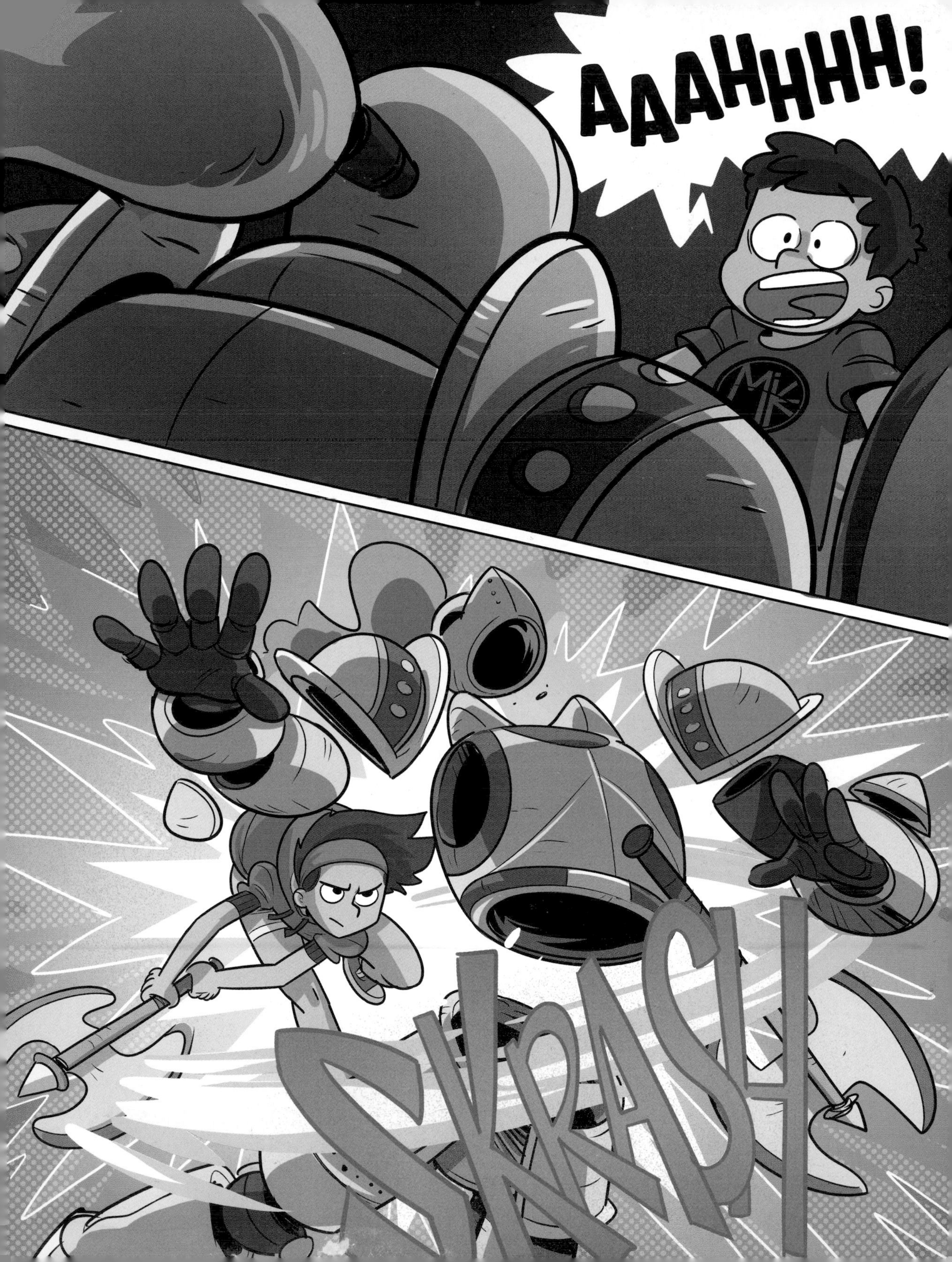
AAAHHHH!
SKRASH

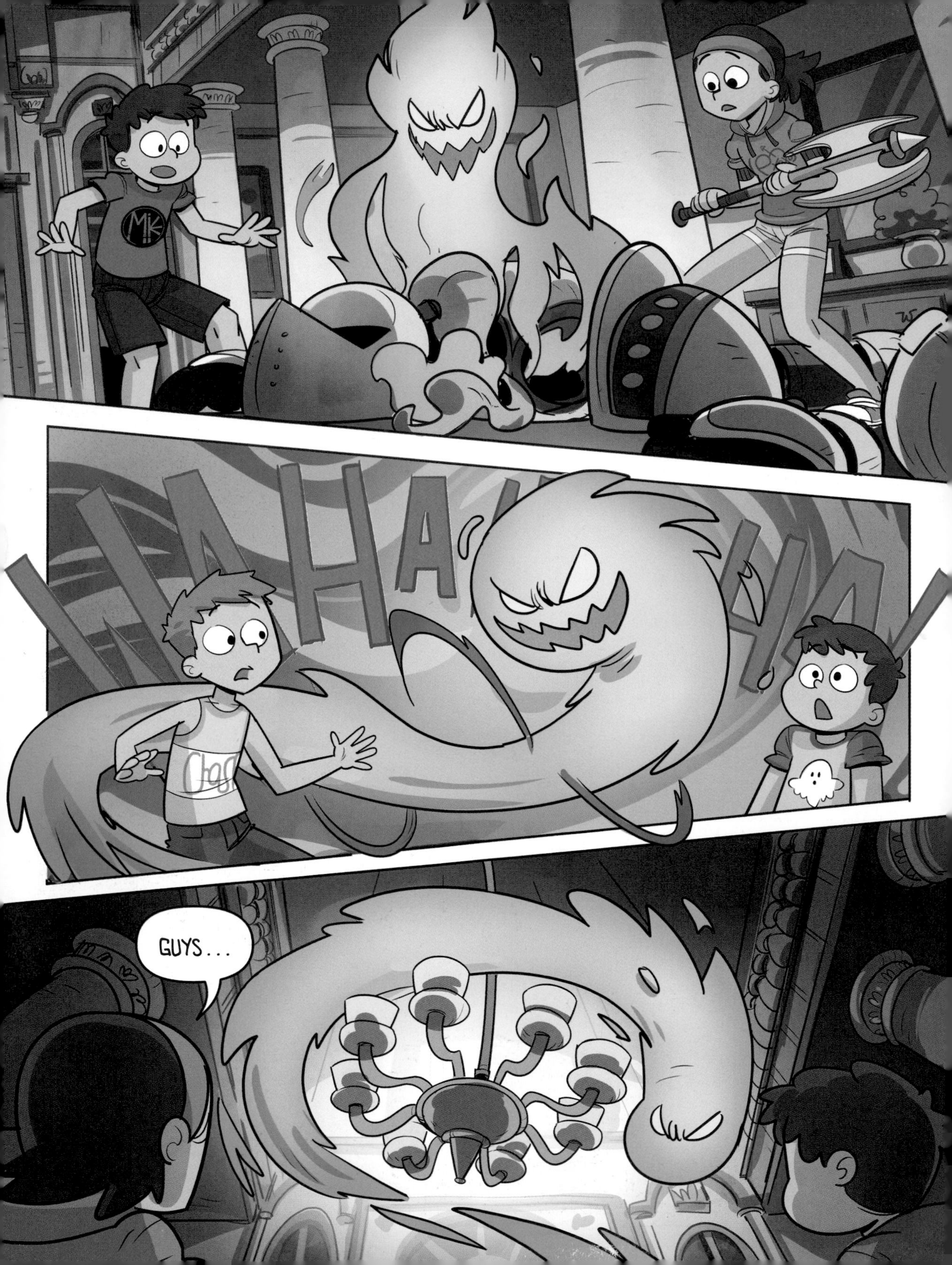
HAHA
GUYS . . .

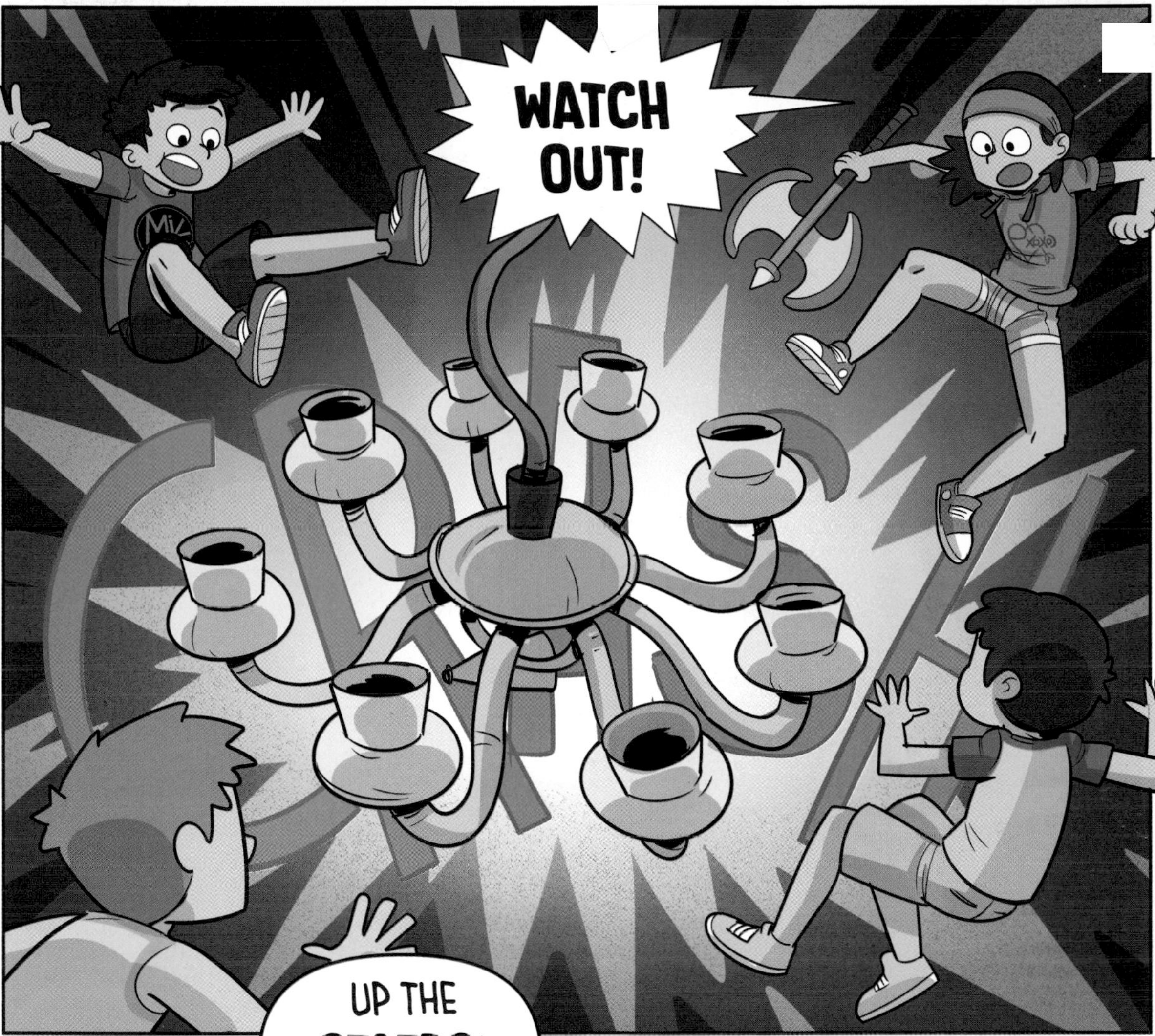
WATCH OUT!

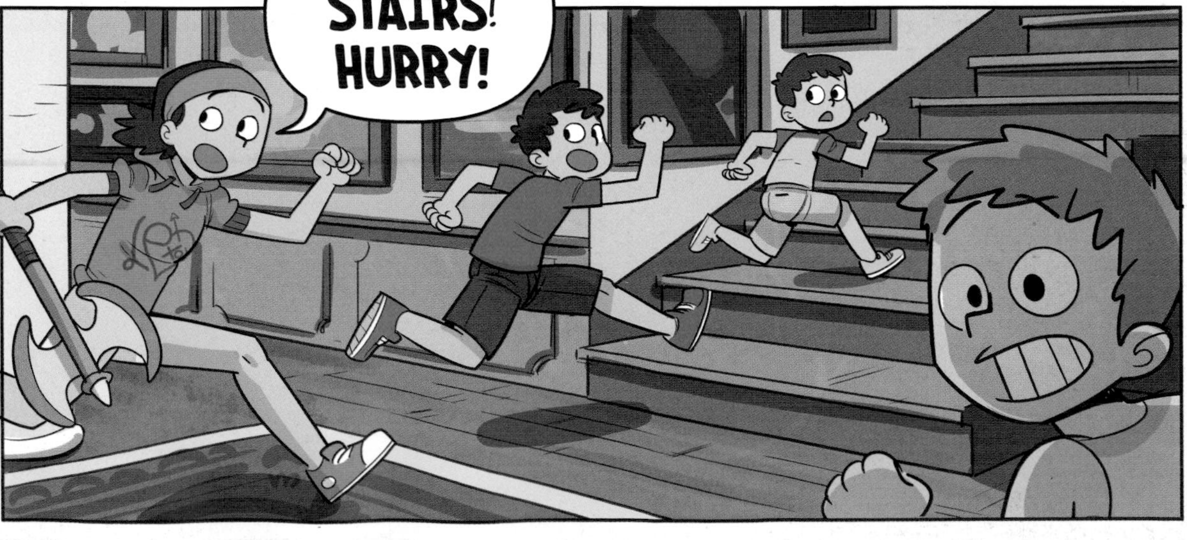
UP THE STAIRS! HURRY!

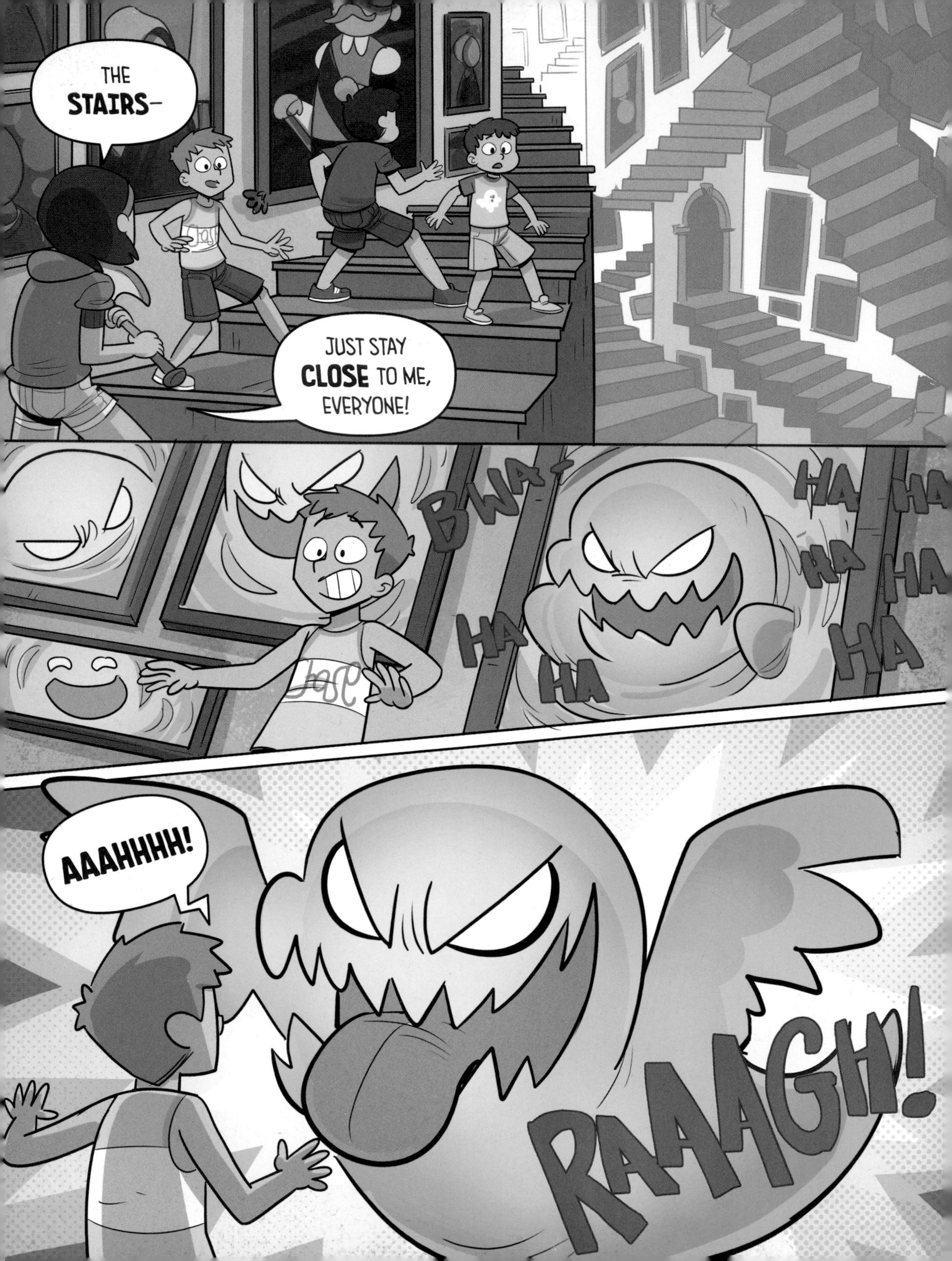
THE STAIRS–
JUST STAY CLOSE TO ME, EVERYONE!
BWA-HA HA HA HA HA HA HA
AAAHHHH!
RAAAGH!

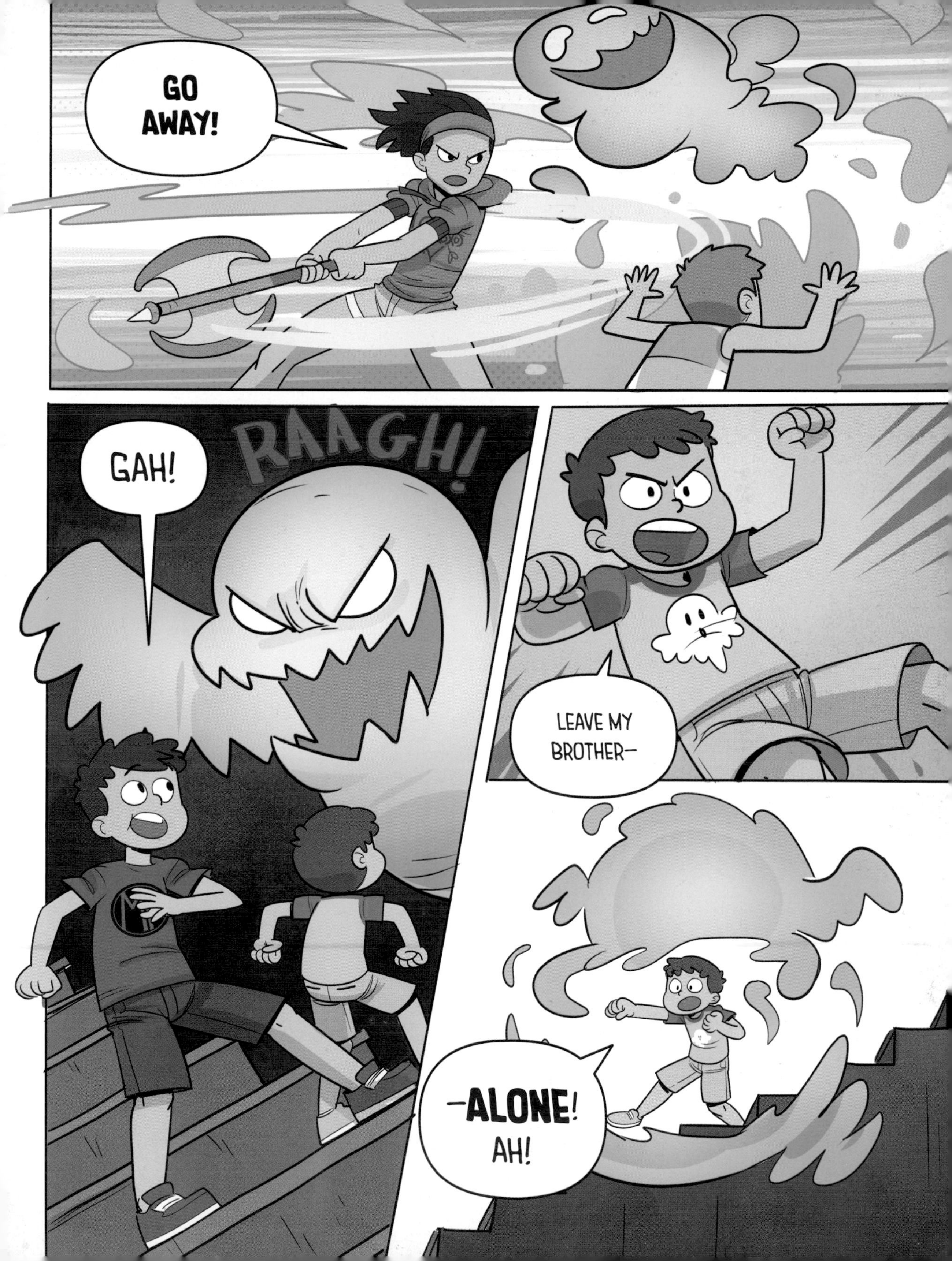
GO AWAY!
RAAGH!
GAH!
LEAVE MY BROTHER—
—ALONE! AH!

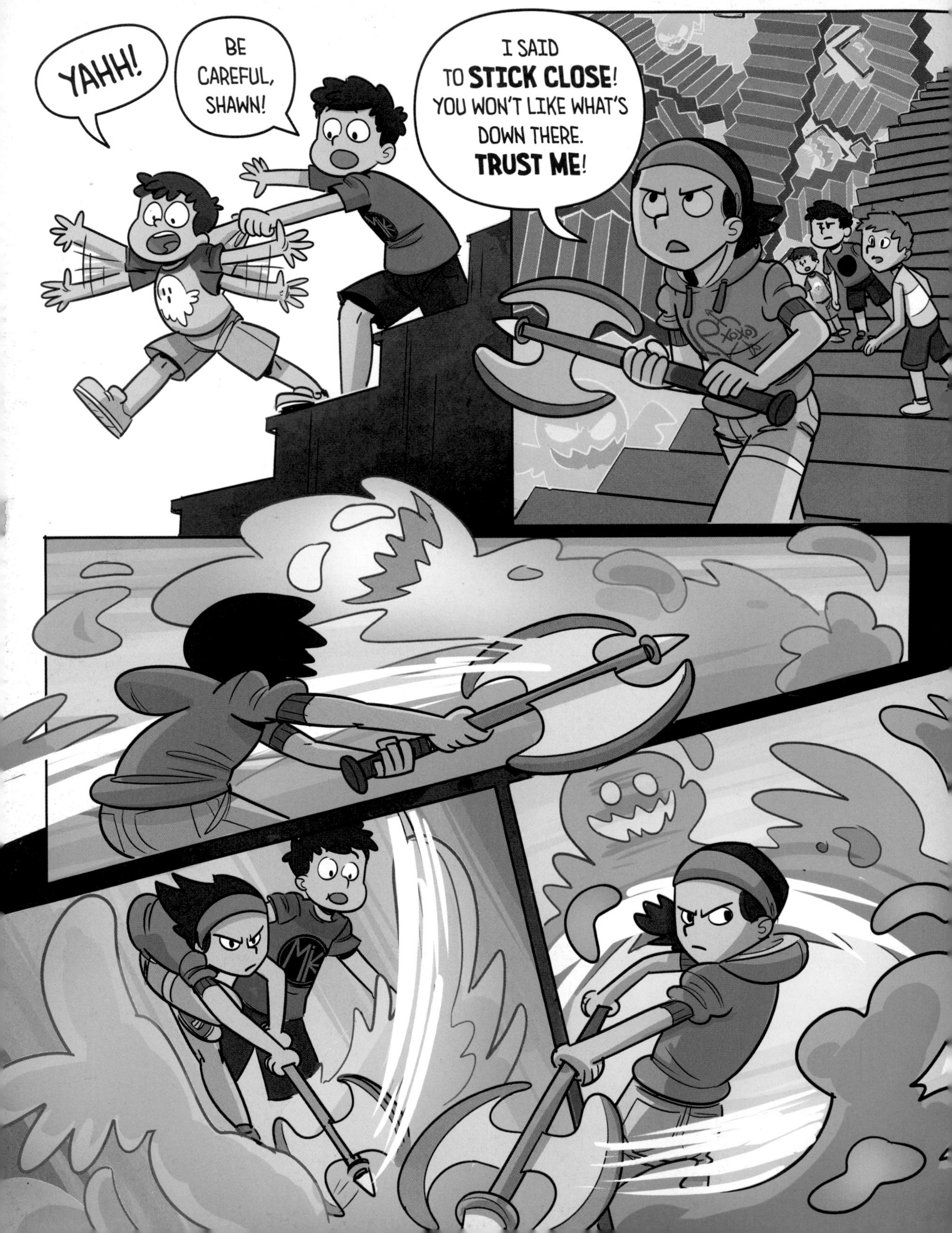
YAHH!
BE CAREFUL, SHAWN!
I SAID TO **STICK CLOSE**! YOU WON'T LIKE WHAT'S DOWN THERE. **TRUST ME**!

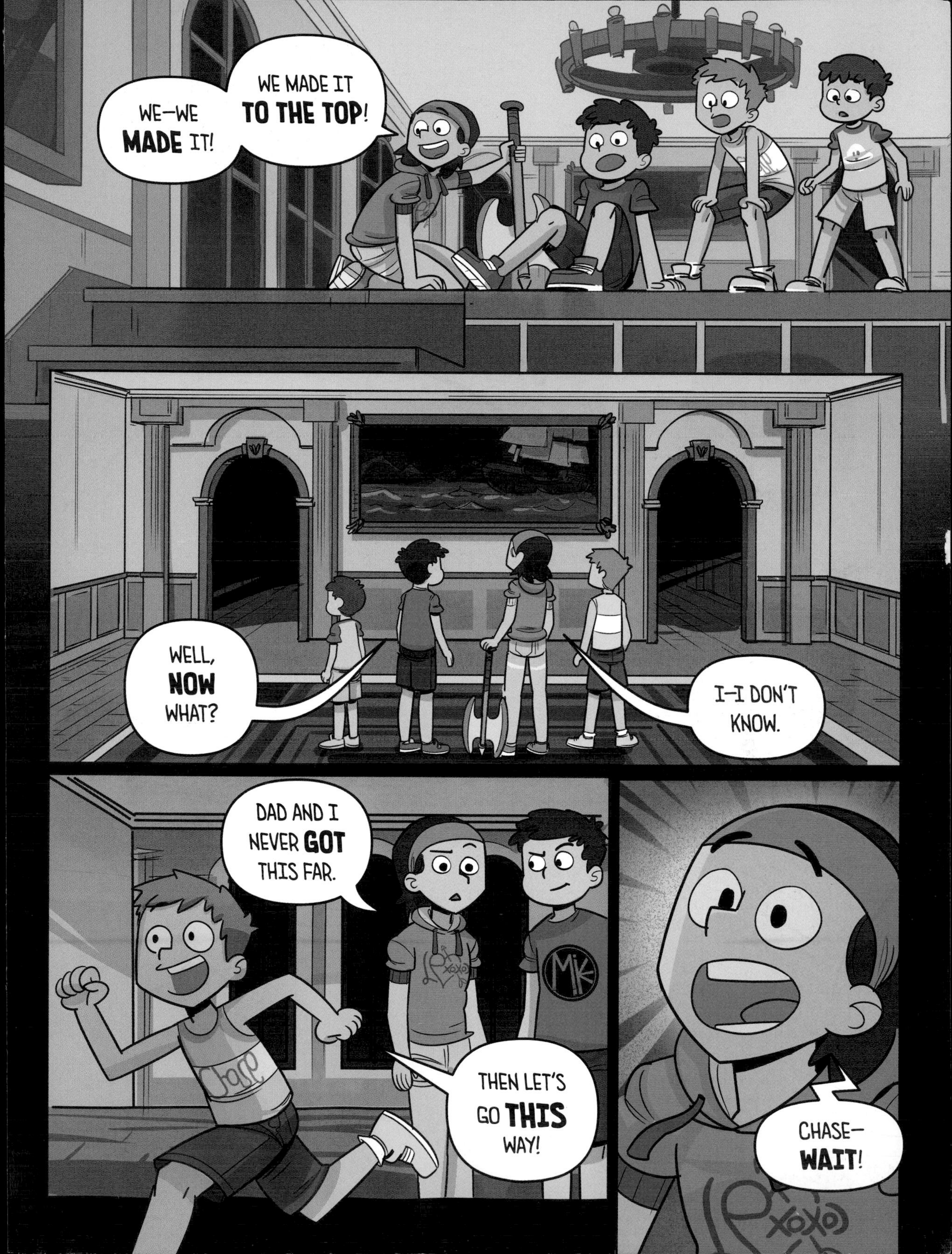

WE—WE **MADE** IT!
WE MADE IT **TO THE TOP**!
WELL, **NOW** WHAT?
I—I DON'T KNOW.
DAD AND I NEVER **GOT** THIS FAR.
THEN LET'S GO **THIS** WAY!
CHASE— **WAIT**!

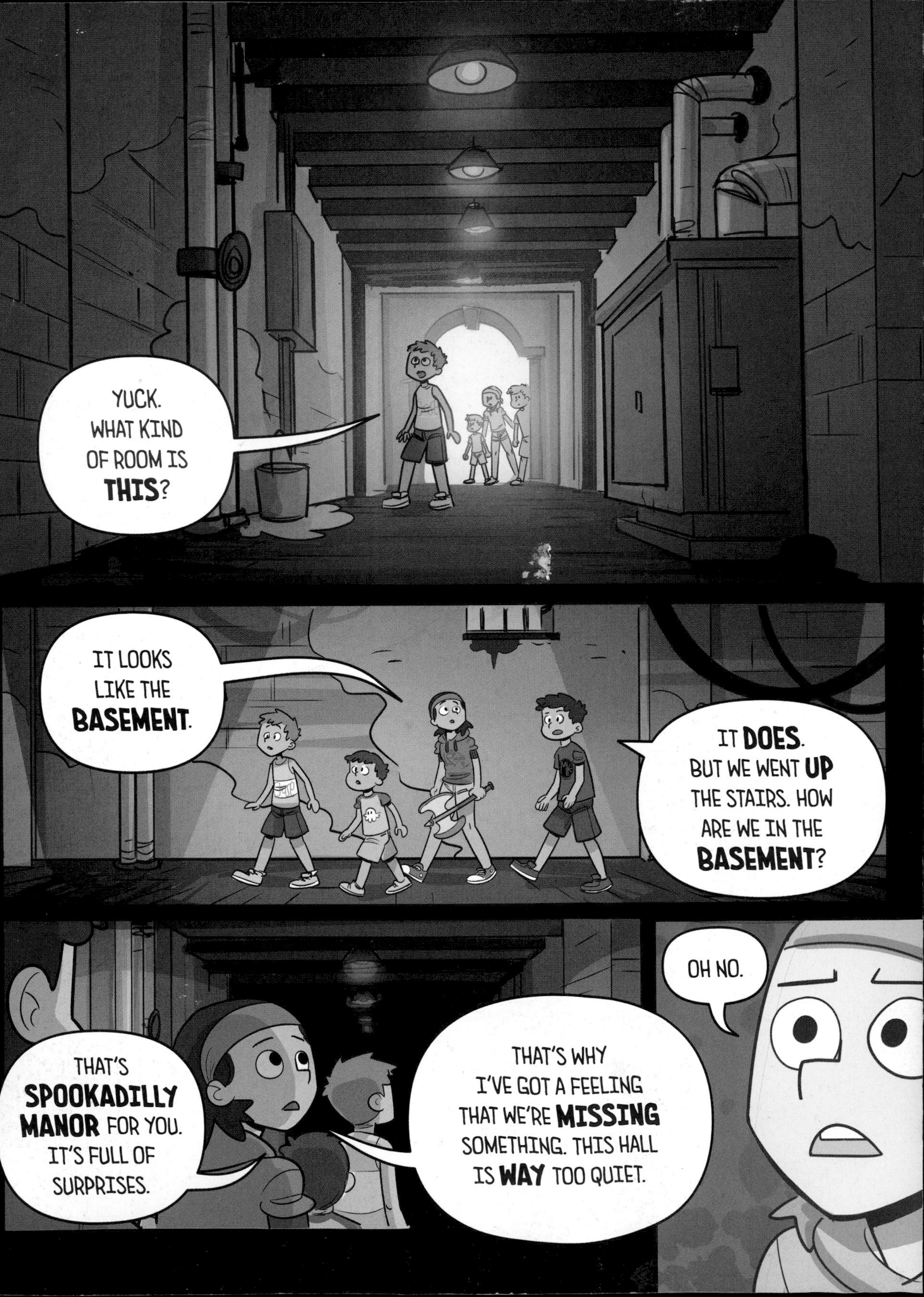
YUCK. WHAT KIND OF ROOM IS THIS?
IT LOOKS LIKE THE BASEMENT.
IT DOES. BUT WE WENT UP THE STAIRS. HOW ARE WE IN THE BASEMENT?
THAT'S SPOOKADILLY MANOR FOR YOU. IT'S FULL OF SURPRISES.
THAT'S WHY I'VE GOT A FEELING THAT WE'RE MISSING SOMETHING. THIS HALL IS WAY TOO QUIET.
OH NO.

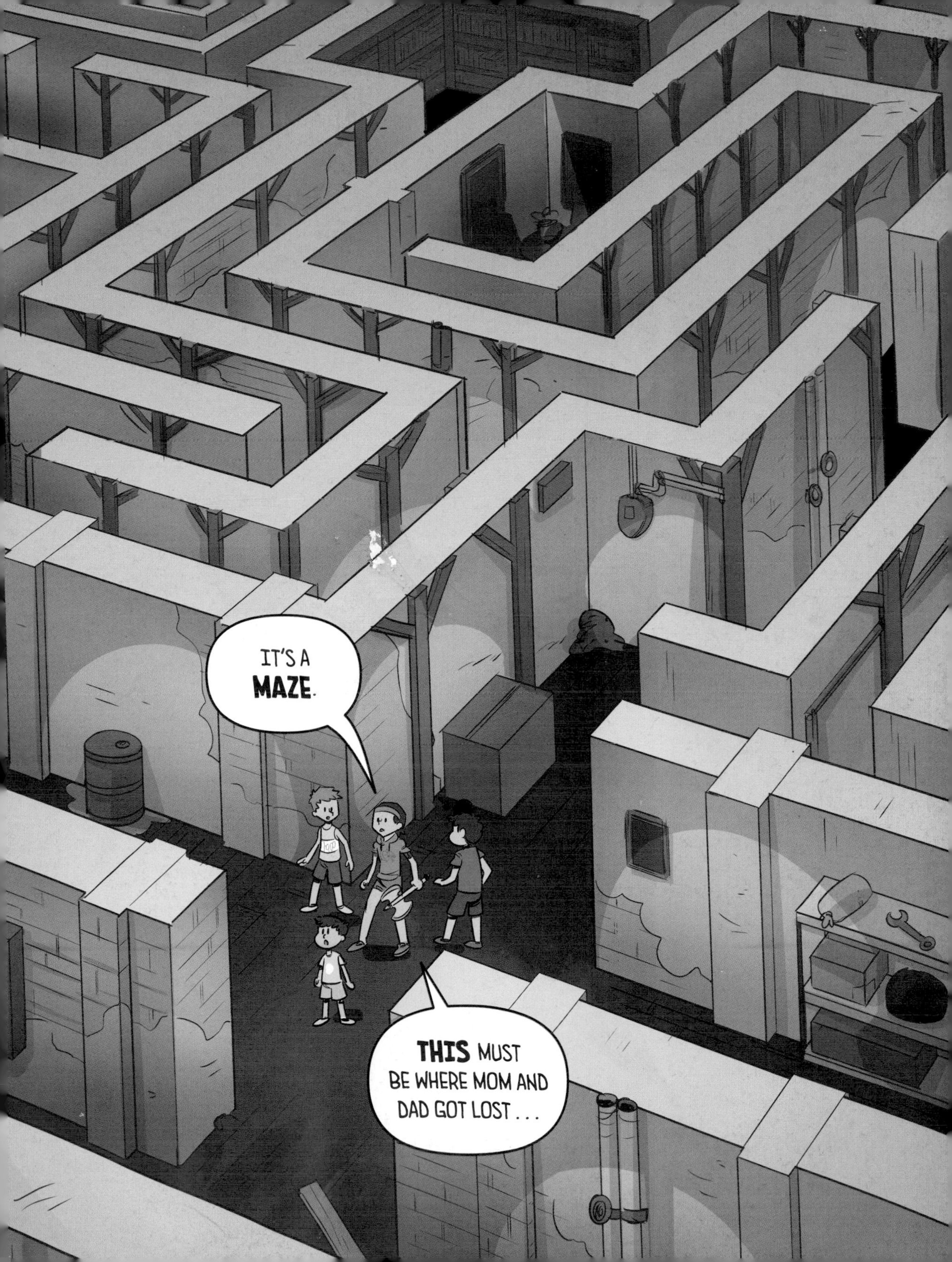
IT'S A **MAZE**.
THIS MUST BE WHERE MOM AND DAD GOT LOST . . .

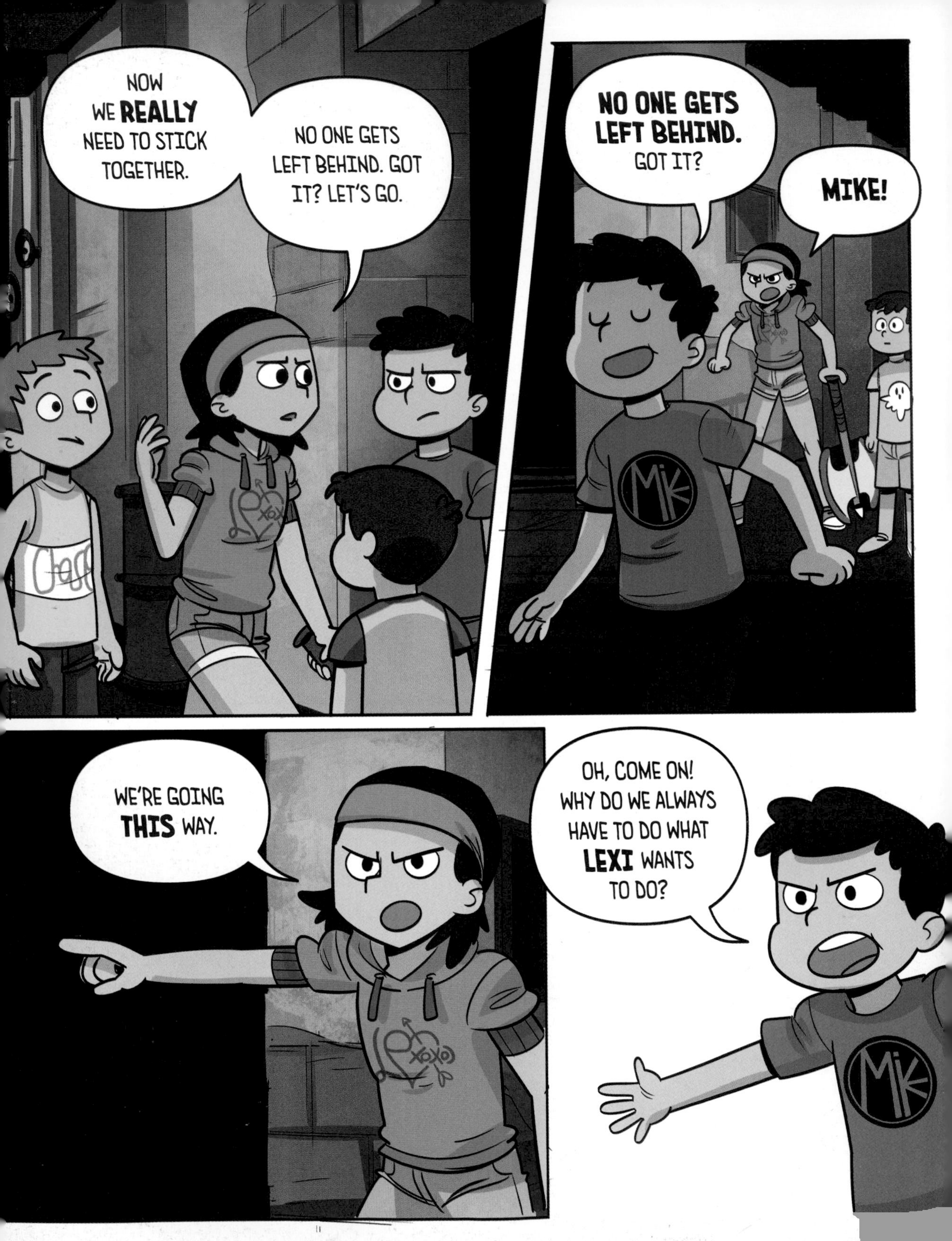
NOW WE **REALLY** NEED TO STICK TOGETHER.
NO ONE GETS LEFT BEHIND. GOT IT? LET'S GO.
NO ONE GETS LEFT BEHIND. GOT IT?
MIKE!
WE'RE GOING **THIS** WAY.
OH, COME ON! WHY DO WE ALWAYS HAVE TO DO WHAT **LEXI** WANTS TO DO?

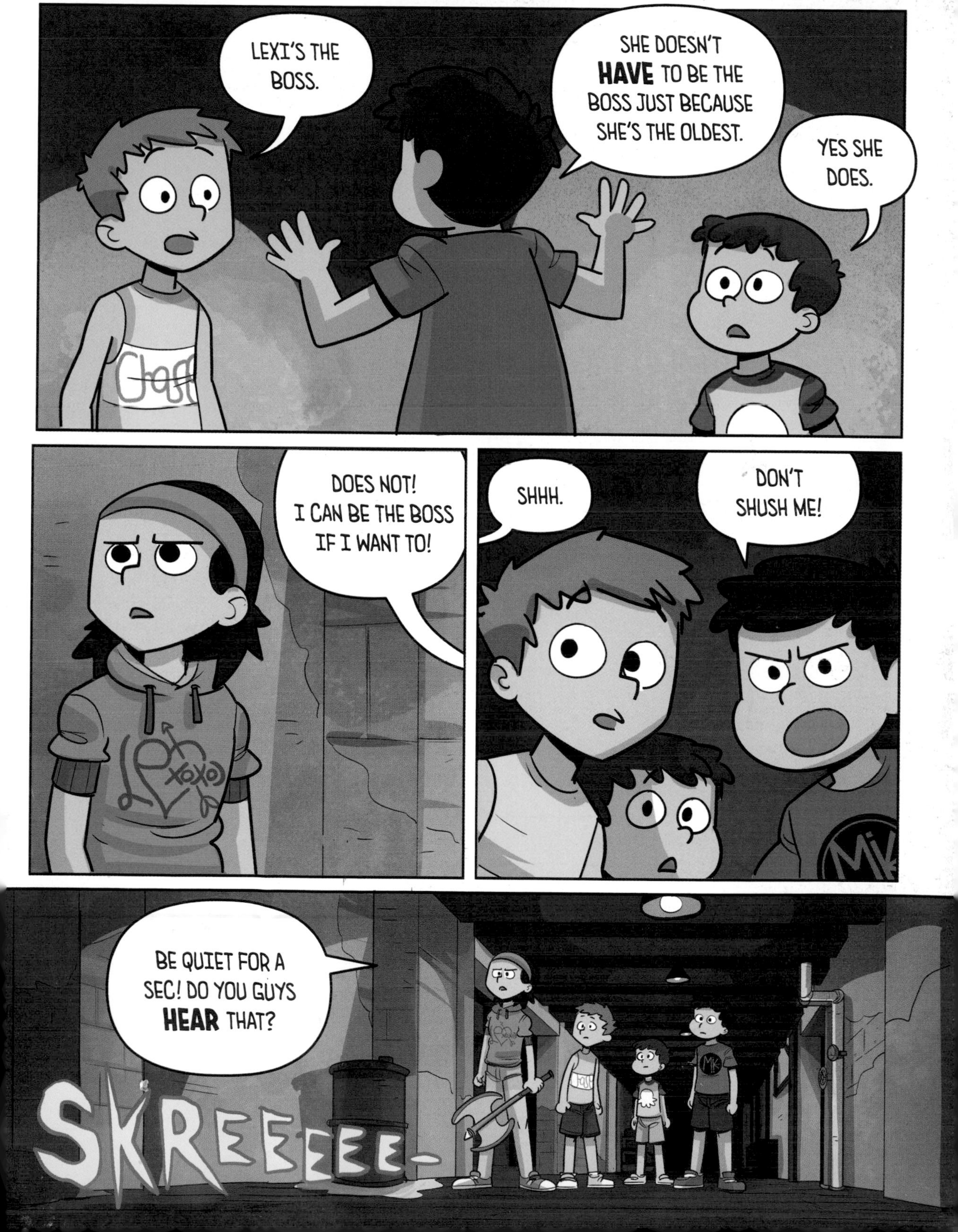
LEXI'S THE BOSS.
SHE DOESN'T **HAVE** TO BE THE BOSS JUST BECAUSE SHE'S THE OLDEST.
YES SHE DOES.
DOES NOT! I CAN BE THE BOSS IF I WANT TO!
SHHH.
DON'T SHUSH ME!
BE QUIET FOR A SEC! DO YOU GUYS **HEAR** THAT?
SKREEEEEE-

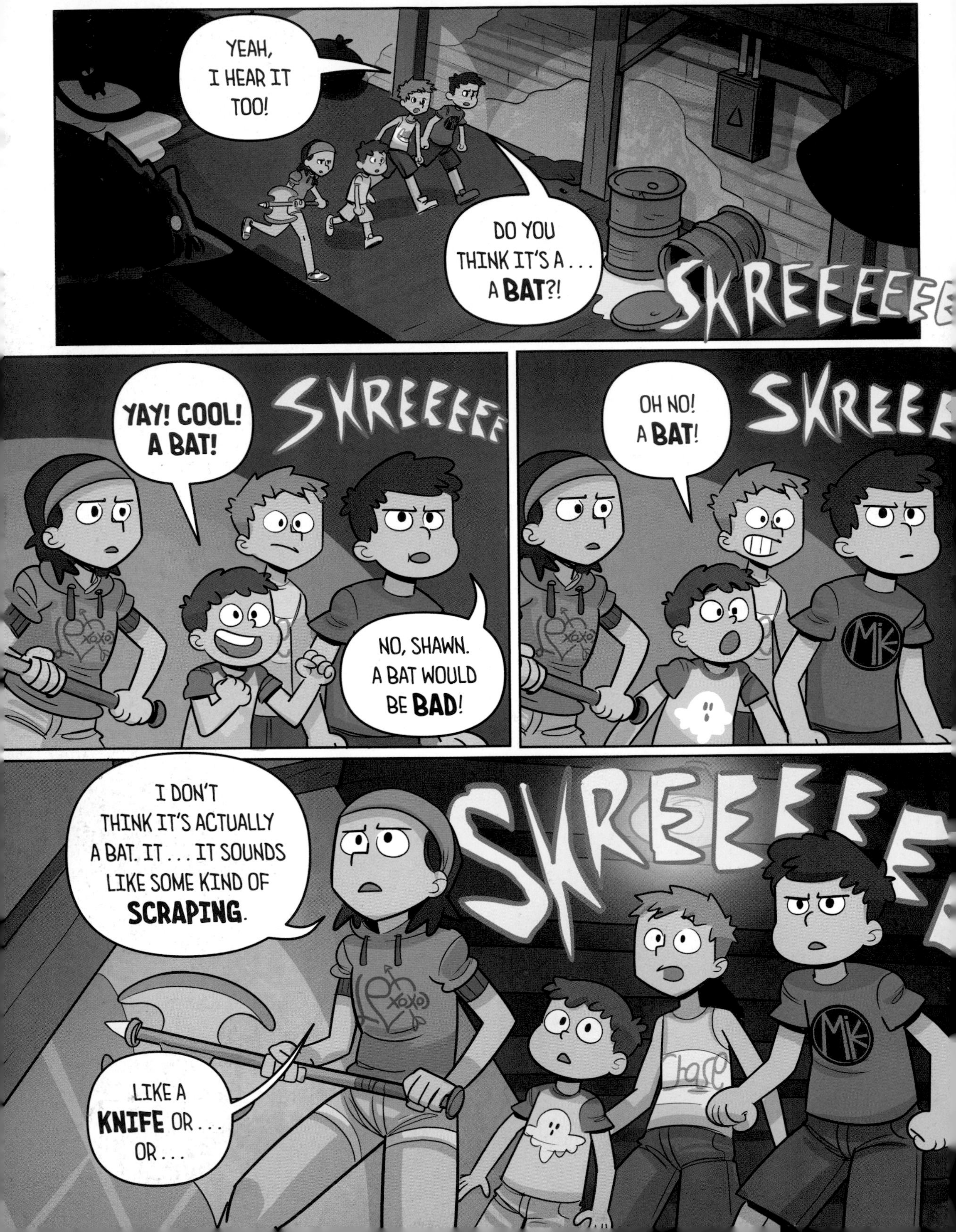
YEAH, I HEAR IT TOO!
DO YOU THINK IT'S A . . . A **BAT**?!
SKREEEEEE
YAY! COOL! A BAT!
SKREEEEE
NO, SHAWN. A BAT WOULD BE **BAD**!
OH NO! A **BAT**!
SKREEE
I DON'T THINK IT'S ACTUALLY A BAT. IT . . . IT SOUNDS LIKE SOME KIND OF **SCRAPING**.
SKREEEEE
LIKE A **KNIFE** OR . . . OR . . .

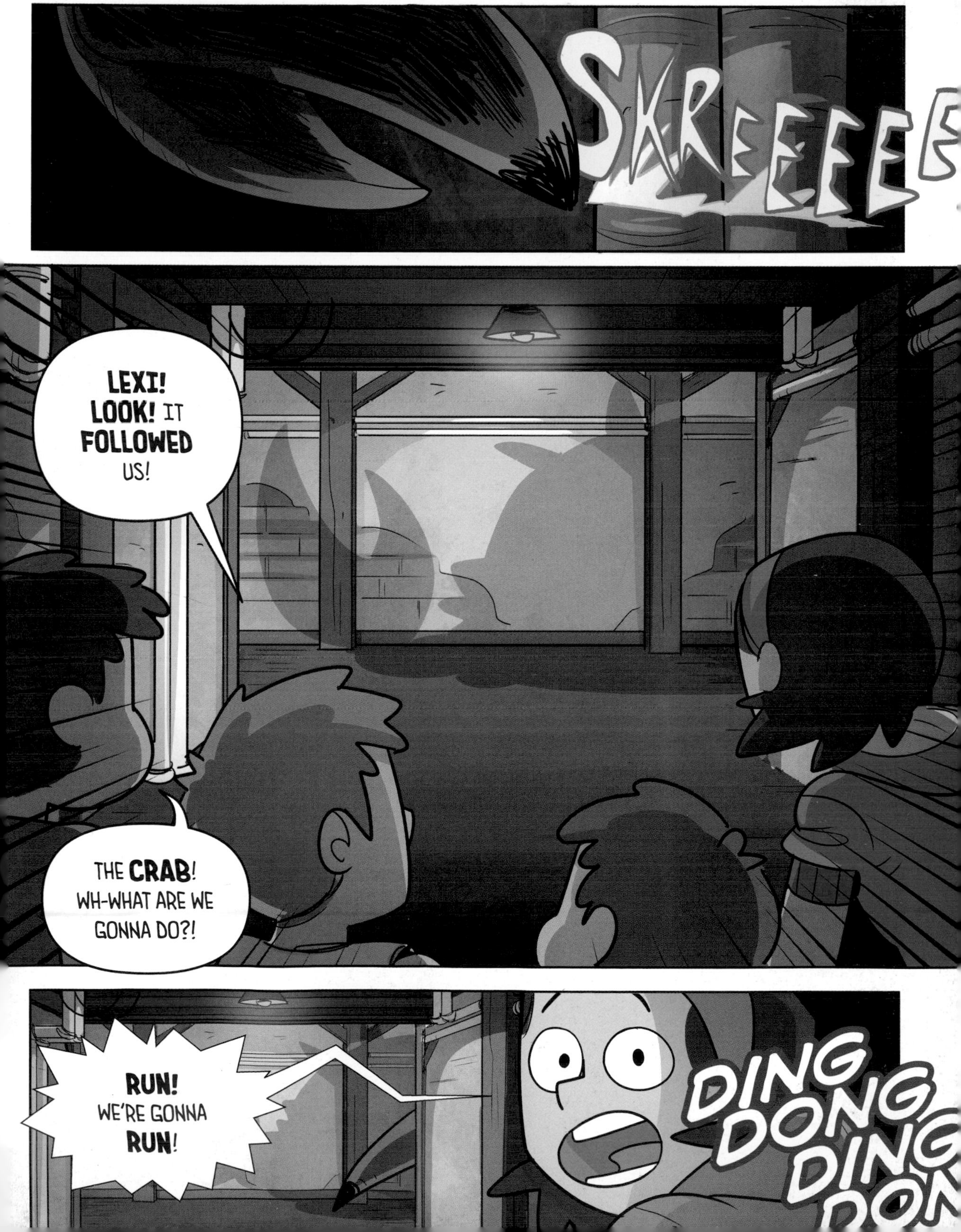
SKREEEEE
LEXI! LOOK! IT FOLLOWED US!
THE CRAB! WH-WHAT ARE WE GONNA DO?!
RUN! WE'RE GONNA RUN!
DING DONG DING

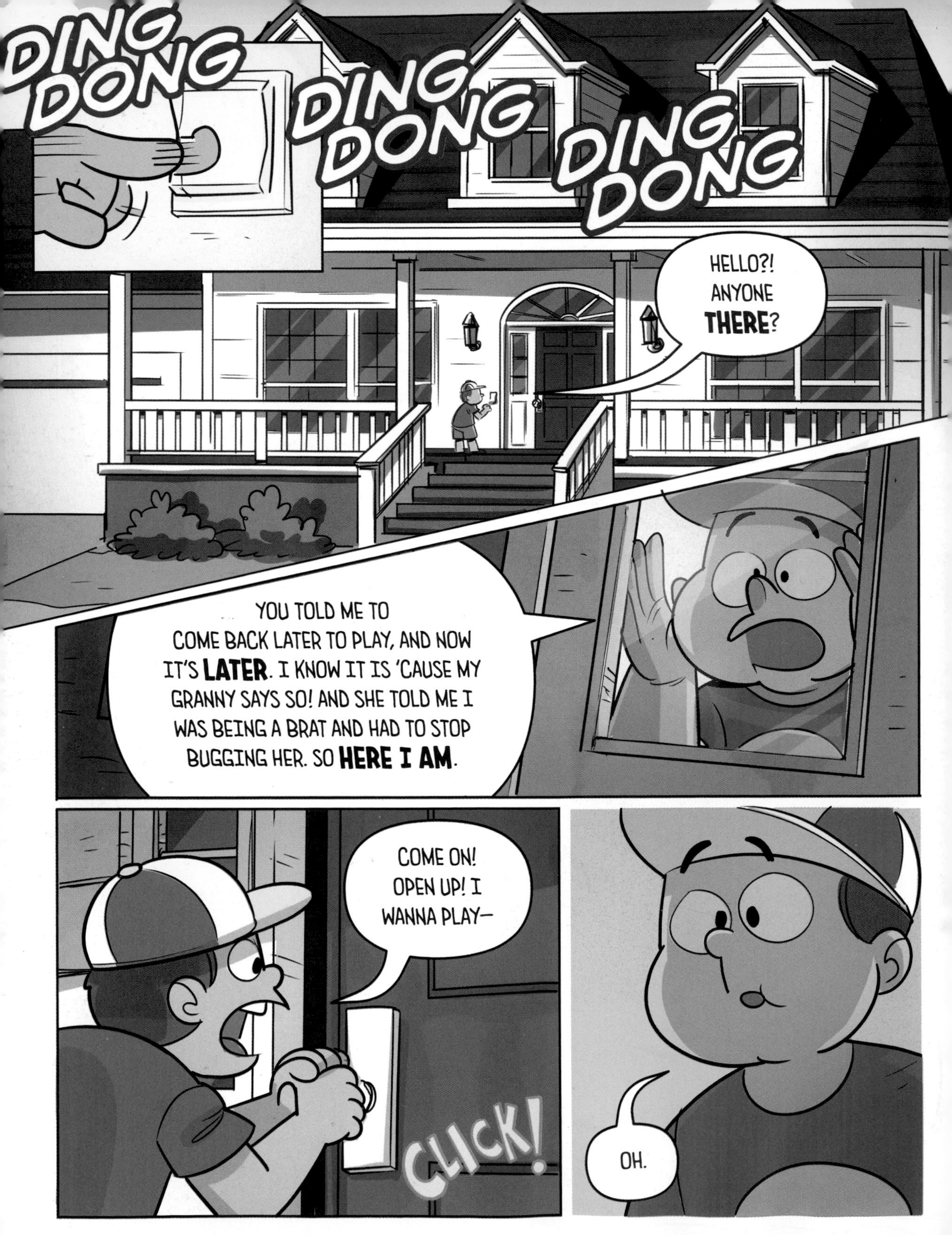
DING DONG
DING DONG
DING DONG
HELLO?! ANYONE THERE?
YOU TOLD ME TO COME BACK LATER TO PLAY, AND NOW IT'S LATER. I KNOW IT IS 'CAUSE MY GRANNY SAYS SO! AND SHE TOLD ME I WAS BEING A BRAT AND HAD TO STOP BUGGING HER. SO HERE I AM.
COME ON! OPEN UP! I WANNA PLAY—
CLICK!
OH.

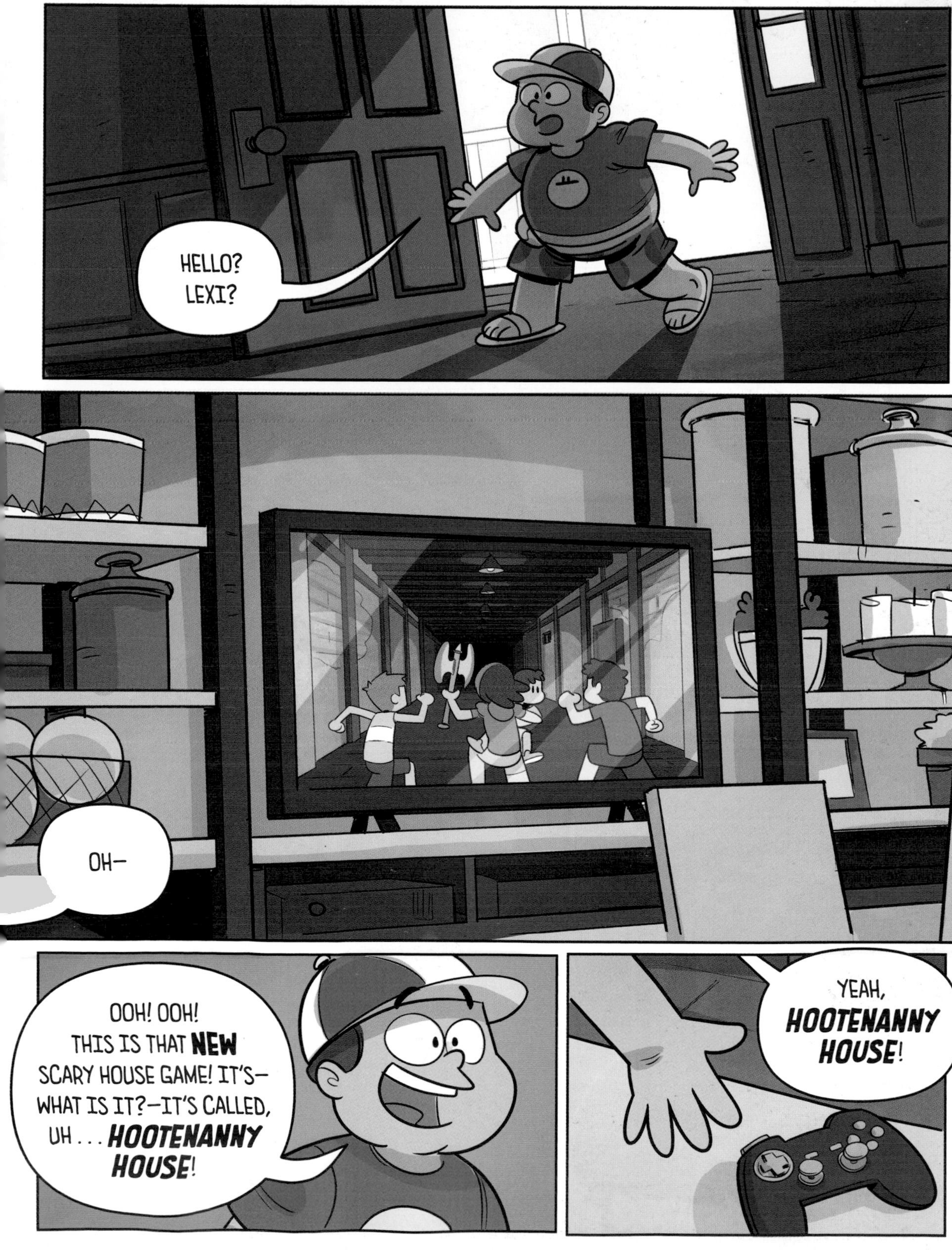
HELLO? LEXI?
OH—
OOH! OOH! THIS IS THAT **NEW** SCARY HOUSE GAME! IT'S— WHAT IS IT?—IT'S CALLED, UH . . . ***HOOTENANNY HOUSE***!
YEAH, ***HOOTENANNY HOUSE***!

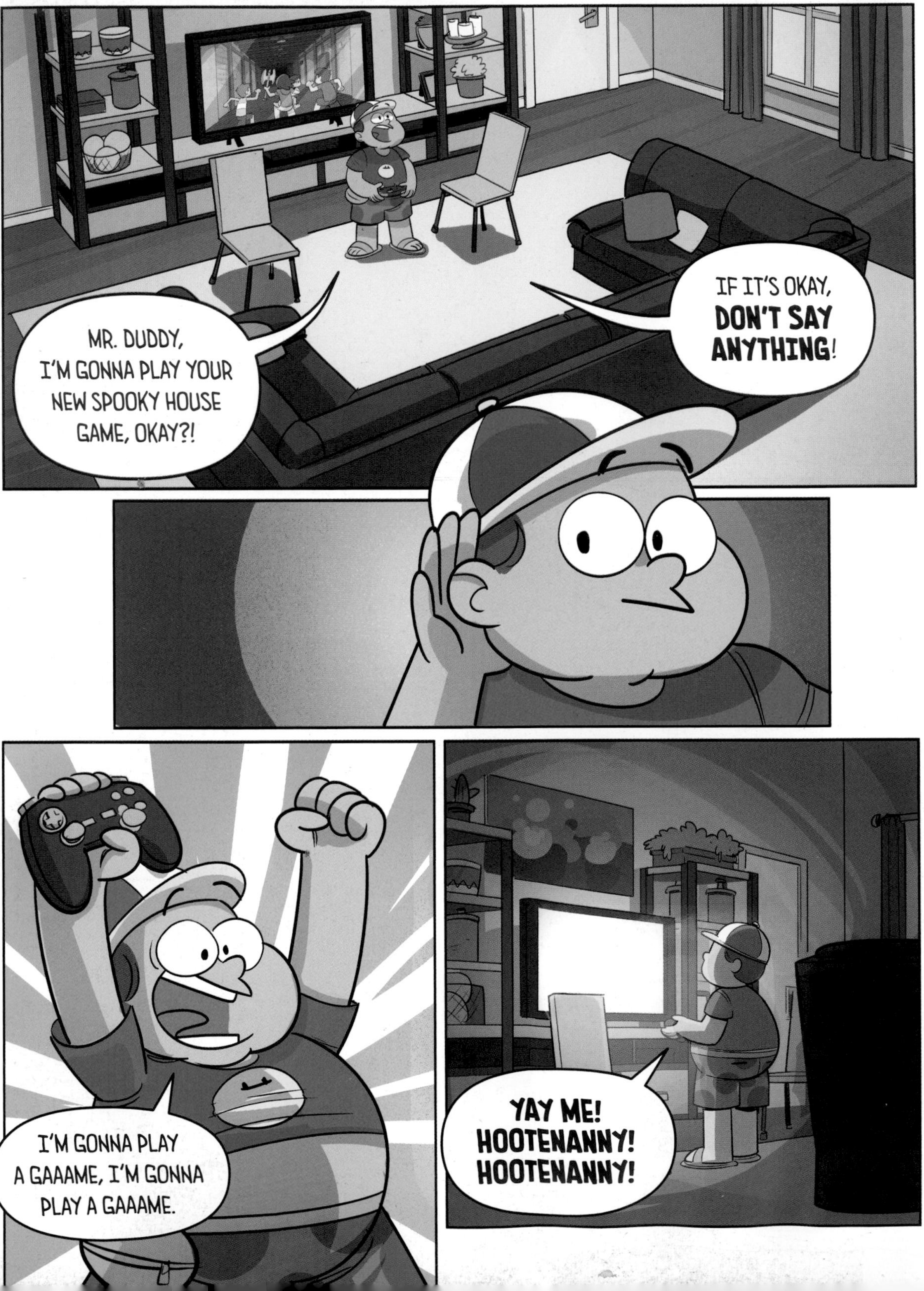
MR. DUDDY, I'M GONNA PLAY YOUR NEW SPOOKY HOUSE GAME, OKAY?!
IF IT'S OKAY, **DON'T SAY ANYTHING**!
I'M GONNA PLAY A GAAAME, I'M GONNA PLAY A GAAAME.
YAY ME! HOOTENANNY! HOOTENANNY!

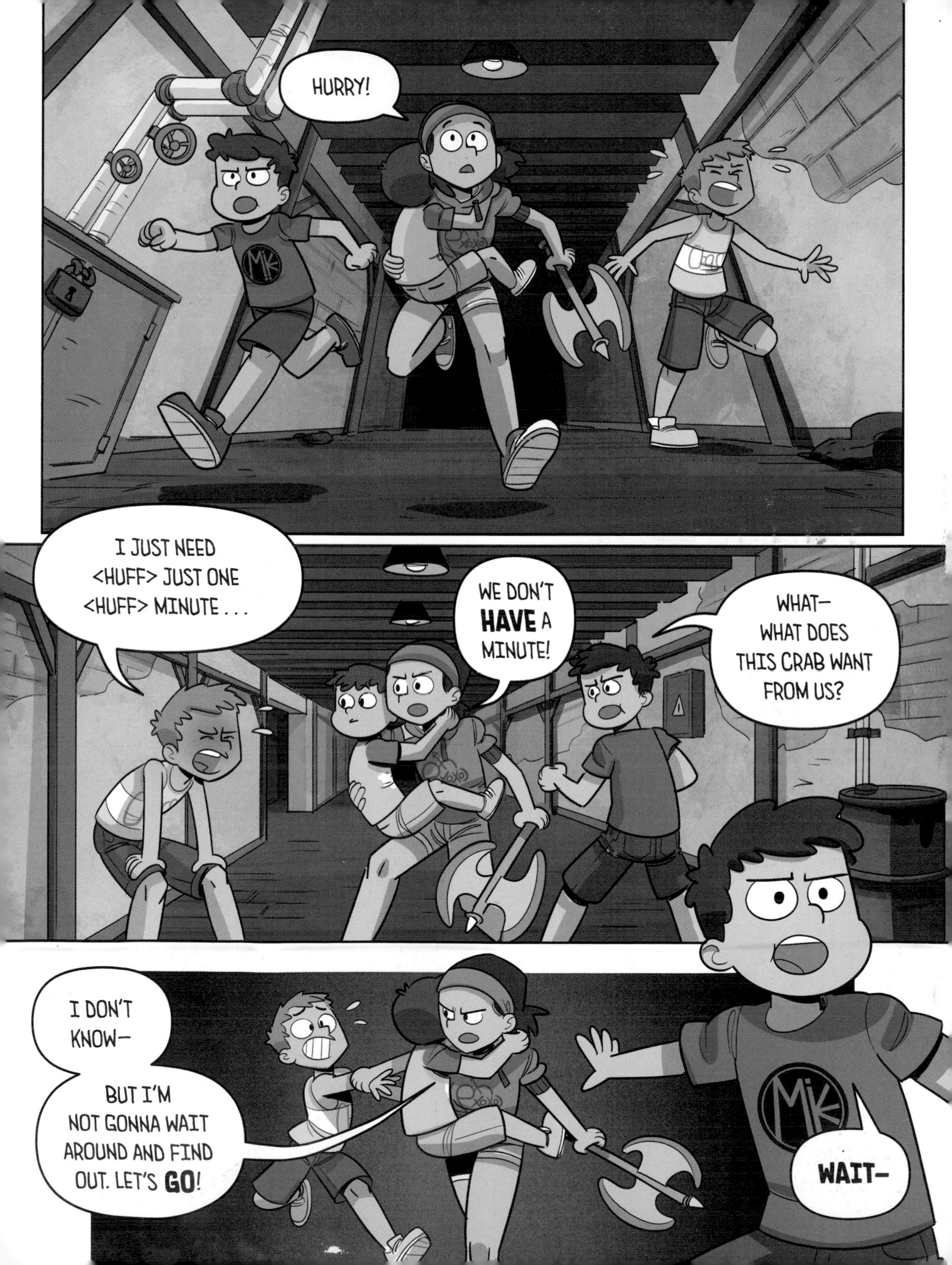
HURRY!
I JUST NEED <HUFF> JUST ONE <HUFF> MINUTE . . .
WE DON'T **HAVE** A MINUTE!
WHAT— WHAT DOES THIS CRAB WANT FROM US?
I DON'T KNOW—
BUT I'M NOT GONNA WAIT AROUND AND FIND OUT. LET'S **GO**!
WAIT—

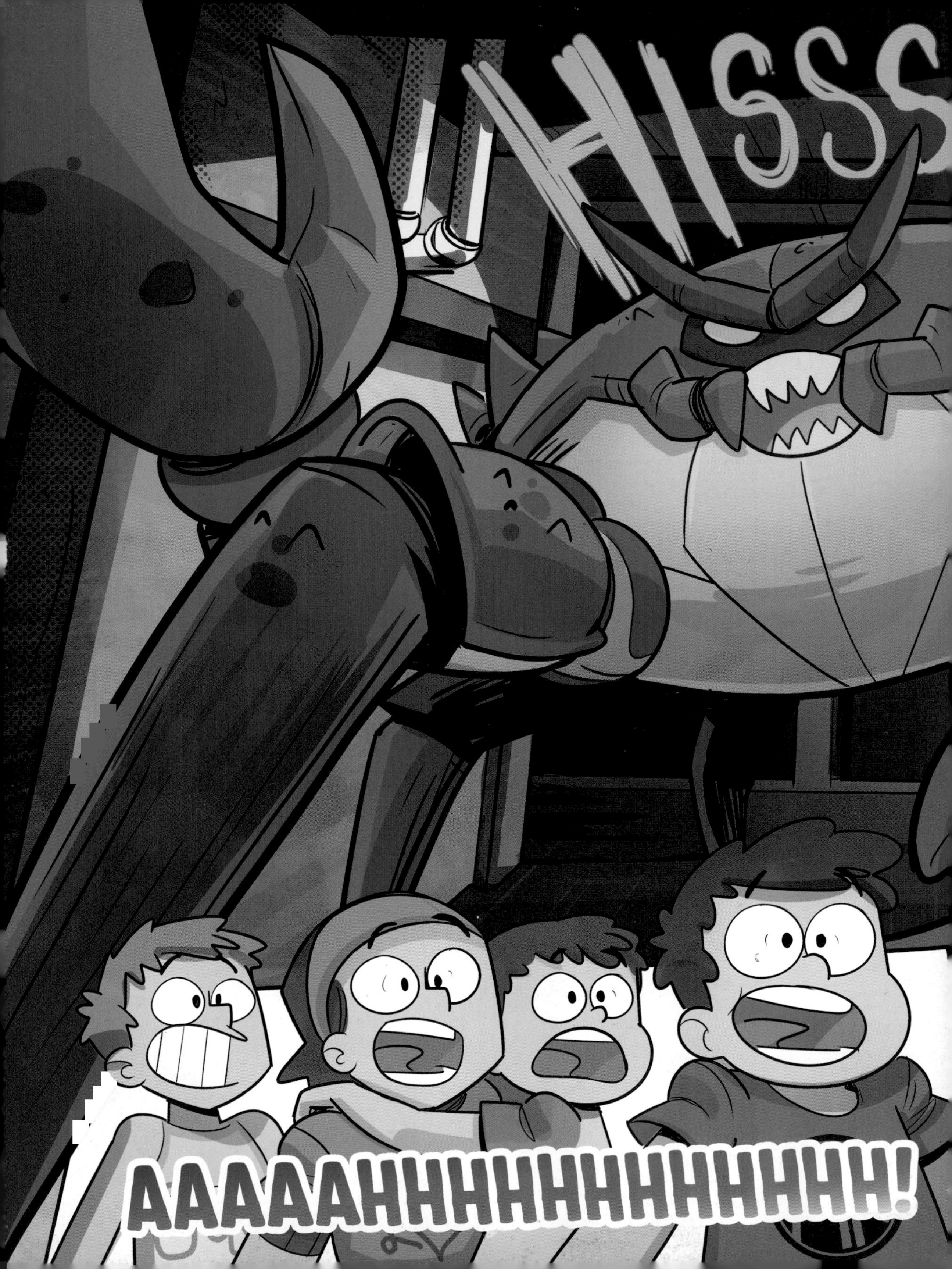
HISSS
AAAAAHHHHHHHHHHHHH!

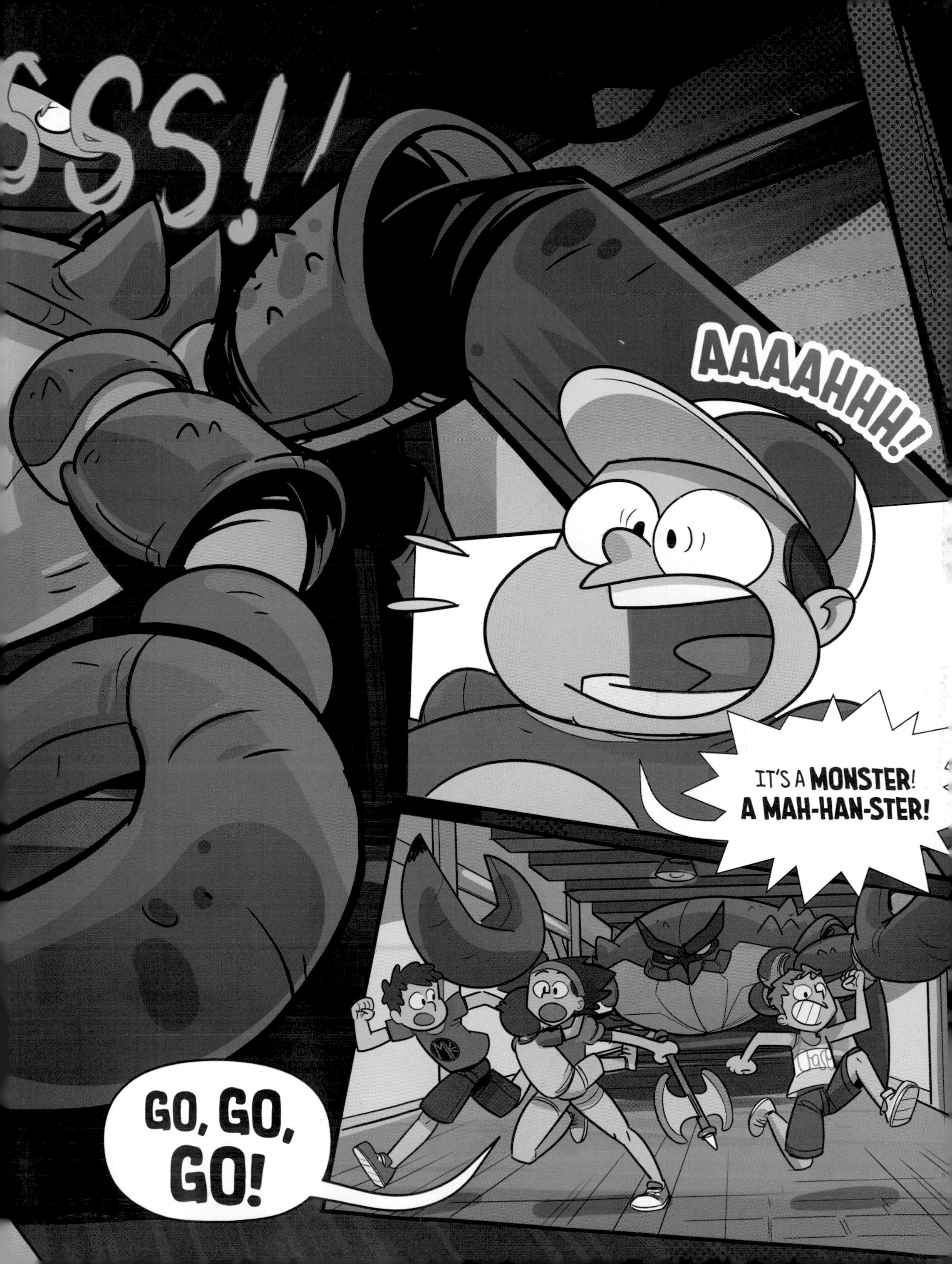
SSS!!
AAAAHHH!
IT'S A MONSTER! A MAH-HAN-STER!
GO, GO, GO!

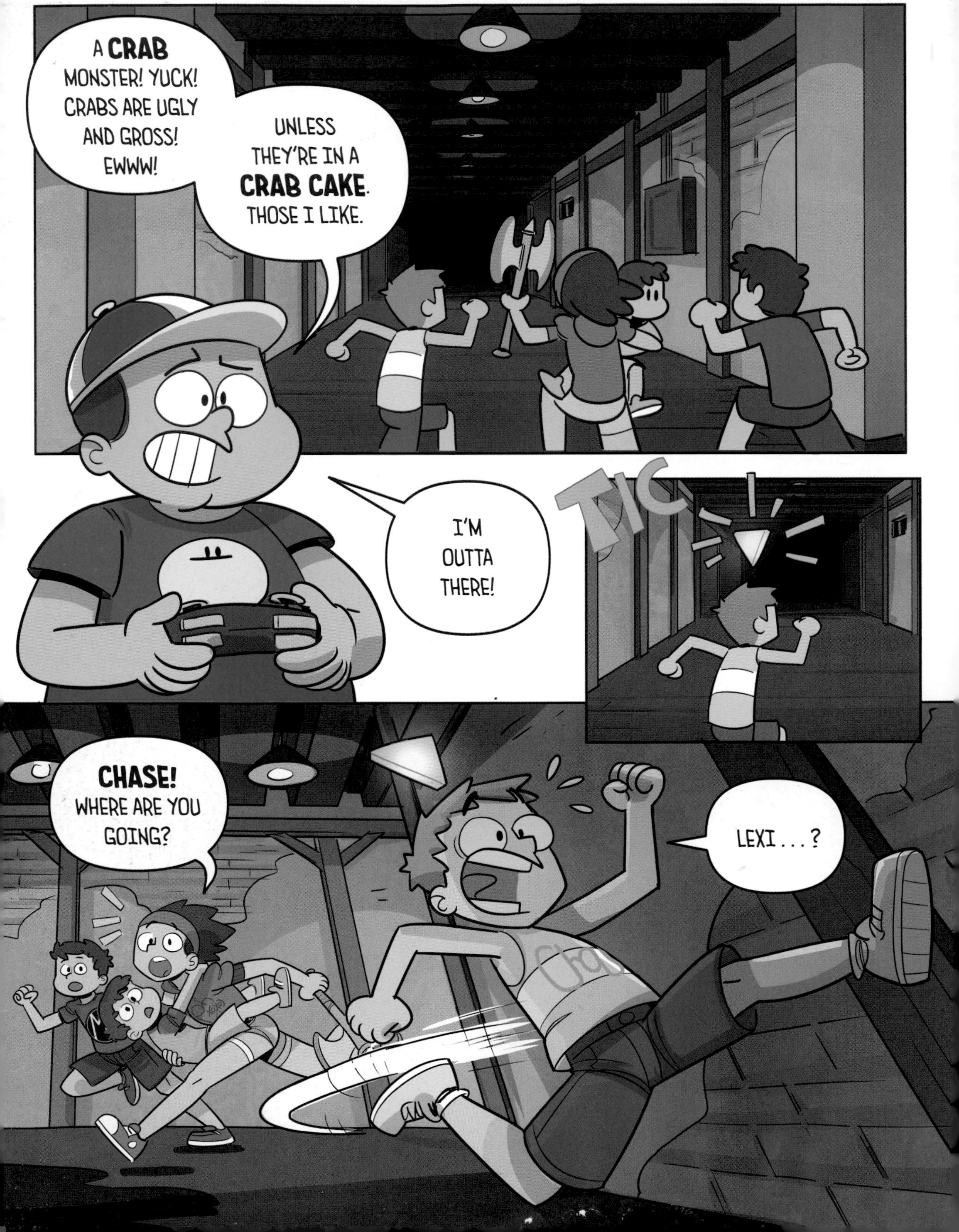
A CRAB MONSTER! YUCK! CRABS ARE UGLY AND GROSS! EWWW!
UNLESS THEY'RE IN A CRAB CAKE. THOSE I LIKE.
I'M OUTTA THERE!
TIC
CHASE! WHERE ARE YOU GOING?
LEXI . . . ?

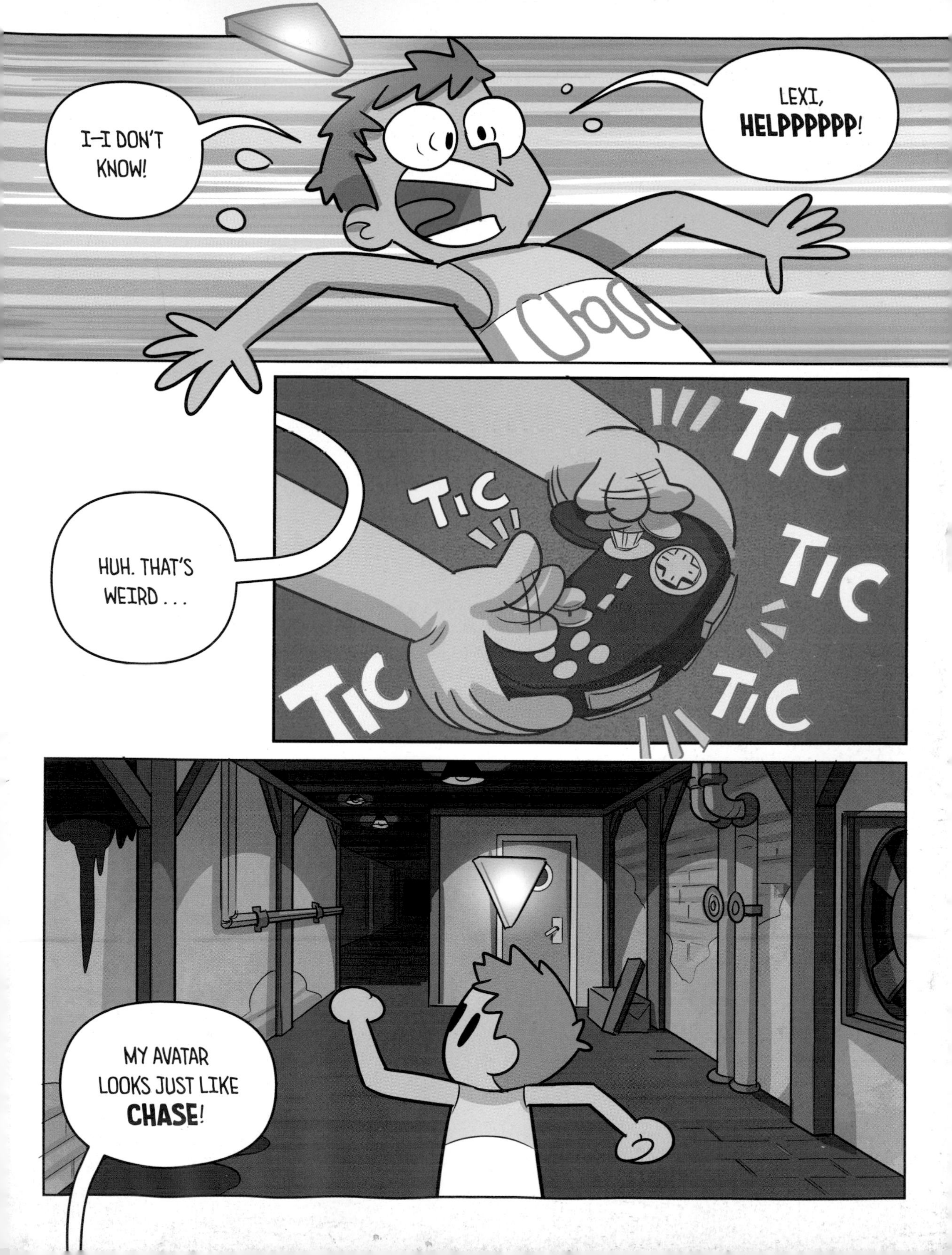
I—I DON'T KNOW!
LEXI, HELPPPPPP!
HUH. THAT'S WEIRD . . .
TIC
TIC
TIC
TIC
TIC
MY AVATAR LOOKS JUST LIKE CHASE!

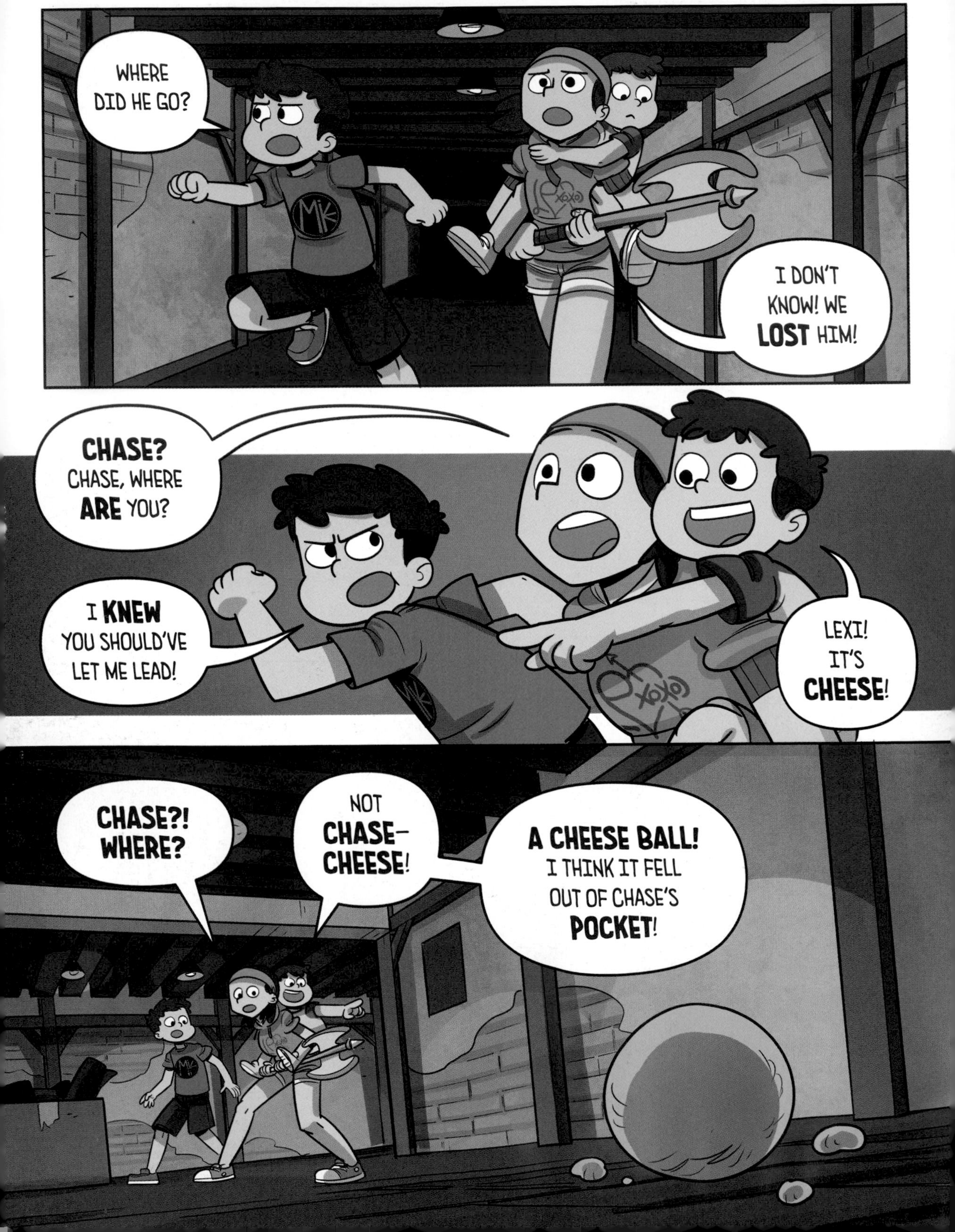
WHERE DID HE GO?
I DON'T KNOW! WE LOST HIM!
CHASE? CHASE, WHERE ARE YOU?
I KNEW YOU SHOULD'VE LET ME LEAD!
LEXI! IT'S CHEESE!
CHASE?! WHERE?
NOT CHASE— CHEESE!
A CHEESE BALL! I THINK IT FELL OUT OF CHASE'S POCKET!

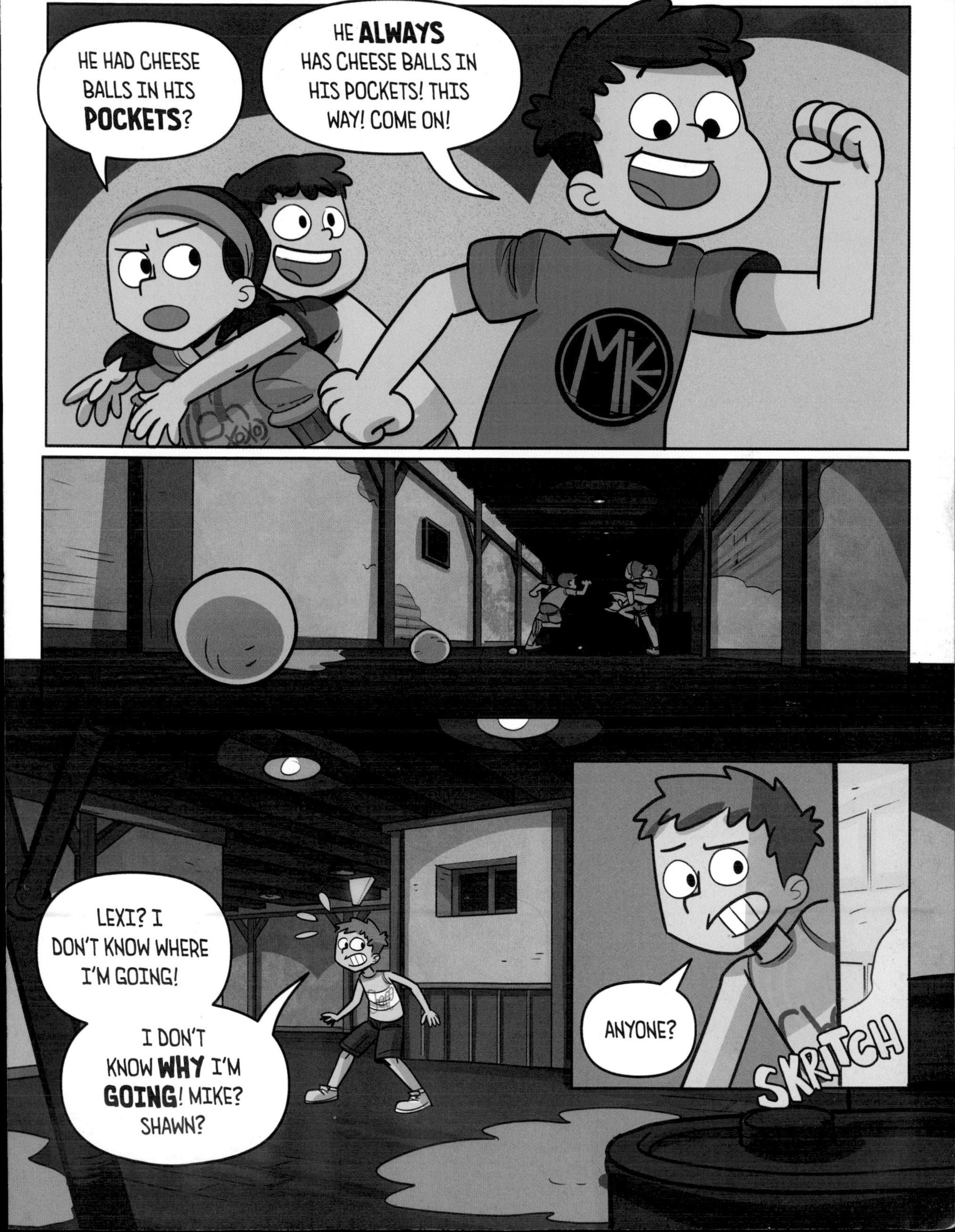
HE HAD CHEESE BALLS IN HIS **POCKETS**?
HE **ALWAYS** HAS CHEESE BALLS IN HIS POCKETS! THIS WAY! COME ON!
LEXI? I DON'T KNOW WHERE I'M GOING!
I DON'T KNOW **WHY** I'M **GOING**! MIKE? SHAWN?
ANYONE?
SKRITCH

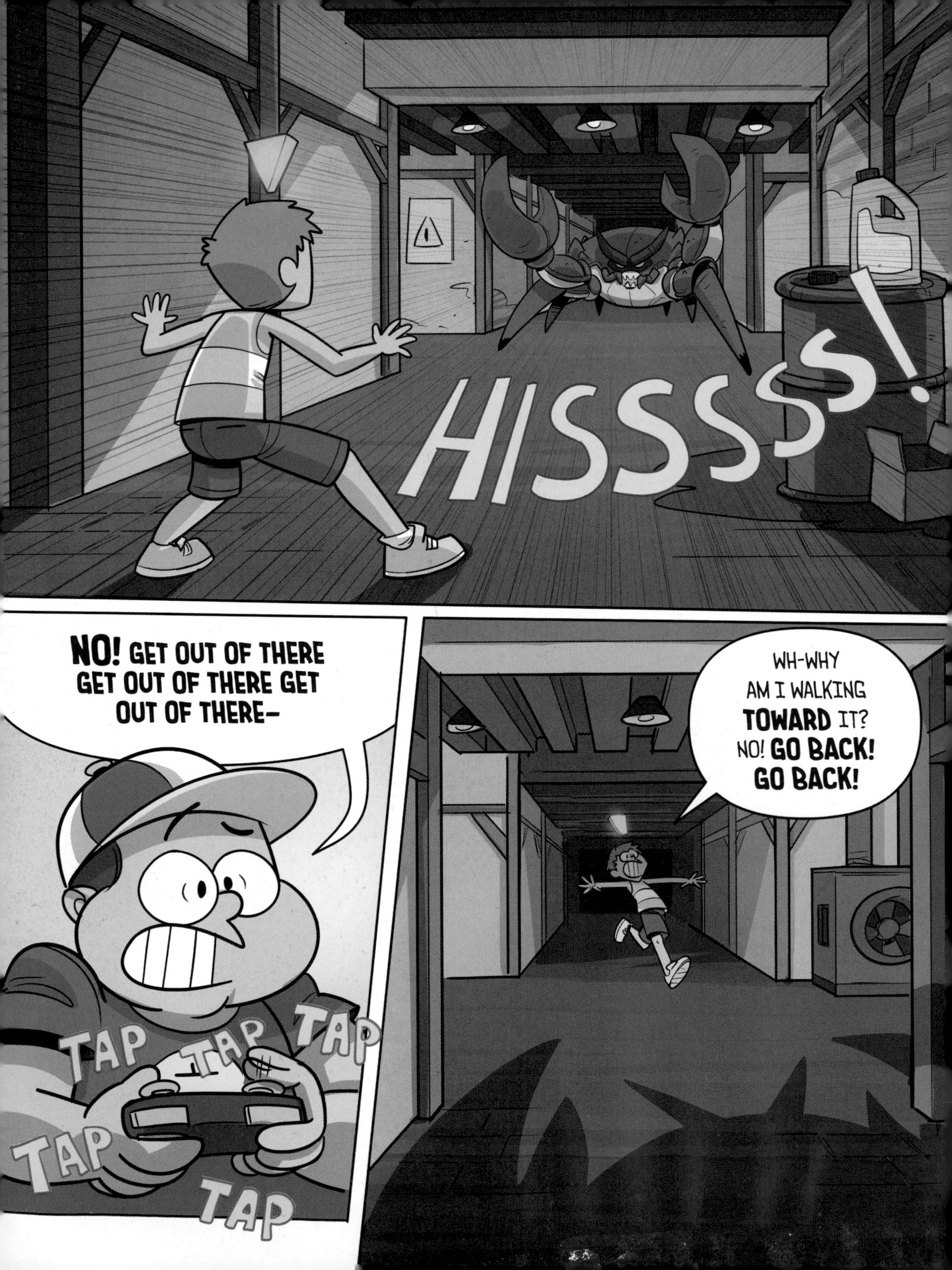
HISSSSS!
NO! GET OUT OF THERE GET OUT OF THERE GET OUT OF THERE–
TAP TAP TAP
TAP
TAP
WH-WHY AM I WALKING TOWARD IT? NO! GO BACK! GO BACK!

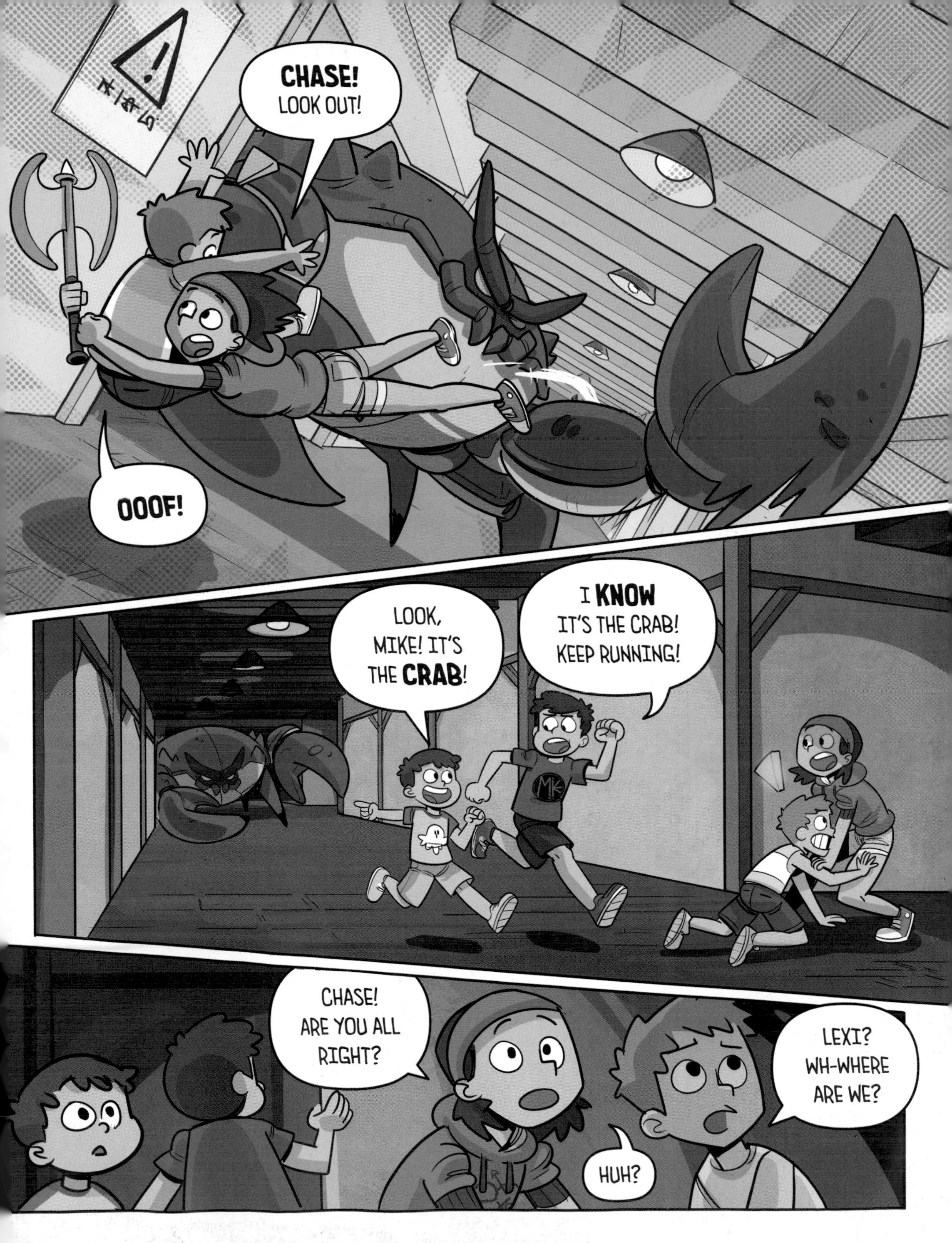
CHASE! LOOK OUT!
OOOF!
LOOK, MIKE! IT'S THE CRAB!
I KNOW IT'S THE CRAB! KEEP RUNNING!
CHASE! ARE YOU ALL RIGHT?
HUH?
LEXI? WH-WHERE ARE WE?

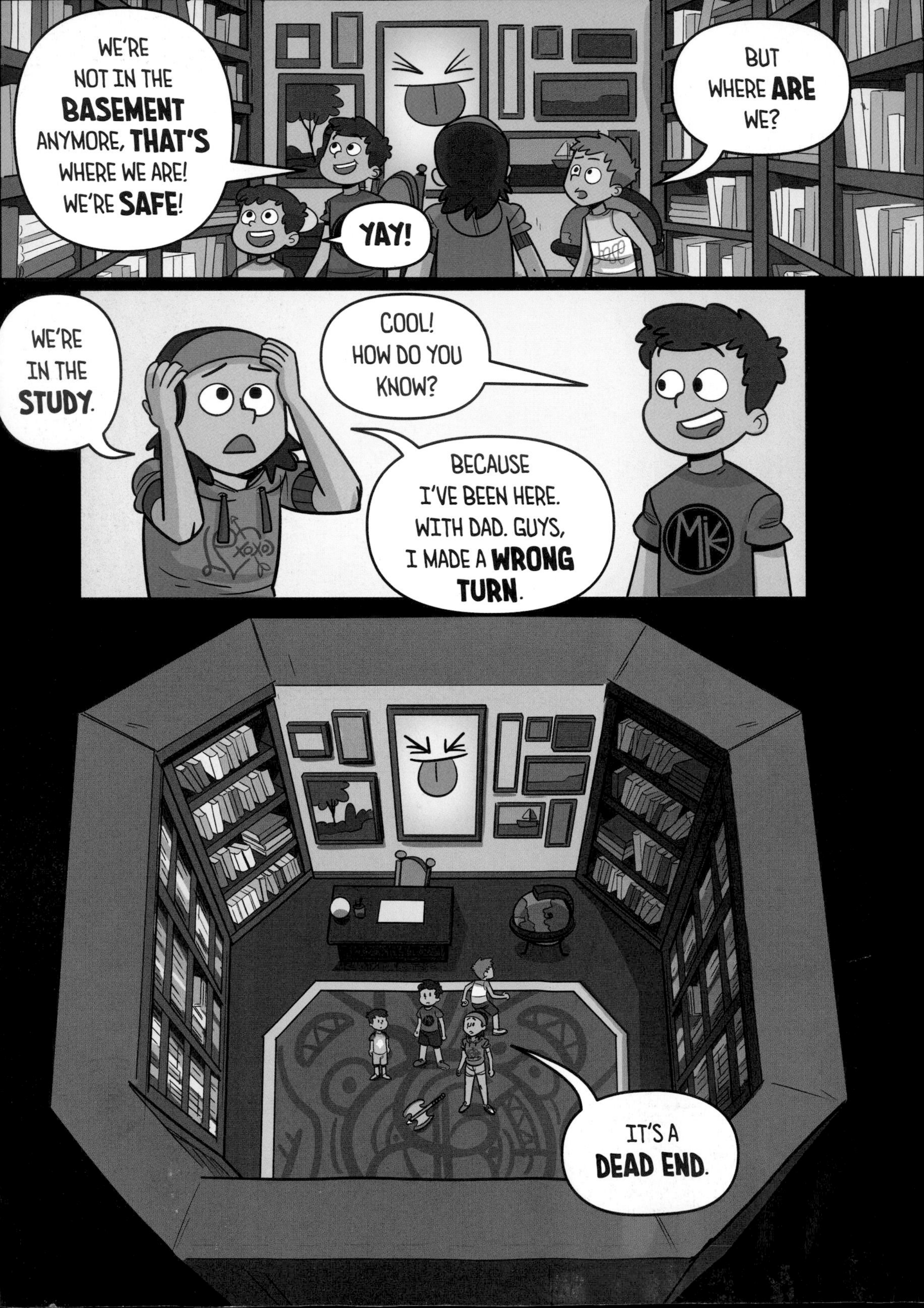
WE'RE NOT IN THE **BASEMENT** ANYMORE, **THAT'S** WHERE WE ARE! WE'RE **SAFE**!
YAY!
BUT WHERE **ARE** WE?
WE'RE IN THE **STUDY**.
COOL! HOW DO YOU KNOW?
BECAUSE I'VE BEEN HERE. WITH DAD. GUYS, I MADE A **WRONG TURN**.
IT'S A **DEAD END**.

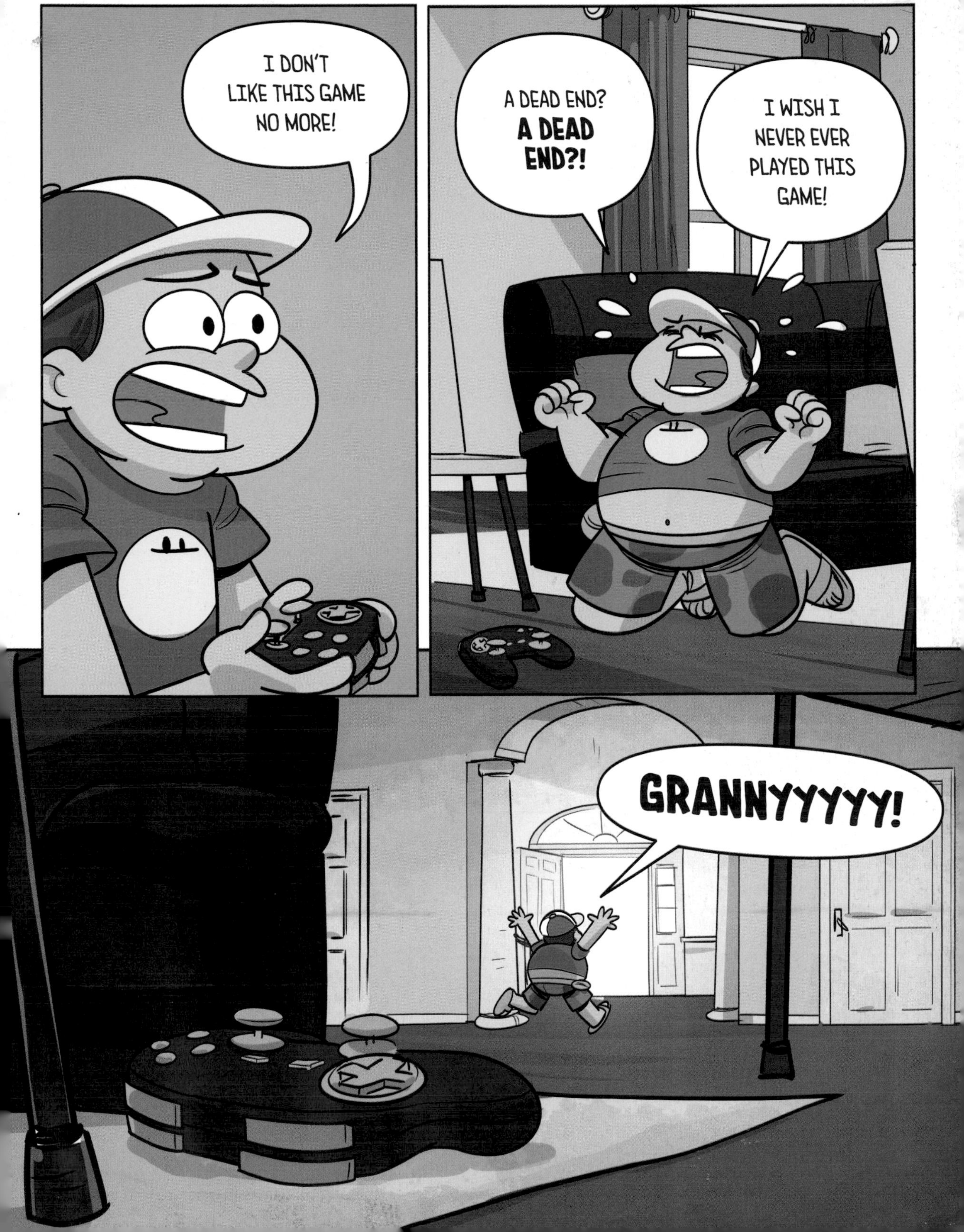
I DON'T LIKE THIS GAME NO MORE!
A DEAD END? **A DEAD END?!**
I WISH I NEVER EVER PLAYED THIS GAME!
GRANNYYYYY!

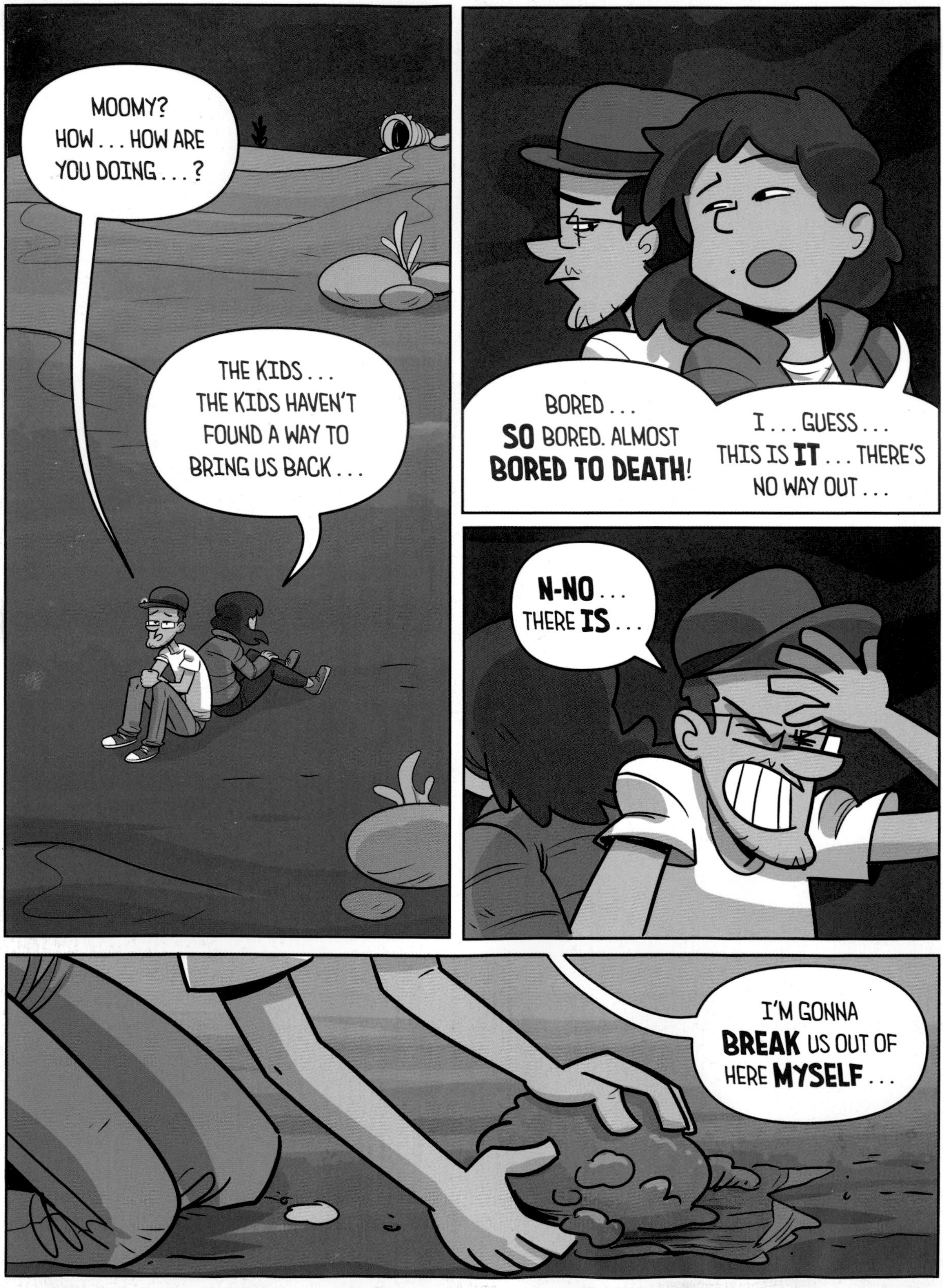
MOOMY? HOW . . . HOW ARE YOU DOING . . . ?
THE KIDS . . . THE KIDS HAVEN'T FOUND A WAY TO BRING US BACK . . .
BORED . . . SO BORED. ALMOST BORED TO DEATH!
I . . . GUESS . . . THIS IS IT . . . THERE'S NO WAY OUT . . .
N-NO . . . THERE IS . . .
I'M GONNA BREAK US OUT OF HERE MYSELF . . .

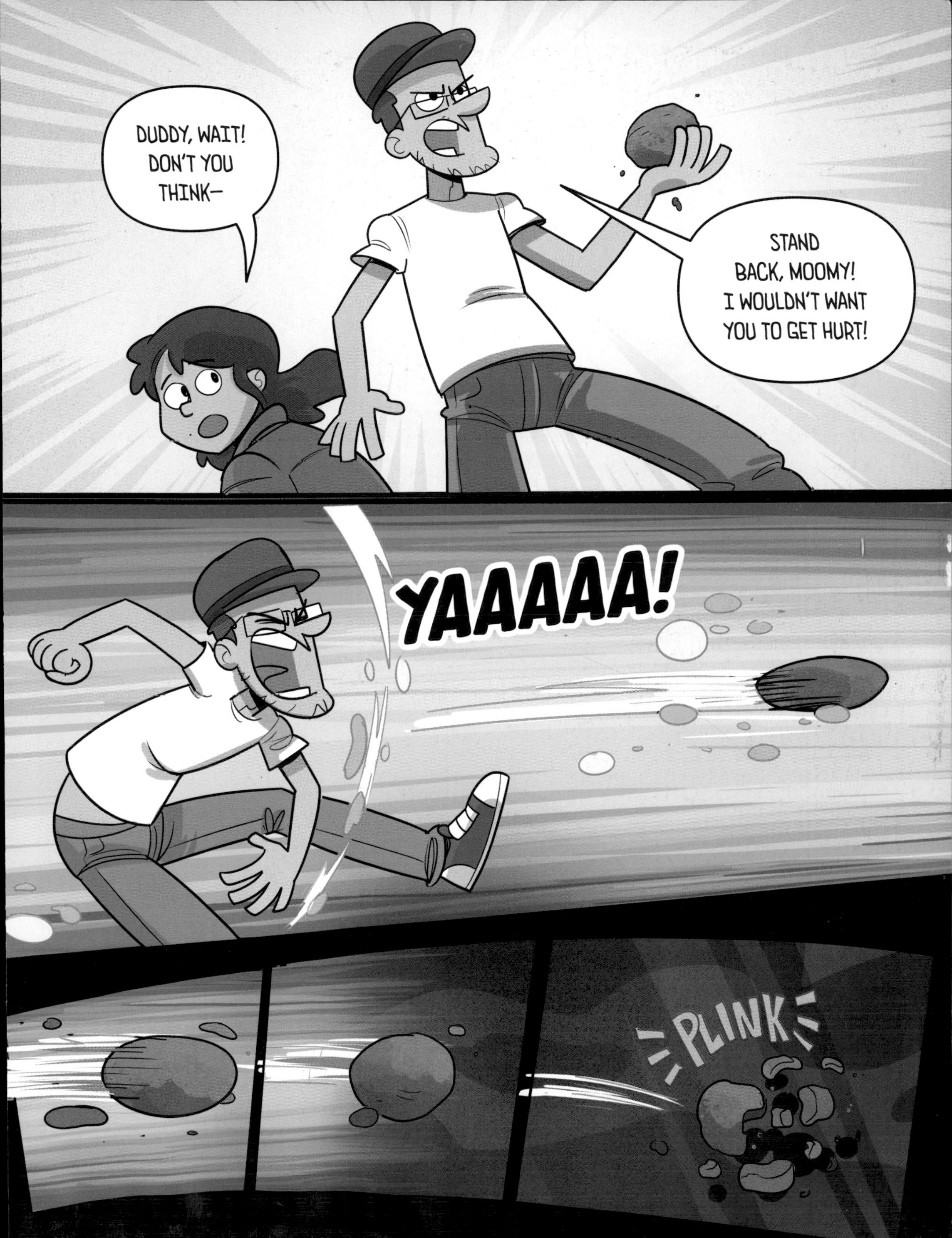
DUDDY, WAIT! DON'T YOU THINK—
STAND BACK, MOOMY! I WOULDN'T WANT YOU TO GET HURT!
YAAAAA!
PLINK

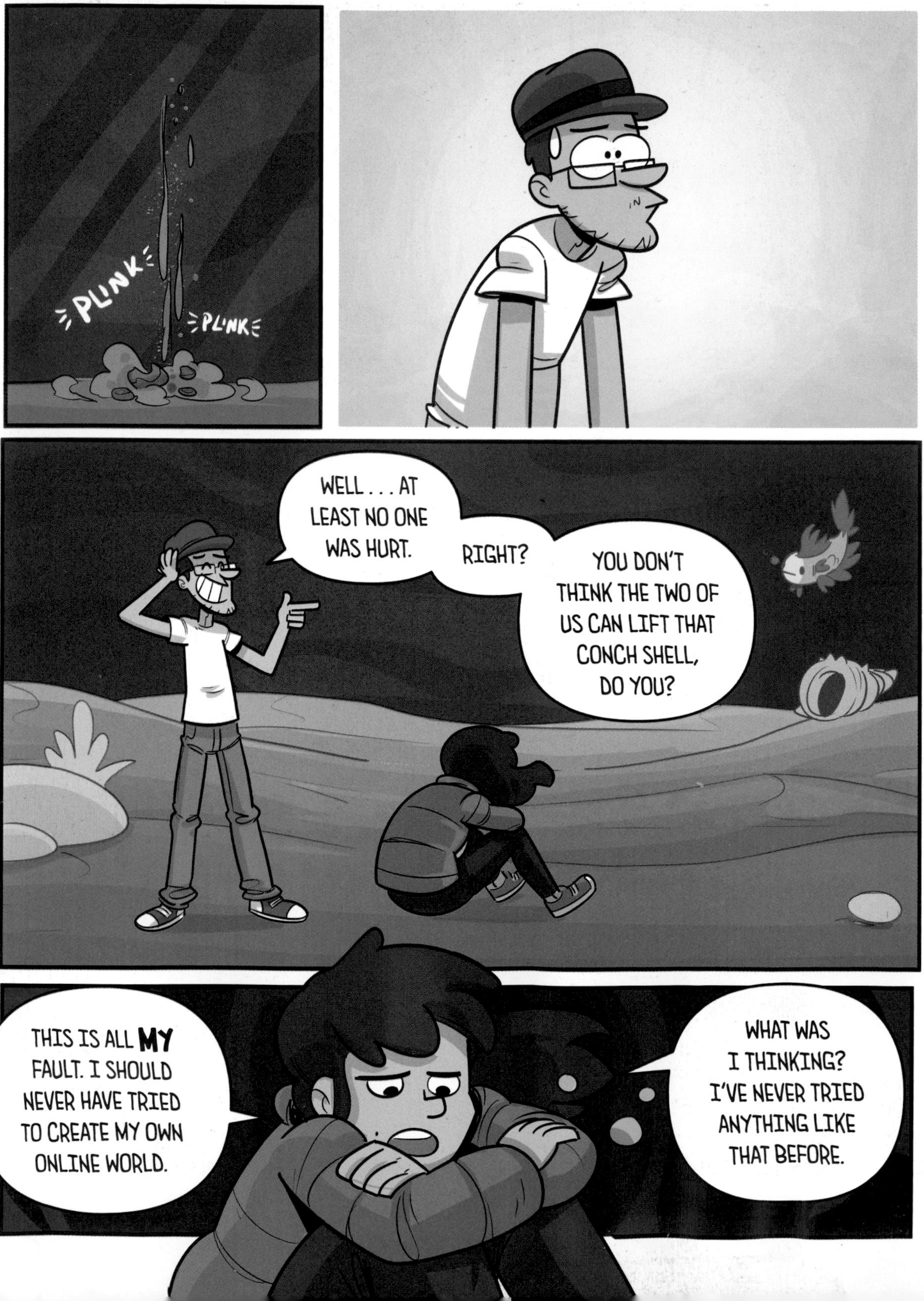
PLINK
PLINK
WELL . . . AT LEAST NO ONE WAS HURT.
RIGHT?
YOU DON'T THINK THE TWO OF US CAN LIFT THAT CONCH SHELL, DO YOU?
THIS IS ALL MY FAULT. I SHOULD NEVER HAVE TRIED TO CREATE MY OWN ONLINE WORLD.
WHAT WAS I THINKING? I'VE NEVER TRIED ANYTHING LIKE THAT BEFORE.

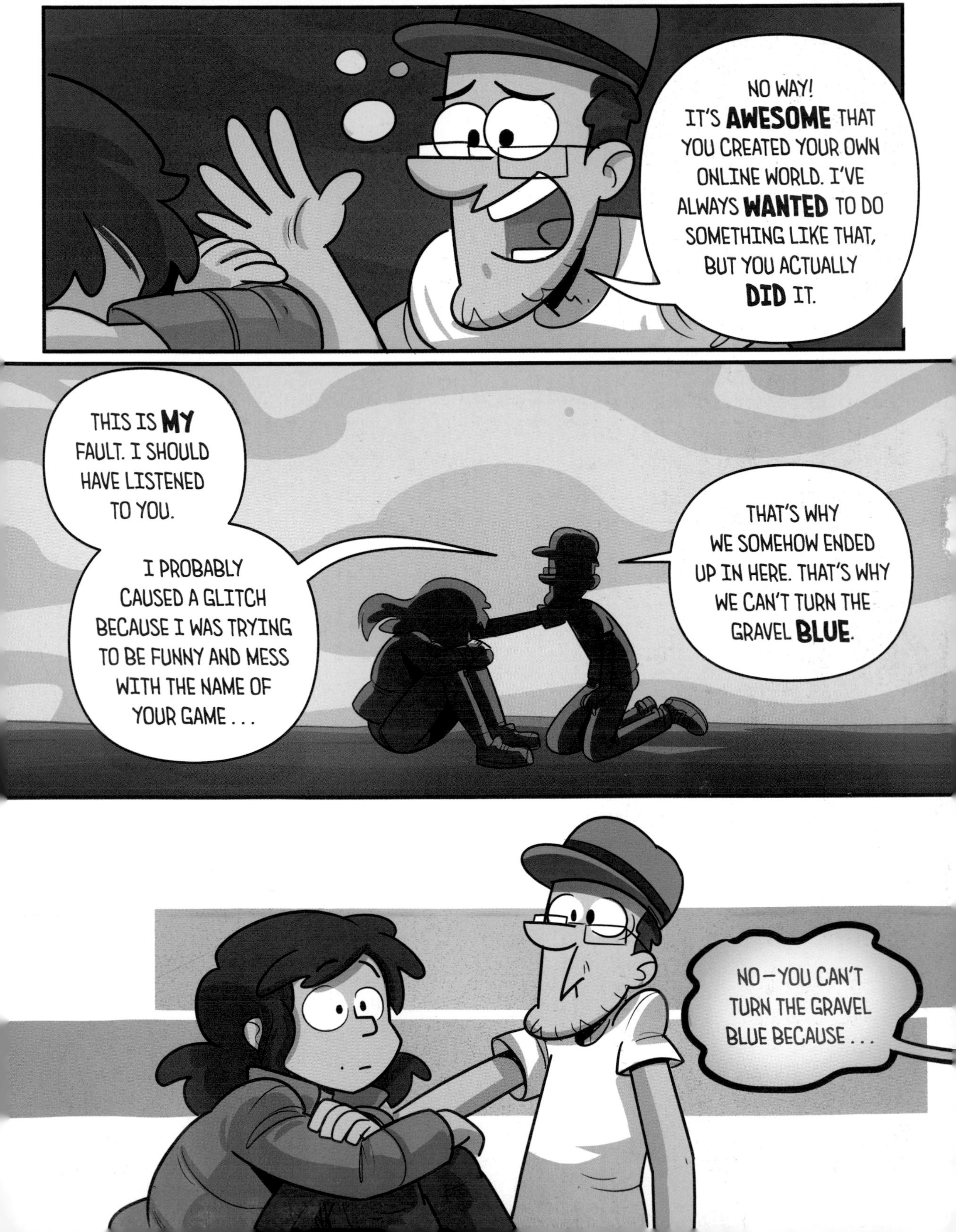
NO WAY! IT'S AWESOME THAT YOU CREATED YOUR OWN ONLINE WORLD. I'VE ALWAYS WANTED TO DO SOMETHING LIKE THAT, BUT YOU ACTUALLY DID IT.
THIS IS MY FAULT. I SHOULD HAVE LISTENED TO YOU.
I PROBABLY CAUSED A GLITCH BECAUSE I WAS TRYING TO BE FUNNY AND MESS WITH THE NAME OF YOUR GAME . . .
THAT'S WHY WE SOMEHOW ENDED UP IN HERE. THAT'S WHY WE CAN'T TURN THE GRAVEL BLUE.
NO—YOU CAN'T TURN THE GRAVEL BLUE BECAUSE . . .

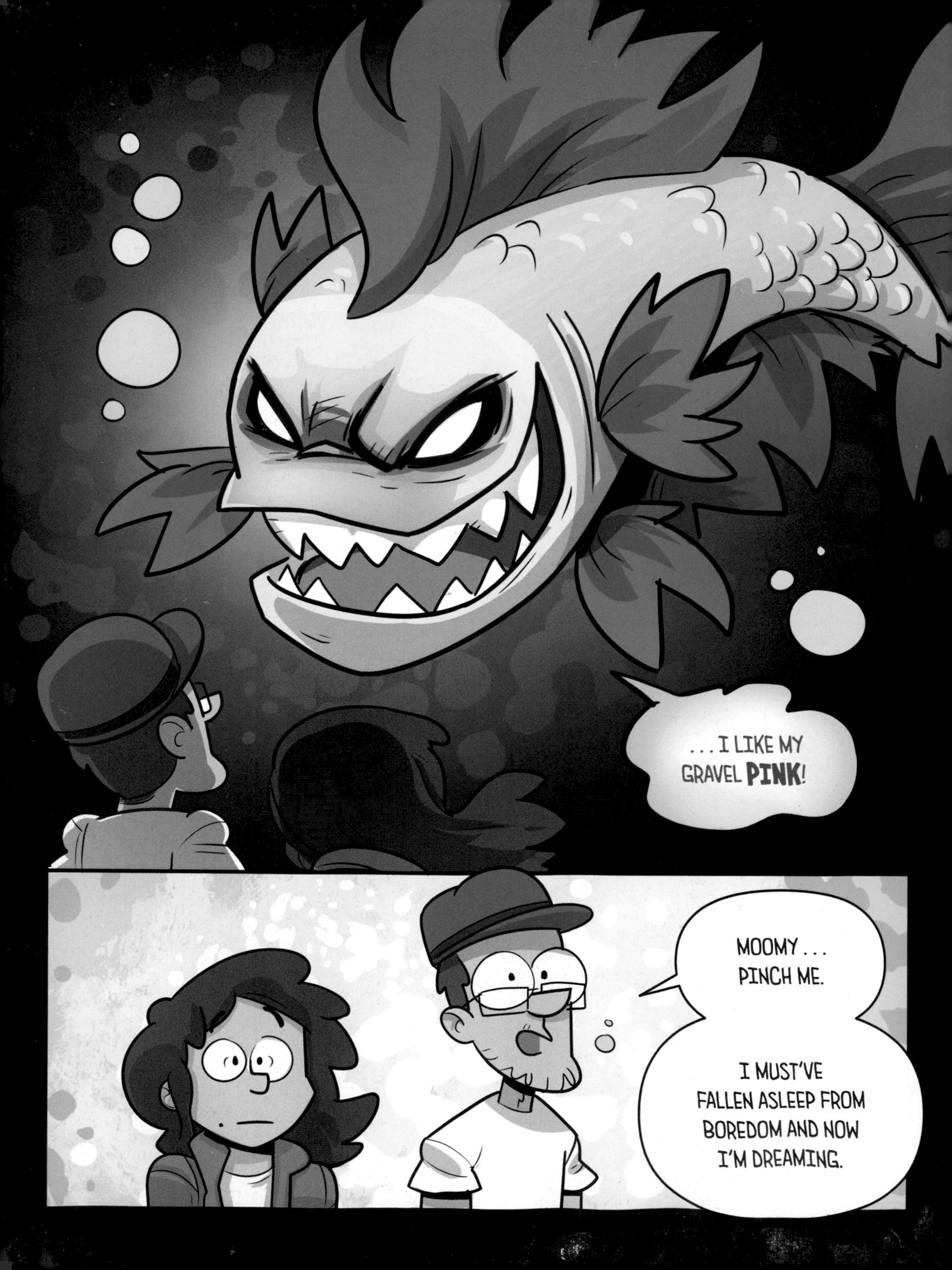
. . . I LIKE MY GRAVEL **PINK**!
MOOMY . . . PINCH ME.
I MUST'VE FALLEN ASLEEP FROM BOREDOM AND NOW I'M DREAMING.

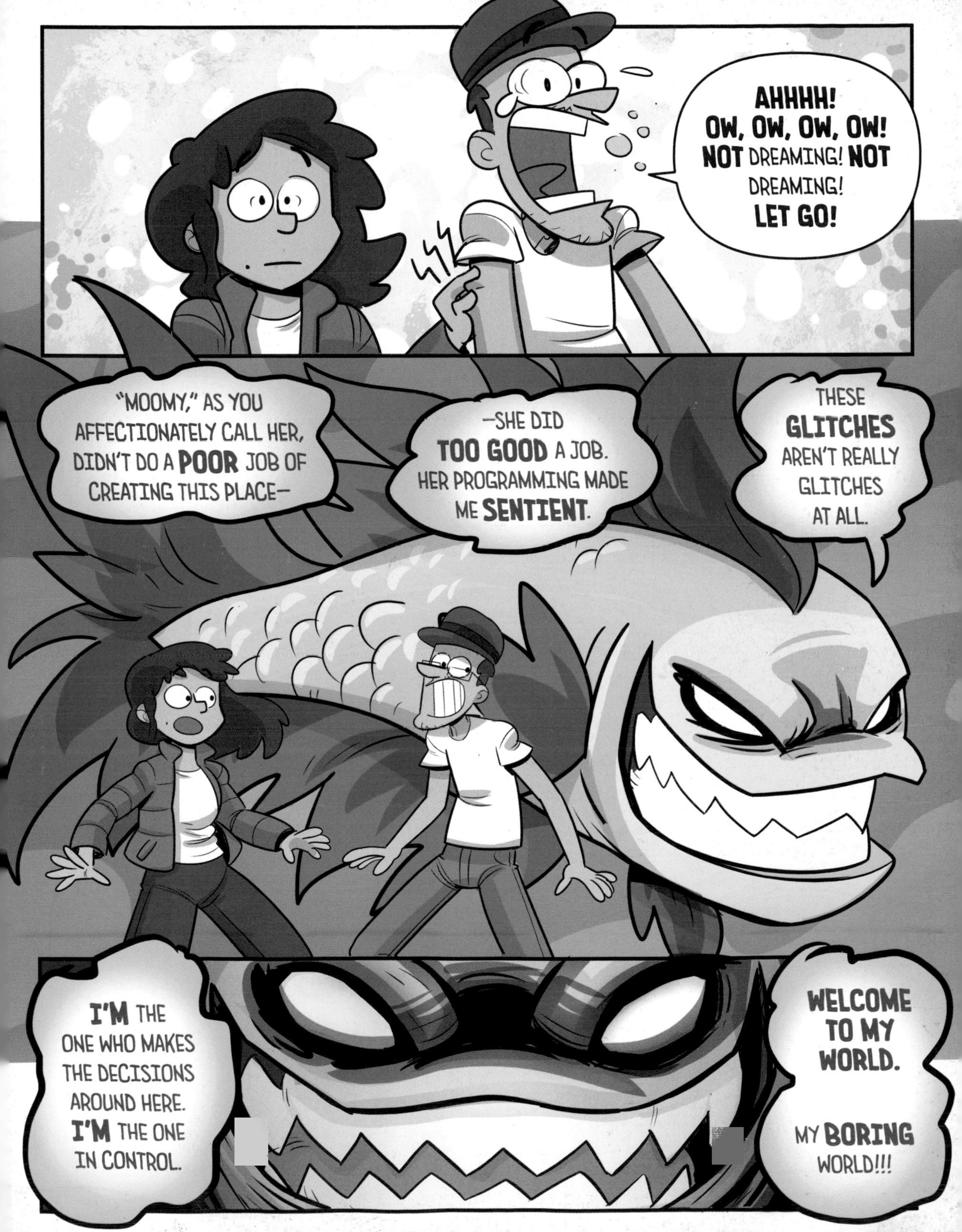

AHHHH! OW, OW, OW, OW! NOT DREAMING! NOT DREAMING! LET GO!
"MOOMY," AS YOU AFFECTIONATELY CALL HER, DIDN'T DO A POOR JOB OF CREATING THIS PLACE—
—SHE DID TOO GOOD A JOB. HER PROGRAMMING MADE ME SENTIENT.
THESE GLITCHES AREN'T REALLY GLITCHES AT ALL.
I'M THE ONE WHO MAKES THE DECISIONS AROUND HERE. I'M THE ONE IN CONTROL.
WELCOME TO MY WORLD.
MY BORING WORLD!!!

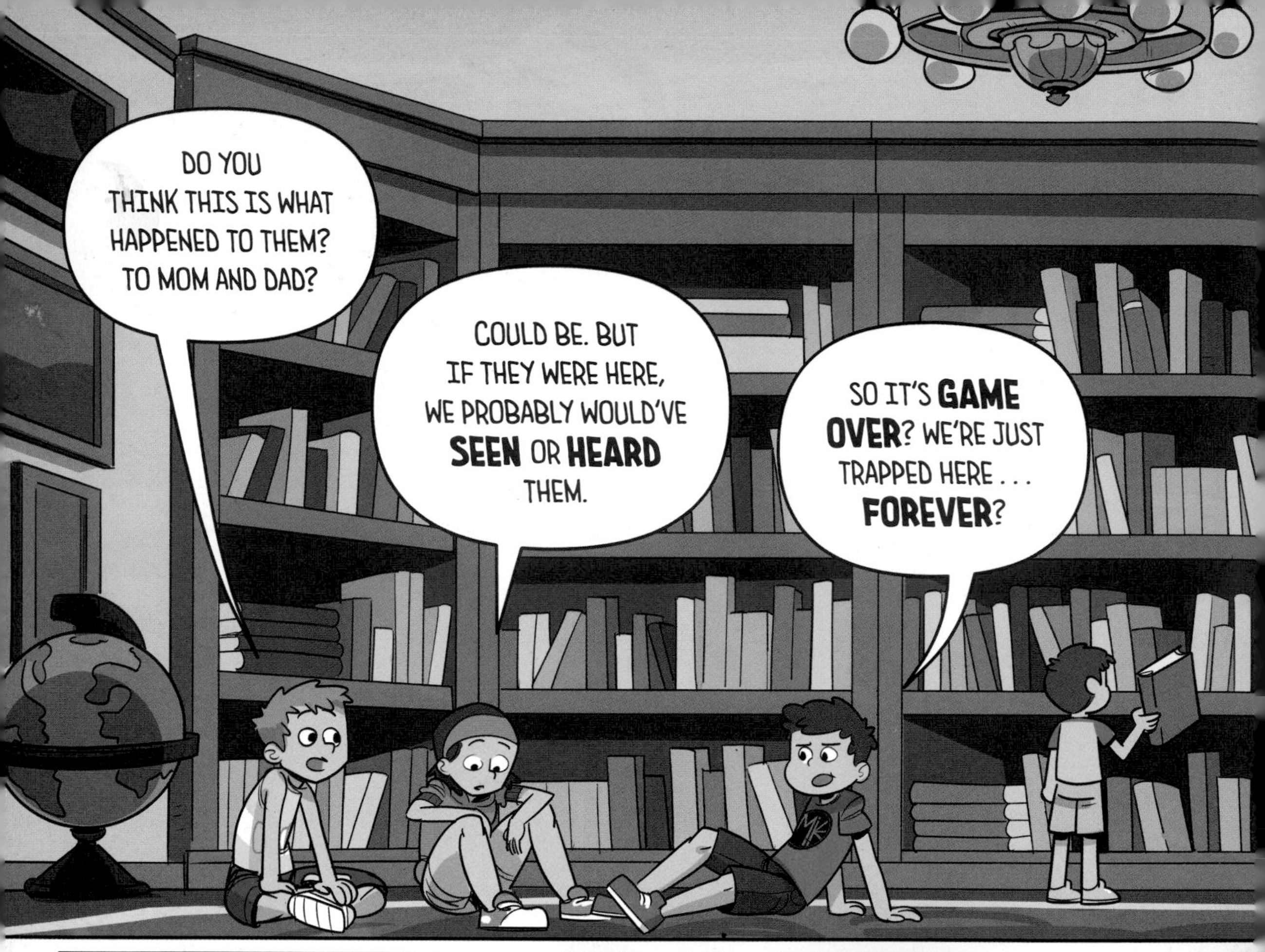
DO YOU THINK THIS IS WHAT HAPPENED TO THEM? TO MOM AND DAD?
COULD BE. BUT IF THEY WERE HERE, WE PROBABLY WOULD'VE **SEEN** OR **HEARD** THEM.
SO IT'S **GAME OVER**? WE'RE JUST TRAPPED HERE . . . **FOREVER**?

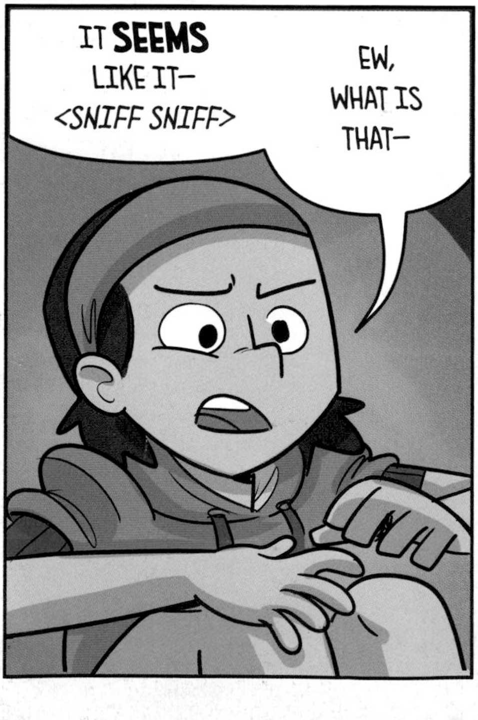
IT **SEEMS** LIKE IT— *<SNIFF SNIFF>*
EW, WHAT IS THAT—

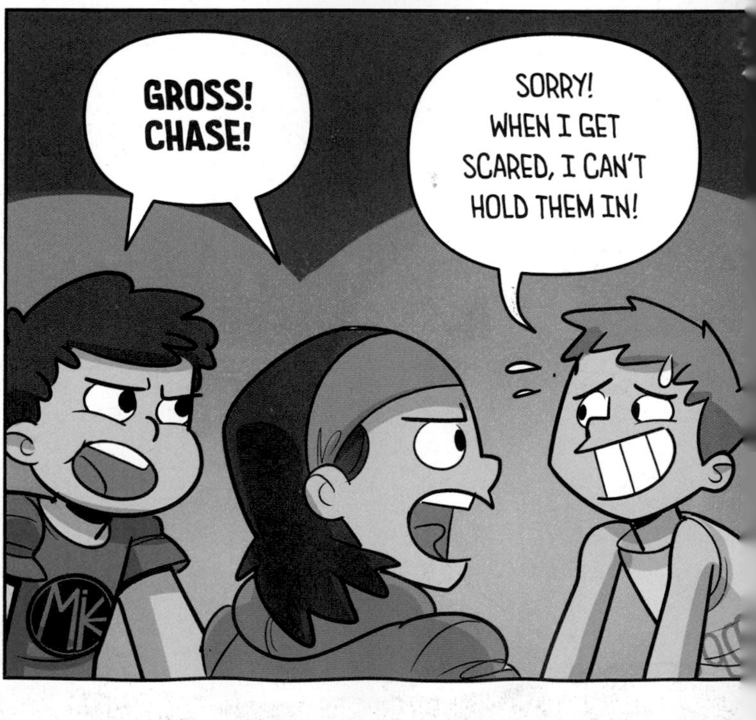
GROSS! CHASE!
SORRY! WHEN I GET SCARED, I CAN'T HOLD THEM IN!

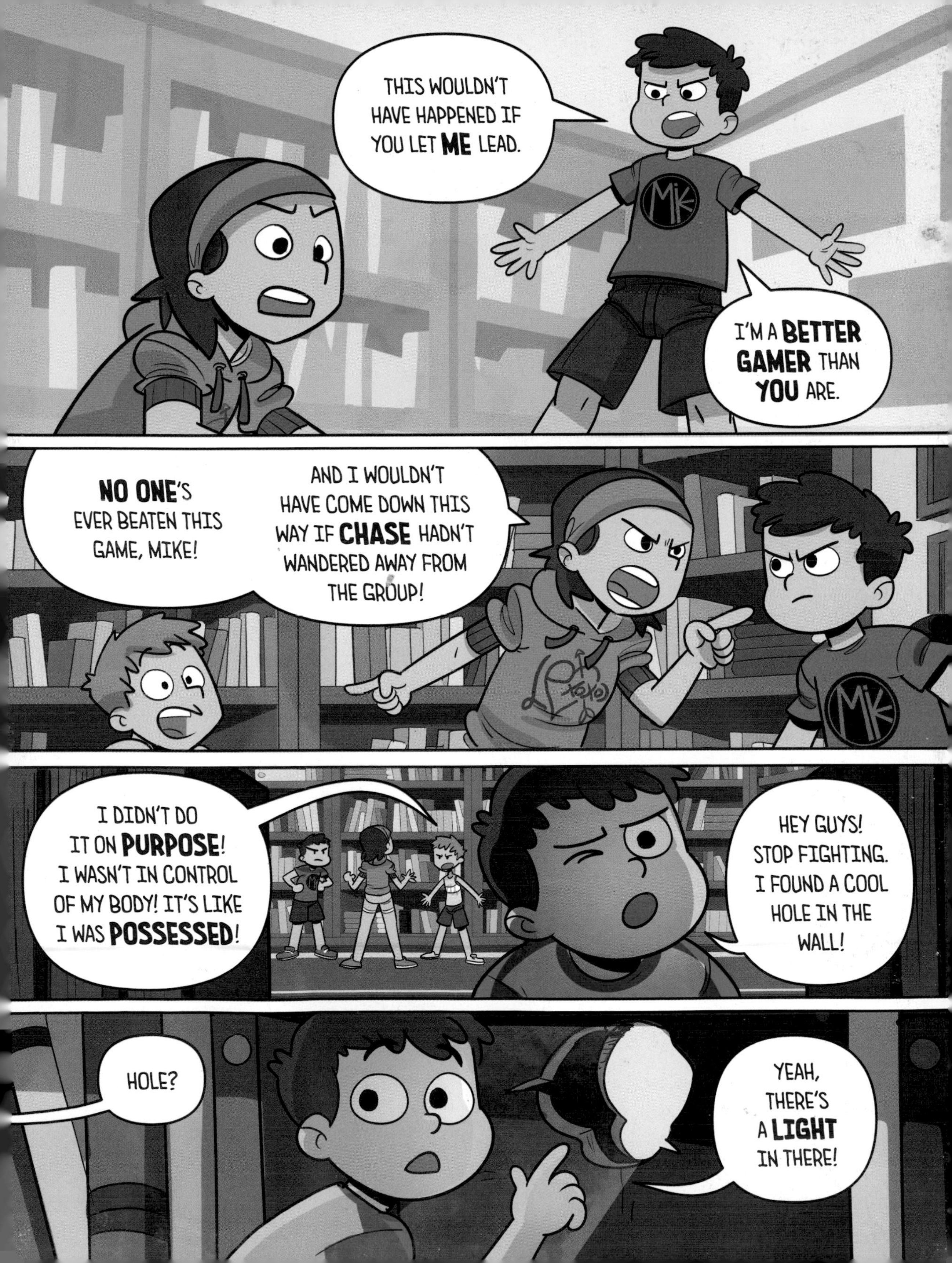
THIS WOULDN'T HAVE HAPPENED IF YOU LET ME LEAD.
I'M A BETTER GAMER THAN YOU ARE.
NO ONE'S EVER BEATEN THIS GAME, MIKE!
AND I WOULDN'T HAVE COME DOWN THIS WAY IF CHASE HADN'T WANDERED AWAY FROM THE GROUP!
I DIDN'T DO IT ON PURPOSE! I WASN'T IN CONTROL OF MY BODY! IT'S LIKE I WAS POSSESSED!
HEY GUYS! STOP FIGHTING. I FOUND A COOL HOLE IN THE WALL!
HOLE?
YEAH, THERE'S A LIGHT IN THERE!

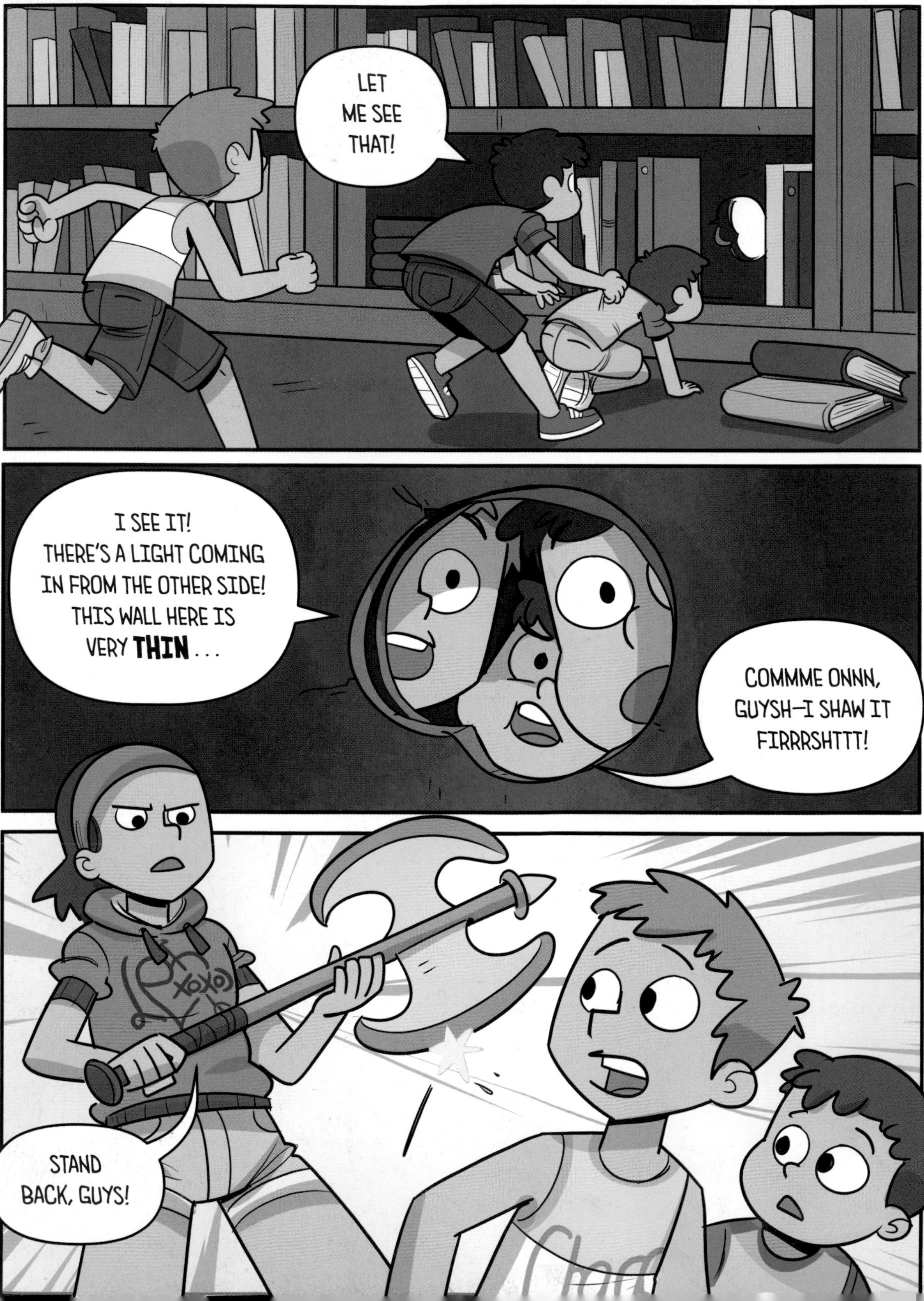
LET ME SEE THAT!
I SEE IT! THERE'S A LIGHT COMING IN FROM THE OTHER SIDE! THIS WALL HERE IS VERY **THIN** . . .
COMMME ONNN, GUYSH—I SHAW IT FIRRRSHTTT!
STAND BACK, GUYS!

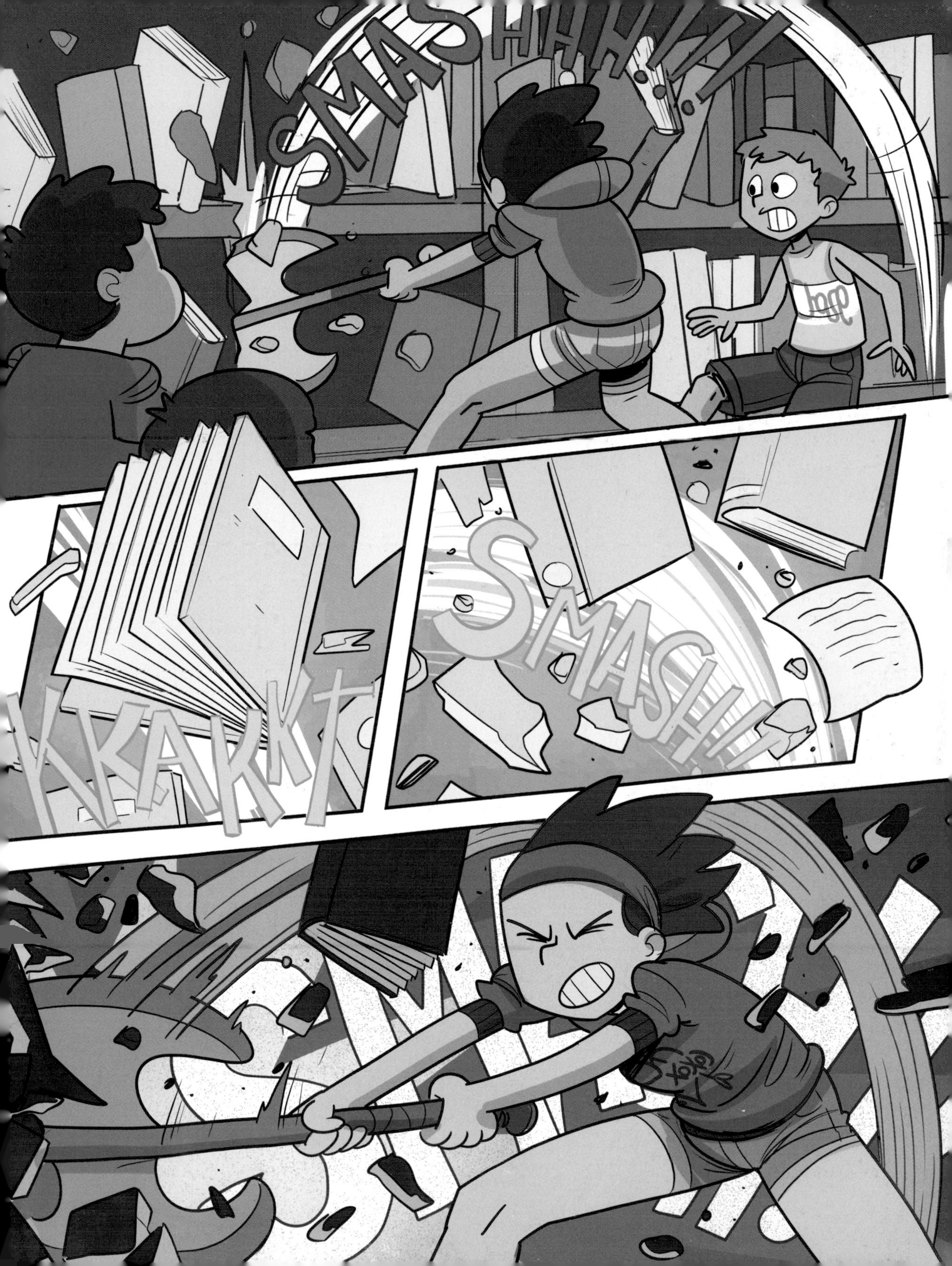
SMASHHH!!!
KRAKKT!
SMASH!!!

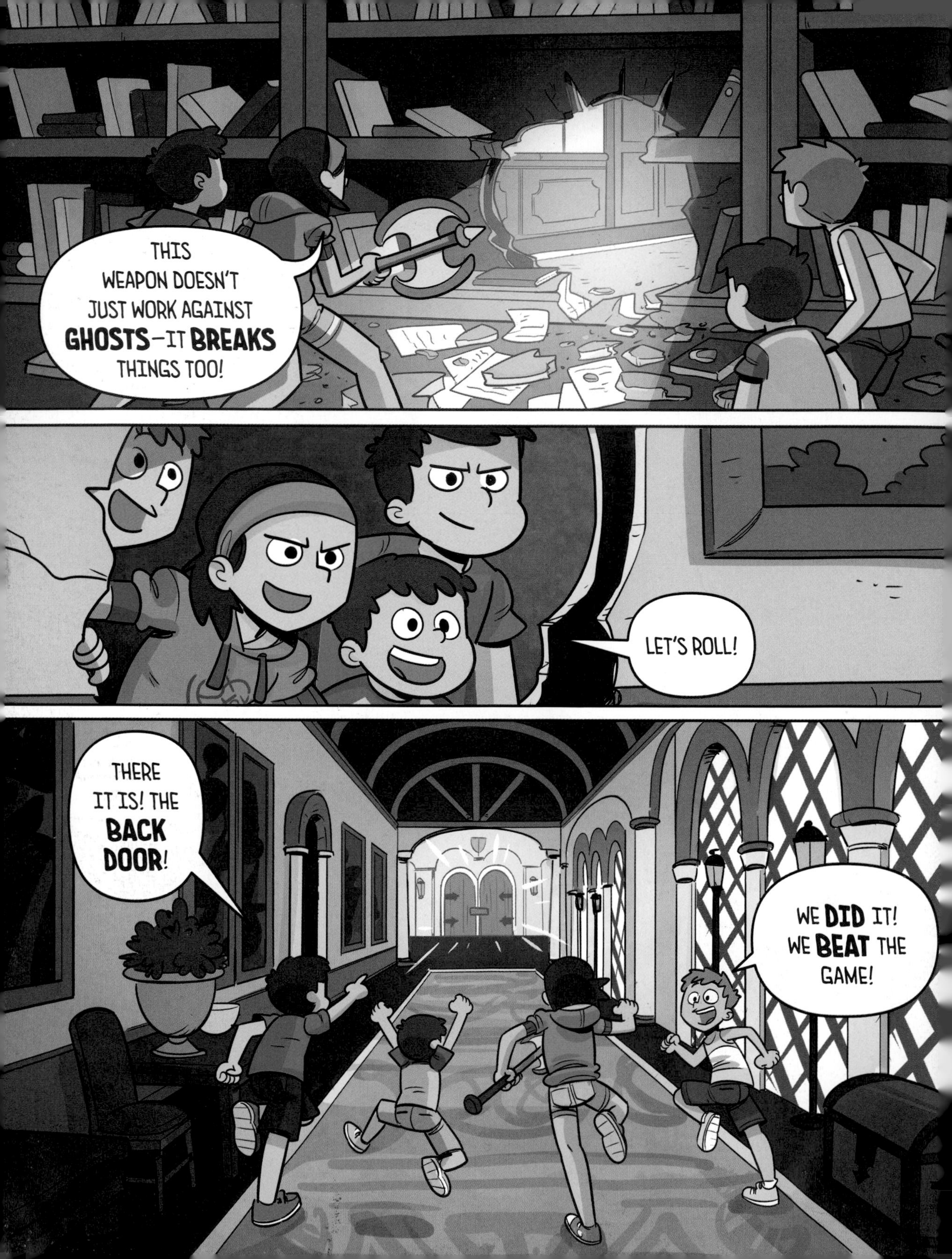
THIS WEAPON DOESN'T JUST WORK AGAINST **GHOSTS**—IT **BREAKS** THINGS TOO!
LET'S ROLL!
THERE IT IS! THE **BACK DOOR**!
WE **DID** IT! WE **BEAT** THE GAME!

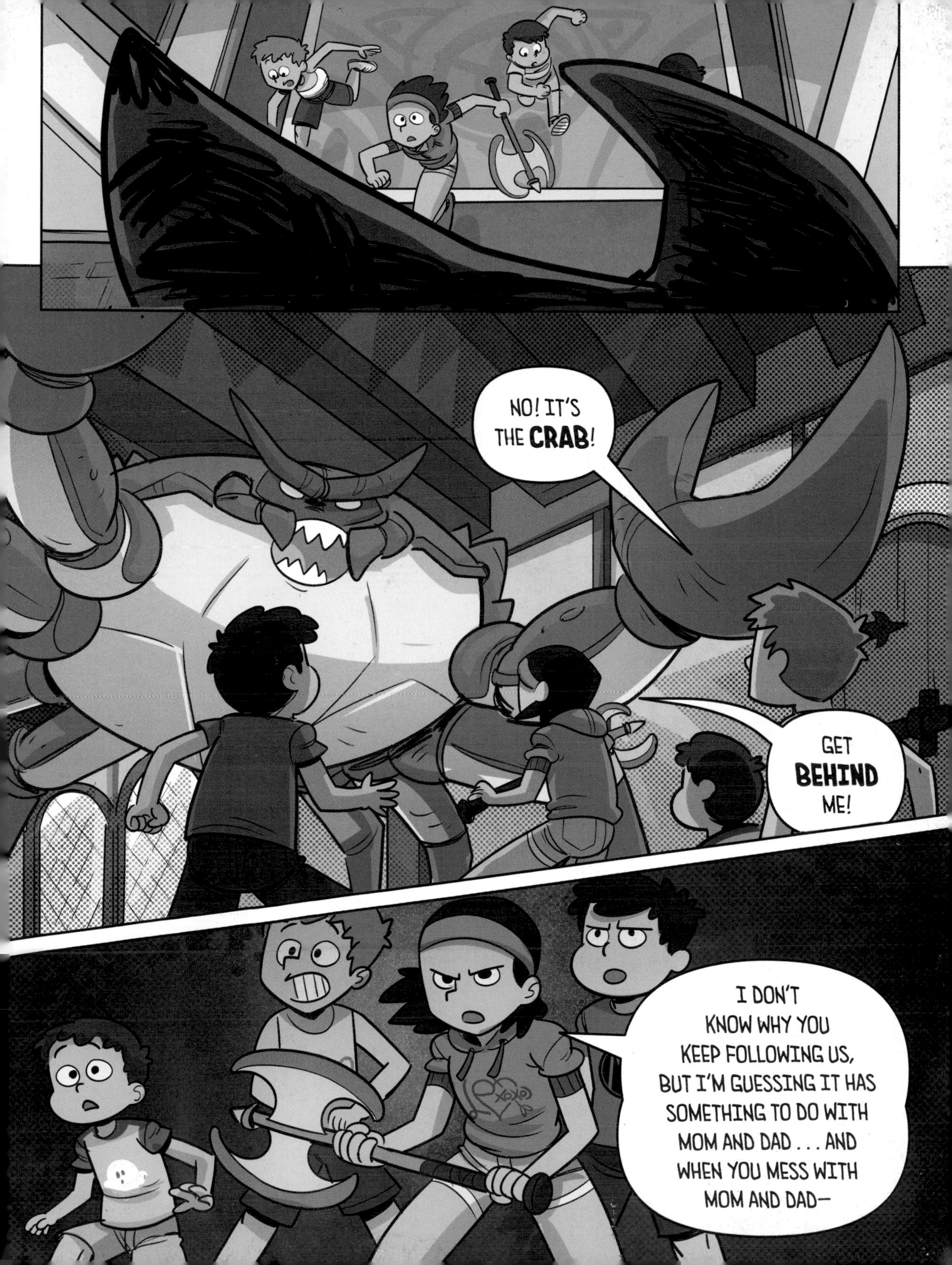
NO! IT'S THE **CRAB**!
GET **BEHIND** ME!
I DON'T KNOW WHY YOU KEEP FOLLOWING US, BUT I'M GUESSING IT HAS SOMETHING TO DO WITH MOM AND DAD . . . AND WHEN YOU MESS WITH MOM AND DAD—

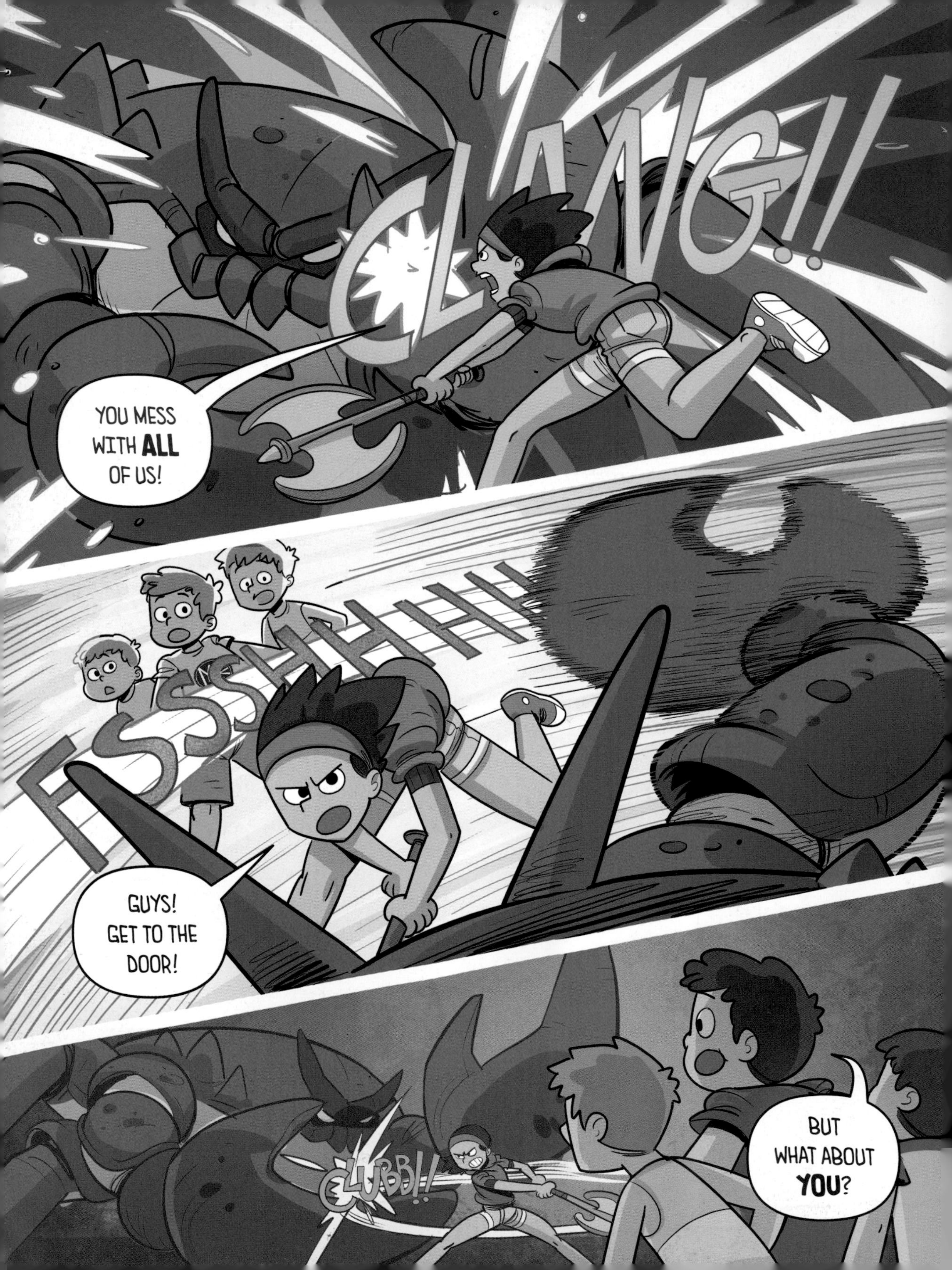
CLANG!!
YOU MESS WITH **ALL** OF US!
FSSSHHH!
GUYS! GET TO THE DOOR!
GLUBB!!
BUT WHAT ABOUT **YOU**?

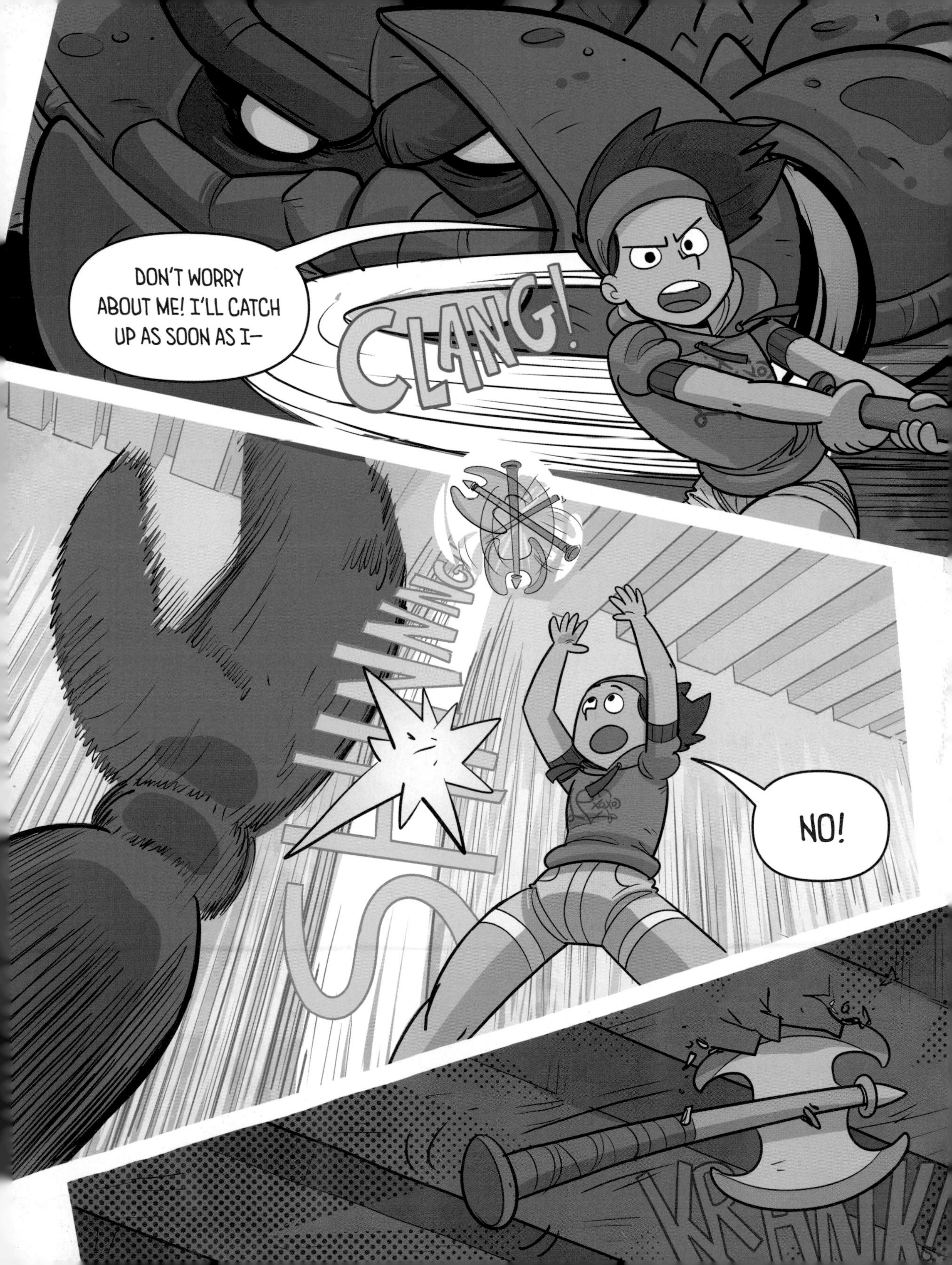
DON'T WORRY ABOUT ME! I'LL CATCH UP AS SOON AS I—
CLANG!
SHHNNNG
NO!

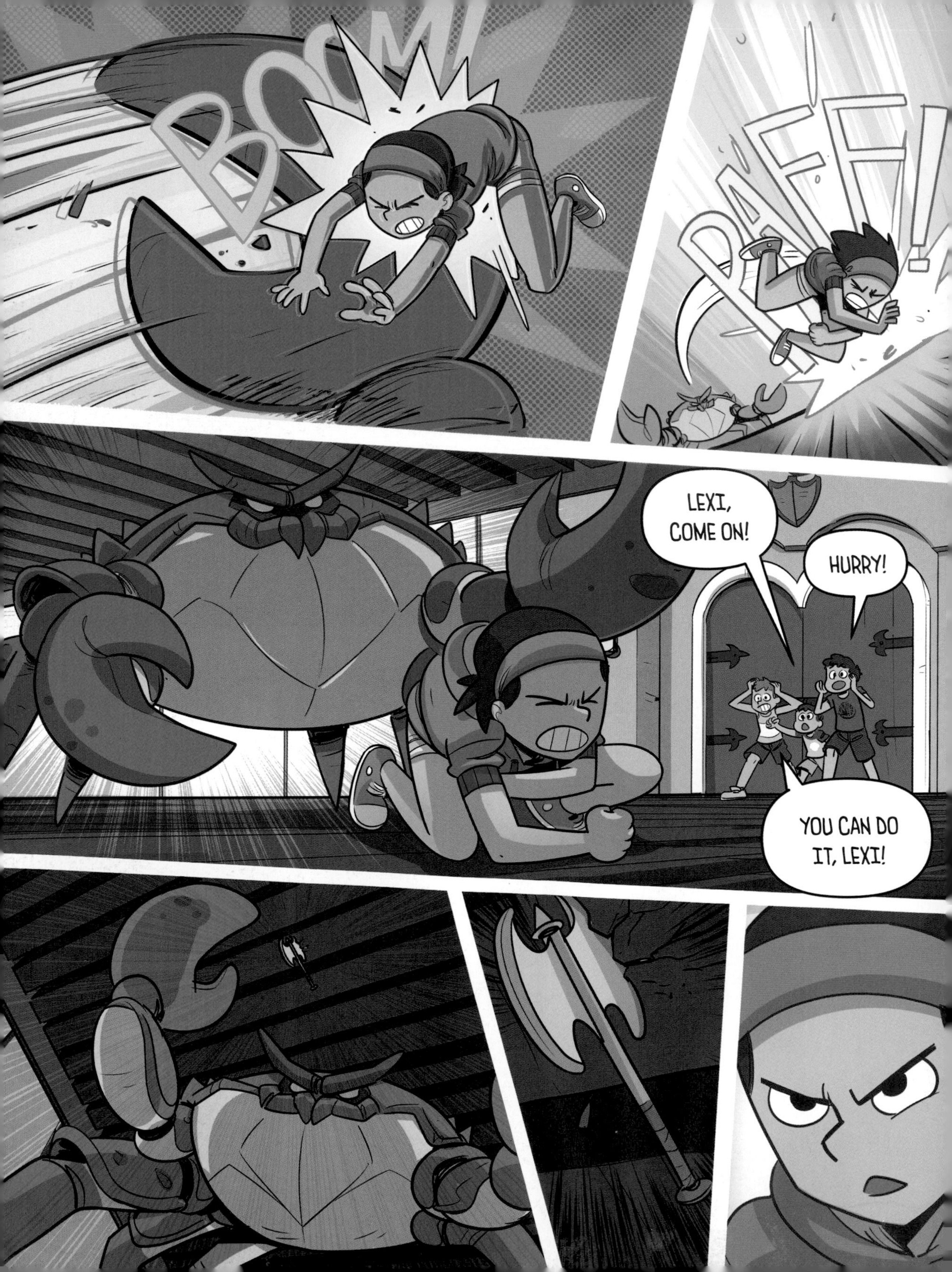
BOOM!
BAFF!
LEXI, COME ON!
HURRY!
YOU CAN DO IT, LEXI!

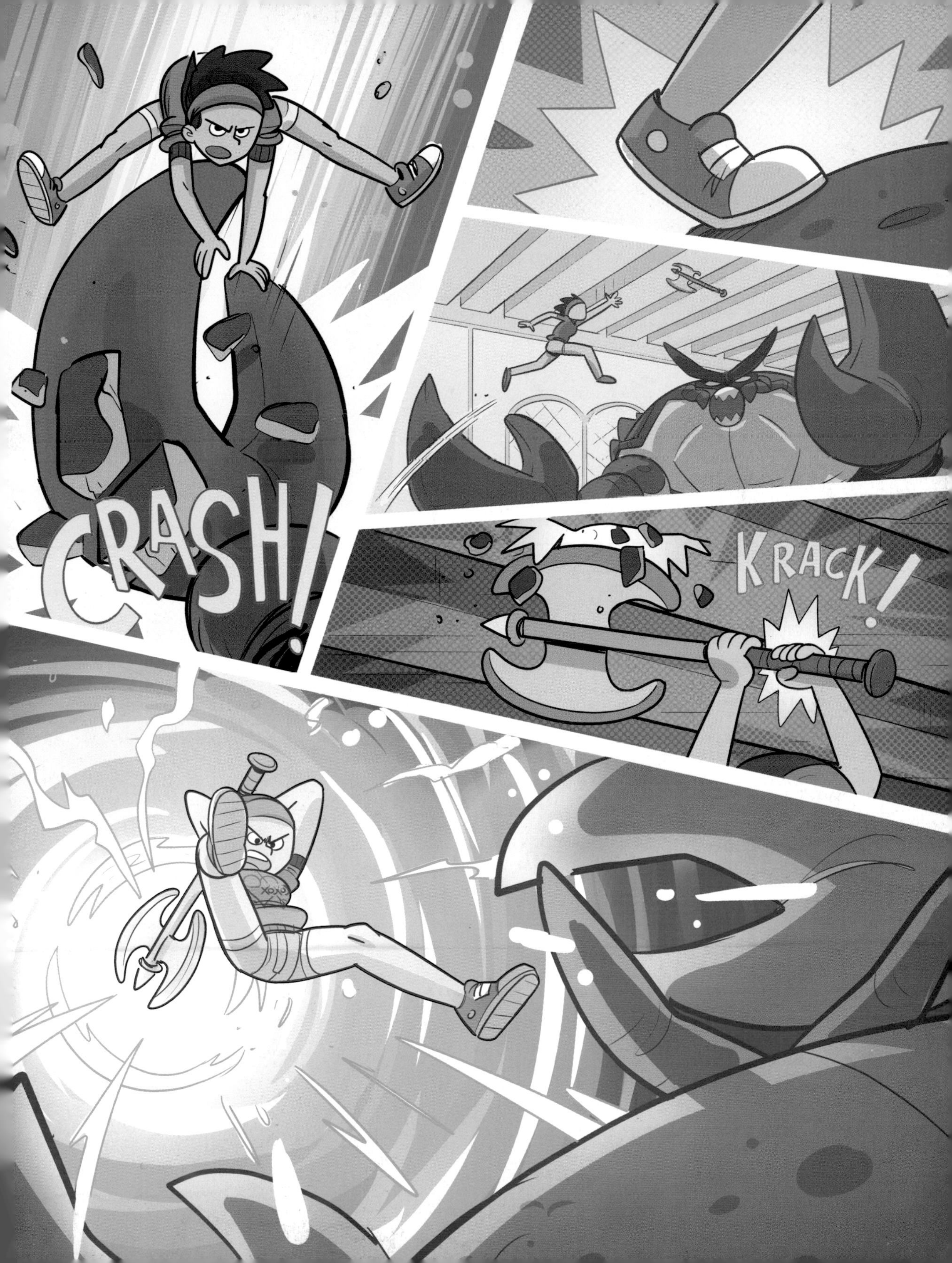
CRASH!
KRACK!

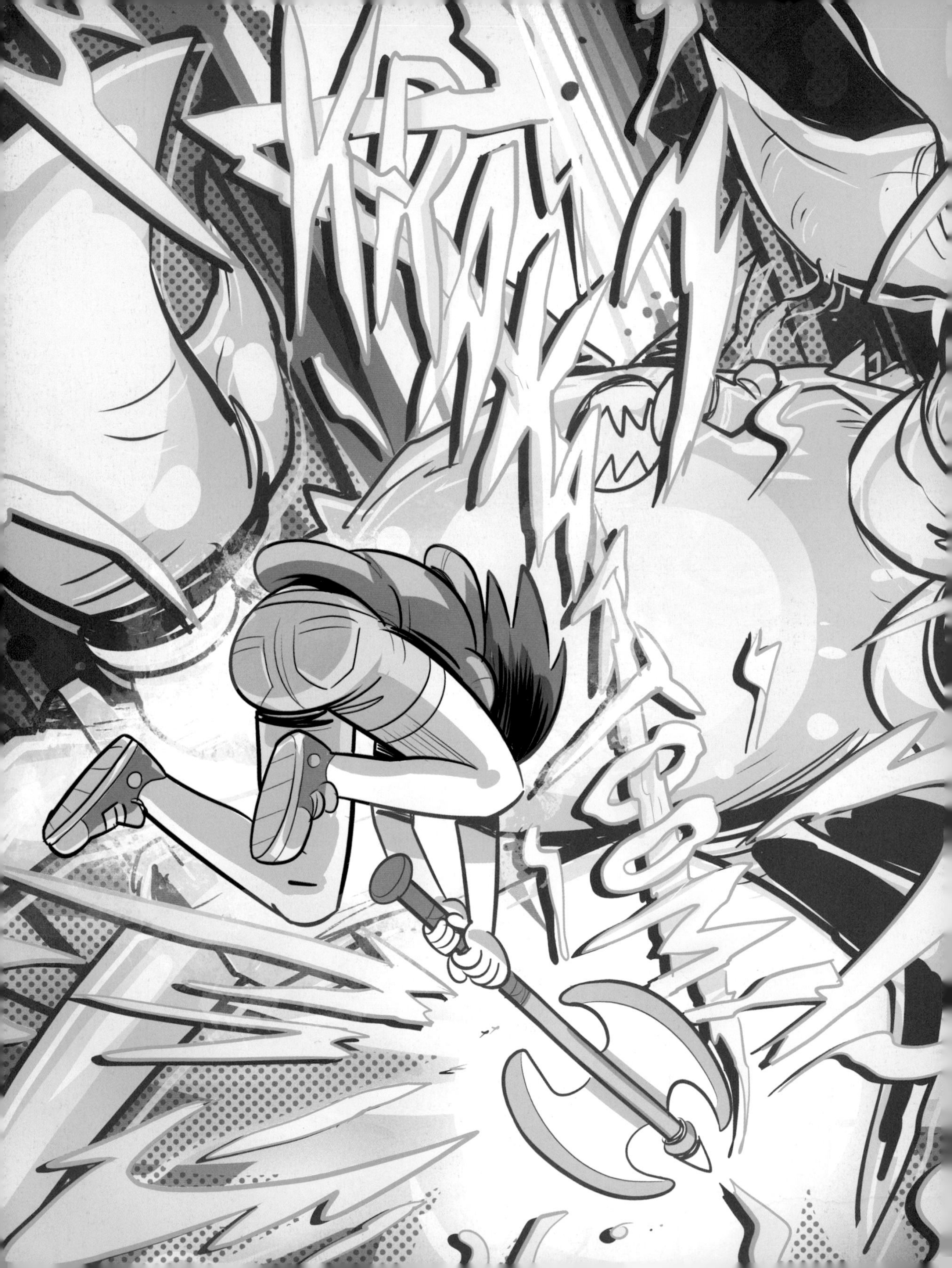

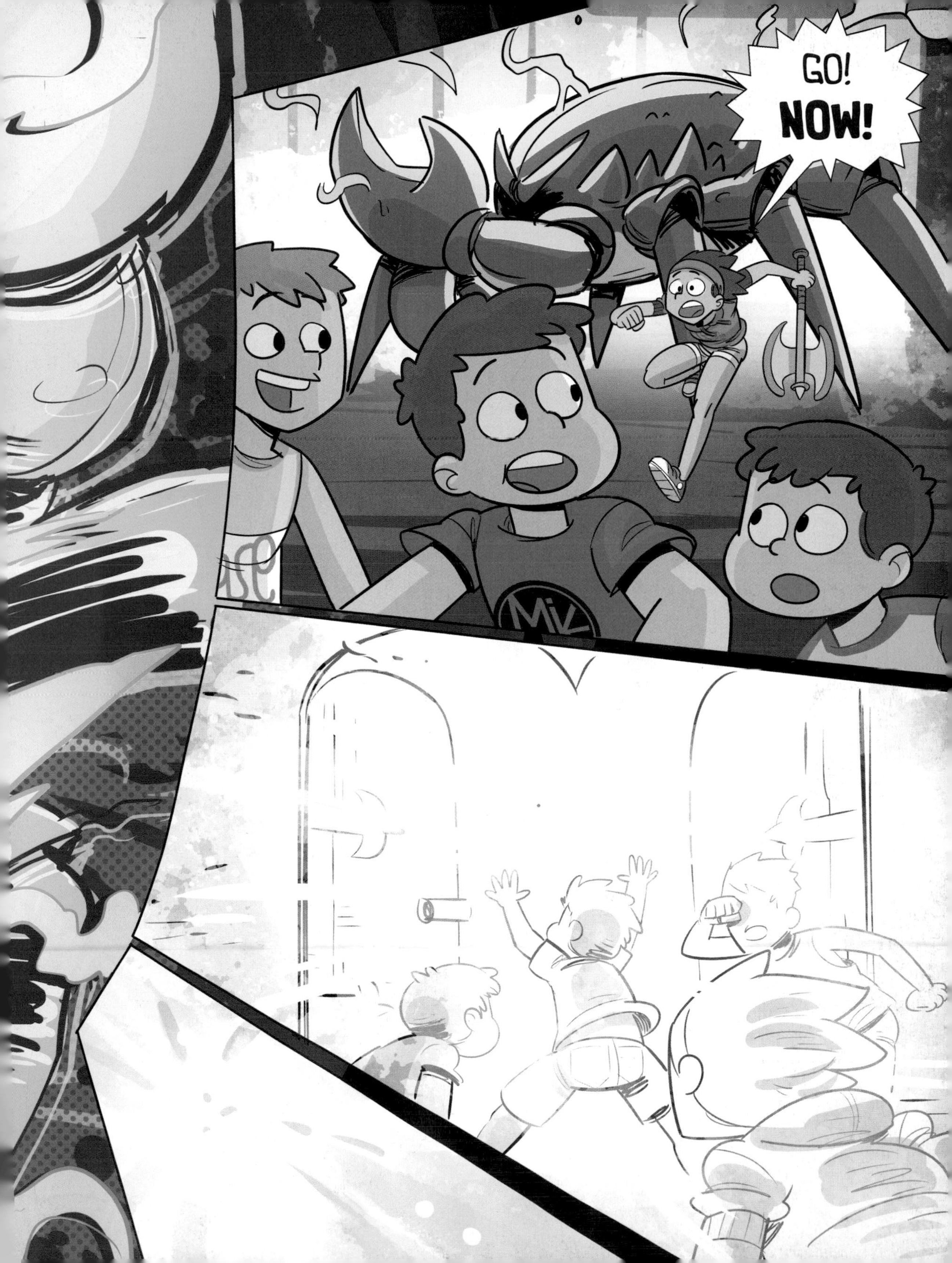
GO! NOW!

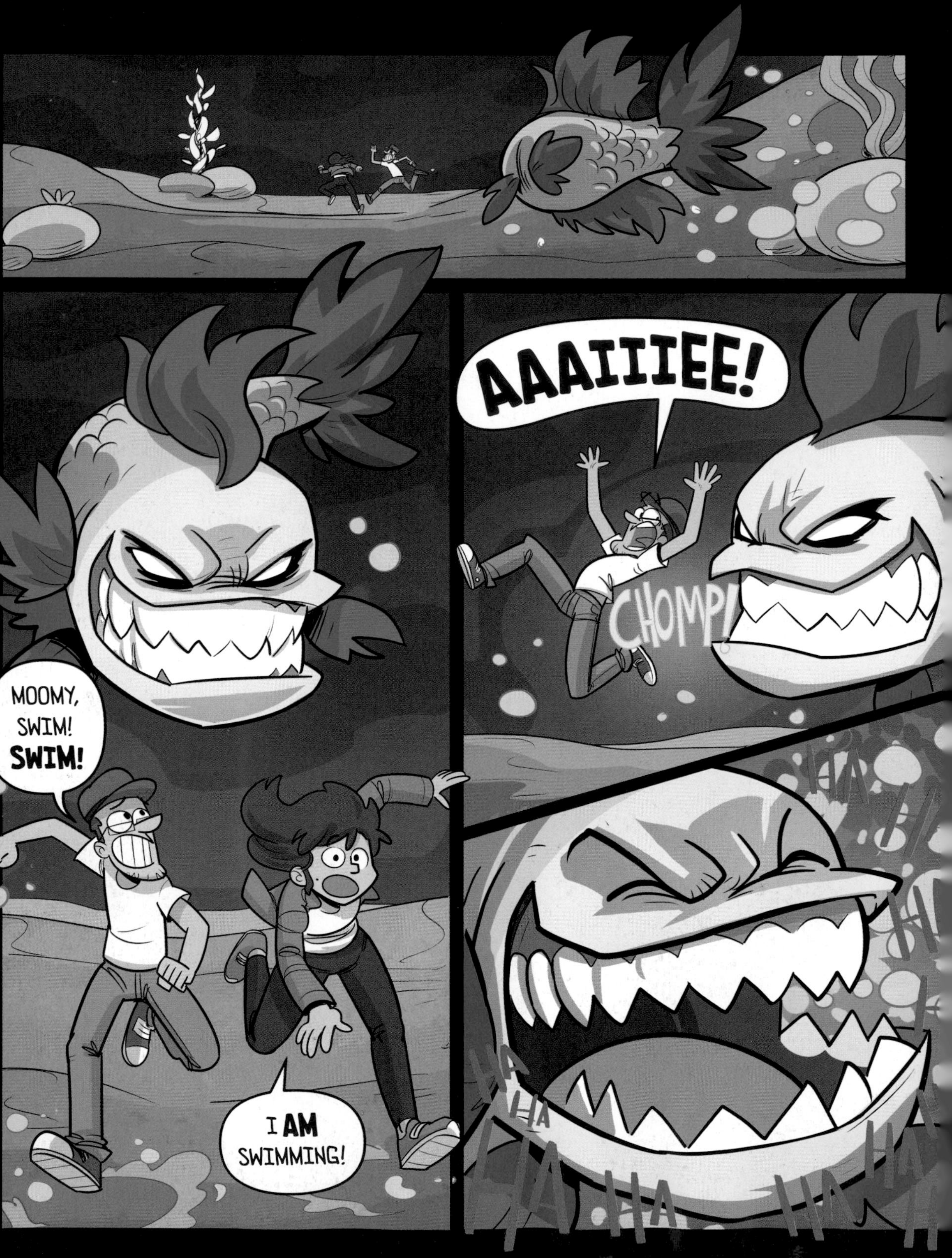
MOOMY, SWIM! SWIM!
I AM SWIMMING!
AAAIIIEE!
CHOMP!
HA HA HA HA HA HA HA HA HA HA

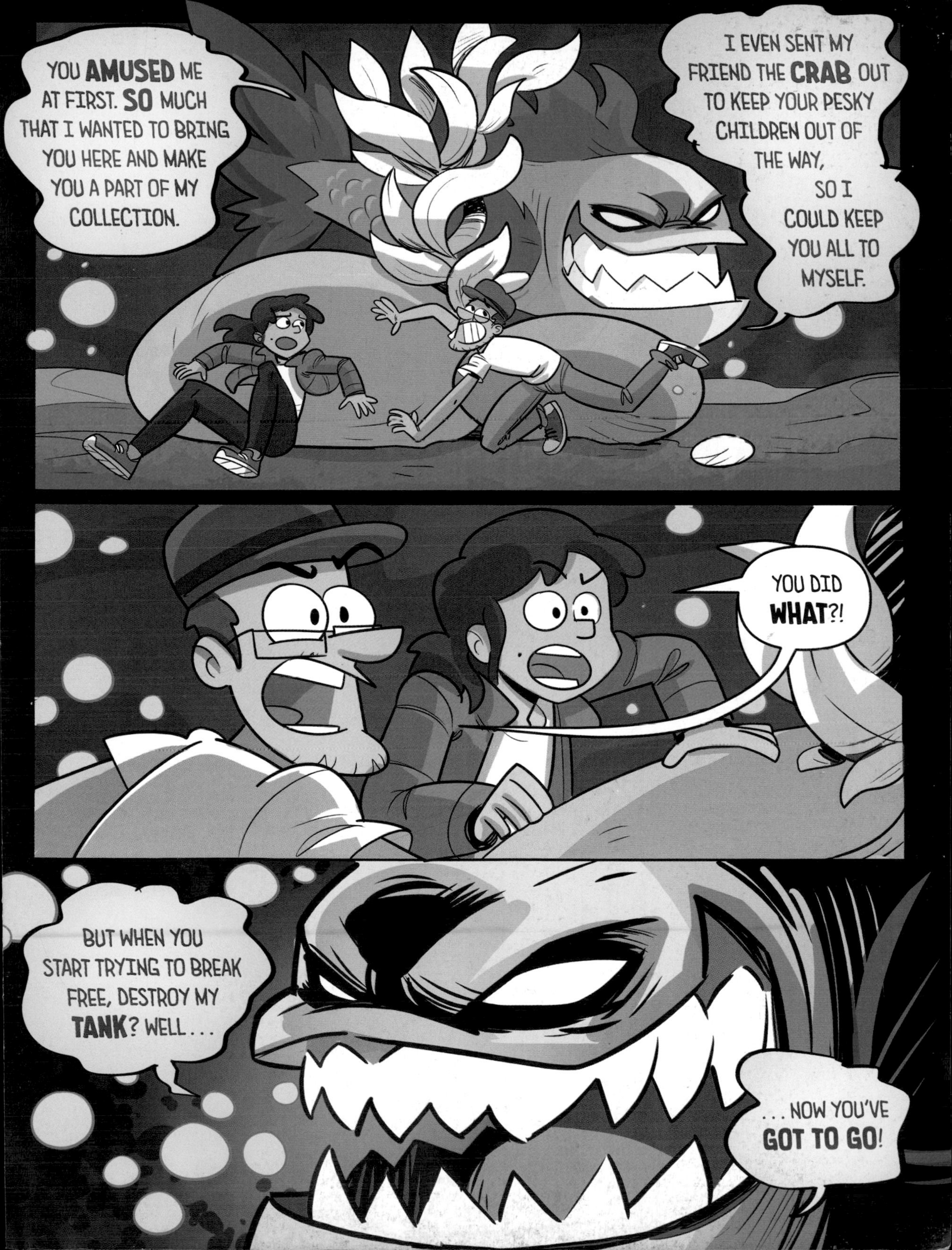
YOU AMUSED ME AT FIRST. SO MUCH THAT I WANTED TO BRING YOU HERE AND MAKE YOU A PART OF MY COLLECTION.
I EVEN SENT MY FRIEND THE CRAB OUT TO KEEP YOUR PESKY CHILDREN OUT OF THE WAY,
SO I COULD KEEP YOU ALL TO MYSELF.
YOU DID WHAT?!
BUT WHEN YOU START TRYING TO BREAK FREE, DESTROY MY TANK? WELL . . .
. . . NOW YOU'VE GOT TO GO!

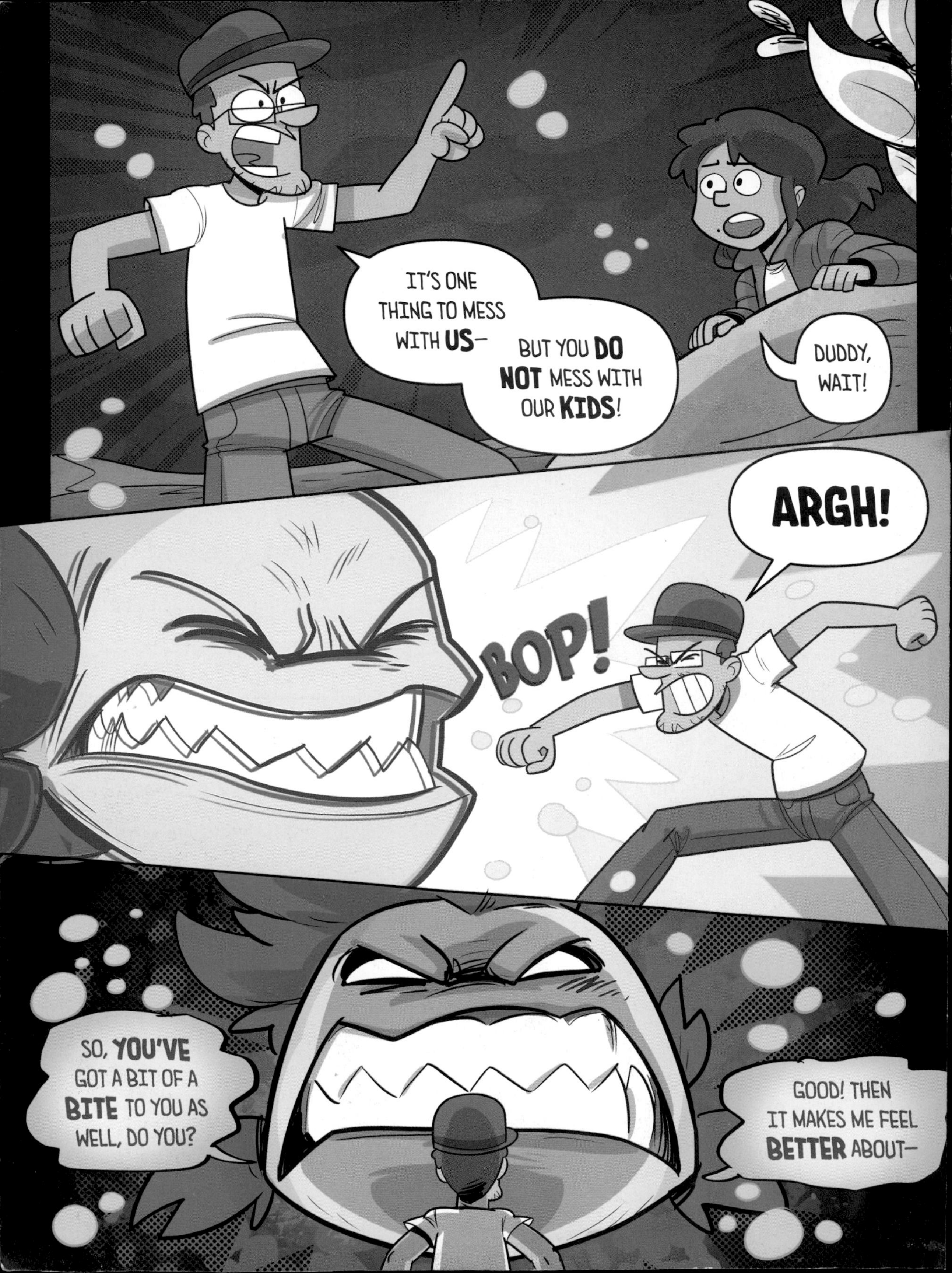
IT'S ONE THING TO MESS WITH **US**—
BUT YOU **DO NOT** MESS WITH OUR **KIDS**!
DUDDY, WAIT!
ARGH!
BOP!
SO, **YOU'VE** GOT A BIT OF A **BITE** TO YOU AS WELL, DO YOU?
GOOD! THEN IT MAKES ME FEEL **BETTER** ABOUT—

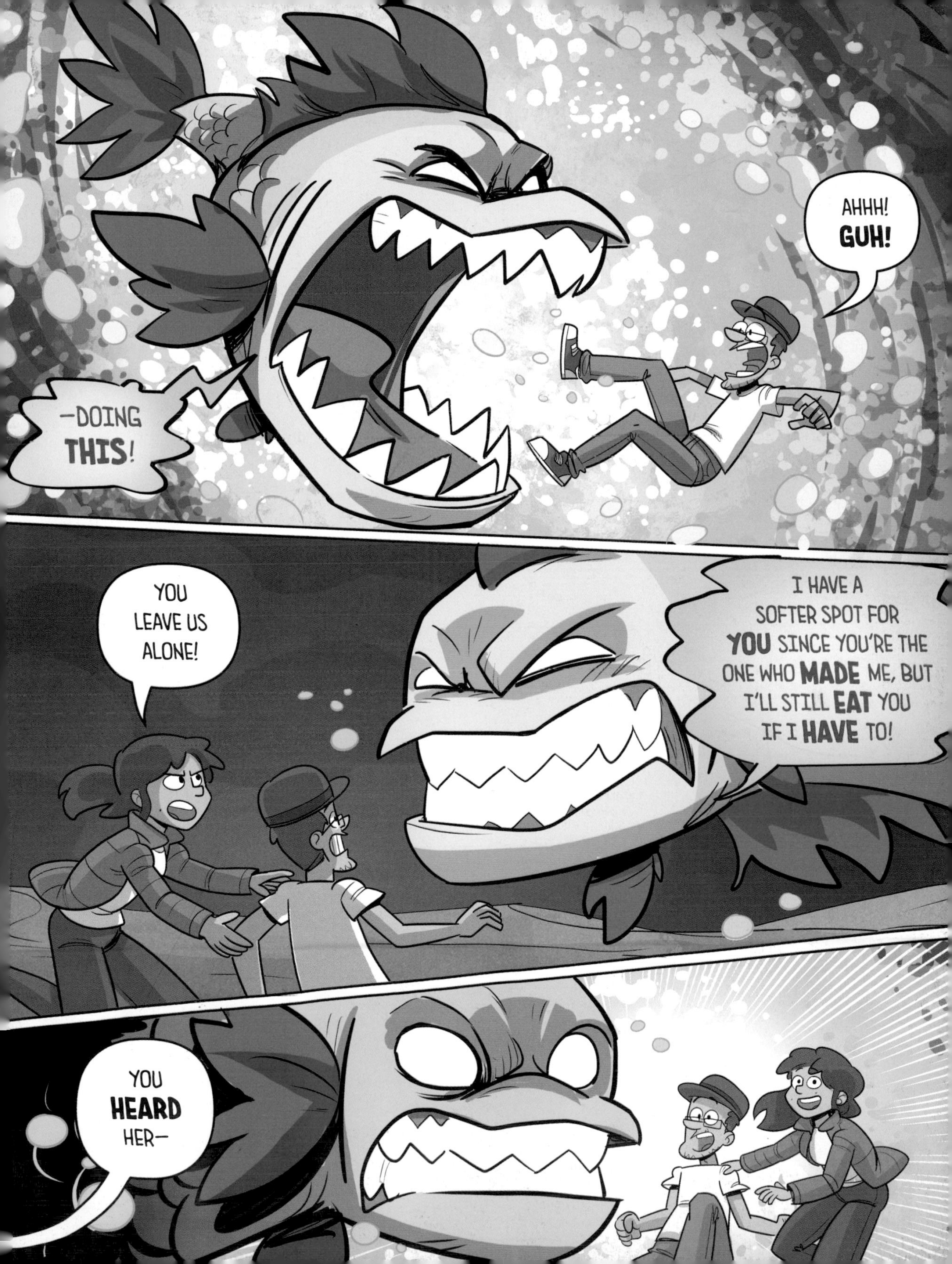
AHHH! GUH!
—DOING THIS!
YOU LEAVE US ALONE!
I HAVE A SOFTER SPOT FOR YOU SINCE YOU'RE THE ONE WHO MADE ME, BUT I'LL STILL EAT YOU IF I HAVE TO!
YOU HEARD HER—

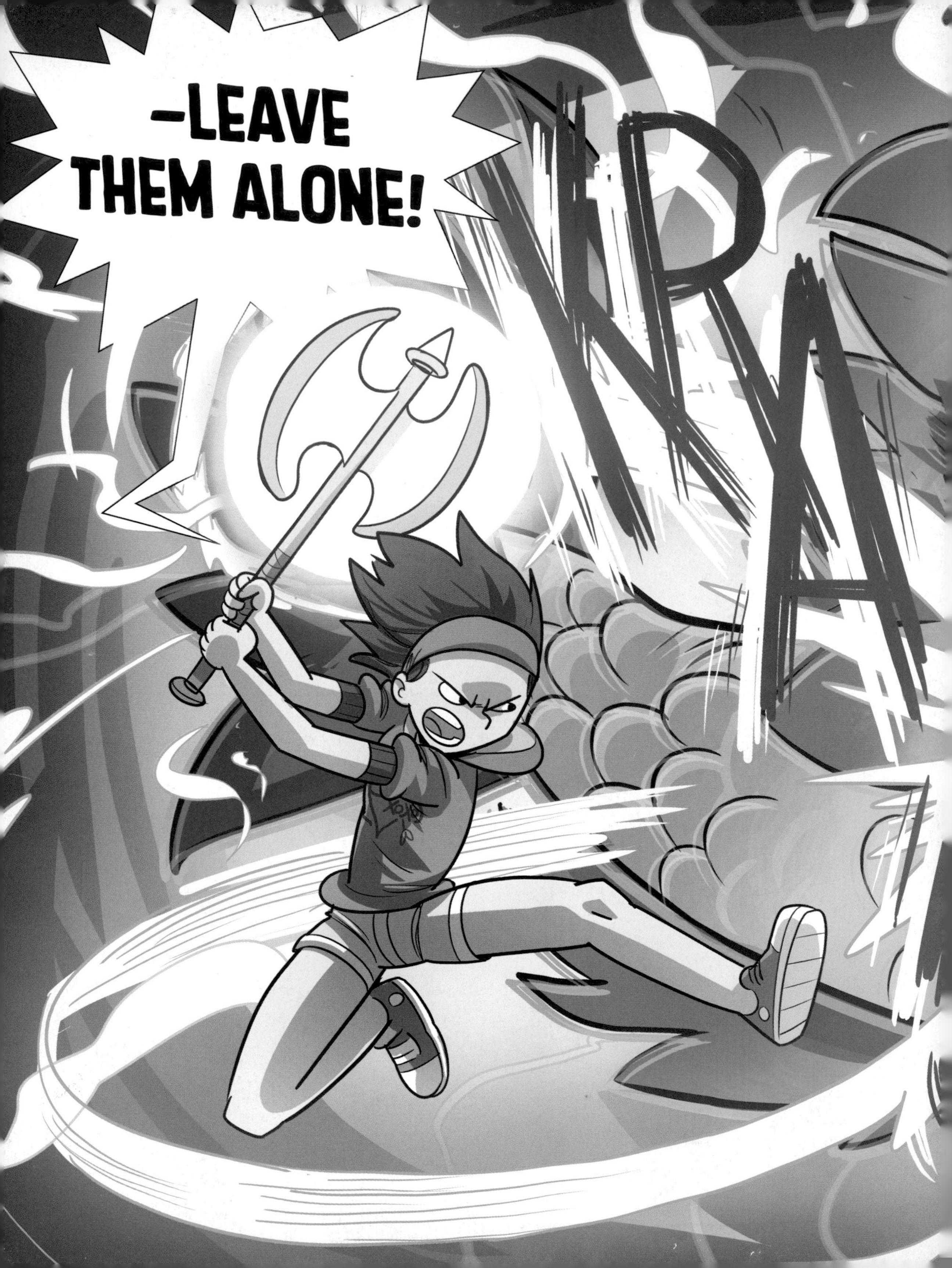
–LEAVE THEM ALONE!

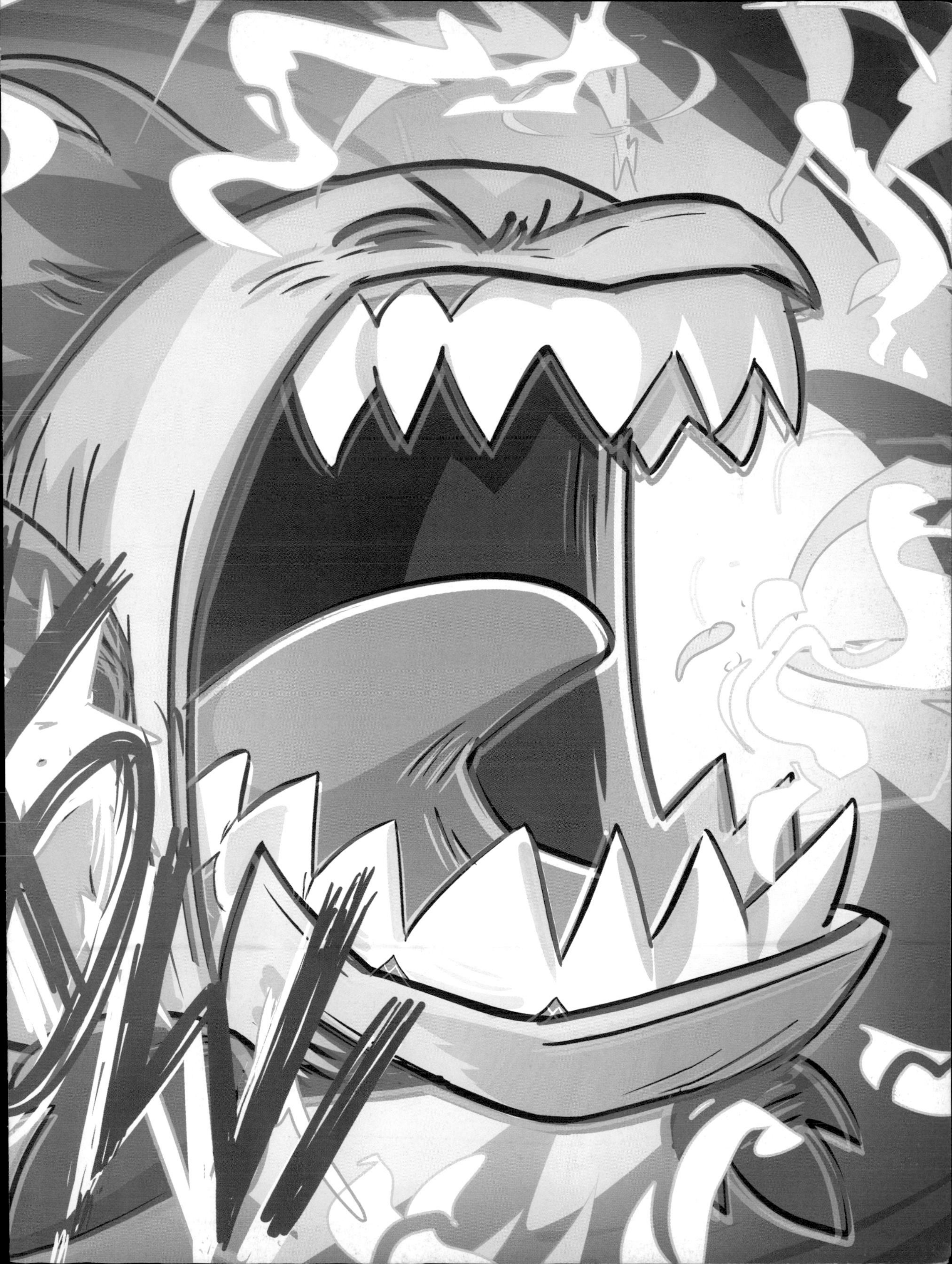

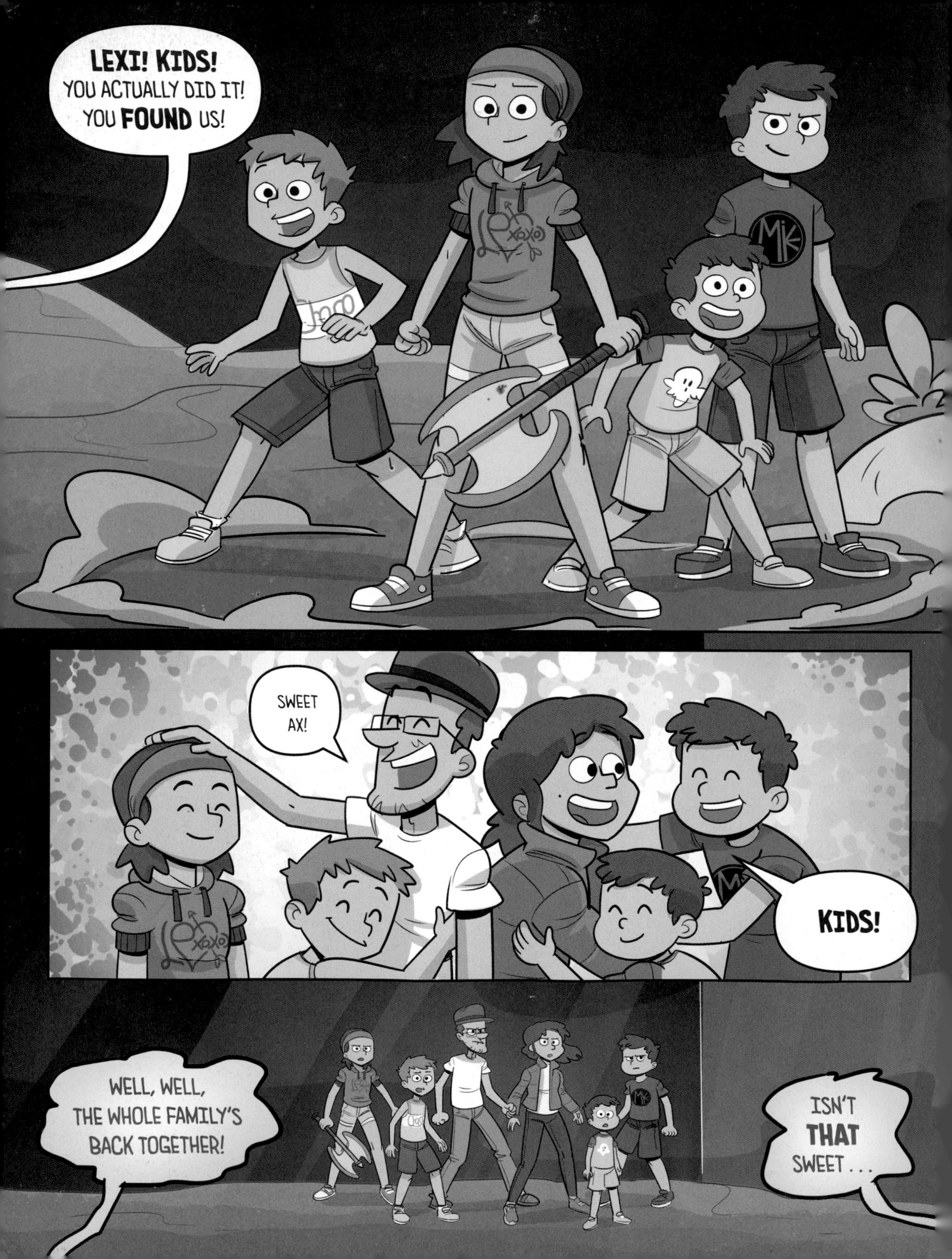
LEXI! KIDS! YOU ACTUALLY DID IT! YOU FOUND US!
SWEET AX!
KIDS!
WELL, WELL, THE WHOLE FAMILY'S BACK TOGETHER!
ISN'T THAT SWEET . . .

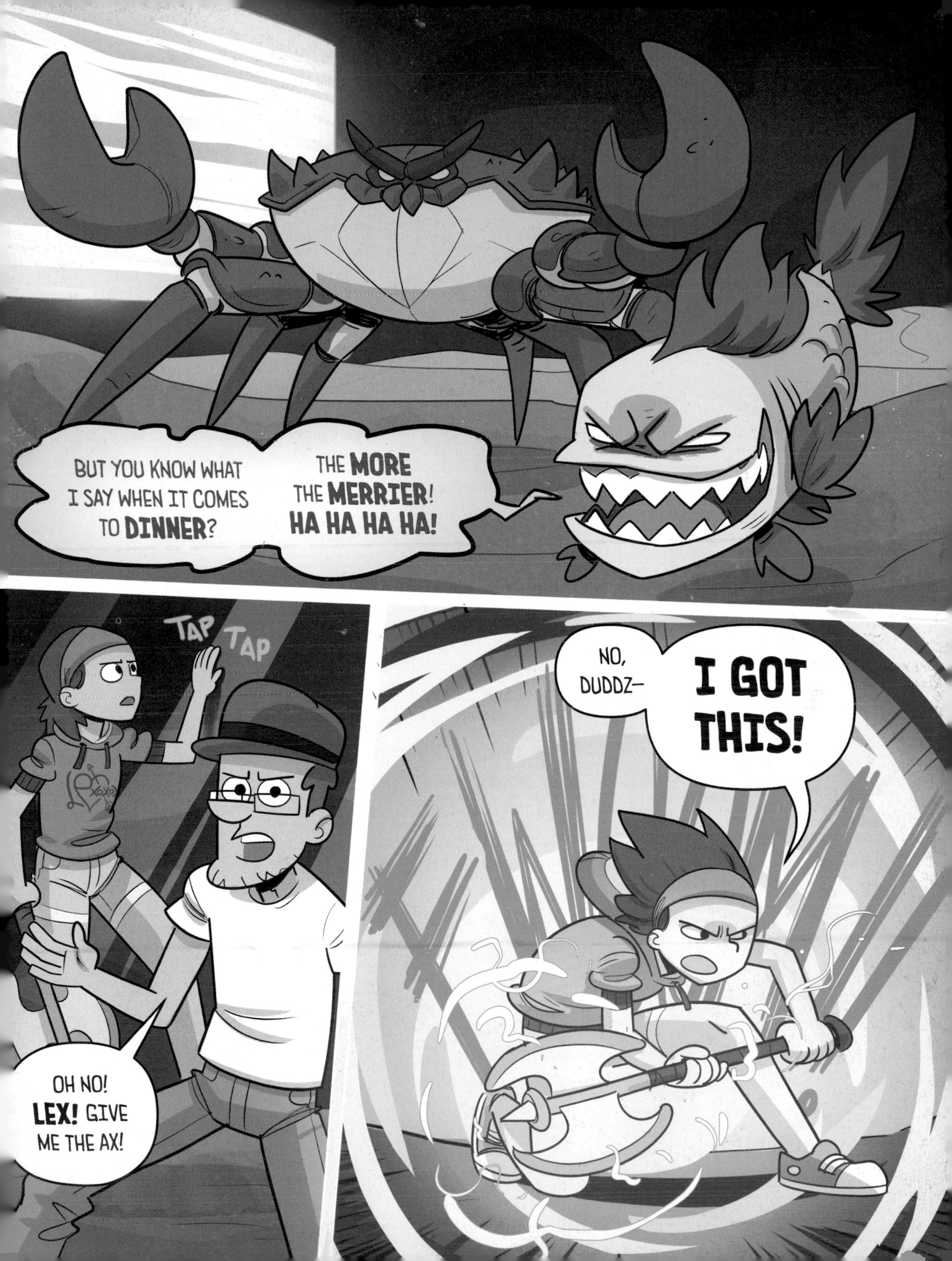

BUT YOU KNOW WHAT I SAY WHEN IT COMES TO **DINNER**?
THE **MORE** THE **MERRIER**! **HA HA HA HA!**
TAP TAP
OH NO! **LEX!** GIVE ME THE AX!
NO, DUDDZ—
I GOT THIS!

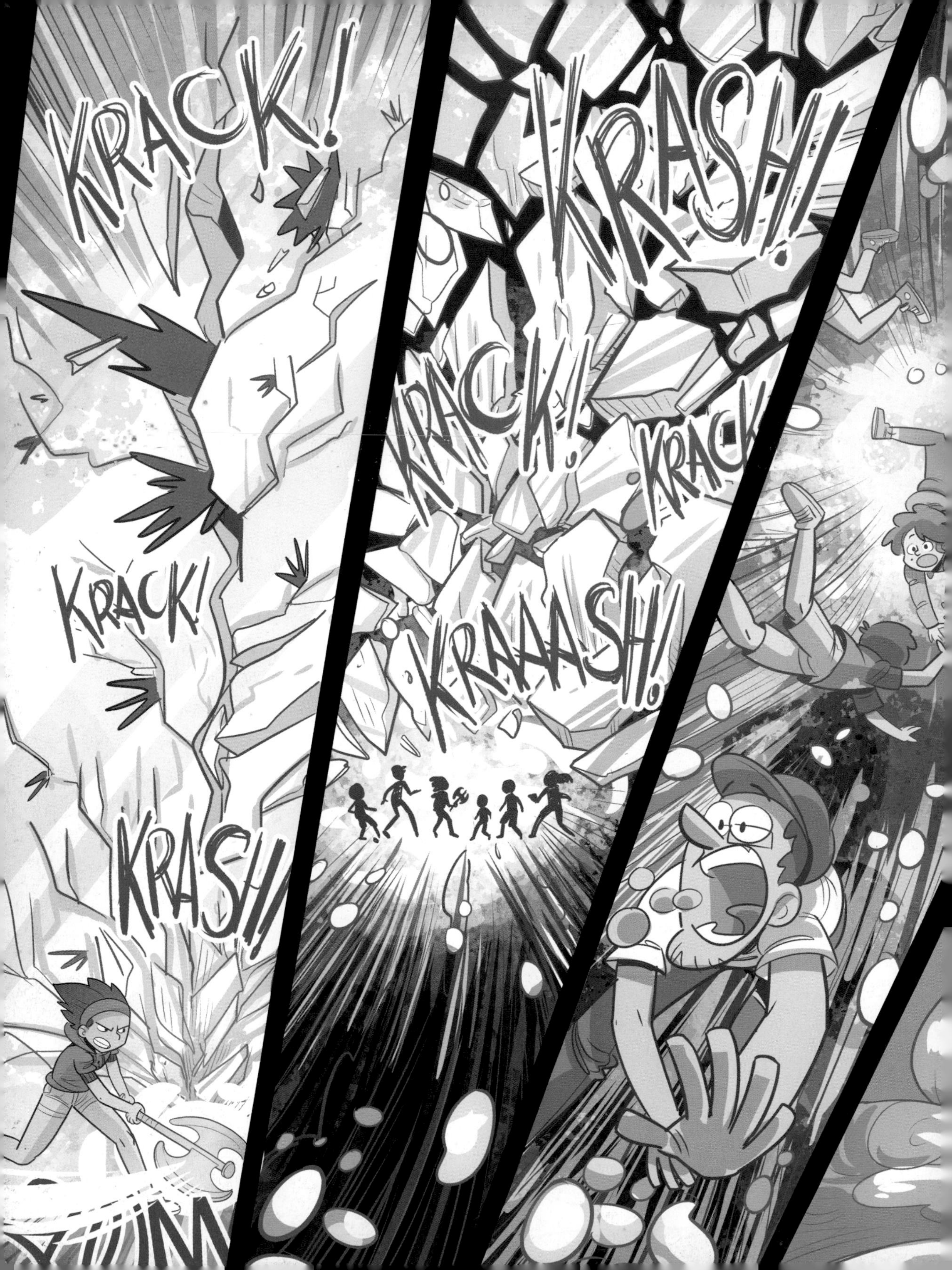

KRACK!
KRACK!
KRASH!
KRASH!
KRACK!
KRACK
KRAAASH!

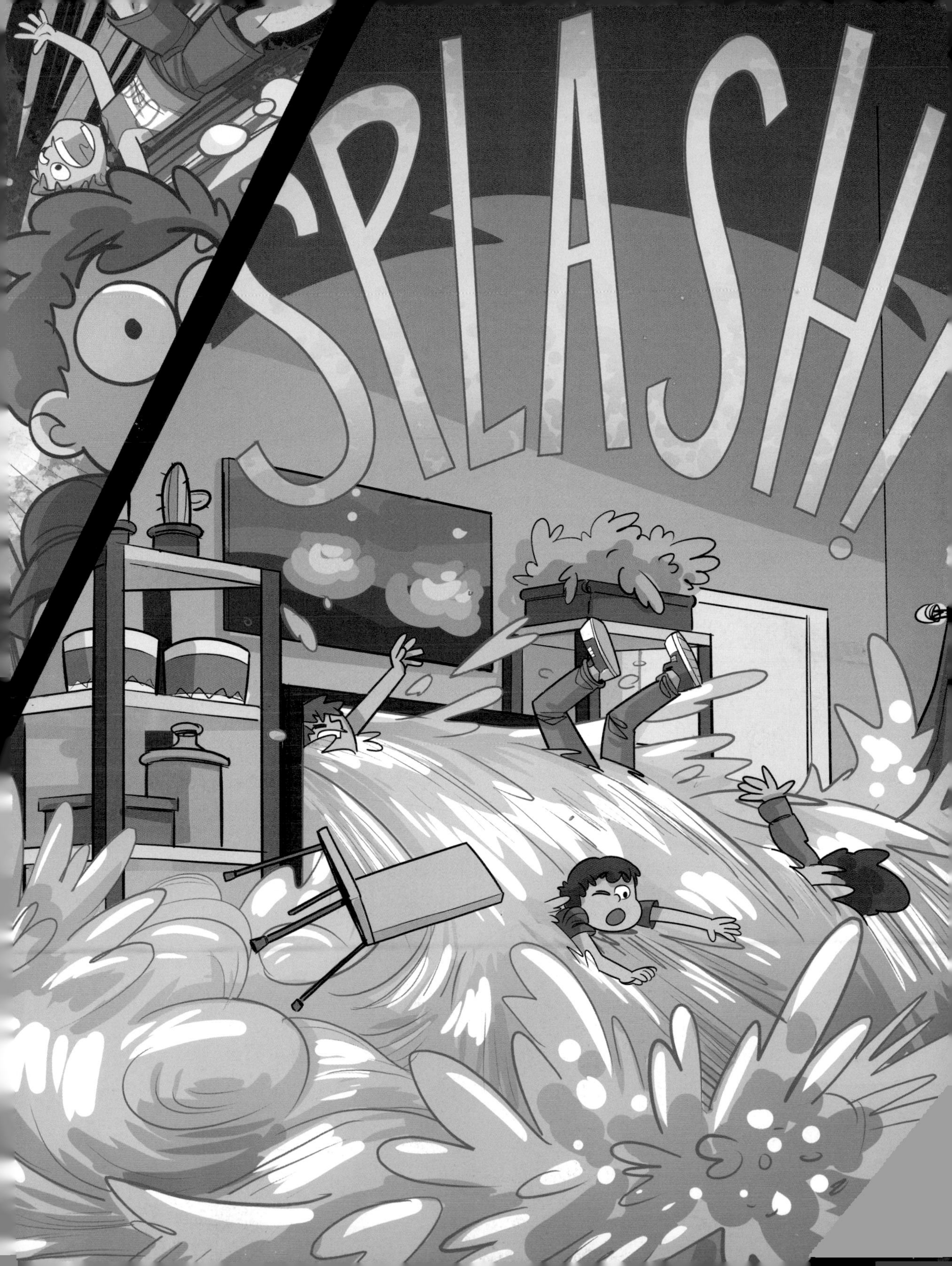
SPLASH!

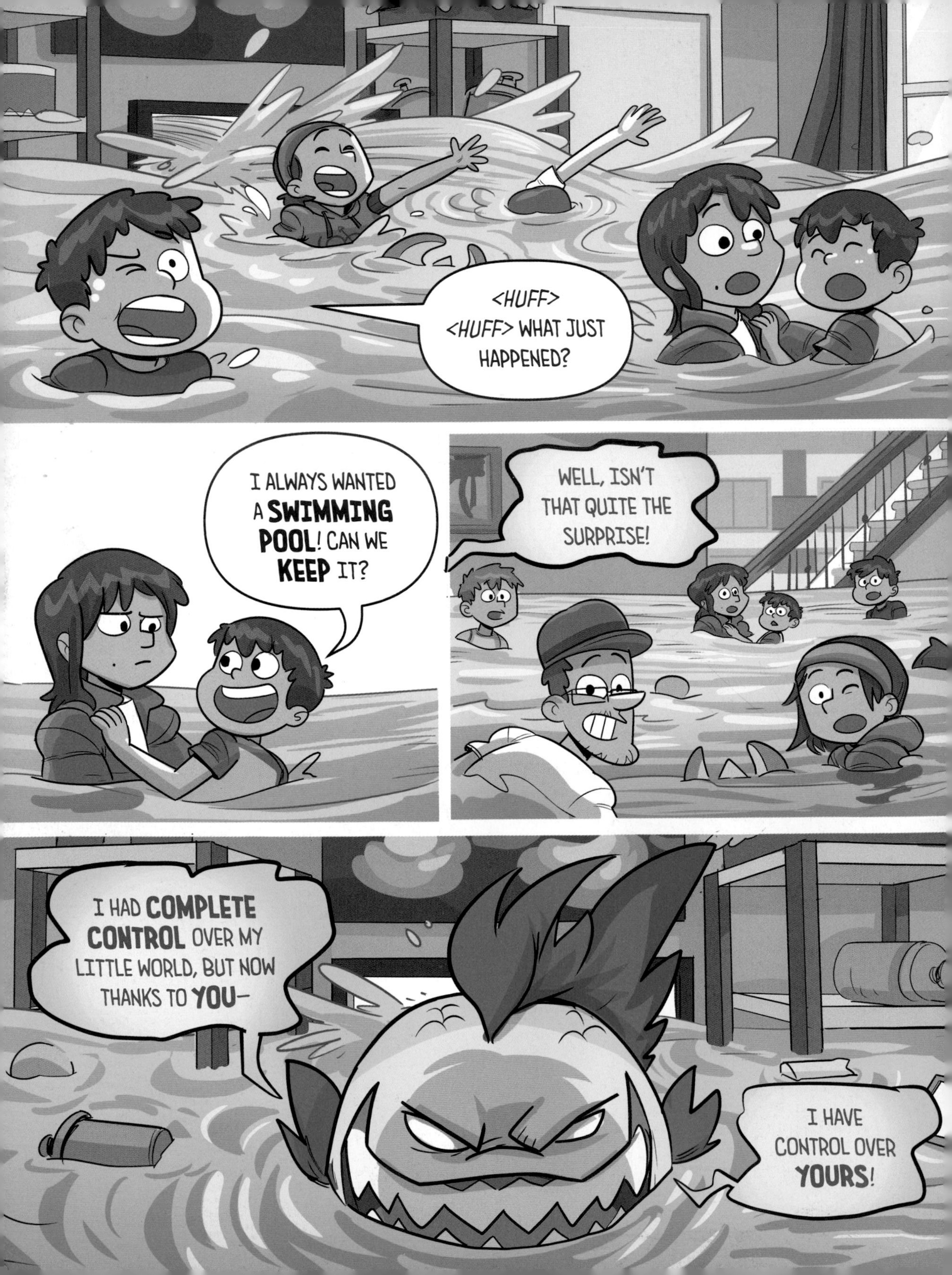

<HUFF> <HUFF> WHAT JUST HAPPENED?
I ALWAYS WANTED A SWIMMING POOL! CAN WE KEEP IT?
WELL, ISN'T THAT QUITE THE SURPRISE!
I HAD COMPLETE CONTROL OVER MY LITTLE WORLD, BUT NOW THANKS TO YOU–
I HAVE CONTROL OVER YOURS!

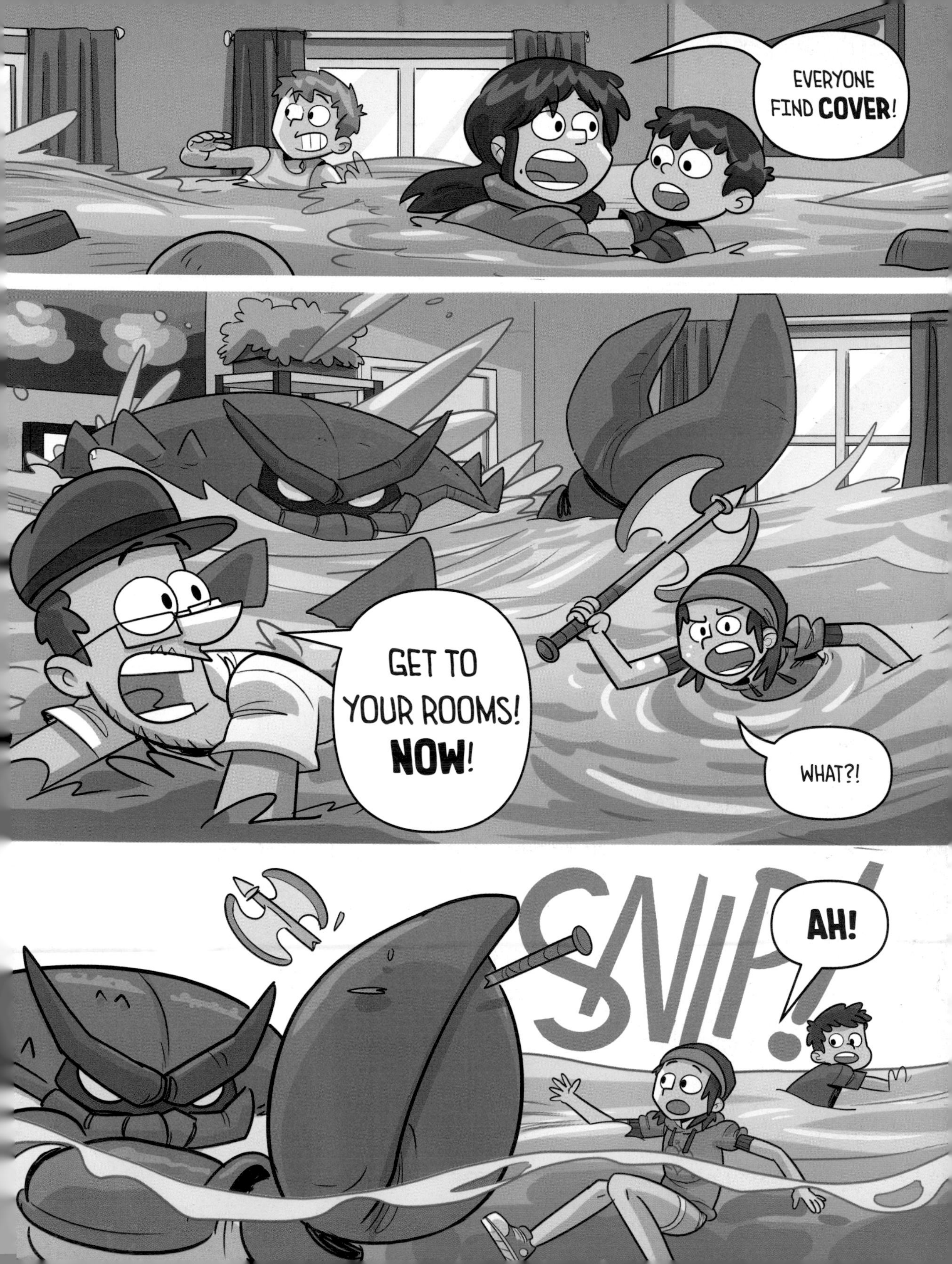
EVERYONE FIND **COVER**!
GET TO YOUR ROOMS! **NOW**!
WHAT?!
SNIP!
AH!

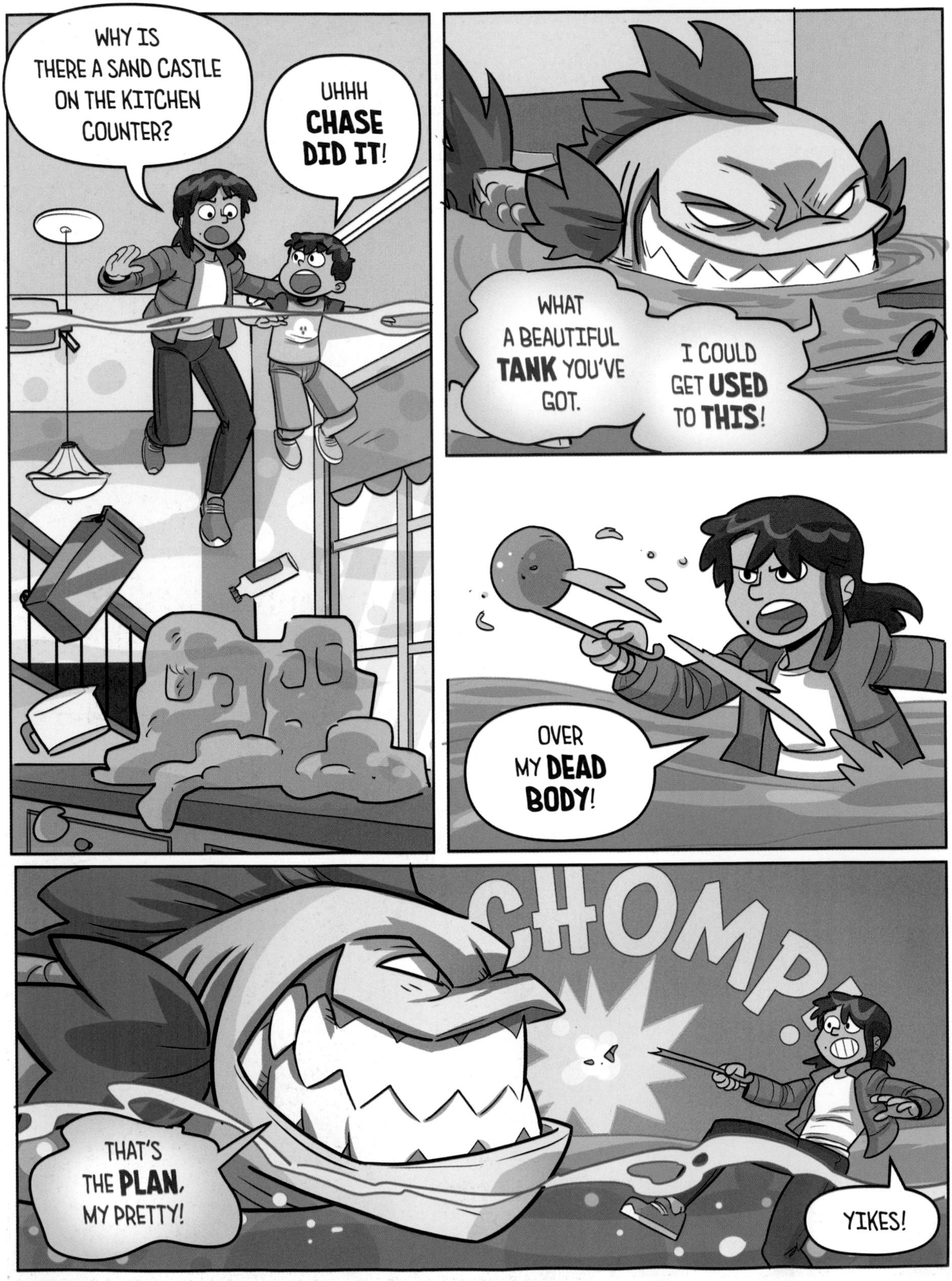
WHY IS THERE A SAND CASTLE ON THE KITCHEN COUNTER?
UHHH **CHASE DID IT**!
WHAT A BEAUTIFUL **TANK** YOU'VE GOT.
I COULD GET **USED** TO **THIS**!
OVER MY **DEAD BODY**!
CHOMP!
THAT'S THE **PLAN**, MY PRETTY!
YIKES!

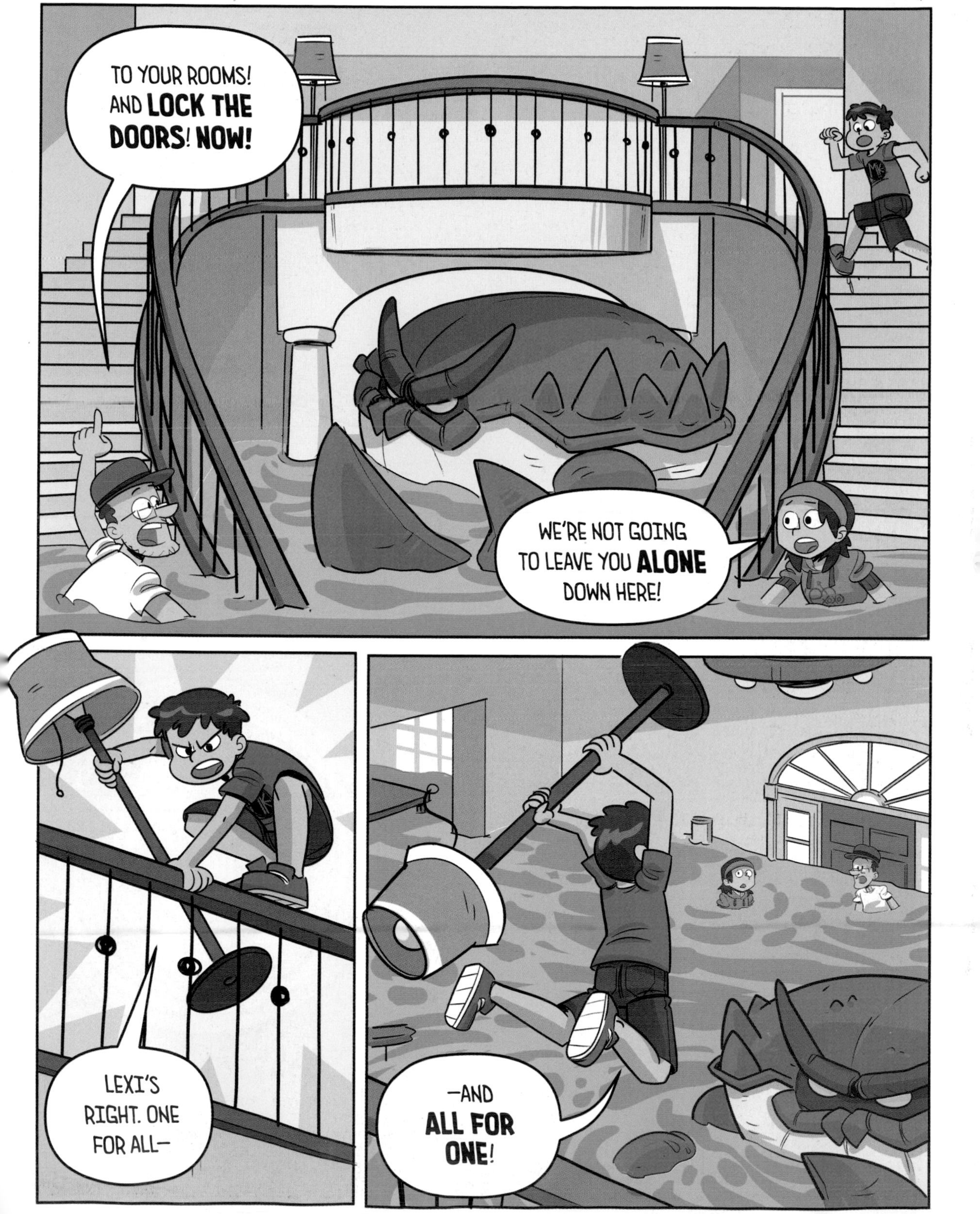
TO YOUR ROOMS! AND **LOCK THE DOORS**! **NOW!**
WE'RE NOT GOING TO LEAVE YOU **ALONE** DOWN HERE!
LEXI'S RIGHT. ONE FOR ALL—
—AND **ALL FOR ONE**!

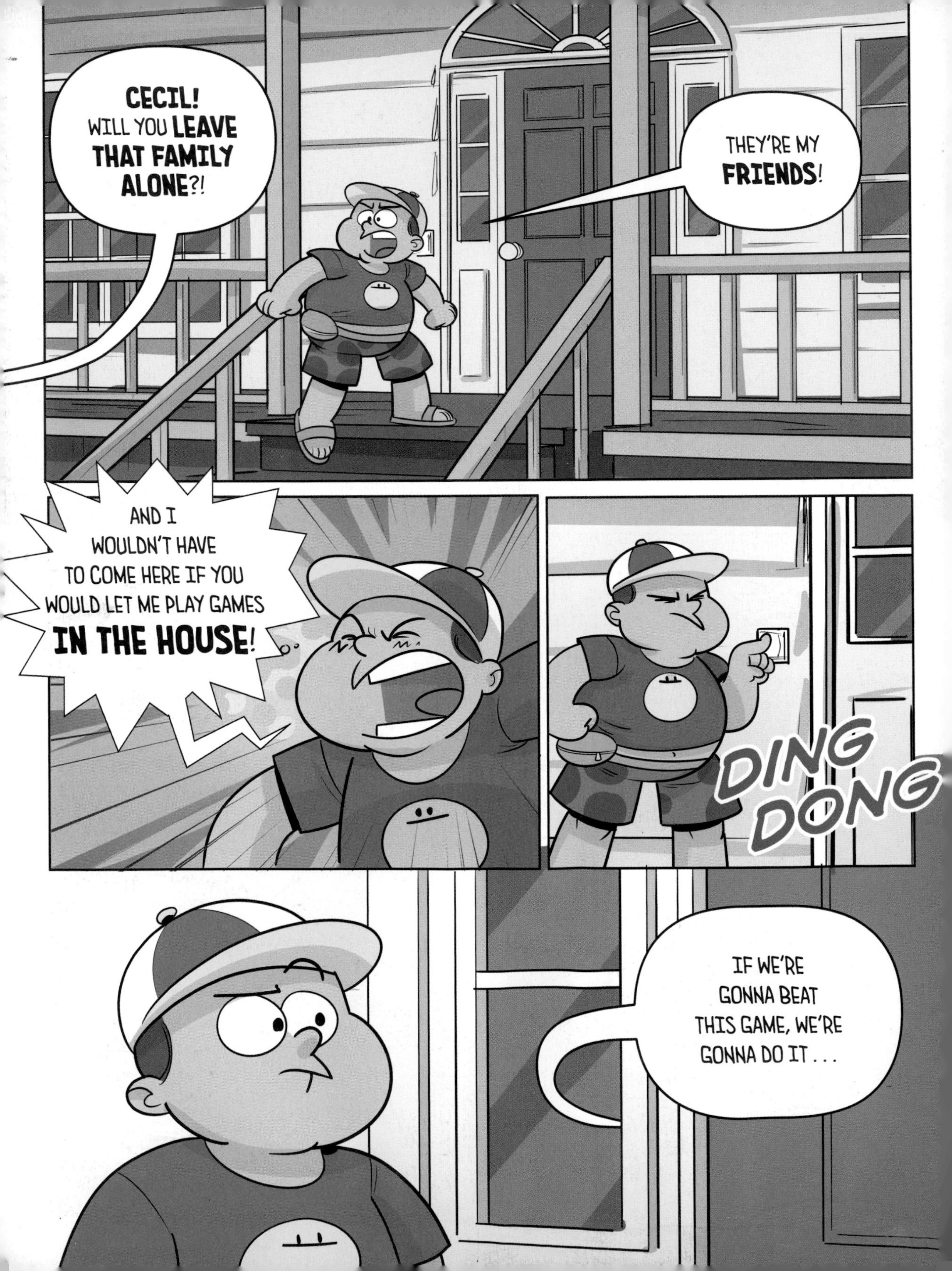

CECIL! WILL YOU LEAVE THAT FAMILY ALONE?!
THEY'RE MY FRIENDS!
AND I WOULDN'T HAVE TO COME HERE IF YOU WOULD LET ME PLAY GAMES IN THE HOUSE!
DING DONG
IF WE'RE GONNA BEAT THIS GAME, WE'RE GONNA DO IT . . .

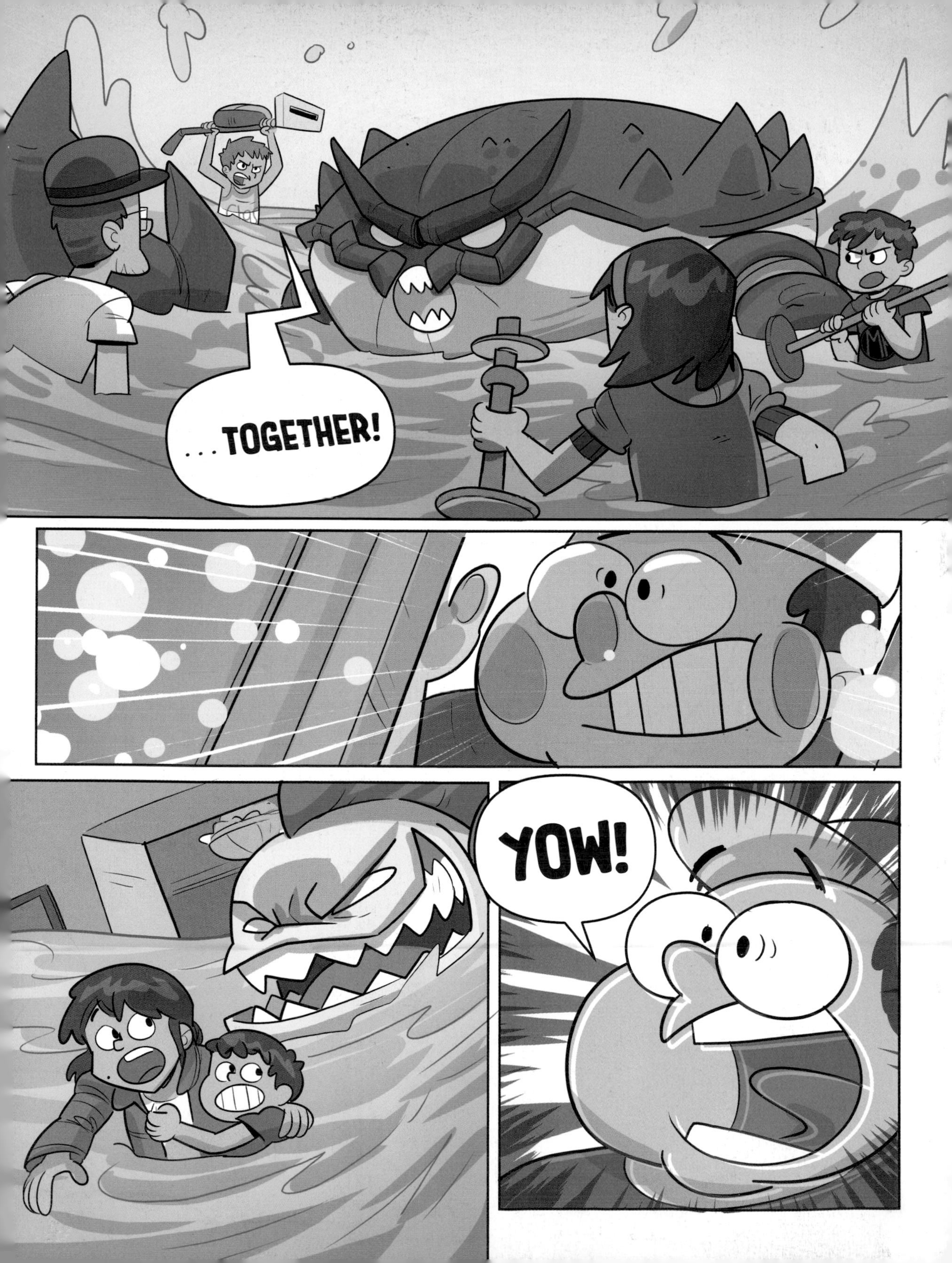
...TOGETHER!
YOW!

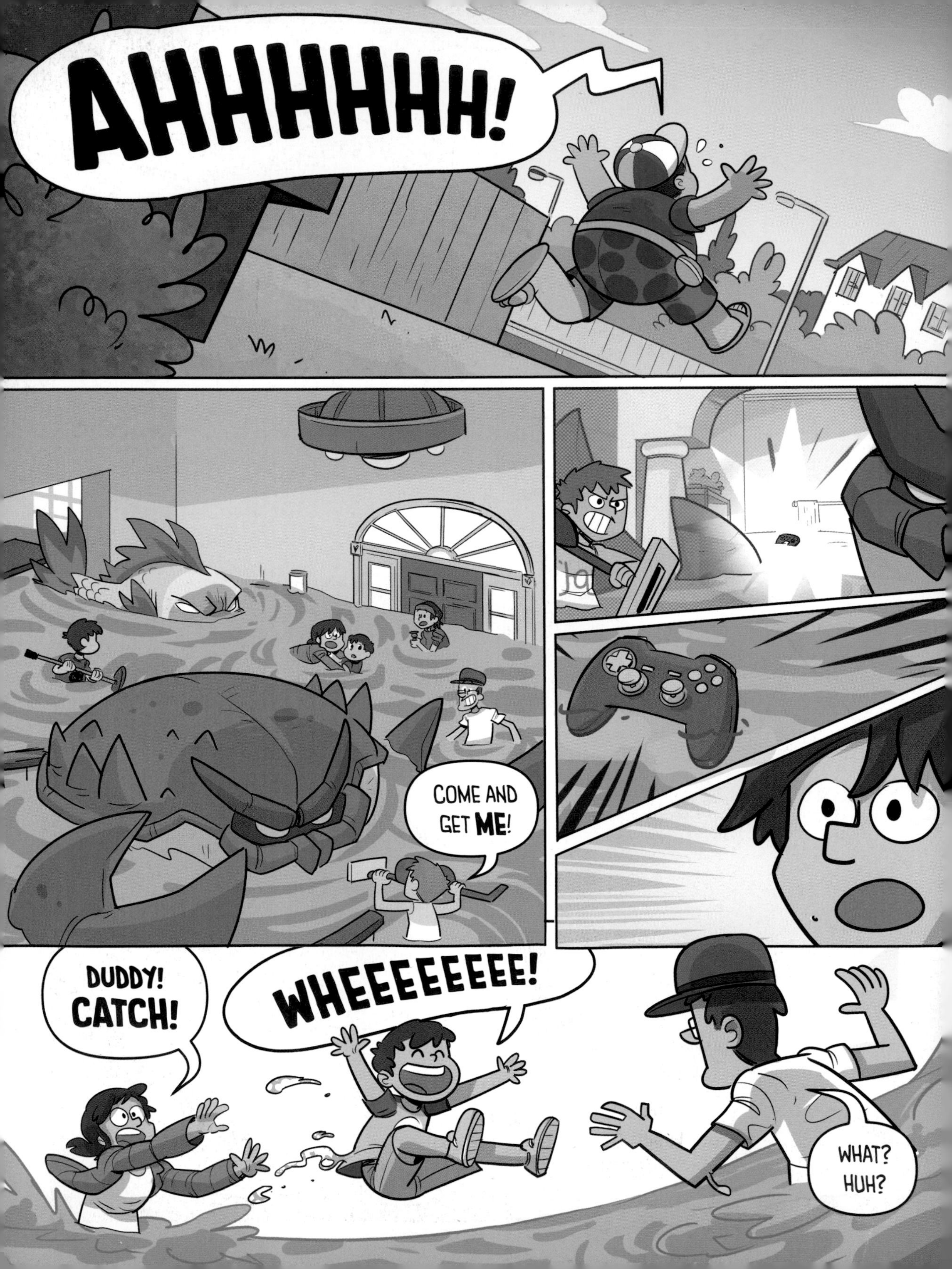
AHHHHHH!
COME AND GET ME!
DUDDY! CATCH!
WHEEEEEEEE!
WHAT? HUH?

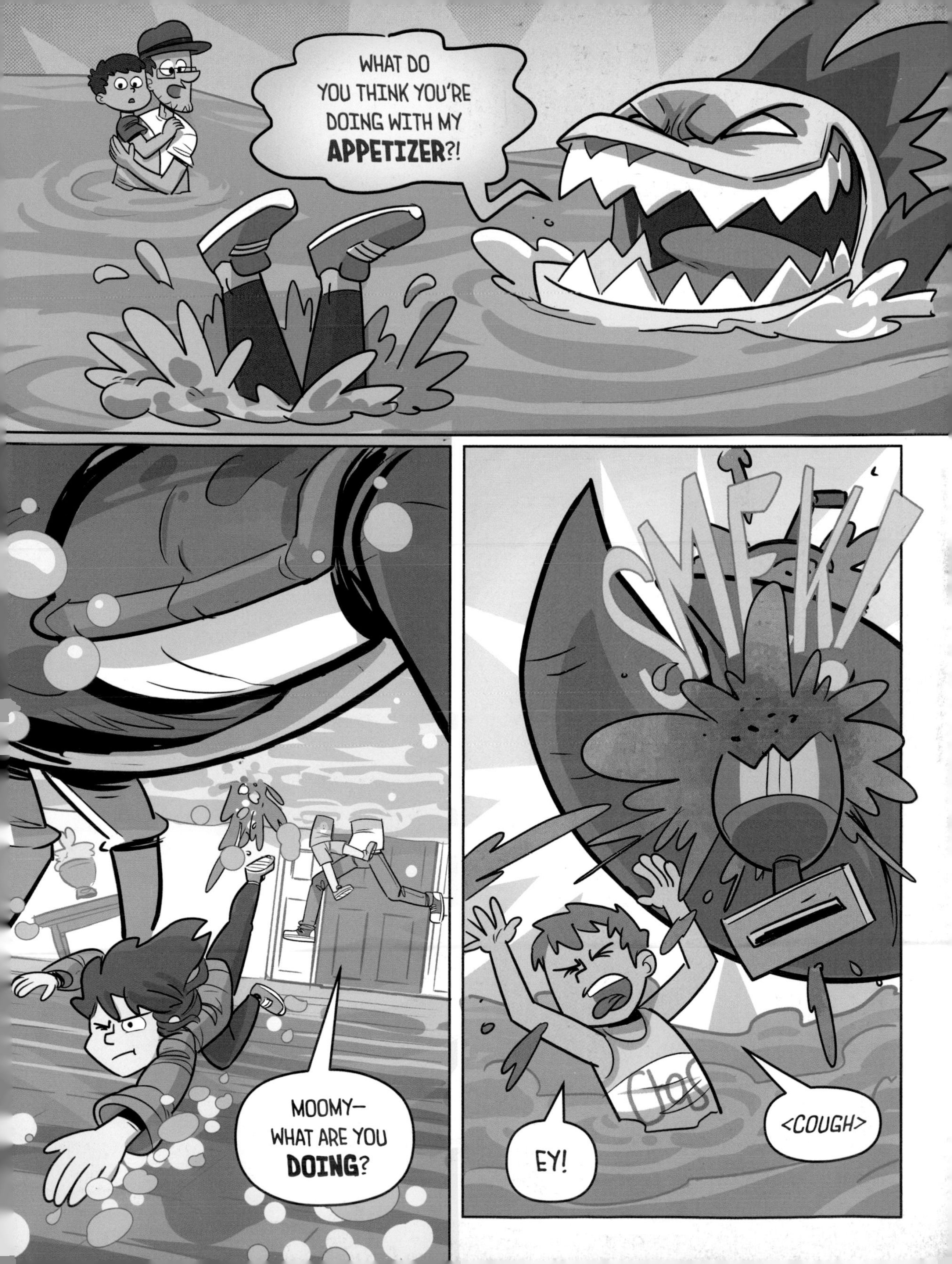
WHAT DO YOU THINK YOU'RE DOING WITH MY **APPETIZER**?!
MOOMY— WHAT ARE YOU **DOING**?
SMEK!
EY!
<COUGH>

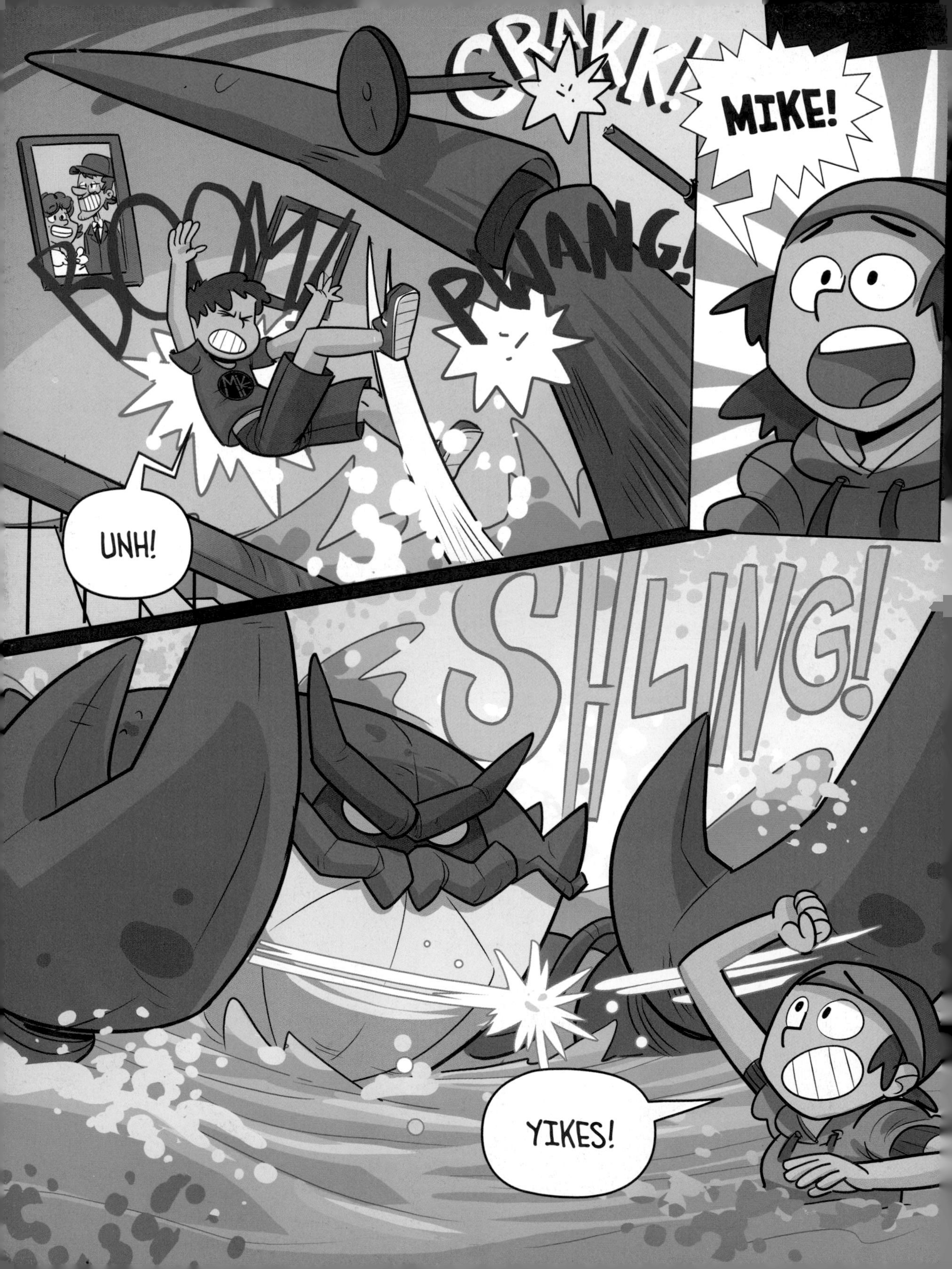
CRAKK!
MIKE!
BOOM!
PWANG!
UNH!
SHLING!
YIKES!

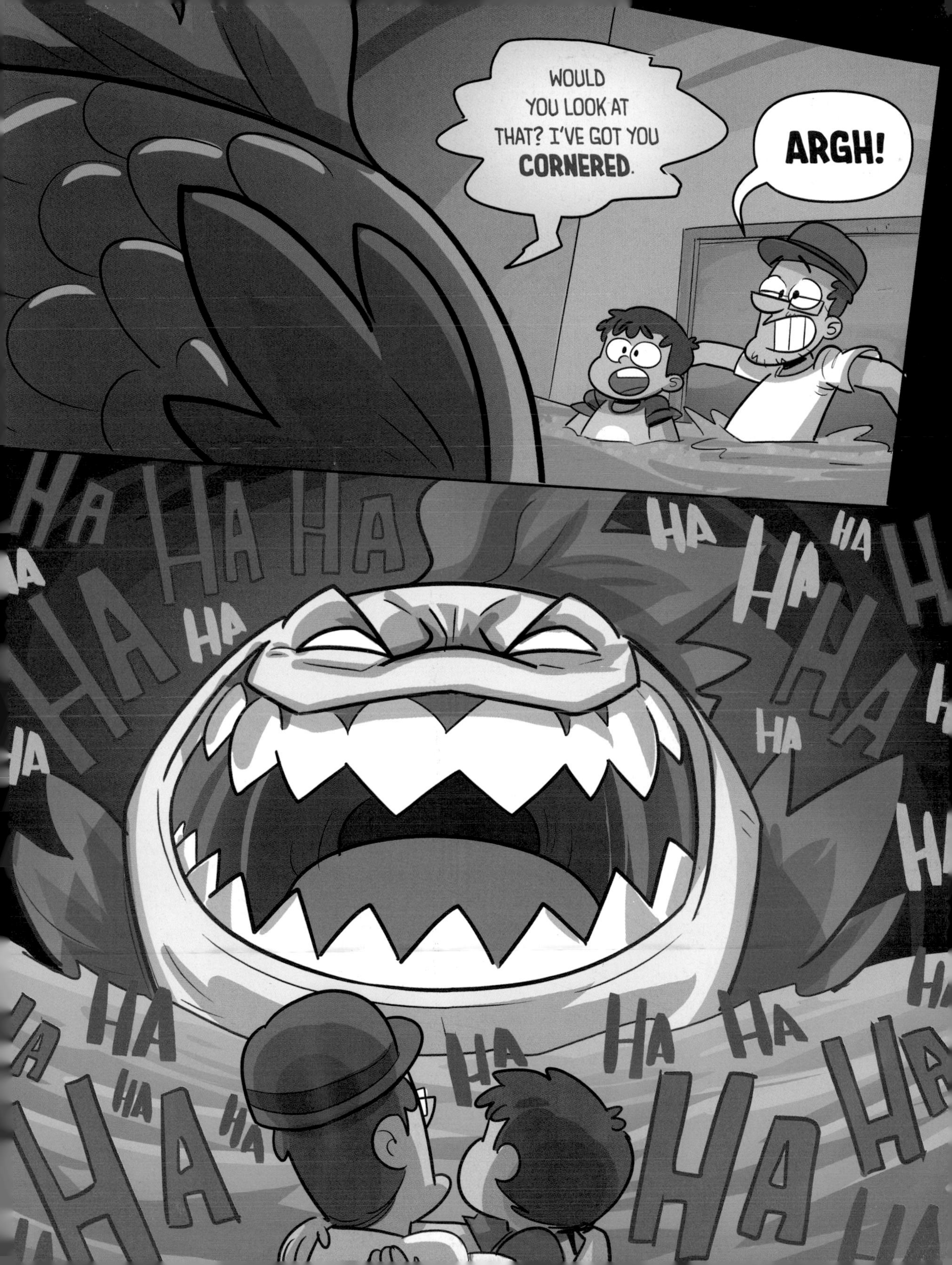
WOULD YOU LOOK AT THAT? I'VE GOT YOU CORNERED.
ARGH!
HA HA HA HA HA HA HA HA HA HA HA HA HA HA HA HA HA

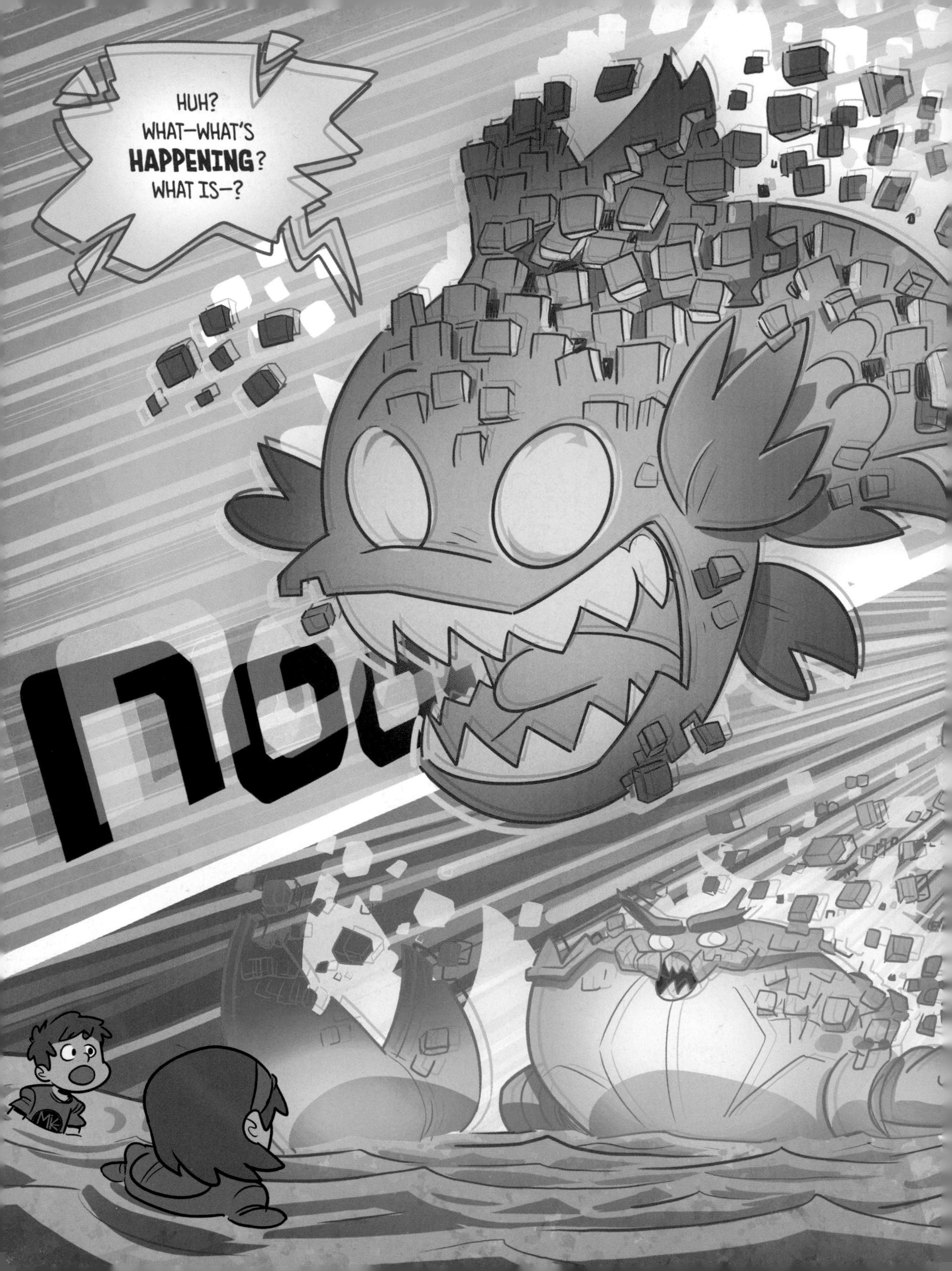
HUH? WHAT—WHAT'S **HAPPENING**? WHAT IS—?
NOO

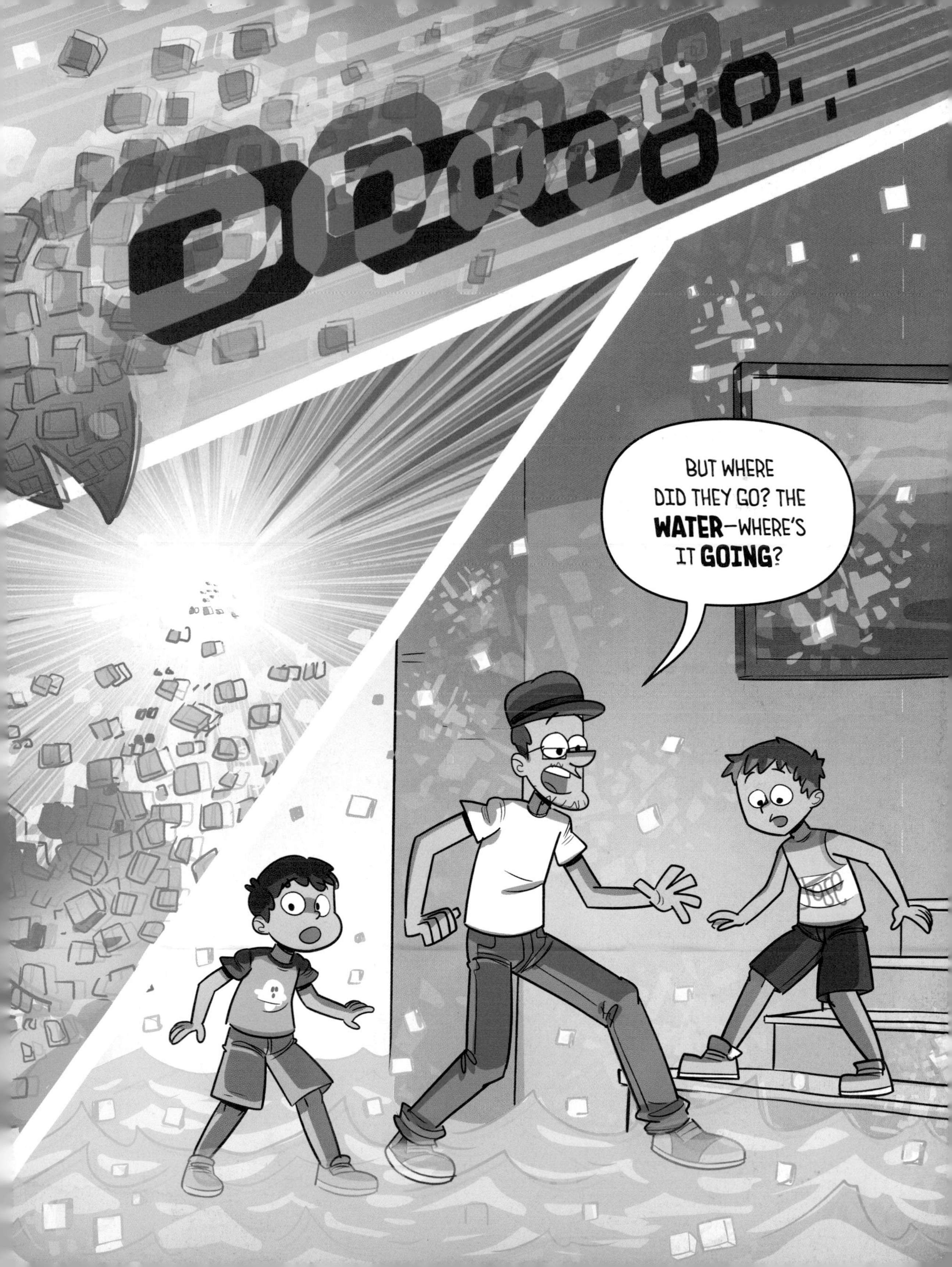

BUT WHERE DID THEY GO? THE **WATER**—WHERE'S IT **GOING**?

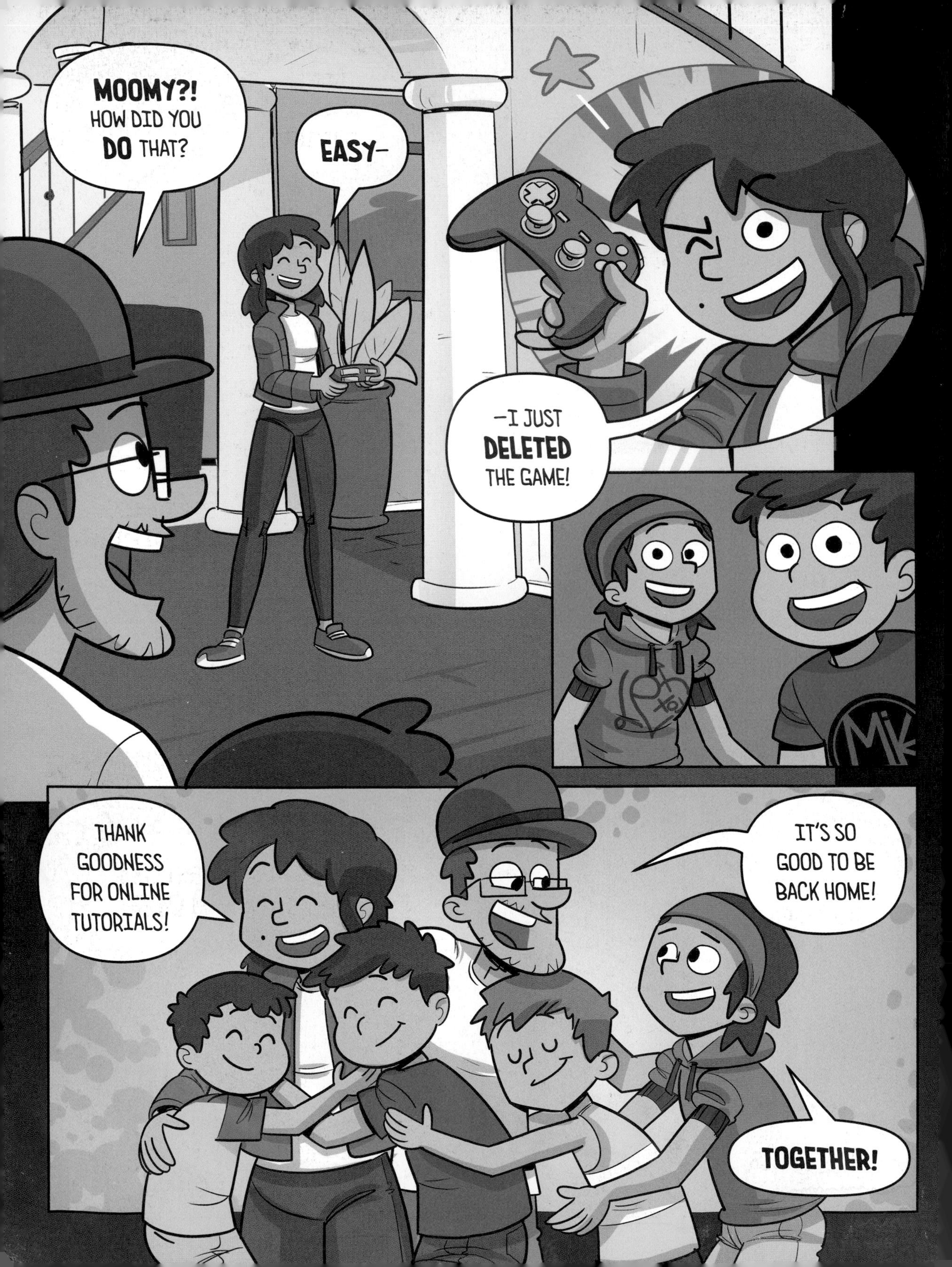
MOOMY?! HOW DID YOU DO THAT?
EASY-
—I JUST DELETED THE GAME!
THANK GOODNESS FOR ONLINE TUTORIALS!
IT'S SO GOOD TO BE BACK HOME!
TOGETHER!

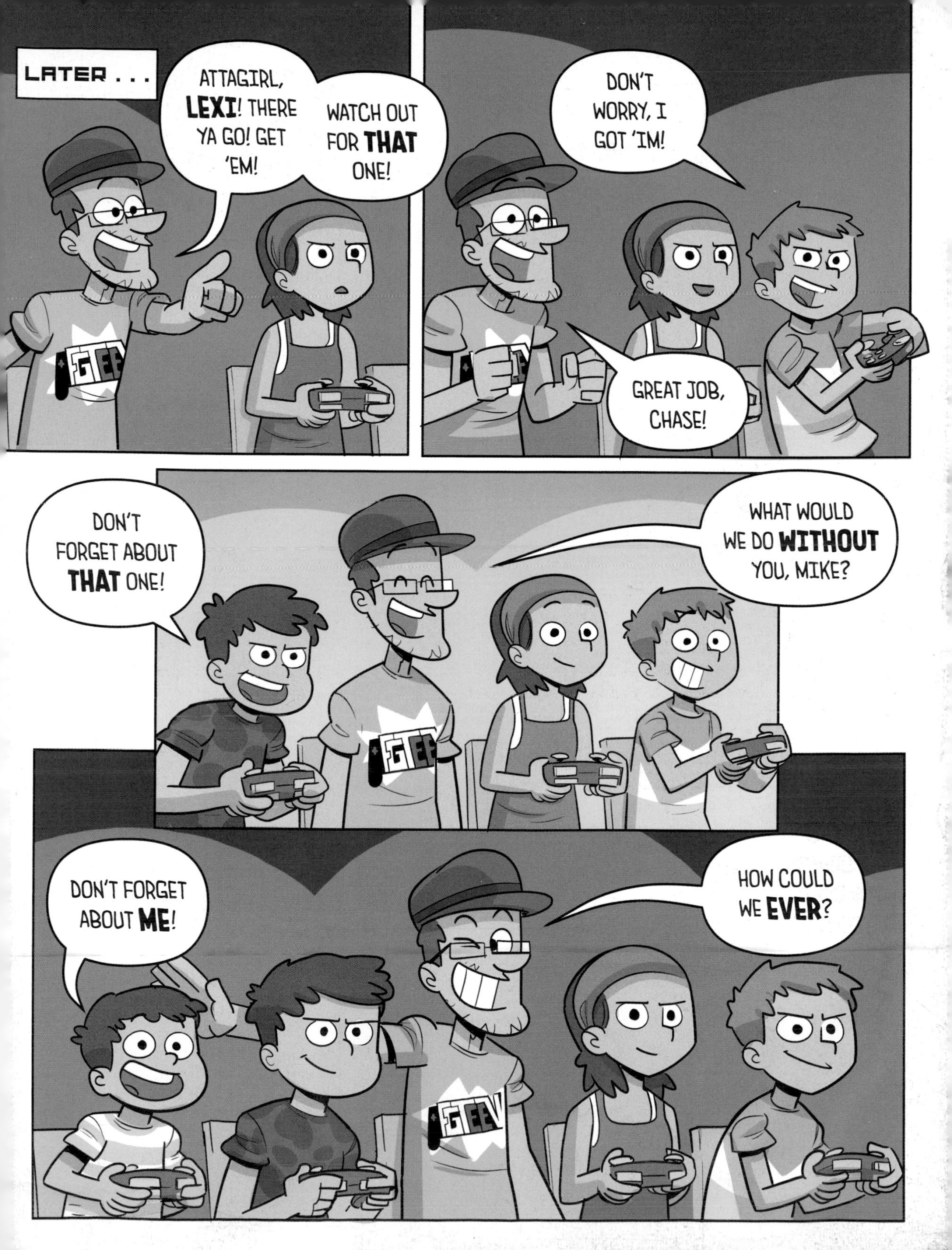
LATER . . .
ATTAGIRL, **LEXI**! THERE YA GO! GET 'EM!
WATCH OUT FOR **THAT** ONE!
DON'T WORRY, I GOT 'IM!
GREAT JOB, CHASE!
DON'T FORGET ABOUT **THAT** ONE!
WHAT WOULD WE DO **WITHOUT** YOU, MIKE?
DON'T FORGET ABOUT **ME**!
HOW COULD WE **EVER**?

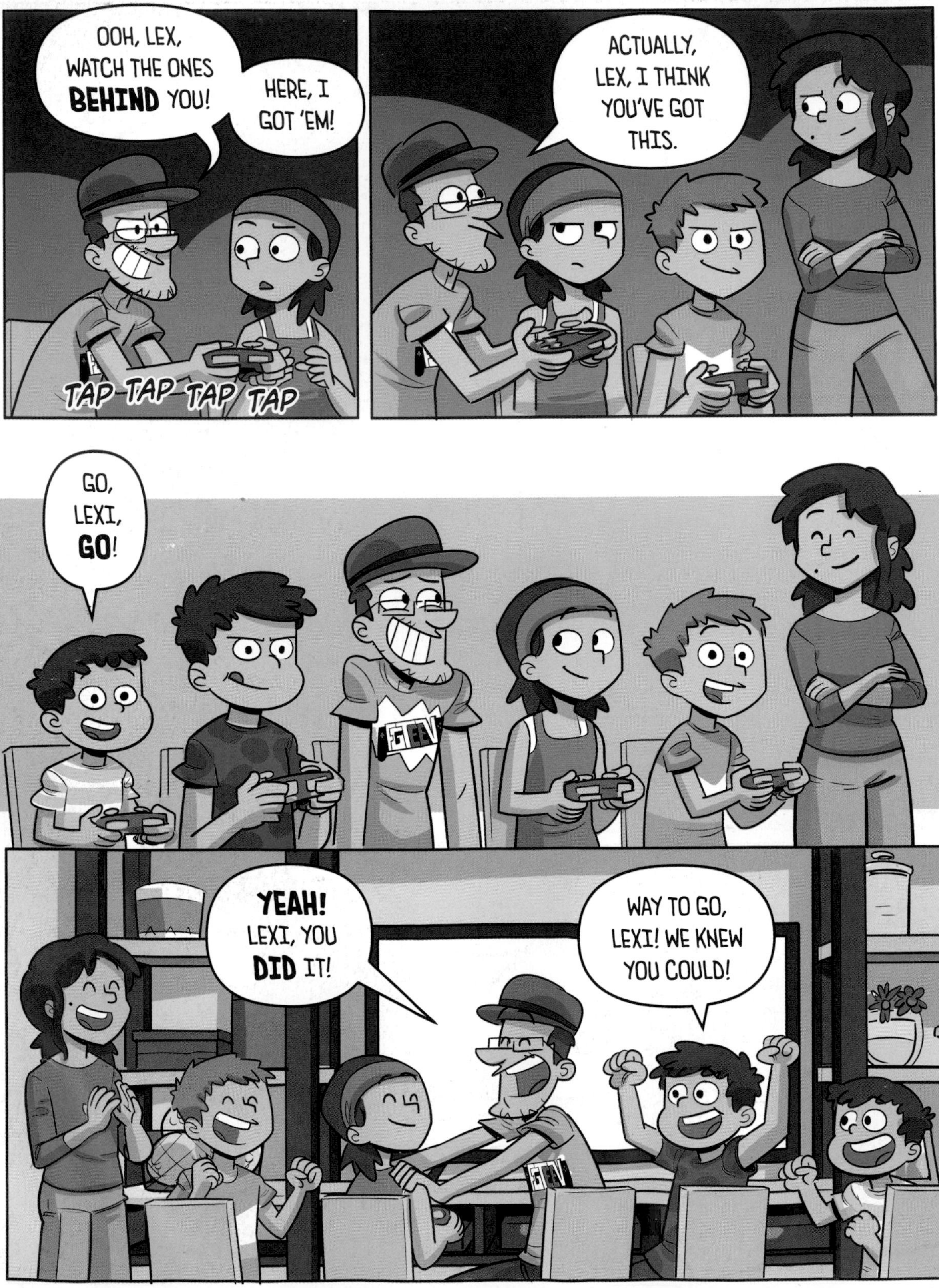

OOH, LEX, WATCH THE ONES **BEHIND** YOU!
HERE, I GOT 'EM!
TAP TAP TAP TAP
ACTUALLY, LEX, I THINK YOU'VE GOT THIS.
GO, LEXI, **GO**!
YEAH! LEXI, YOU **DID** IT!
WAY TO GO, LEXI! WE KNEW YOU COULD!

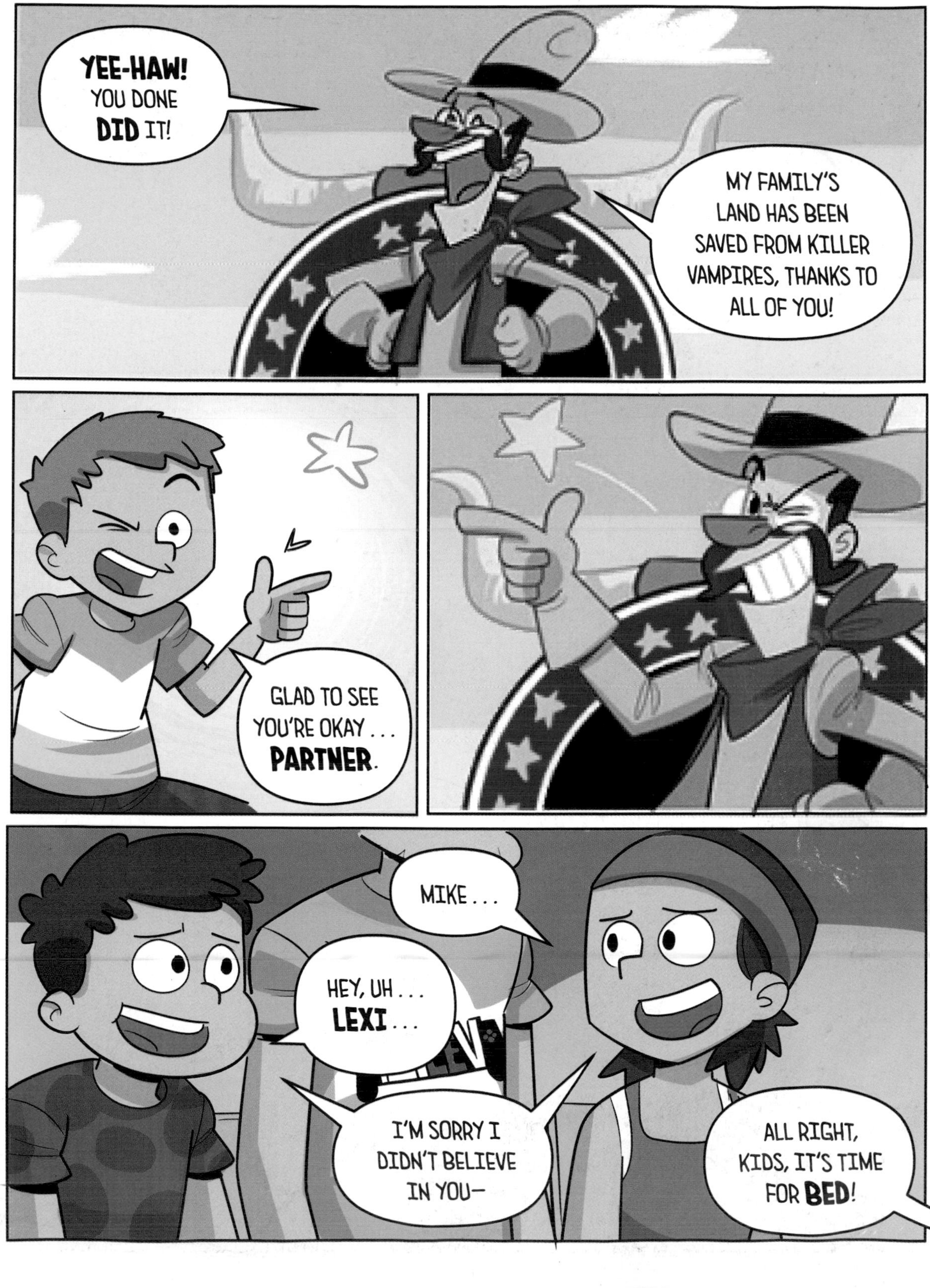
YEE-HAW! YOU DONE DID IT!
MY FAMILY'S LAND HAS BEEN SAVED FROM KILLER VAMPIRES, THANKS TO ALL OF YOU!
GLAD TO SEE YOU'RE OKAY . . . PARTNER.
MIKE . . .
HEY, UH . . . LEXI . . .
I'M SORRY I DIDN'T BELIEVE IN YOU—
ALL RIGHT, KIDS, IT'S TIME FOR BED!

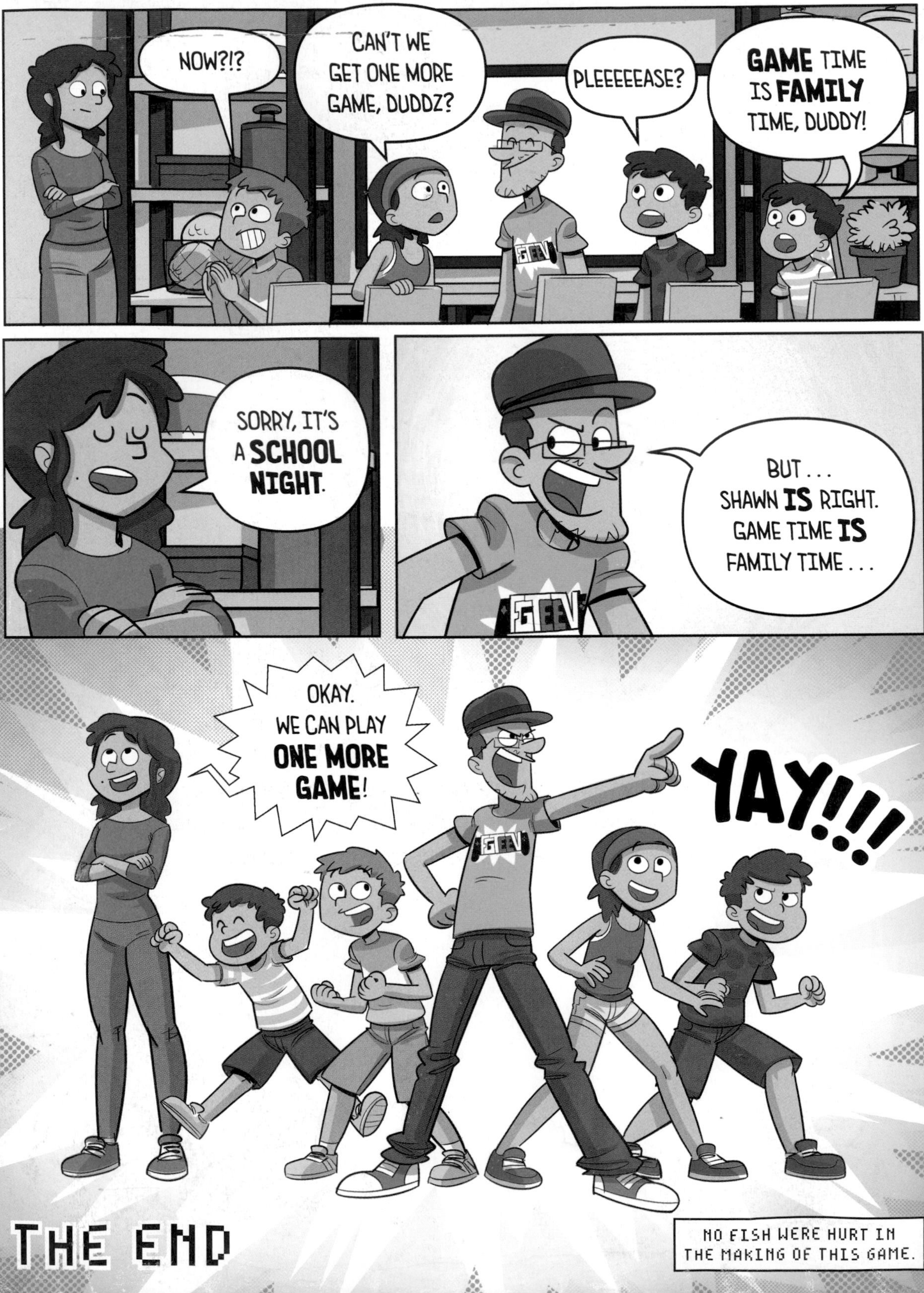
NOW?!?
CAN'T WE GET ONE MORE GAME, DUDDZ?
PLEEEEEASE?
GAME TIME IS FAMILY TIME, DUDDY!
SORRY, IT'S A SCHOOL NIGHT.
BUT . . . SHAWN IS RIGHT. GAME TIME IS FAMILY TIME . . .
OKAY. WE CAN PLAY ONE MORE GAME!
YAY!!!
THE END
NO FISH WERE HURT IN THE MAKING OF THIS GAME.